TWINS OF FATE

Self-Published by
Sarah M. Wasson

DEDICATION

This book is dedicated to Paul, my loving husband, critique partner, and scene enhancer, and to my father, without him consistently placing fantasy books in my hands, my love for fantasy and sci-fi would never have grown.

EPIGRAPH

Forgotten Kingdoms lost to tyranny, the realm of beasts, and the realm of magic fade away.

The birth of twins in the darkness of night, upon uniting, the fates of the Royal Lines shall intertwine.

Infinity embraced; royal birth rights restored.

CHAPTER LIST

Gods & Goddesses
in Ombrasia

Grielan - the God of the Afterlife
Oshan - the Goddess of Life
Ahara - the Goddess of Healing
Iton - the God of Wisdom

Spirit Helpers of the Gods

Isoa - the Herald of Death
Mortal form is a hyena
with unblinking black eyes that walks upright like a man.
Chihara - the Essence of Life
Mortal form is a pure white stag
with silver antlers and emerald eyes.
Rei - the Blessing of Wellness
The mortal form is a silver fox
with an enormously bushy, blue-tipped tail and blue eyes.
Minori - The Seeker of Truth
Mortal form is a phoenix with gold eyes.

OSHANA
The Wyvers fortress
Sanctuary of Iton
Ombrasia's Gate
Griffin's Keep
Brisbin Ocean
Wyvern Empire
Monastery of Iton
Black Mountains
Sapphire Mountains
The Craig's
The Waste
Threndy
Brighthane Forest
Kingdom of Evansshire
Line Shuck
Creekside
Verdale
Blackbane River
Firestrum Ranch
Esther's Cottage
Evans Creek
Inn
Lower City
Kingston
N
E
S
W

The Beginning

ELLIOT wrung his hands together, looking nervously at his bedroom door. Moaning came from his room, but he was not allowed to enter. He sighed deeply and continued his pacing back and forth across the floor.

"Elliot, you're doing yourself no favors, my son. Sit, the child will come when he comes." His father told him from where he sat in front of the crackling fire, puffing on a pipe.

Elliot looked at his father sitting beside the blazing hearth. He shook his head at the absurdity of a fire on such a warm summer day but said nothing and continued pacing around the room.

Suddenly, a scream wrenched from the bedroom. Elliot froze momentarily and then rushed to the door. He turned the knob, but it wouldn't turn. The midwives had locked him out of the room after his fourth interruption of the night.

"Those midwives know what they're doing; you must trust them. She will be fine. I watched your mother give birth to the first two of you. I was glad to be left out of the room for the other three. Your wife is strong; she will be fine." He heard his father's voice from behind him.

"You don't know that." Elliot threw his arms in the air. He walked closer to his father, lowering his voice, "A woman her age should not be having children. We didn't even think she could have children. We've tried for so many years that we gave up. And now she's getting to the age where she should not be able to have children, and she gets pregnant." His face was getting flustered and reddening. Elliot was visibly frustrated at being powerless to do anything about the situation.

"The gods are surely punishing me for something. I would have been more than happy to live out the rest of our lives, just the two of us. It has been a good life," Elliot started pacing again, raking his hands through his hair and shaking his head. "But Maya always wanted children."

Maya screamed again, and then a baby's cry could be heard. Crying and laughter came from inside the room, but the door remained locked.

Elliot froze again before the door, counting his heartbeats until Alma, the head midwife, emerged from the room carrying a tiny baby wrapped in a blanket.

"Mr. Keifman, I present to you your son," she said proudly, stretching her arms out to hand him the tiny bundle.

Elliot hesitantly accepted the baby, holding the baby close so he wouldn't drop him. "My son," he whispered in disbelief. He looked up at the midwife with wide eyes, afraid to ask. At first, he just stared at her and his baby, his gaze shifting back and forth between them, his mouth half-open, struggling to get the words out. "How is she?" He finally managed, his tone still meek, half the words catching in his throat.

The midwife touched his shoulder, looked him in the eyes, and said, "She did fine. She will have a complete recovery." She held her hands back out for the child.

Elliot looked at his son one last time with a small smile, tugging at his lips, "My son." Then, he handed the child back to the midwife. She retreated into the room and shut the door.

Elliott crossed the floor and sat heavily in the chair beside his aging father. "It is a good omen to have a firstborn son. Elliot, I was graced with you first, so I should know." He chuckled to himself.

"How long do you think it will be before she's up and moving?" Elliot asked his father.

"Every woman handles it differently, son; she'll be up when she's up." His father shifted his position on his chair, getting comfortable near the fire.

Alma returned to Maya's bedside. As she was about to hand the child to her, she noticed she had broken out in a sweat again. "Is everything okay, my dear?" She asked.

"I don't know. This doesn't feel right." Suddenly, Maya screamed again as another contraction grabbed hold of her abdomen.

"I think there are two," one of the other midwives said in a hushed voice.

Alma rushed to the end of the bed. "It can't be," she mumbled. A moment later, another baby was born, this time a girl.

Maya started weeping, "No, not twins. Not twins," she paused as sobs overtook   her, "Please, you have to help me," she whispered to the midwives. "I can't lose them both. No one but us four know about the second one, please," she begged in a hushed whisper. Why now, now of all times, to have the twins I wished for? Wished for so many years, she thought to herself. Now, in this place, they are nothing but a curse. Twins with a doomed fate. She glanced over at Alma holding her son; she closed her eyes and tried to think of nothing but him.

All three midwives shared a look and nodded their heads with grim expressions. Sophia, the youngest of the three, bundled the new baby tightly in a blanket, draped a bunch of other blankets on top to hide her, and exited the bedroom. Elliot was on his feet next to the door again.

"Is everything all right? Is Maya okay?"

"Oh sure, right as rain," Sophia responded.

"Why did she scream again?" he asked, his voice elevating.

"It was just the afterbirth, sir, nothing to worry about, sir. If you will excuse me, I have to get this outside and get it washed." She lifted the bundle of towels and blankets a little higher, then curtsied and exited the house.

Elliot sighed deeply again and sat back down. He placed his elbows on his knees and hung his head. "Well, I certainly won't be able to endure all this stress again."

His father laughed and slapped him on the back. "It never gets any easier, son, that's for sure."

Sophia deposited the dirty blankets on the porch and rushed into the forest with the infant held tightly to her chest. She ran swiftly, guided only by the partially obscured full moon. She had to get deep into the woods so nobody would hear the baby when it started to cry. Sophia cried as she ran. It just wasn't fair. This tiny girl had done nothing wrong. But if the Council knew twins had been born, both would be put to death. Twins were forbidden because of the bond that twin siblings shared, a magical bond, it was thought, and magic was strictly prohibited in the Kingdom of Evansshire.

Sophia tripped over logs and thorny underbrush but continued deeper and deeper into the forest. When she finally stopped, she listened for the sounds that people made, ears piqued for any sign of activity. But the forest was as still as the air, and the only sounds being heard were that of the owls, crickets, a lone wolf in the distance, and the wind rustling through the full foliage of the trees in early summer.

She knelt beside a giant redwood tree and gently placed the baby on the ground. A sob ripped through Sophia; her whole body quaked with fear and sorrow. How could her homeland be so cruel to innocent babies?

Still kneeling on the ground, she bowed and said a silent prayer, hoping that any God listening would spare this child from its sealed fate. "Goddess Oshan, Goddess of Life, please send your spirit helper to protect this young one. Chihara, the Essence of Life, please spare this tiny baby girl," she whispered. "Please, someone help this innocent life! Her only crime was being born a twin." She said a little too loudly.

Sophia clamped her hand over her mouth and looked around frightfully. She froze, listening for any sounds.

Satisfied she was alone, she looked at the infant one last time; the moon broke free from the clouds and bathed her in a silvery glow. Sophia was amazed that she still hadn't uttered a sound since leaving the womb.

A high-pitched fluting whistle reverberated throughout the forest, shattering the calm evening. Sophia's feet faltered at the sound. The guttural grunting of a stag in rut seemed to vibrate under her very feet. Her heart skipped a beat. The rut didn't take place until fall. Stag bulls were silent this time of year. Could it be? Could Oshan's Essence of Life spirit helper have heard her prayers and, at this very moment, was rescuing the infant? She sent a quick prayer of thanks to the sky but couldn't linger any longer.

As quickly as she arrived, she returned to the village, leaving the poor baby alone in the forest. Its fate, now sealed.

PART ONE

Keelan

CHAPTER

-1-

KEELAN rushed through his small village, weaving in and out through the people walking down the street, jumping over lazy dogs, and avoiding horse-drawn carts rolling down the middle of the road.

"Keelan, wait up," someone yelled from behind him. He turned his head briefly to see two kids from school chasing after him. But neither could keep up. He laughed but did not stop; he was too excited and had to get home.

Twice a year, his mother journeyed to Kingston, home of the King, to get more supplies for her healing lotions and tonics. This was the first year Keelan would be allowed to join her.

Ever since he was old enough to attend the village school, he dreamed about the day he could join his mother outside of the village. At eight–after joining school–he begged his mother, saying he was old enough to go with her.

Patting him on the head, she chuckled and said, "When your schooling is done, you will be old enough to join me."

That day had finally arrived; now that he was thirteen, his elementary schooling was complete. He knew how to read, write, and do arithmetic, a subject he felt was totally unneeded in the world, but trudged through it, and today was their last day of school. Now, it would be up to the children's parents or other tradesmen in the village to continue their education or assist them with getting a livelihood of their own. Most children followed in their parent's footsteps, but some more adventurous types would seek other apprenticeships.

Before leaving school, his teacher had asked him what he wanted to be, and he quickly responded,

"An adventurer."

To which, of course, the teacher giggled at and said, "You have never even been outside the boundary of our village; how could you possibly know you want to be an adventurer? No, learning to be a healer like your mother or a farrier like your father is the right job for you."

Keelan scowled at his teacher, knowing she wasn't aware of what she was talking about.

Today was the day that he was finally able to leave his village for the first time and see what it was like to be an adventurer because in his heart… he knew that was what he was to be.

Keelan grew up as an only child in a cozy village in the Kingdom of Evansshire. His elderly parents were loving and supportive, and even though they lived meager lives, he had a very happy childhood.

His mother, Maya, was the town's healer; she knew how to make simple healing lotions and tonics and could cure most of the everyday injuries and sicknesses. However, if the injury was too complicated, the patient had to be rushed to Kingston, or a full-fledged Kings Healer was brought in.

His father, Elliot, was one of two blacksmiths in town. His father specialized in farrier and equipment repair whereas the other blacksmith crafted weapons and tools, farrier was only a side job for him. Besides the farrier, Elliot, operated a small stable with a few horses that people could borrow and boarded the horses of any travelers coming through the village. Keelan kept busy most of the day between helping his parents and attending school.

As he rushed through town, he stole quick glances at the shops and people he passed. The bakery next to the seamstress and potter and the

Inn along the main road. About two dozen residences branched off onto smaller roadways and paths that stretched away from the main road through town.

The council hall in the middle of the village was situated next to a small fountain. It was the focal point of the town. The council representative, Consul Tybard, stood in front of a gathering group of villagers and spoke to a Knights patrol that was passing through town. Keelan slowed slightly as he took in the sight of the seven hard-faced knights. They wore travel armor made of mostly thick leather with accents of once shiny metal in critical places. Three men stood beside them with their wrists shackled. Their faces were downcast and one was visibly shaking.

Keelan thought briefly about stopping to get a better look, but then he remembered he was going to Kingston, and the capital was filled with knights and the crimes of those three were none of his business. He smiled broadly, waved to a knight glancing his way, and then quickened his pace.

Keelan skidded to a halt as he neared his father's shop, mindful of avoiding his disapproval for rushing through town. He quickly smoothed down his clothing, brushed off the dust from his pants and boots, and splashed water on his face from the trough to cool his flushed cheeks.

He walked slowly into the stable to find his father working hard hammering out another pair of shoes; the mare that the shoes belonged to was waiting quietly beside him.

"There you are, my boy, man the bellows for me."

Keelan dropped his books next to a wagon wheel that his father had been repairing and rushed over to the furnace; he pumped on the bellows to get the coals white hot. When the fire was stoked enough, Keelan grabbed the tongs and held the shoe for his father to hammer into shape. His father was quiet and rarely spoke while he worked, so Keelan patiently watched and helped him complete all the shoes. He then watched him nail them onto the horse's hoof.

"Did somebody rent Marigold?" Keelan asked his father, "I haven't seen you put shoes on her in a long time."

His father took a long drink of water from his canteen and splashed some across his face before answering, "No, your mother is going to use Marigold on this trip; Honey's due to give birth any day now. Do you think you can handle Marigold for your mother?" his father asked him.

"Yes, of course, Father. Marigold is a sweet horse. She'll get us there and back, no problem."

His father clapped him on the back, "Let's go see if your Ma has anything ready for dinner yet."

"It is a little early for that, isn't it, Father?"

"Maybe, let's see if there are any sweets then," he laughed.

Maya hummed a little as she completed the list of supplies she needed to buy when her husband and son entered the door.

"There you two are," she replied as they walked in.

"Are you about ready to go?" Elliot asked.

"I'm putting the finishing touches on my list now; we will leave in the morning. The stew is almost ready, but I think you could have some pie on the sill while you wait," she winked at her son.

How does she always know when I'm in the mood for sweets? He thought to himself.

Early the following morning, Keelan's mother shook him awake. He bolted upright, startled and groggy; he was up half the night wondering what this trip would be like and what adventures he would be having.

"Quickly get dressed. I want to be gone before the sun rises," she said to him.

Rubbing what little sleep he received from his eyes, he swung his feet over the side of the bed. He looked outside to see that the sky was still dark, but a hint of light was on the horizon.

Keelan padded over to his dresser and found a brand-new pair of green pants, a matching green vest, and a dark brown cloak. He carefully picked up the cloak, admiring it. It was the finest piece of clothing he'd ever seen. He brushed his fingers across the material.

Definitely waterproof, he thought to himself.

Fully awake now, he threw the pants on, found a light brown shirt in his drawer to wear underneath the vest, and grabbed the cloak before bounding out of his room.

His father was in the kitchen making them breakfast. He turned and looked at his son, "Wow, fine new clothing you have there, my son."

Keelan beamed at his father and looked at himself in the living room's looking glass,

"Where did Ma get these?" he asked with apparent astonishment.

In contrast with the tan of his shirt, the green of the pants and vest brought out the green flecks in his eyes. Looking at himself one last time, he smoothed his wild brown hair down before returning to the kitchen.

"Your mother's been saving," was all he said.

His mother exited her bedroom wearing very similar attire, but instead of pants, she wore an ankle-length skirt, "Oh good, they fit perfectly," she said looking at Keelan, "Come quickly, let's eat and then be on our way."

After a hasty breakfast, they made their way out the front door; Marigold was already hitched to their wagon and loaded with supplies for the trip.

"This is everything I need for my shop. Make sure you get everything on the list," his father said with a smile.

"I will, no problem; thank you, Father."

"Take good care of your mother!"

Keelan watched his parents embrace, and then his mother stepped into the wagon. Before Keelan knew it, they were on their way.

At midday, they stopped by a small pond to let Marigold rest.

"So, how long will it take us to get there?" Keelan finally asked his mother.

"I was wondering when you were going to ask me that. We should be there by this time tomorrow."

"We will spend the night out under the stars?"

"No, there's a small inn that we will stay at. We should get there before dark today."

Keelan frowned but then nodded his head, "Okay, I guess it's still an adventure," he said. Maya smiled at her son.

When they arrived at the inn, a stable boy greeted them, "Welcome back, Mrs. Keifman. I see you brought your son along this time," He looked at Keelan, "Nice to meet you, lad."

"Nice to meet you too," Keelan said with a smile.

Maya grabbed their bags, patted him on the head, and entered the inn. The inn was bright and cheery, with a whole wall of windows overlooking the dusty road. A dozen or so tables were scattered around the large open room with fireplaces on both sides. Only a few tables were taken. A couple of people glanced their way but ignored them for the most part. A petite woman standing next to the bar greeted them with a smile.

"Welcome back, Maya. I have your usual room ready for you."

"Thank you so much. Patty, I'd like you to meet my son. This is Keelan. Keelan, this is Patty. She runs this inn."

"Nice to meet you, ma'am," he replied politely.

A large, burly boy about Keelan's age approached, took the bags from Maya, and led them upstairs.

"Supper will be ready in about half an hour, ma'am," the boy told them, and left the room.

"So, what do we do first when we get to the capital?" Keelan asked as he bounced on the straw bed with soft, fluffy feather pillows.

"Well, the first thing we'll do is get settled into an inn without a broken bed," she smiled as he stopped bouncing, "and then we will see my very good friend. He taught me everything I know about healing."

Night slowly descended, and candles were lit throughout the inn. Keelan yawned and stretched, looking around the common room, the dice game he was playing with his mother was long forgotten.

The hushed conversations of the other travelers stopped as three knights walked into the room. They stood in the doorway scowling as they surveyed the inn patrons. Patty rushed up to them and showed them to a table in the back corner of the inn. The burly boy, Patty's son, hurried to the table with ale and stew. The knights sat without a word and shrugged off their cloaks. The officer scowled at a few of the patrons before returning his eyes to his companions.

The soft conversations resumed, and everyone ignored the three newcomers. Keelan stared at the knights, marveling at their confident movements and steely glances.

"Come, we have a long day ahead of us," Maya said. She placed a couple of coins on the table and headed for the stairs.

Keelan walked behind her without taking his eyes off the three soldiers. One looked up from his pint and locked eyes with Keelan. A slight grin curled his lips into a crooked smile. He nodded to Keelan before roaming his eyes across the room once again.

As Keelan hit the pillow, he fell asleep almost immediately and began dreaming of a grand quest and traveling through the countryside to save his kingdom and win favor from the King.

CHAPTER

-2-

KINGSTON was huge.

Keelan's head swiveled left and right as Marigold plodded down the main road leading into the Capital. Maya glanced at her son's amazed expression.

"Not what you were expecting?" she smiled.

Keelan turned his gaze to her, his eyes wide and mouth gaping open, "I knew it was big, but not this big."

"This is only Lower City; wait until tomorrow. I will take you close to the castle," She pointed to the left, "Now that is a huge building. See there,"

Keelan eyes followed her outstretched arm. To the left of Lower City was an enormous mountain. A road wound up the mountain and disappeared into a large crevasse.

"You see there? That is the way to the actual city of Kingston. This," she swept her hand in front of them, "is its own town, Lower City, but most people lump them together. Our inn for tonight isn't far now. We will go into Kingston proper tomorrow. That's where my friend lives."

Keelan was speechless. He couldn't keep his eye off the mountain towering above with its rocky slopes jagged and steep, casting long shadows over Lower City. Wisps of mist curled around its peaks. The city before him was smaller than Kingston. How did people not get lost every day?

As they arrived at the mouth of the jagged canyon, the sun peeked over the eastern horizon, casting a golden glow on the rugged landscape. A towering wall stretched across the chasm, reaching heights that made anything Keelan had ever seen before look short. It was the only entrance into Kingston, standing as a barrier.

"They say it's over seven stories high," his mother whispered. "The sentries chosen to guard it train for two years before they are honored with this post."

"Seven stories high!" he repeated. The gate in the middle of the wall would have easily let ten of their wagons go through side by side without touching them. Keelan strained his neck, trying to see the top of the wall. Royal knights guarded the entrance and seemed to be everywhere. Several officers spoke with travelers and looked inside the wagons as they rolled up.

"Purpose?" An inspection officer barked at them when they neared the front of the line.

"Supplies and visiting a friend," Maya said calmly.

"Friends name? Supplies needed?"

"Healing and farrier supplies for Creekside. My friend is Healer Jonal."

The officer glanced at Maya for the first time.

"All clear!" A knight shouted from the rear of the wagon. Keelan spun around, surprised to see someone standing on the back of their wagon. The knight jumped down and walked to the next wagon in line.

"You have three days." The officer handed a scroll to Maya and waved her through the gate.

"They tell us how long we can stay?" Keelan asked.

"Kingston is kept quite secure and has stringent rules. Three days is more than enough time."

Keelan nodded. "Does he know your friend?" He turned around in his seat, his gaze fixed on the gate and wall as they rode past. Maya shrugged, "I wouldn't be surprised if he did."

They lumbered through the narrowing canyon. Even though the cobblestone path was plenty wide enough for their wagon, the sheer height of the cliffs made Keelan feel as if they were being squeezed in. Bright torches lined the path, casting flickering shadows along the canyon walls. Keelan couldn't help but be amazed at the sight of knights standing guard at every turn.

The wall and gate alone should be enough to stop any invading force, he thought to himself.

Finally, the canyon's end could be seen. The high mountains that circled the valley gave the illusion of dusk instead of dawn. The city was situated in the middle of the valley and was surrounded by woods and farmland.

The focal point of the valley was the magnificent white castle sitting on a small hill. As the sun peaked over the imposing mountain tops, the points of the castle's twisted spires, with their royal blue and yellow flags, caught the first light. Keelan was mesmerized as he watched the whole castle slowly illuminate and sparkle.

Maya continued along the main roadway, heading straight for the castle. Keelan kept looking around in utter amazement. "I thought Lower City was huge!" he exclaimed.

Maya chuckled softly, "Well, I will tell you a secret, my son. I was raised in this city, and when I left it, I couldn't believe so few people could feel safe living without the security of a city like this."

"Truly, you lived here. But why is it a secret?"

"Few people from Kingston ever leave. And those that do are not usually well-liked outside of the city. I don't think anybody would truly hold it against me, but it's fun having your own little secret sometimes," she winked and smiled at him.

The anticipation grew in Keelan as he asked, "How much further to your friend's house?"

"Not much further, he lives on the innermost ring," She continued, "The city is arranged in rings. This road that we are on is called the Grand Staircase. Because it goes from the canyon all the way to the castle. The first ring is where most of the inns are located to house travelers when they first arrive. The two rings we are passing now hold most of the working-class people who keep the city going. The next ring is where most of the shops are located: the bakers, the seamstresses, the blacksmiths, and every other business that is needed. The final ring is where most of the merchants and the upper class live, and then you get to the castle itself, where only the Council and the King live."

Keelan nodded, "So, your friend lives in the upper-class ring? Is he wealthy?"

"Some would say he is, but he lives a simple life."

The wagon creaked to a stop in front of a small single-story home nestled between a long row of two-story houses. The tiny cottage appeared to be the oldest in this section.

"Here we are," Maya hopped down and tied Marigold to the hitching post. "Come on, Keelan."

Before they could proceed further, a voice called them, "Maya Flim! You made it!" Keelan turned around to see an aging man with messy gray hair and a long, wild gray beard standing at the front door.

"Jonal! It's so nice to see you again. And, you know, Flim is not my last name and hasn't been for near thirty years," she smiled as she walked up to him. He grabbed her shoulders and brought her in for a big hug.

"You will always be little Maya Flim to me." His gaze fell on Keelan, "Now, this must be young master Keelan," he smiled broadly.

Maya grinned and nodded her head toward Healer Jonal while Keelan's eyes widened to the size of saucers as he looked at the strange man.

"Don't be shy, boy. Come shake my hand. I don't bite." Healer Jonal said, breaking Keelan's trance.

Taking a deep breath, Keelan walked up to him.

"Nice to meet you, Healer Jonal," he said quietly.

Jonal shook Keelan's hand. "Healer Jonal Bertelsen at your service, but my friends call me Jonal." He smiled at him and opened his front door wide, "Come, come. You must be tired from your journey. I have supper just about ready, and I insist you spend the night here instead of the *Humble Pony*."

Keelan tilted his head to one side, "The *Humble Pony*?" He asked.

"That's the inn I always stay at when I come here. Come on. I need to sit on a chair that doesn't sway and hit bumps."

While they ate, Jonal and Maya caught up on local news from around the capital and surrounding towns.

With a full belly of mutton, roasted vegetables, and warm, freshly made bread, Keelan fell asleep in front of the fireplace with Jonal's cat curled up in his lap.

Keelan woke the following day to the sound of a tea kettle whistling. He yawned and stretched his arms and legs. With sleepy eyes, he looked around at his surroundings. He was in a small room with nothing more than a bed against the wall and a desk under the window.

He hopped off the bed to get ready for the day. After opening his bag and putting on fresh clothing, he left the room.

"Good morning, Keelan. Did you sleep well?" Jonal asked, standing before the fire, stirring something in a large pot.

"Yes, sir," Keelan sat down at the kitchen table.

"Posh, I'm not a sir. Call me Jonal or Bertelsen if you must, but never sir."

"Yes, si… Okay, Jonal," Keelan said with a grin.

"Much better. Hungry?"

Keelan nodded.

Jonal spooned out a large helping of oatmeal into a bowl and handed it to him. "I have strawberry and blackberry jam or honey in that cupboard over there."

Keelan grabbed all three and placed them on the table. "Oh, is Marigold still hitched out front?" he jumped from his seat.

"Sit, sit. No, I made her comfortable in my stable behind the house after you fell asleep. Eat your breakfast."

Keelan sat back down, "Thank you for doing that, but you should have woken me; it is my job to take care of Marigold."

"Nonsense," Jonal dismissed him, "It was my pleasure to help. I don't get very many visitors, you know."

Keelan placed a large dollop of strawberry jam in the middle of his oatmeal and then stirred it in.

"Good morning, gentleman," Maya greeted them entering the room.

"Good morning," Keelan and Jonal said together.

"That smells wonderful. Is there enough for one more?" She asked.

"Of course, and some Kingsberry tea just the way you like it."

"Oh, Kingsberry, my favorite."

"What is Kingsberry? I've never heard that." Keelan leaned closer to his mother's cup to smell the tea.

"It is a special hybrid berry developed especially for the King. It only grows here in Kingston. Would you like to try some?"

"Yes, please."

"So, what is your first stop today?" Jonal asked Maya, while Keelan sipped on the tea.

"I want to stop by Sally's first and then Jarod's. Those two stops will take most of the day. We will get Elliot's supplies tomorrow and stop at Esther's…"

"Esther's? That old witch! Truly child, my supplies are far better than anything she produces," Jonal grumbled.

"Now, now, my friend. You used to get along with her, and you know better than anyone that her pox cream is the best there is." Maya smirked.

"Psst, that was a long time ago," he crossed his arms across his chest.

"And her pox cream?" Maya asked, smiling.

"Psst, it's all right, I suppose," he said quietly.

Maya bellowed out a loud laugh, "Just all right? High praise from a grumpy old wizard."

"Wizard?" Keelan whispered.

Jonal and Maya shared a quick look, and Jonal cleared his throat loudly.

"Just a figure of speech, Keelan. Now, I think it's time to get going."

Maya and Keelan left Jonal's house, walking down the street to return to the Grand Staircase. From there, they made their way over to Sellers Row.

Sally's shop was called Herbs and Things. There was a large sign above the door showing numerous herbs.

When they entered the shop, their noses were assaulted with dozens of scents, making Keelan sneeze immediately. Maya laughed, but even she sniffled.

A very tall, slender woman was standing behind the desk in the middle of the room, grinding up something with a mortar and pestle. Looking up from her work, she smiled, "Maya, my child, you're back."

Keelan looked at his mother and then at the lady, seeing little age difference between the two. "Why is she calling you child, Mother? She's not any older than you; I would say she's younger," Keelan whispered.

Maya chuckled, "She's actually quite a bit older than me. She has some amazing herbs that help her stay young-looking."

Keelan looked at the woman with astonishment, "Why doesn't everybody use those herbs?"

"Not everybody could afford them, and I'm very greedy." Sally laughed "So, what will it be today?"

Maya and Sally broke away from Keelan and got to work filling two large bags that Maya had brought. Keelan walked around the shop, looking at the different vials and pouches of dried herbs, lotions, and tonics; most of them he recognized, but there were a few here and there that he had no idea what they would do or even how to pronounce.

He made a slow circle around the shop. It was a small shop, and before long, he returned to where he started. The minutes dragged on, and he soon found himself extremely bored. He heard a rustling sound near the back room; slowly, he approached the sound. He peered into the back room, not wanting to trespass, but his curiosity was mounting. *What was making all that noise?* He glanced into the back room and saw a large burlap sack shaking and shuddering. The sound was coming from inside. He kept staring at the sack, wishing he could get closer to investigate. Suddenly, he heard a squeak and four ferrets tumbling out of the bag. They didn't appear to notice that he was there and just kept rolling around on the floor, rough-housing. Laughing at the antics, Keelan knelt and made clicking noises to get their attention. The ferrets stopped and looked at him all at the same time. He continued to make the little clicking and popping noises, but none of them took any steps toward him.

He looked back at Sally, "Excuse me, ma'am, did you know you have ferrets back here?"

She looked up and smiled at him. "Yes, those are mine. You can go there if you want to. They are quite friendly. Well, all except for number four."

"Number four?" Keelan asked.

"I'm not very good at naming things, so their names are one, two, three, and four. Number four is the black one. The other three will come when you call them by their number or name, as it were."

Still on his knees, Keelan nudged forward to get closer to the ferrets and then sat on his behind cross-legged.

"So, which one of you is number one?" He asked. A tan ferret perked up and ambled toward him. It got within a foot of him before it stopped and sniffed the air in his direction. "Don't worry, I won't hurt you," Keelan smiled at him. Number one reached forward and gently sniffed his hand.

Suddenly, one of the other ferrets rushed up and jumped into his lap. "Whoa, okay, so are you number two or three?" he asked. The ferret just looked at him, "Number two," he said. A white ferret standing next to number four squeaked and rushed toward him. "Okay, so I take it your number two. So that would make you, number three." Soon, he had three ferrets in his lap. They rolled around, squeaked, and tried to get his attention while keeping the others from getting pets. Number four stayed where he was, looking at his three companions and the newcomer.

"It's okay, number four. I won't hurt you." Keelan stretched his hand away from the other three ferrets toward the shy black one, "It's okay, come on," he said softly. Slowly, the black one inched toward him until he was just within reach and sniffed his fingers.

The little black ferret continued to sniff his fingers while inching closer until he was almost standing at his side. "Come on, now." Keelan started to mutter under his breath. Keelan, engrossed in his interaction with the ferrets, remained unaware that Sally and his mother had stopped to watch. Sally glanced at Maya and arched her eyebrow, "Would you care to explain?" she whispered; Maya shook her head.

Finally, the shy little black ferret got close enough and allowed Keelan to pet it for a moment before he scurried away, leaving his three siblings with the boy. Keelan shrugged and went back to petting the three in his lap.

"Okay, Keelan, I'm all done here," his mother said finally. "Can you carry this bag for me, or should we drop it off at Jonal's?" Keelan picked up the bags and tested their weight by bouncing them back and forth in his hands.

"I think I got it, Ma. It's not too heavy," she smiled at her son. As they stepped out, he looked up at the sky; it was nearing midday. He had no idea they'd been in that shop for so long.

"Let's get a bite to eat before heading to Jarod's store," his mother said.

"Sounds good to me, Mom."

Jarod's store turned out to be a tailor. Jarod, his wife, and two eldest daughters ran the store together.

"Good afternoon, Jarod," Maya greeted him. Jarod was a short, round man with little hair left on his head. He had a cheerful and kind face.

"Good day to you too, Maya; this must be Keelan. I've heard so much about you," he said with a smile. He looked back at Maya, "I have your order ready, but I may have to get a bigger size for your son."

"That is to be expected. He is a growing boy, and you never know how much they're going to grow year by year."

Jarod walked into the back room and emerged with a large parcel. He placed it on the counter and opened it up. Inside were two new shirts for Keelan's father, a couple of new dresses, a pair of pants, and a couple of shirts for Keelan. Jarod handed Keelan the clothes, "Head to the back room and change into these. Let's see how much we need to adjust them."

Keelan did as instructed. The black pants fit fine at the waist but were a little short at the ankle, and the shirts were just too small. He squeezed into the blue shirt, anyway. He stepped out carrying the bronze-colored shirt as he returned to the main room.

Maya gasped, looking at him, "Oh my, those are way too small."

"Now, now," Jarod said as he pulled another parcel from under the table and handed it to Keelan, "Try these on, boy." He winked.

Keelan returned to the back room to try on the next set of clothing. These fit perfectly. When he entered the main room, his mother clapped. "Oh, Jarod, you are the best," she said with a smile. "Those fit perfectly."

"Well, it has been a whole year since I've seen you last; he was bound to be bigger than you thought he would be. And I made the seams a little bit larger on these, so if you have to, you can take them out just a little bit here and there until he just wears them out."

"Again, I can't tell you how happy I am. Until next year." Maya said with a slight wave. Done with the receiving, Maya and Keelan prepared to leave.

"Safe travels," Jarod said, as he saw them making their way out.

"You mentioned to Jonal those were going to be our only two stops today," Keelan said, "What are we going to do for the rest of the day?"

"Well, just like our home village, Kingston has a yearly festival, and we are just in time for it." Maya smiled.

Keelan's eyes lit up, "What kind of festival do they have?"

"Here, in the capital, they celebrate the start of summer. Let's get all this put back, grab Jonal, and head to the main square."

With an energized spring in Keelan's step, they hurried back to Jonal's.

CHAPTER

-3-

JONAL was already waiting for them with a large bag slung over his shoulder. They exited the street Jonal lived a crowd walking up toward the castle.

"I thought the main square would be in the town," Keelan stated.

"Since this is Kingston, our main square is at the castle." He glanced down at Keelan and smirked, "You are in for a treat, my boy."

It appeared the entire town was headed up toward the castle, and everybody was in their best attire. Keelan was suddenly very thankful he decided to keep on the new clothing he had tried on just a short while ago. The men and boys all wore dark pants of black, brown, or dark green with colorful shirts, and the women and girls wore brightly colored ankle-length skirts or dresses. Most of the younger women and girls wore large frilly hats with feathers sticking out of them; the older women carried umbrellas to shade themselves from the summer sun. Keelan saw his mother looking at him. She winked and then put her eyes back toward the road.

So, she planned this the whole time and kept it a secret, he chuckled to himself.

When they finally got to the castle mound, they were greeted by the biggest staircase he had ever seen. Twenty people could walk up the stairway side by side easily. Made of solid stone, the steps led all the way up the hill to the front of the castle.

"So, this is why the road is called the Grand Staircase," he said out loud.

"Yes, my boy, this is where the road gets its name from. Everybody who's anybody will be here tonight; no one will miss this affair. And anybody smart enough will have something here to sell," he patted the bag on his shoulder.

At the top of the stairs, Keelan found himself in a large rectangular garden. It was filled with flowers of all kinds and colors, creating a beautiful scene. The air was sweet with the scent of blossoms, and the sunlight made everything look vibrant.

On the far side of the garden stood the castle, gleaming white under the bright sunlight, almost blinding to look at. Royal blue and yellow flags fluttered in the gentle breeze, adding a regal touch to the surroundings.

People dispersed, some wandering alone or in small groups, mingling throughout the garden. Jonal led Keelan and his mother closer to the castle. "Do we get to go inside?" Keelan asked, hoping the answer would be yes.

Jonal shook his head, "Only into the courtyard, my boy, that is where most of the festivities will take place; we will head in there momentarily. But first, I want to see if I can lighten my load," he said with a hearty chuckle. Keelan watched as he walked over to a bench, opened his bag, and laid out various things he had brought: a few lotions, different tonics, and some cylinders that appeared to have powder in them.

"What are these?" Keelan asked curiously.

"Just a few things that I sell here every year. Your mother always refuses to take my advice and bring a few things to sell."

Maya shook her head, "I'm here buying things, not selling. That would take way too much time for me to prepare both."

Jonal opened one of the tonics and held it under Keelan's nose, "Can you identify this?" he asked.

Keelan took a hesitant sniff, knowing full well that sniffing certain things too deeply can be dangerous. "Go ahead. It's not dangerous." he smiled, looking at Keelan's hesitancy.

Keelan took a small sniff. He wiggled his nose a bit and said, "That one is used to cure headaches,"

"Are you sure?"

Keelan nodded so Jonal opened a powder next, "How about this one?" He held it under his nose.

Keelan sniffed it and frowned, "I don't know what that one is, sir."

"Are you sure?" He held it closer to his nose. Keelan took a bigger sniff. "I'm sure, but it smells like honey."

Jonal patted Keelan's head, "Good nose, my boy. This is a good powder to place on bee stings; it removes the pain."

In no time at all, Jonal sold everything he brought with him. He slung his empty bag over his shoulder and declared, "Now we have some spending money; let's go eat," he grabbed Maya by the arm and Keelan around the shoulders and led them toward the castle.

The castle was breathtaking. It was made of shiny white marble with gold and silver decorations. Bright blue and yellow flags fluttered everywhere. As they got closer, Keelan noticed three layers of protection at the courtyard entrance: fancy gates, a big heavy gate that could be lowered quickly, and huge black oak doors.

The decorative gates were white iron woven in an intricate scrolling that looked like ivy with blue and yellow leaves strewn throughout. Keelan looked at the gates intently, fascinated by the craftsmanship. The thick portcullis was drawn about halfway up. As Keelan walked under them, he saw the gates shimmer and slowly start to rise. A Royal officer shouted at the guard manning the wench to stop moving it. The guard looked around, confused; his hands were at his sides, unmoving. Keelan watched the exchange, equally confused. Keelan locked eyes with the officer and smiled weakly at him. The officer's eyes narrowed, and then he pulled a small scroll from his breast pocket and scribbled down something. Keelan looked around and noticed his ma and Jonal was several yards ahead of him. Quickly he followed the adults through the gates into the grand courtyard.

The courtyard was almost as big as the receiving garden they had just come from. Fruit trees were planted all along the high walls, making a beautiful ring around the courtyard. In the center of the square was a large stage where musicians played. Jonal led them to the right-hand side of the courtyard, where food vendors had set up tables and carts. The various smells coming from the vendors instantly make Keelan's mouth water.

"What would you two like?" Jonal asked them.

"What do you suggest?" Maya asked.

"I was hoping you'd leave it up to me." Jonal's face lit up and he led them quickly to a cart near the rear of the group. "We will take three specials, my good server," he told the vendor. He smiled and handed them three sticks with various chunks of meat and vegetables.

"That'll be six coppers," the vendor said. Jonal gladly handed over the money and accepted the kabobs.

Keelan took a bite of a piece of meat at the top. His eyes widened with surprise. It was slightly sweet and spicy but delicious. He wanted to devour it in one bite. As he ate he looked around at the vendors' tents. Each vendor had a table or two set up to display their wares or food. Brightly colored awnings were placed above most of the tables with thin poles holding them up. They walked to the wall surrounding the courtyard to avoid the crowds of people. While Jonal and Maya spoke quietly, Keelan walked closer to the wall. Something caught his eye. Something was sparkling in the light of the torch. He knelt and brushed the dirt off the partially buried object. It was a pin that looked like it could have belonged to a knight. Something to hold their cape around their neck. It was old and worn. Keelan held it up to the torch light, there was an image etched into one side, but he couldn't quite tell what it was. Jonal called to him, making him jump. He absentmindedly tucked the pin into his pocket before returning to Jonal and his mother. Together they slowly returned to the courtyard's center.

Suddenly, a loud gasp came from the left-hand side of the stage. Red, blue, and green sparks shot into the air, and then a cacophony of clapping could be heard.

"What's going on over there?" Keelan forgot about the meat stick in his hand.

"Well, I don't know. Let's go find out." Jonal replied.

As they neared the large crowd, they saw a man wearing a long dark blue robe with a large blue hat that was pointed at the top like a cone. He danced around, flourishing a large stick in his hand, calling out strange words, and sparks were flying from his stick.

Keelan stared in shock, "Is that real magic?" he whispered.

Jonal laughed, "No, my dear boy. He is nothing but a trinket-store performer. He uses tricks and illusions. Nothing he does is real. He preys on those that want to be manipulated and gives them what they crave," he scoffed.

Keelan nudged and squeezed his way through the crowd to get a better look. The odd man with the funny hat continued dancing and chanting; suddenly, a bouquet of flowers appeared in his hand, and the crowd clapped loudly again. The performer covered the flowers with a scarf and waved his stick above it, repeating obscure words, and when he pulled the scarf off, a white dove fluttered and flapped in his hand. The crowd broke into cheers, and Keelan clapped and whistled along with them.

"Nice tricks, huh," Jonal said to him.

Keelan looked up at him with his eyes wide in disbelief, "I didn't know anyone could do this. He is amazing."

"Well, his outfit is utterly ridiculous. I mean, look at that hat; what is that thing? Tell me what practical purpose that hat serves." He grumbled, looking at excited Keelan. "Come on now, let's see what other shows are going on,"

Jonal led them to the rear of the stage. Another act was going on, one with trained animals.

The entertainer had a group of dogs and cats performing tricks, making them jump through hoops and walk on narrow boards between platforms. His only way of communicating with them was by calling their names and using a whip to guide their actions. While most of the children watching were highly impressed, the adults seemed less captivated by the performance. More booths were set up on this side of the courtyard. A face painting booth and Kiss the Maiden seemed to be the most popular.

The far side of the courtyard held the last stage. On it was an old man and a young woman. The man was telling everyone that the young girl could read minds. The old man blindfolded the young woman. Then he walked through the crowd and asked her if he was standing next to a man or woman. She always answered correctly.

"He's giving her the answers! I know he is!" Keelan stated.

"How can you tell?" Jonal leaned toward him to hear him better.

"He's changing how he asks her, is this a man or woman, or is this a woman or man, depending on who he is standing next to. The first thing he says is the correct answer."

"Very good, my boy," Jonal praised. "Do you think you could do better than her?"

Keelan looked at him puzzled and shrugged, "I can try, I guess." Keelan closed his eyes and focused on the man's voice.

The old man swayed through the crowd and stood beside a man. Before he could ask the young woman, Keelan answered, "Man,"

"Woman," he said next. "The man is wearing a red shirt; the woman is wearing a peach dress," Keelan continued, his eyes still closed as the old man swayed in the crowd. "The woman is pregnant with twins."

A few people around Keelan gasped as he opened his eyes. The crowd's gaze fell on the woman. She seemed quite petite and feeble. There was no way of telling she's pregnant – and even if she was, it was clear she wasn't aware. With fear and excitement in her eyes, she took a few steps near Keelan,

"Say. Is that true? How do you know this?" The young woman's voice was laced with fear. Her eyes darted around the crowd to see who had heard Keelan's words.

Several people standing next to them glanced at Keelan with fearful eyes.

"What does this boy speak of?" one man in the crowd asked. "Is that true with this one? She's pregnant with twins as he says?"

Jonal grabbed Keelan's shoulder and Maya's hand, "Was nothing, nothing. It's just a silly game we play." He laughed, "This boy. A silly one, I tell ya." He looked at Maya, "Come on now, Maya. Off we go! Enjoy the show, rest of you all."

He dragged them through the crowd of people back to the food vendors.

"What happened?" Keelan asked, as Jonal dragged him through the crowd, followed by Maya. "Jonal, how did I know that about the woman?" Keelan asked in a hushed voice.

"Just your imagination, my boy. How about some dessert?" Jonal said to distract him.

Maya gave Jonal a very frightful look but said nothing. Jonal only raised his eyebrows but remained silent as well.

"Dessert! Yes, please." Keelan beamed with happiness.

They wove their way between the merchandise and food vendors, stopping now and then to look at what somebody was selling. As the sun started to set, everybody started walking toward the castle.

"Where is everybody going?" Keelan asked.

"The King is going to be addressing his people; come on. Let's see if we can get a good look." Jonal led them toward the castle, weaving their way through the crowd.

At the top of the main castle gates was a large balcony. The doors behind the balcony slowly opened, and three people walked out. A short, plump, balding man approached the railing, "Here ye, here ye. I present to you your king, King Percival Theodric, 2nd of his name, ruler of the Kingdom of Evansshire, your lord and liege," he yelled. The crowd erupted into cheers—the throng of people pressed in close to Keelan until everybody stood shoulder to shoulder. Without warning, Keelan was struck in the back of the head; he stumbled forward, pushing the person in front of him, who looked back and glared at him.

"Sorry, sir," Keelan stammered. He looked behind him and saw a young boy swinging his feet wildly while sitting on somebody's shoulders. With his attention briefly occupied, he was surprised when the crowd suddenly quieted. He looked at the balcony to see the king and queen standing at the railing. The king was a regal-looking man appearing to be in his late forties, with blonde hair and a neatly cut blonde beard. The queen stood next to the king, a large smile plastered on her face. She wore a bright blue dress trimmed in yellow, the Royal colors. The color of her dress made her red hair stand out and shine. The king had his hand high in the air, asking for quiet. He finally spoke when it was so quiet that you could hear a pin drop.

"Thank you all for coming to our fair city and celebrating the Summer Festival with us. I enjoy seeing so many of you here coming from near and far. Please enjoy the rest of your evening and have a prosperous harvest this year." The King and Queen waved again and then started to depart the balcony. When they reached the large doors, a trumpet sounded, and a flourish of hundreds of birds, bright blue and yellow in color, flew from the castle walls into the sky. The crowd erupted into cheers and laughter, waving their hands at the display of birds being released.

"What are those birds?" Keelan asked.

Jonal frowned and looked at Maya, "I have no idea. I've never seen a bird like that before."

"Me neither, very strange," Maya replied.

"Come, you both have a long journey ahead of you."

Keelan stared up at the birds a moment longer, watching them disperse into the night, *Strange bird to be flying at night,* he thought.

Jonal grabbed Maya and Keelan's hands, and they walked back to his house together.

CHAPTER

-4-

WHEN Keelan and Maya woke the following day, Jonal was nowhere to be found. Maya said it was nothing to worry about. After getting ready, they headed out for the day.

Their main priority was to get the supplies for Elliot. Maya had Keelan hitch Marigold up to their wagon for this stop. The farrier supply was on the first road ring in Kingston, next to all the Inns. When they arrived, Keelan took his father's list out of his pocket and handed it to the farrier master.

"It'll take me a little while to gather up all this," He said examining the list "Why don't you go into the house, and my misses will make you a cup of tea."

Maya smiled. Not surprised at the hospitality. "Thank you, sir. Very kind of you," Maya replied.

Keelan and Maya made their way to the house. They knocked on the door and waited for the Farrier's wife to open the door.

"Hello there. Name's Annabelle," She shook their hands and took them inside a cozy cream and blue-colored house. Annabelle directed them to the table.

Within a few moments, she had a cup of tea in front of them before she bustled out the door to do her daily chores.

Once Keelan was assured they were alone, he whispered to his Ma, "Can we talk about what happened last night?"

Maya acted casual. She shrugged, "I don't know what you're talking about, son."

"Ma." Keelan gave her a look.

"Alright, well, nothing happened last night. We had a lovely evening with a friend and saw some performances."

"You know that's not what I meant. How did I know those things?"

"Just a lucky guess, Keelan. Nothing more. Don't read between the lines too much." She laughed it off.

Keelan frowned; he was positive he *knew* that stuff. It was not a lucky guess or his imagination; but for now, he decided to obey his mother's wishes.

Shortly after they finished their tea, their order was complete. The farrier and his workers loaded the wagon. Maya thanked them for their hospitality, shaking hands with Annabelle, and then climbed into the wagon. Keelan grabbed the reins and gave them a gentle flick,

"Let's go, Marigold." He said, as Marigold sluggishly started to walk down the street.

"Where to next mother?"

Her mother scrolled through the other lists. "That's it for this town."

"You had mentioned to Jonal we needed to see somebody named Esther?"

"Yes, we still need to see her, but she doesn't live in Kingston."

Keelan nodded, "Is she in Lower City?"

"No, she lives further away. We'll head there tomorrow. For now, we will return to Jonal's and wait for his return."

They had already reached home and unpacked all their stuff when Jonal returned. The sun was setting, and Kingston was quickly being cloaked in darkness. Several men walking on long sticks were making their way up and down the streets lighting lanterns.

"Forgive my absence today," Jonal said, making his way inside the house and spotting them in the living room. "I had some business I had to take care of. I bet you two are starving, though."

"I could eat," Keelan said shyly.

Jonal chuckled heartily, "Well, come into the kitchen, my boy. I have a feast waiting for us in this basket." He held up a large basket in front of him.

And it was indeed a feast. Jonal had spread all different kinds of food on the table. As they ate in silence Keelan kept looking between his mother and Jonal, waiting for one of them to say something, but neither did. They had never eaten in silence before.

After dinner, Jonal entered the living room, lit the fire, sat in his chair next to it, and picked up a book and a pipe.

Maya grabbed a book off the shelf and sat in the chair beside him. Keelan again looked between the two adults, trying to figure out the change in their attitudes. He couldn't feel any weird tension, but both of them were acting differently. He could tell.

I must speak to her tomorrow. How did I know those things, and what were those strange birds? He shrugged.

Dismissing the thought for now, Keelan went to the bookshelf, picked something he thought he could understand, and sat on the floor beside the fire.

Keelan read the first page, then the second, and before he could proceed, he was already dozing off. He got up and excused himself as he made his way to bed.

Jonal looked up from his book and watched Keelan walk down the hallway. When the door shut, he shifted his gaze to Maya and cleared his throat.

"I have nothing to say," she said, blandly.

"How can you say that child?" Jonal threw his hands in the air, "Keelan is obviously…. special!"

"He is not. He is just a boy with an overactive imagination," she snapped.

"I knew somebody else that was just a small child once, with an overactive imagination," he said mockingly.

Maya closed the book and got up and looked at him, "Jonal, you know the atmosphere we live in and my past. Please do not make this an issue. It was just a coincidence." She put the book back on the shelf. "Keelan has been spared my fate."

Jonal stared at her for a few more minutes before he nodded, understanding the gravity of the situation. "You're gonna have to talk to him someday, though. He deserves to know your past." He paused before adding, "His past, Maya."

"Right," Maya nodded firmly, "That I shall do when the time is right." She walked toward the bedroom. She was dreading this conversation and wanted it to be over.

"And when will that be?" She heard Jonal's voice from the living room.

"Whenever I deem it to be." She whispered to herself.

After saying their goodbyes to Jonal, they headed out of Kingston. The journey through the canyon seemed to take no time at all this time. At the massive main gate, Maya had to show her admittance scroll. "This is so they make sure we didn't overstay our welcome," Maya told Keelan.

The inspection officer scowled but didn't reply; instead, he waved her through.

Lower City was just as busy as when they traveled through it a few short days ago.

"Why is it so much busier here in this smaller city?" Keelan asked.

"Oh, it's really not smaller. Many more people live and work here. They have whole buildings that are like Inns, but people live in them full-time. It's like several small houses all in one big building. Some of them are three stories tall," she leaned over toward him and whispered as if it was a grand secret.

They traveled through Lower City and then continued traveling out into the countryside. After midday, they stop to give Marigold a break. Maya pulled out a basket Jonal had given them, handed a small sandwich to Keelan, and took one for herself.

"How much further to Esther's?" Keelan asked.

"Not too much now."

"Is she close to a town?" He munched on the sandwich.

"No, she lives out here all on her own. She says she likes the solitude."

Just before dark, they came upon a small cottage at the forest's edge next to a small babbling brook. An old woman was hunched over a garden, picking herbs and vegetables. She looked up and shielded her eyes from the setting sun with one hand while holding her other hand out in front of her. She cast them a curious glance before she seemed to recognize Maya, then broke into a large smile and started to wave.

"You made it, dear girl!" She yelled.

Maya smiled and waved.

"I told you I would be stopping by this summer." She said, as she reached the old woman.

"You did, you did. But I sometimes can't trust my own recollection with my failing memory." She stated with a soft chuckle.

"Esther, this is my son, Keelan." Maya directed her attention toward him.

"Nice to meet you, ma'am," Keelan said.

Esther stared at Keelan without saying a word for a few moments. A small smile crept onto her face, and she turned to Maya, "You did not tell me all about your boy, now did you?"

Maya's eyes widened and she looked at Keelan, "Why don't you go unhook Marigold? We will be staying here for the evening. There's a small pen in the back of the house. She will be fine there tonight," she said to Keelan hurriedly. "Esther, why don't I help you prepare some dinner?" Maya said, ignoring Esther's original comment.

Keelan looked between the two adults, confused as ever.

Why does everyone that she introduces me to, talk about me like I am some sort of strange or special person? He shrugged and got to work unhitching the mare.

The rest of the evening was spent with small talk that Keelan had heard numerous times over the past few days. Thankfully, Esther had a small family of cats that lived in her house, and he busied himself by playing with the kittens. After eating dinner – in silence again – Maya and Keelan went to sleep.

The following morning, after Maya had gathered all the supplies she needed from Esther, it was time to say goodbye again.

"It was good seeing you again, Maya, and meeting you for the first time, Keelan. I know this won't be the last time I meet you, my dear boy." Esther stood from her rickety chair on her front porch and walked over to their wagon to shake hands. She grimaced as she walked, leaning heavily on her cane.

"If you don't mind me saying, ma'am. My mother's friend, Sally in Kingston, has a wonderful product that keeps her looking and, she says, feeling young. I really think that you should get some, ma'am." Keelan said shyly.

"Oh, I do, my boy," she cackled, "I already do," she walked back up the steps of her porch as she laughed almost hysterically.

When they were almost out of sight of Esther's cottage, Keelan turned to get one last look.

"She's a very strange lady," Keelan remarked.

Maya laughed loudly and clapped him on the back, "That she is, that she is."

"Where to now?" He focused his attention on the road.

"We will be going back home now. We will stay in a small village tonight and should be home by dark tomorrow."

"It will be good to be home," he frowned.

Maya glanced at him from the side of her eye, "Have you not enjoyed yourself?" She asked him.

"Oh, I've had a great time, mother. I'm just not used to meeting new people, that's all, and I miss father."

She patted his arm, "Me too, about your father, that is. Before you were born, your father used to come with me."

Keelan's frown deepened.

"Oh, don't feel bad. It was his choice to stay home. I told him we would go together when you turned five, but he declined. He says he gets more work done when I'm not there," she laughed heartily.

Keelan laughed now, "But he doesn't work while you're gone. At least, not that much. We do more fishing, hunting, and lazing around."

"I know, but it is time well spent. Just a father and his son."

CHAPTER

-5-

THE small village was most definitely small. Less than a dozen cottages surrounding three larger buildings and a central well and a clock tower. Keelan thought Creekside was small, but when compared to this one, it was a metropolis.

"An inn with a stable, a mercantile, and one other building. That's it?" Keelan asked, surprised,

"Yup, that's it. This is Verndale. The other building is the meeting hall." Maya said, "Let's go see if the inn's kitchen is still warm."

When they neared the stable, a boy Keelan's age greeted them. "How many nights?" He asked.

"Just tonight. A little extra grain for her, please."

He nodded before beginning to unhitch Marigold from the wagon, while Maya and Keelan grabbed their bags and lugged them up to the inn.

The inn was two stories with a small but cozy common room. The smell of freshly made bread wafted through the air. Keelan's stomach growled loudly.

A boisterous laugh came from the kitchen a moment before a large, barreled man walked through the door. "I think someone's hungry!" He exclaimed. Keelan's face heated.

"Don't be embarrassed, boy. I was once a growing boy. Come, sit. I will bring you out a large helping." He nodded to Keelan and smiled at Maya.

The innkeeper brought out two large bowls of stew, a whole loaf of bread with a wedge of cheese, and a pitcher of lemonade. "The road is dusty business. I'll have your room ready for you when you finish here. No rush, take your time."

"Thank you, Ken."

Ken, the innkeeper, nodded and returned to the kitchen.

"Stop here often, ma?"

Maya smiled, "Eat up, long day again tomorrow."

"After we eat, I'm going to check on Marigold, okay?" Keelan said around a mouthful.

"Take her some of this wonderful bread; she'll love it."

"Hi, girl." Keelan greeted Marigold. The mare nickered softly to him. "Here you go," he held out the bread for her.

She sniffed it once before taking the whole piece in one big bite. The chestnut mare munched on the bread noisily, shaking her head up and down, causing her flaxen mane to bounce.

"Are you feeling rested and ready for one more day of travel?" He asked her. She snorted and tossed her head from side to side; Keelan chuckled. "I'll take that as a yes."

Keelan froze when he heard a faint snorting snicker. He spun around, searching the darkness, "Who's there?" No one answered. He roamed his eyes around, trying to pick out movement. "Show yourself!"

The person snickered again, "Where are you?" He called out.

Finally, a petite girl around his age walked out from behind a large hay bale; she had slightly curly, dark brown hair and sun-kissed tanned skin.

Keelan stood next to Marigold, still holding her halter, one hand stroking the mare's white muzzle. "Who are you?" He asked once again.

"Who are you?" She retorted back, smirking.

Frowning, Keelan answered, "My name is Keelan Keifman. Who are you?"

"Shaylee Faeven," she replied.

"Shaylee, it's nice to meet you." He nodded, "Do you live here in Verndale, or are you passing through like me?"

She shook her head, "Just visiting; I don't live far from here." Her gaze fell on Marigold, "Do you understand her?" She asked, slowly approaching the mare.

"No, I just like to talk to her. What are you doing hiding in a barn?"

"I was chasing after Lyra."

"Who's Lyra?"

"My vaskakat."

"What's a vaskakat?"

Shaylee grinned and flipped her hair off her shoulder. A tiny white kitten was tucked under her hair.

Keelan's eyes widened. "Can I pet her?"

Shaylee shrugged and took a couple of steps closer to him. Keelan reached his hand out to let Lyra sniff him. She leaned forward, sniffed his fingers, and abruptly hissed, leaped off her shoulder, and flew into the rafters.

Shaylee laughed, "She doesn't like very many people. I wouldn't be too upset."

Keelan's mouth dropped in surprise, "Did that cat just fly?"

"She's not a cat; I told you she's a vaskakat."

"A vaskakat? I've never heard of such a thing. How does a cat have wings?"

The vaskakat sat in the rafters, looking down at the two kids. Keelan stared in open awe. The kitten was pure white except for the tips of her ears, which were black and were much more pointed than a typical cat's ears. The ends of her wingtips and tail tip were also black.

Shaylee whistled, and the kitten soared down and perched on her shoulder again. Shaylee smiled, her eyes twinkling.

"Wow, your eyes have green flecks in them," Keelan noted.

"So, what? All Elvenfae's have eyes like mine."

"I've never heard of Elvenfae. What Kingdom are you from? My eyes have green flecks in them, and I'm from Creekside."

"I'm from Threndy; it's not very far from here. And, Elvenfae is not a place; it is what I am."

Keelan looked clueless.

"My mother is a fairy, and my father is an elf." Shaylee added.

He looked at her, trying to judge if she was serious. Before she could add anything, he laughed out loud. "Elves and fairies aren't real. If you don't want to tell me where you're from, that's fine. You don't have to make things up."

Shaylee squinted her eyes, ready to say something, but suddenly, she wrung her hands in front of her and looked around the barn nervously. "I guess I should be going," she said quickly.

"Keelan, where are you?"

"Oh, that's my mother. I better get inside. It was nice meeting you, Shaylee."

"It was nice meeting you as well, Keelan." She narrowed her eyes again and took off at a run out of the barn, around the corner of the inn, and disappeared.

Keelan returned to the inn to find his mother standing on the porch looking around for him. "There you are. Where have you been?"

"I was in the barn. I met a girl with a weird-looking cat."

"Well, come back inside. It's getting dark, and you can tell me all about your new friend."

Keelan jumped up the stairs two at a time, rushing inside. Maya looked out into the yard; several bushes next to the stable were in full bloom, and deep purple petals framed a strange flower. She paused and looked at it.

"Ma?"

"Coming." Her attention diverted to Keelan's voice as she shrugged off the feeling.

Maya was sure she had not seen those flowers there before.

Maya led Keelan up the stairs of the tiny inn and opened their room door for him. Once inside, she handed him a mug of cocoa. He inhaled the steam and smiled.

"Mint cocoa, my favorite."

"Put your night clothes on and tell me about this girl."

Keelan changed into his nightshirt and pants and joined his mother beside the small fireplace. She sat in the room's only chair, sipping her tea so Keelan sat on the floor at her feet.

"Where is your friend from?" Maya asked after a moment.

"She said she's from Threndy. I've never heard of that place. Have you?" he asked, looking up at her.

She winced slightly before answering, "I have; it's not far from here."

"That's what Shaylee said."

"Shaylee…" She whispered, "That's a pretty name."

"She told me some strange things, though."

Maya kept her gaze locked on the fire even though she could feel Keelan's eyes on her. "What did she tell you," she said softly.

Keelan narrowed his eyes, "Ma?" He said, wanting her eyes to be on him,

"I'm listening." She replied, her gaze fixed on the fireplace.

Why is she suddenly acting so weird? He thought.

"Okay," He sighed, "Anyway, she said she was an Elvenfae, her mother is a fairy, and her father is an elf, and her cat wasn't a cat," he continued with the same excitement. "It's a vaskakat, which looks like a cat with wings and can fly."

Maya slowly drank out of the mug in her hand. Keelan waited for her reaction, but instead, she closed her eyes and sighed, "Oh, I see," she finally replied. "What did this Elvenfae look like?"

Keelan smiled, satisfied that his mother was paying attention. "Well, kind of like me, I guess. She looked to be about my age, with long brown hair, but it was her eyes that startled me the most. She has green flecks in her eyes, just like me."

Maya snapped her gaze to Keelan, "Green flecks, huh? That is rare." She shifted her posture toward Keelan, "Tell me about this vaskakat?"

"Well, like I said, it is a cat with wings." His mother's sudden interest was putting him off.

"Be more descriptive, Keelan."

"Okay," He sat straight. It did not feel like a fun conversation any more. "It had long white fur, with very pointed ears that were tipped black. The tip of its tail was black, and the ends of the feathers on its wings were black, too. Oh, and did I say it had wings, Mother? It flew to the rafters and then flew back to her."

"Are you sure it flew and didn't just jump?"

He shook his head, "It didn't jump. No way. That rafter was way too far up there. It had to flap its wings to get there."

Maya nodded, "It has been a long time since I have seen a vaskakat."

"You've seen one before?" Keelan scrambled to his knees, placing his hands on his mother's knee.

"I used to have one, but, oh my, that was a long time ago. I wasn't much younger than you." She seemed relaxed now. "Ferret," she added, sitting back in a comfortable position again.

"I'm confused. Did you have a ferret or a vaskakat?"

Maya laughed, "No, his name was Ferret. He was brown and black with a hint of gold threaded throughout his short coat and long, bushy tail. He was such a mischievous little character." She smiled and shook her head at the memory.

"What happened to him?"

"What… oh, what happened to him?" She repeated, a little distracted. "He ran away one day." She paused and looked at Keelan again, "What did she call herself again?"

"Shaylee."

"No, who was she, an Elven fairy?"

"Elvenfae is what she said."

"Now, that is something I have never heard of before."

Keelan frowned, "Ma, you're not listening! She said her mother is a fairy, and her father is an elf!" He exclaimed, "I thought those were just fairytales."

"Well, yes," she said, and the twinkle in Keelan's eye disappeared. "And no." She added.

"What?" He elevated his voice and the twinkle returned to his eyes again.

"Calm down, let's retire for the evening," She got up from the chair, "We can discuss this later, but not where anyone can hear us, understand?"

He nodded, "Um, yeah, I guess so."

Early the next morning, they were back on the road and headed toward Creekside. Keelan looked around to make sure no one else was in sight. Once confirmed, he decided to see what his mother knew about elves and fairies.

Just as he opened his mouth to start asking the questions that had been rattling through his brain all night, his mother spoke first.

"I think it is time for a pop quiz," she said. Keelan groaned. "Tell me what you would use for a colicky infant," she said.

Keelan racked his brain, trying to remember the remedy, "Oh, I remember… that is… what is it?" He asked himself, "Oh yeah, you can try either basil, fennel seed, or peppermint made into a tea and then cooled to drink."

"Very good."

For several hours, Maya continued to quiz her son on different remedies, medical procedures for healing cuts and bruises, the best places to find specific herbs, and how certain herbs were prepared. The questions kept coming, and Keelan couldn't get a word in edgewise.

When the conversation paused, and Keelan thought he would finally get to ask some questions, other travelers appeared on the road.

He could not ask his questions since they had an audience. He grumbled to himself but didn't say anything out loud.

The rest of the trip, somebody was always within earshot, either behind them or in front of them, and then they reached Creekside.

Upon the sight of their house, both of them suddenly felt relaxed. Keelan could see his father standing at the door. He waved excitedly. His Ma and Father hugged before Marigold was put up and the wagon was unloaded, it was then time for a quick dinner and to bed; it had been a long day, and still, his questions went unanswered.

"Good morning, son," Keelan's father smiled, "It's so good to have you and your mother back,"

"Where's Mother?" Keelan asked, entering the kitchen.

"Oh, people have been missing her. She had to leave early to hand out remedies for those people who had been requesting her services while you two were gone."

Keelan sighed but said nothing else to his father; after all, he didn't know if his father had any information on elves or fairies and figured it would be best to talk to his mother first.

"We also have a lot of hard work to do, my boy. Now that you are officially done with school, I need your full-time help at the farrier shop. How does that sound?"

"I'm ready," he replied. His father smiled and dished out their breakfast.

Days turned into weeks of the same routine - wake up, his mother already gone for the day, head out to the farrier shop with his father, shoeing horses, training a few horses that came through, and general tidy and clean up.

Whenever he did try to speak to his mother about elves and fairies, she would make vague comments or repeat something he heard in a fairy tale, but she would always hint there was more to it but never elaborate.

After about a month of this, he decided to start taking matters into his own hands. Any free time he got, he went to the local library, a tiny building near the meeting hall with a small collection of books. He found a few books on fairies and elves, but most were stories he'd already heard.

He found a few books discussing the Kingdom of Evansshire's founding. He found those more intriguing, but soon he grew tired of searching for answer. There just weren't enough books on the subject in the library.

Winter came and went, and soon Keelan gave up learning more about elves and fairies, as just the daily activities to keep the family afloat took all of his energy and that of his parents.

CHAPTER

-6-

WHEN spring finally arrived, Keelan grew anxious to join his mother on her next visit to the Capital. He thought they might have more books; surely, they have more extensive libraries. With his desire to learn more about elves and fairies reawakened, he found himself getting his chores done much quicker than usual so he can have spare time to visit the library.

The day before his mother was set to leave, someone new moved into town.

Keelan was in the farrier shop hammering out a couple of shoes for a skittish gelding that belonged to a traveling merchant. His father voice drifted to him from outside the shop, "Come out here, son. I want you to meet someone."

Keelan placed the shoe and hammer down and went out front to see his father. His father was standing next to a massive man with flame-red hair and light brown eyes that almost had a yellow tint to them.

"Keelan, I want you to meet Douglas Firestrum and his son, Lance. They just relocated to Creekside and are bringing their ranching operation here."

"Welcome to Creekside, Mr. Firestrum." Keelan smiled, "What kind of ranch do you have?" he asked.

"We raise cattle and horses, my boy." Douglas replied, "And that's why I'm here. I was told your father was the best farrier in town.

Keelan chuckled, "Well, there's only two."

Douglas winked, "That's beside the point. I didn't get recommendations from inside this town. I was told over at Lower City that there is no better place to get your horses shod than with the farrier, named Elliot, over in Creekside. I've been searching high and low for just the right town."

Keelan beamed up at his father; he was well known and held in high regard all the way to the Capital.

"And I hear that you, my boy, are starting to be a fine horse trainer."

Keelan's face reddened, "Well, horses just seemed to respond well to me. That's all," he replied, shyly.

Douglas boomed out a deep, bellowing laugh and clapped his hands together, "I'm looking forward to this being a beautiful working relationship."

Keelan looked up at his father, puzzled.

Elliot looked at Douglas making his way back a few feet away from them to their wagon. He leaned in, "We have our work cut out for us, son. He has eight horses that need to be shod right away and four wagons to repair, and he's expecting at least three foals here in the next couple of weeks. So, both of us are going to be kept really busy."

"But I'm leaving with Mother in the morning," Keelan reminded his dad.

"I'm sorry, son, plans have changed. We can't pass up on an opportunity like this." Elliot dropped his shoulder. "Besides, you know your mother has two apprentices now. They will be accompanying her on this trip."

"Three women traveling alone. Is that safe?" Shock and sorrow gripped his expression.

"As safe as when she travels by herself, but don't worry, one of the girls has an older brother who will accompany them. So, it'll just be the boys here at the house, but we're going to keep plenty busy." His dad responded, excited for the new opportunity.

"Okay then," Keelan said disappointedly, his eyes glazed over, "When do we get started?"

"Oh, don't worry, my child!" He patted Keelan's head, "You'll get plenty of opportunities to go with your mother later down the road. But you know this," He pointed at Douglas, who was busy taking stuff out from his wagon, "This happens rarely."

Keelan nodded, trying to hide his disappointment. He didn't want to make his father sad, "You're right."

"Good!" His father beamed, "We'll start the first horse tomorrow. He will also have the wagons dropped off first thing in the morning. Why don't you take Lance and show him around town? Take the rest of the day off; you deserve it."

As Keelan turned around to leave, a young boy walked up to them. He had a striking resemblance to Douglas.

"Hello." He said, looking between Elliot and Keelan.

Elliott looked down and held his hand out, "Hello there. You must be Lance?"

Lance nodded. Elliot introduced himself and Keelan to Lance.

"Would you like me to show you around town, Lance?" Keelan asked.

"Sure, I don't know where anything is, so it'll be nice to get the lay of the land," Lance said.

"Okay, well, let me get cleaned up, and then I'll show you around."

Maya arrived home with her herb collection basket in hand. She smiled and waved before continuing to their home. Douglas's head swiveled to follow her. He narrowed his eyes and then nodded. "I'll see you this evening, Lance."

As Keelan and Lance walked toward the town center, Keelan couldn't help but notice Lance's expensive-looking attire. His britches and boots seem to be of finer quality than the ones his mother had bought him in Kingston several months ago.

"So, what brings you to Creekside?" Keelan asked.

Lance seemed startled by the question and looked around nervously before answering, "Uh, my dad just wanted a change of scenery, I guess. He isn't really telling me much - he just said, Son, we're moving," he chuckled dryly.

"Wow. That must have been weird."

Lance shrugged. "So, what do you do for fun around here?" he asked, changing the topic.

It was Keelan's turn to shrug, "Well, not much. I spend most of my time working with my father. I guess I go down to the Creek whenever I can. It's really nice in the summer."

"Oh, that sounds like fun. Why don't we head there now? To the Creek?"

"Okay," Keelan led him passed the Council Hall and into the surrounding woods. They could hear it babbling against the rocks that lined the edge as they neared the creek.

Even though it was called a creek, it turned into a rapid-filled river during the summer runoff. Despite this early in the spring, the banks were starting to swell.

"Oh, wow, I wasn't expecting it to be this big. That's not a creek; why don't they call it Riverside?" Lance said, amused.

"From what I was told, this area's first settler was someone traveling through and got snowed in. At that time of the year, it was just a creek, but it helped sustain the family through the harsh winter, so they decided to stay and called their encampment Creekside. When the town built up around it, the name just stuck."

Lance nodded. He looked around and grabbed a couple of stones. Sitting down at the bank, he tried to skip them across the rolling water. His last rock hit the top of a fish, which made the fish jump out of the water and roll in the air. Both boys broke out laughing.

Maya left the following morning with her two apprentices and their guardian chaperone. The two apprentices were Keelan's age, and he remembered them both from school. Lea was a short, plump girl with strawberry blonde hair and pale blue eyes. She smiled and waved to Keelan, her freckled face scrunching up as she smiled. Joy and her brother, Owen, had dark skin and black curly hair that shined in the early morning light, both were taller than average and slender. Owen was twenty and already had a wife and two-year-old son. Owen nodded to Keelan, but Joy ignored him like always. Her dark brown eyes found his, but she quickly looked away and started to say something to Lea, making the other girl frown.

Keelan watched with sadness as they rolled out of the yard and down toward the town. He looked forward to spending time with his mother again like he did almost a year ago. His father approached from behind and patted him on the back, breaking him out of his thoughts.

"Since we're both up and at'em, might as well get going today; it's going to be a long one."

Keelan nodded and followed his father to the shop.

True to Mr. Firestrum's word, he arrived first thing in the morning with four wagons and eight horses to be shod. Douglas and Lance each drove a team of two horses with a wagon, and then two additional men drove the other two. Riding horses were attached to the rears of each wagon.

"Here they are. How long do you think it'll take you to get all this done?" Douglas asked.

Elliot went around to each horse, picked up every hoof, and then looked at the damage done on the wagons. "My boy and I can have this done fairly fast." He gave it a bit more thought, "I'd say about two weeks."

Douglas scratched his chin, "I think that should suffice. I'll let you boys get to it." Mr. Firestrum's ranch hands were already mounted on their riding horses when Douglas mounted his. "Oh, and Master

Keifman, would it be too much of an imposition to allow my son to observe your work today."

Elliot looked at the boy and then back at his father, "It wouldn't be too much of an imposition, not at all."

Douglas glanced at his son and nodded. "He needs to learn some skill, and he just doesn't seem to want to work with cattle yet." He looked at Lance, "I'll see you at dinnertime, son." Mr. Firestrum and his ranch hands rode away.

"Okay, Keelan, why don't you and Lance start unhitching all the horses and put them in the back pen? I'll start on the first wagon, and you pick which horse to start with. You can show him around the shop as well."

"We're on it, Father," Keelan said.

Lance followed Keelan to the closest wagon. He appeared to be quiet and reserved, which suited Keelan just fine.

With Lance's help, they were able to finish two horses on the first day.

The next several days went the same; Lance arrived early in the morning and assisted Keelan in shoeing the horses or helped Elliot with the wagon repairs. He was a quick learner and quite strong for his age. He was able to handle the bellows much better than Keelan could. Keelan and Lance spoke occasionally, but most of the time, Lance kept to himself.

On the final day, with only one horse left to shoe and one wagon left to fix, Keelan took a break from the forge to help a traveler with their horse.

"I don't know what got into him," the stranger said. "We were just riding along the road, and all of a sudden, he bucked me off. I didn't see any snakes in the road and didn't hear anything in the woods. It was like he saw a ghost or something. There must be something in his hoof."

Keelan nodded and walked over to the horse. He ran his hand up and down his neck and forehead, whispering to it. The stranger leaned over to Lance and whispered, "What's he doing? Trying to talk to the horse?"

Lance shrugged, "I don't know. Sometimes, he whispers to the horses; it seems to calm them, I guess."

The man harrumphed but didn't press it any further.

Keelan ran his hand down the nervous horse's side and down the flank toward the tail, all the while muttering softly to it. The horse's ears flipped in his direction, and his hide quivered under his touch, but the horse did not shy away from him. Keelan walked behind the horse and started the same process from the tail to the head. When he reached the middle of the saddle, he paused and ran his hand under the blanket; he quickly went to the other side, uncinched the saddle, and slid it off the horses back.

"What's the meaning of this?" the stranger asked his face turning scarlet, "Why are you unsaddling my horse? I told you there's something in his hoof, and you haven't picked up a single foot!"

Keelan ignored him as he gently placed the saddle on the ground. Next, he pulled off the blanket and laid it on the saddle. He felt around in the saddle blanket until he pulled out a large sticker and held it up for the stranger to see.

"Looks like a burr got in the blanket. It must have worked its way free," he said as he handed the large sticker to the horse's owner.

"Well, I'll be. If I got poked in the side with this, I think I would go bucking around too." The stranger was startled at Keelan's way of working but he let out a chuckle, "Thank you, my boy that was fine work you did there. The man fished in his pocket, pulled out a silver coin, and handed it to him.

"I'm sorry, sir, I don't have change for this. I can't possibly accept more than a copper for what I did here."

"Nonsense, my boy, what you did was priceless to me. I thought I would have to get a new horse!" He pointed at the horse, "I thought this one was lame." He whispered to Keelan.

Keelan smiled, pocketed the coin, and saddled the man's horse. In no time, the man was trotting down the road. He turned around to see Lance staring at him. "What?"

Lance shook his head, "I've never seen anybody understand horses so well. Even my father and his ranch hands couldn't have done what you just did in so little time."

Keelan shrugged but didn't reply. The rest of the afternoon, Lance was much more talkative; he asked Keelan if he'd ever been outside of Creekside before, and Keelan was happy to tell him of his trip to Kingston. Well, most of it anyway; his encounter with Shaylee, he kept to himself.

With the last wagon and the final horse complete, Lance was set to return to his ranch.

"My father requested that one of you come to the ranch with me to receive payment," Lance said. Elliot splashed water on his face to cool himself down and then looked over at Lance and then at his son.

"Keelan can go with you." Elliot said.

"I'll saddle up Marigold right now," Keelan replied, grinning ear to ear.

The Firestrum's ranch was on the outskirts of town, close to the edge of the Brightbane Forest, the gateway to the Black Mountains. No one else lived this close to the Black Mountains. They were said to be cursed, and anyone who entered never returned.

Mr. Firestrum said he didn't believe all the superstitions regarding the forest and the mountain, and the land was cheap. He even laughed heartedly when he said he hoped the superstitions stayed alive to keep people away from his herds.

Once they left the town proper, the road to the Firestrum's ranch became old and rain-worn as nobody else ventured down or maintained it. As the Firestrums hadn't lived in town very long, their house was still under construction, and they were living in a series of tents. It seemed their priority had been getting the barn and corrals up and running. Keelan gazed out at the field and saw at least a hundred cows grazing within sight.

"How many cows do you have?"

Lance's face scrunched in thought, "I think Father said close to 500 currently."

"500 cows!" Keelan said, amazed. "I've never heard of a ranch having that many before. How do you feed them all?"

"Well, right now, they're just out grazing in the pastures, but Father has been cultivating a few pastures so we can get hay for the winter. He's hoping to be able to maintain the whole herd all winter. There's a big market for cows in Kingston and surrounding areas, and he doesn't plan to only sell to Evansshire."

Keelan thought, *I didn't think anybody was allowed to sell anything outside Evansshire, but what do I know?*

Keelan looked around at all the black and tan cows in utter amazement. He couldn't believe this wasn't even the whole herd.

They rode up to the barn, parked the last wagon next to the other four, and unhitched the team. One of the ranch hands came out to assist and took the horses away for them.

Lance looked around, trying to spot his father, "There he is," he pointed out into the field.

Keelan saw a large black horse with an even larger man on its back. That was most definitely Mr. Firestrum. Keelan thought his father was a large man until he met Douglas. He was an imposing man at 6'6" and probably 250 pounds of muscle. But then, when you took in his slightly yellow eyes, he just looked eerie. Lance had dark reddish-brown hair and blue eyes. Even though both boys were the same age, Keelan could tell that Lance would be bigger than him.

Lance hopped on his horse and gestured for Keelan to follow him; they set off to meet with Mr. Firestrum at a canter.

"Was that the last wagon I saw rolling in?" Douglas asked when his son approached.

"Yes, sir. All eight horses and four wagons complete." Keelan nodded firmly.

"In just under two weeks, just as your father promised. Can't thank you boys enough. Let's head back to the tent, and I'll get you all squared away." He kicked his horse into a fast gallop, and the three raced back to the tents.

"Lance, go check on the mares. I'll just be a few moments."

Lance nodded his head. "Come on, let me show you the mares that will give birth soon."

Both boys made their way inside the massive barn. There were twelve stalls, all of which were full of horses. The four stalls on the furthest end were the largest. Four mares with enormous bellies stood quietly in their stalls. "These three should be given birth any day," he motioned to the three closest to them. "The one over there in another couple of weeks."

All the horses the Firestrum owned were of the finest looking quality, and all were either black or chestnut.

In a corral outside the barn, a horse stomped, snorted, and then screamed. "What's going on with that one?" Keelan asked.

"Oh, that's just Untamable," Lance said.

"Untamable, that's a weird name."

"Well, he doesn't really have a name. That's just what we call him. Nobody can even get close to him without him trying to kill you."

"Can I see him?"

Lance shrugged, "Sure, I don't see why not. Come on."

Untamable was in a fairly small corral with an extremely tall fence. One of the ranch hands was sitting on the fence, trying to get a rope around his neck. Untamable bucked, snorted, and screamed as he evaded every attempt. A couple of the other ranch hands who had stopped their work to watch the antics laughed and snickered.

All except for the one trying to capture Untamable; he was growling in frustration. "Damn horse, just won't sit still. Just doesn't know what's good for him. Just look at him; look at the condition he's in," the hand complained.

Keelan looked over at the sorry-looking horse. He appeared to be about five years old and well-fed, but his coat, mane, and tail were just in shambles. He could not determine precisely what shade of brown his coat was; it was so dirty, with clumps of winter coat clinging to it. His mane and tail were just a mass of rats' nests and mats.

Keelan and Lance walked up to the fence and peeked through the slats. The ranch hand looked down at the boys but said nothing. Lance motioned for the ranch hand to stop trying to catch Untamable. Keelan climbed to the top of the fence and locked eyes with the horse.

Untamable stopped bucking and rearing and stilled, just looking at Keelan. He stomped a front hoof into the hard, dusty ground and snorted. Keelan started to whisper to himself. The horse stilled further and stopped snorting and tossing his head. It took a hesitant step forward. Without even thinking, Keelan flipped his legs over the top of the fence and dropped down into the pen. A couple of the ranch hands rushed forward and shouted, "Get out of there."

Lance held up his hand and told them to wait.

Still whispering mostly to himself, Keelan took a couple of cautionary steps toward Untamable with his hands outstretched. Untamable tossed his head and snorted but did not retreat. Slowly, step by step, Keelan walked the short distance until he stood within reach of Untamable. With his hands in the air to show Untamable he meant no harm, he took one step at a time, making sure he didn't spook him. The horses' ears flicked back and forth nervously, and he expanded his nostrils in a deep breath. Keelan froze, he outstretched his hand, just inches from Untamables' muzzle.

After a brief moment, Untamable closed the distance and pressed his muzzle against Keelan's hand.

"Unbelievable!" one of the ranch hands exclaimed.

Keelan moved his hand up Untamables' forehead, brushing off caked-on mud and dirt. He noticed some white fur underneath all the crud and brushed a little harder to reveal a white mark perfectly in the middle of his forehead in the shape of a sword. Untamable snorted but didn't retreat. Keelan continued to whisper and moved his hand down the horse's neck to rest on his shoulder.

Keelan looked over at the ranch hands and Lance staring in awe, watching him approach a horse no one had been able to touch before. "I don't think Untamable fits him anymore," he said, winking at Lance.

Douglas had joined his son and was shaking his head in disbelief. "If I hadn't seen it with my own eyes, I wouldn't have believed it! A boy of thirteen tames the Untamable!" He laughed. "So, what will you name him, boy?" he asked.

"Me? Name him?"

"It's only fitting that you should get to name your own horse," he said with a smile.

"Oh no, I can't afford a horse like this," Keelan said, sadly.

"No one said I was selling him to you, Keelan. I'm going to make you work for him. If you can train him and gentle him to saddle, then you will have earned him. Nobody else can handle him; it's obvious you two were meant for each other."

Keelan smiled proudly. He looked at Untamable.

"His name is Rogue."

"Well, why don't you give Rogue time to think about his new station in life and come on out here so we can get you all set up and get you home?" Keelan complied and hopped out of the fence enclosure.

"You can keep him here until he's rideable. I'll work it out with your father for you to be here every day bright and early working with him. From the connection I can see that you two have, it shouldn't take long before you're riding him down that road.

"Take this sack and give it to your father. This should be more than enough to cover all the horses' shoes and wagon repairs." He started making his way out. "My son told me that you had a way with horses. I'm glad I got to see it in action for myself." He shook his head, still amused. He turned around to look at Keelan, "Why don't you stay for dinner, and then you can be on your way."

"Thank you, sir, I would like that." Keelan said, before looking back at Rogue, his own first horse.

CHAPTER

-7-

OVER the next several months, Keelan would wake early and eat breakfast before saddling Marigold and riding to the Firestrums ranch.

He worked with Rogue until they finished the task Keelan had in mind for the day, or until their mutual patience wore thin.

Today was one of the days that patience was running out.

"Come on, Rogue, just go through the puddle," Keelan begged the horse again.

He was astride the blood-bay horse with a perfect white sword on his forehead. Rogue's actual coloring became evident after a particularly hard rain about two weeks prior. Now, Keelan had a new puzzle on his hands: getting Rogue to tolerate water, whether touching the horse with it or taking a dip on its own accord. The small puddle was about six feet across, two feet wide, and no more than a few inches deep. Rogue pawed and snorted but refused to step foot into the puddle. Keelan gently nudged Rogue's side with his heels, trying to get him to take a step forward. Rogue took one step, then another, and suddenly took a flying leap, sailing through the air over the puddle.

Keelan grabbed a hold of the saddle to keep from falling off at the sudden movement. Lance and one of the stable hands laughed from their vantage point. Keelan only frowned and shook his head at his horse.

"Well, that's one way to get over the puddle," he muttered under his breath. He walked Rogue in a large circle and headed back toward the puddle once again. He dismounted when they reached and attempted to lead Rogue across the puddle this time. Keelan put both feet in and splashed around in the puddle, "See, it's not that deep; what are you so scared of?" he said to the horse. Rogue reached down, sniffed the water, and took a few hesitant steps toward it.

Slowly, Rogue put one hoof in the water with his head lowered down just inches above the water.

With one hoof in the water and then two, Rogue took a giant sniff and pawed at it; when the water splashed him in the face, he screeched and threw his head back, almost jerking the reins out of Keelan's hands.

"Whoa," Keelan said as he got a tighter hold of the bridle. Keelan started to whisper and mutter softly under his breath; Rogue immediately calmed down. Rogue stood still, not stepping further into the water but not retreating. After a moment, Keelan glanced over at Lance.

"What are you saying to him when you start whispering like that?" Lance asked.

Keelan looked at Lance, puzzled, "What do you mean?"

"Well, whenever Rogue starts misbehaving, you start whispering, and he immediately calms down. Same with that horse with the saddle burr that you helped a while ago. You started to whisper and mutter quietly, and the horse immediately calmed."

Keelan thought about the last few moments to try to recall what he had been doing. "I didn't realize I was saying anything."

Lance raised his brow, not buying it. "Explain what happened just now. You walked him over to the puddle; he splashed himself and reared back. Then you started to whisper. What were you thinking?"

"Hmmm, I was just thinking that he needed to be calm and at peace with the situation."

"What about that horse with the bur in its saddle blanket?"

Keelan thought for a moment before he replied, "With that one, I guess I was thinking, what is going on with the horse? Where was his pain? As I was looking him over, I was just, for lack of a better word, directed to the saddle blanket. I instinctively knew something was wrong there, and it was not in his hooves."

"So, you're telling me the *horse* was *telling* you where it was having problems?"

"Oh, that's ridiculous." Keelan laughed, "I can't talk to horses, Lance."

"Well, you may not be able to talk to them, but somehow you communicate with them. It's the same way when you first met Rogue. He instantly had a connection to you and responded to you immediately."

Now, it was Keelan's turn to frown. "Well, I think I have some things to think about now. I think this is a good place to stop for today. I better return to my father's shop, but I'll see you tomorrow."

Over the next few days, Keelan continued to work with Rogue and tried to concentrate on everything he did. He could never hear himself whisper to the horse, but Lance told him it happened every time. All he remembered of the incidents was that a sense of peace washed over him as he concentrated on the horse. But he was not conscious of any whispering or muttering that he did. What he was doing bothered him, but since he could not hear himself do it, he decided to continue training with his instincts and not let it bother him because, obviously, it was working.

At one point, he even tried to have Lance stand beside him to see if he could hear what he was saying. Lance said he could hear him but did not understand what he was saying. It was like he was speaking a different language and one that he could not pronounce or repeat. It was almost like the minute he heard the words, he forgot what they were.

On the eve of Keelan's Name-Day, his parents gave him an unexpected gift. After working with Rogue all morning, he had just arrived at the farrier shop to find his mother and father smiling at him on the front porch. He looked at them questioningly and approached them.

"What are you both doing out here?"

"Waiting for you," Elliot replied.

Keelan's brow shot up as he looked back in forth between the two, "Did I do something wrong?"

Maya smiled at her son, "Why would you think you've done something wrong?"

"I don't think I have," he replied. "But I've never seen both of you stand on the front porch this time of day."

"Well, as you know, tomorrow is your fourteenth name-day, and we thought we'd do something special for you. You have been a mighty big help around the house and in the shop this past year. You're almost a man and ready to go out on your own. So, to celebrate, we are giving you the rest of the day off and the next three."

Needless to say, Keelan was shocked. "Four days off? Wow," He scratched his head, "Uh, what will I do?"

"We thought you and Lance would like to go hunting together. You have a fine new horse that I have been told is ready for his first outing away from a pen, and we thought this would be a perfect opportunity for you."

Keelan smiled broadly. "That'll be fun. I can't wait to tell Lance. He came into town a bit ago; I hope I can find him before he heads back to his ranch."

He started to run toward the house before he heard, "Hi, Keelan," Lance said from inside Keelan's house.

Keelan slid to a halt. "Hey! It's you!" Keelan said in surprise. "What are you doing here?"

"I'm here for the surprise; what else? And my father has one for you as well back at the ranch. We can ride double on my horse."

Keelan grinned as his father winked at him, "Let me grab my bow and bedroll, and we'll head out. If that's okay with you?" he asked his parents.

"Of course. I also have a few supplies packed for you." Maya reached up on her tip toes to kiss Keelan on the cheek. "I hope you have a good time, Keelan. You deserve it." She handed them a large sack of food, "Now look after each other, alright?"

Keelan rushed into the house, quickly grabbed his bow, quiver, bed roll, and cloak, and rushed back out of the house. Lance was already mounted and waiting for him. He removed his foot from the stirrup and held his hand out to help Keelan hop on the back of his horse. Once Keelan was situated holding his two bags, Lance spurred his horse into a brisk trot.

Back at Lance's ranch, Douglas Firestrum was waiting for them outside the barn. On the ground next to him was a small bundle draped in a cloth. Keelan and Lance both dismounted from Lance's horse and walked over to Mr. Firestrum. Lance had a goofy smile plastered on his face.

"What's going on?" Keelan asked.

Douglas grinned and grabbed the edge of the cloth, pulling it back to reveal a black saddle. "Happy name-day, Keelan."

Keelan's face beamed. He loved the attention he was getting from everyone. "Oh, wow. You didn't have to get me anything!" He exclaimed as he ran his hands down the fine leather of the new saddle.

"Nonsense. A man with a fine horse, needs something to sit him with. Also, you've done a marvelous job with Rogue. He is now yours."

"I guess I am a man now," he chuckled. "Thank you, sir, I will take very good care of him."

Douglas nodded, "Go get Rogue saddled, men." He laughed loudly, "And get yourself a fresh horse, Lance. Now, get going."

Lance smiled broadly, "Going, going."

"Oh, and Lance?"

Lance skidded to a halt and turned to look at his father.

"I have something for you in the tack room."

Keelan grabbed his new saddle and headed over to the corral that Rogue occupied. Rogue nickered and flicked his head in his direction. "Let's see how this looks on you, boy," Keelan said.

When Rogue was saddled and ready to go, Lance approached, leading his horse.

"You got a new saddle too?"

"Yeah, looks just like yours, only tan."

"That makes sense; a black saddle on a black horse - it would just blend in. Are you ready?" Keelan grinned. He was too excited.

"I'm ready. Where too?"

"I know the perfect place. We'll have to hustle to get there before dark, but I think we can make it."

"Lead the way!"

And off the boys went.

Lance and Keelan took off down the road at a quick canter. Just before the edge of town, Keelan veered to the left to follow a game trail that was his father's favorite.

Once in the woods, they had to slow to a jog, but it was still an excellent ground-covering pace.

They reached Keelan's favorite camp spot just as the sun drifted below the trees. They gathered wood to start a fire and slept under the stars for the first night.

"So, what's the best thing to hunt this time of year?" Lance asked.

"Mostly rabbits, but maybe we'll get lucky and see a badger or a fox. If we go a little deeper tomorrow, we might be able to come across a boar or an elk."

"Well, then I say we go a little further; I wouldn't mind boar for dinner tomorrow night." Lance winked.

Keelan nodded as he grabbed the bag his mother had given him and fished out some jerky and biscuits. "Here you go, this will do us for tonight."

Lance accepted his portion. They sat in front of the fire, enjoying the solitude of the evening.

Keelan had forgotten all about elves, fairies and talking to the horse.

By midday the following day, they had traveled deep into the forest, now they were far from town. The pine trees bent slightly at their tips from the gentle breeze. Flowers and berry bushes were in full bloom. Small animals scurried about and became more prevalent the further from town they went.

"Leaving before sunup was a good idea, I think," Lance stated in little more than a whisper. Songbirds sang in the treetops demanding attention and undisturbed by the boys passage.

"Yeah, if you're too close to town, the big animals stay away. We'll see more action out here; I say we go a little further before we start making our way back."

Suddenly, there was a loud crash to the right. Lance and Keelan both grabbed their bows and nocked an arrow. They saw quick movement dashing between the bushes; a small brown animal was making haste away from them.

"Boar," Keelan whispered.

"At least three," Lance whispered back.

At the same time, both boys turned their horses and went into pursuit. The boars crashed through the thicket trying to evade their pursuers.

Before long, the boar broke from the forest into a small meadow.

The boys on the backs of their well-bred horses exploded into the meadow keeping the boars in sight. Keelan and Lance both targeted a different boar and loosed their arrows simultaneously; their arrows thudded into the sides of their target in quick succession of each other.

"It was almost like we rehearsed that," Lance laughed.

Keelan dismounted quickly and dispatched his kill as Lance did the same with his.

"I think the edge of this meadow will be a good place to spend the evening while we prepare these. We'll eat some and take the rest home," Keelan said.

"Sounds good to me. I think I smell some water in the distance there," Lance pointed to the far edge of the clearing.

"It's probably the creek. It winds its way through the forest. That would be a great place to spend the night."

CHAPTER

-8-

THE full moon shone brightly as it peaked over the tree line, overshadowing the stars. The two boys sat beside their fire, roasting a fresh boar haunch. Little did the boys know the smell from the roasting boar was leading four mercenaries right to them.

The tantalizing scent of sizzling meat emboldened one of the warriors, causing his stomach to growl. He slowly approached the clearing, keeping the bright moon at his back to conceal his passage. He peered into the darkness and quietly crept back to his gang, laughing in his mind.

He knelt in front of the seated men resting from their long journey. "General, there's only two of them, and they're roasting a boar," he sneered.

"Only two?" General Lucas questioned. "With such a large fire?"

"Two rich boys. That's it. Should be easy pickings," the scout replied.

"I could use a little sport to increase my appetite," the newest gang member said with a wicked grin.

"Young ignorant fools. Krull and I will approach using the moon to blind them. You two stay back in the shadows and come in from the sides after we approach."

"Should we wait for the others?"

Lucas shook his head, "Nah, they're hours behind us, and this way, there's more boar for us. Two rich boys shouldn't be too much for the three of you."

His three men smiled, nodding, their eyes gleaming in the bright moonlight.

"Let's eat."

"Hello the camp," a deep voice called from somewhere in the dark.

Both boys jumped to their feet. Keelan stared wide-eyed in the direction the voice came from. Lance used his hand to shield his eyes from the fire, trying to adjust his night vision.

"Who's there? Show yourself," Lance said.

Two rough-looking men in dirty clothing emerged slowly from the darkness. One of them smiled, showing numerous missing teeth in his sinister grin.

"We were hoping we could share your bounty with you; we haven't eaten for several days," General Lucas said.

"We have plenty to share," Keelan replied. Lance reached over, placing a hand on Keelan's arm. Keelan looked at his friend; he shook his head slightly, mouthing, *Caution.*

Several snickers could be heard coming from the forest. Keelan looked around nervously.

Another man materialized from the shadows. He smiled and said, "Share? We will take it all."

Lance suddenly jerked toward the horses, but a fourth man appeared from behind a tree.

"We have no coin; help yourself to some meat and be on your way," Lance said.

Keelan glanced at Lance, uncertain how he could sound so confident and calm. Keelan had never found himself in such a perilous position.

The four strangers slowly circled them, brandishing their weapons.

Keelan held his hands out in front of him, "Wait, wait, wait, we're unarmed. There's no need to attack us; just take what you want and leave," he said.

"Unarmed? How did you take those animals down, then?" one of the bandits asked.

"With bows," Keelan pointed over by the horses.

"We'll give you a fighting chance." Krull and the General threw their swords at the boys' feet, backing up a couple of steps to sit on a log next to the fire, crossing their arms. "Pick 'em up, boys; let's even the odds," the general said, lifting a flask to his lips.

Lance and Keelan stared at each other. Lance reached for one of the swords and then hesitated.

"Wishing you were suckling your mother right now, don't you, boy? Pick it up!" He roared.

Lance picked up both swords and handed the shorter one to Keelan.

Keelan gulped as he accepted the sword. He wrapped his fingers around the leather-wrapped hilt. Though it was shorter, it was heavier than he had expected. He didn't struggle to raise it before him, but he was not comfortable with it either.

Lance gripped his sword with confidence that Keelan didn't feel. "Do you know how to fight?" Keelan whispered to him.

"Be fearless. Follow my lead."

The newest mercenary pointed his sword at Keelan, turned his head to his leader, and started to laugh, "Like taking honeyroot from a baby."

Lance lunged to his left toward the distracted mercenary before Keelan, bringing his sword down in a sweeping arch—his sword bit into the man's shoulder, slicing to the bone down to his ribcage. The man had no time to react to the ghost-like movement. He swore loudly, dropping his weapon to cradle his almost severed arm.

"Me arm!" he screamed as he stumbled backward, tripping over a rock and falling to the ground.

Lance continued the momentum of his slashing movement, swinging himself in a circle and bringing his sword up to block the blade of the fourth man. They met with a clash of steal.

The General and Krull sprang from the log, pulling out their long daggers and advancing toward Keelan.

Keelan's first movement was to retreat closer to the horses. Although the thick, heavy brush behind the horses offered no escape.

Krull advanced on Keelan while he continued to back up.

"You're not going anywhere," he smirked, looking at the seemingly scared boy.

Keelan turned, keeping the thicket to his rear as he faced Krull. He planted his feet, gripping his sword before him, his hands starting to shake. With adrenaline and fear rushing through his veins, the inexplicable happened.

Krull grinned, spat on the ground, and lunged, stabbing at Keelan with his dagger. Time seemed to slow; Keelan lifted his sword, hitting the blade and almost knocking it out of Krull's hand as he jumped backward.

"Stronger than you look, boy," Krull glanced at his sword and then at Keelan.

Krull advanced again. Keelan reacted to his every stab and slash. He wasn't sure what was happening, but somehow, he could see what Krull would do moments before he did it.

The first mercenary whom Lance dispatched regained his footing and started making his way to the tree line.

"Coward, get back here and fight!" General Lucas yelled.

Krull broke through Keelan's weak defense, and the tip of his dagger bit into his cheek. Keelan cried out in shock and pain.

The general laughed, leaving Krull to deal with the whelp. He turned his attention to the other boy. His man was holding his own, but it looked like his endurance was wearing out.

Lance heard his friend's cry of pain and reacted without thinking of what he was about to do.

A primal roar ripped from his throat as he moved impossibly fast, slashing the grunt bandit across the stomach. The Man doubled over as his innards started to protrude from the slash.

The General rushed over, picking up a sword as he went. He lifted the sword overhead, intending to dispatch the boy. Lance spun, raising his sword; their blades slid down each other until their hilts locked. Lance gagged as putrid breath wafted toward him.

Lance pushed the General backward. He swung his sword in a blur of motion, slicing the General's arm and chest. Lucas pulled a small ball out of his pocket and threw it on the ground. A cloud of smoke exploded in between them. Concealed, the general melted into the trees and retreated.

With both of his opponents no longer a threat, Lance moved to help Keelan. He slashed Keelan's bandit across the backs of his knees. With a scream of agony, the mercenary crumbled to the ground. Keelan was in mid-swing with his sword, with the bandit on the ground, grabbing his sliced legs; he didn't see Keelan's sword arching toward his head. With a clean slice, the man's head was lopped off.

"Oh!" As the head rolled toward him, Keelan exclaimed, "How, what, oh…" he tried to make sense of the situation.

Keelan jumped backward before the head hit his foot. He retreated several steps. Before he could proceed, he could feel his stomach churning. Keelan bent over and emptied his stomach on the ground. He looked up at Lance; his face pale, eyes wide, and breathing hard.

"It's okay, Keelan, take a deep breath."

"I've got a lot of questions, but right now," he licked his lips, "I just want to get away from here," he said, his voice shaking.

Lance reached into his pocket pulled out a scrap of cloth and handed it to Keelan. Keelan nodded his thanks and pressed the cloth to his cheek to stop the bleeding.

"I agree, we should leave this place. Why don't you pack up and saddle up the horses? I'll do something with these," Lance gestured to the two dead warriors.

Keelan nodded numbly and went to work.

After Keelan had the horses saddled and all their gear and the meat secure, he looked around for Lance but couldn't find him. The last time he saw Lance, he was dragging the last body deep into the woods. Suddenly, he heard what sounded like a raging fire. Smoke billowed up from the trees in the direction he last saw Lance. He made sure the horses were tied up securely before he ran in the direction of the fire. Just as he broke through the trees, Lance appeared.

"Are you okay? Where did all that fire come from?"

"I piled up the bodies and then set them on fire," Lance replied.

Keelan's eyes grew wide. It sounded unreal to him. "Well," he tried to sound as normal as possible, "That sounded like more than just a little fire; that sounded like an inferno like a whole house was being burned down,"

"Oh, that," Lance looked back into the forest, appearing to be a little nervous before answering, "One of them must have had an oil lamp or something in their bag. I burned all their possessions with them, too. That was a little startling, though, I have to admit. But don't worry, I ensured the forest won't catch fire."

"Oh, okay." He gulped down, almost forgetting what he had to say, "Well I prepared everything for us to leave. It's pretty dark, but I think we can make it a little way before we should stop for the night. We can just set up a cold camp, get a couple of hours, and then head back at first light."

"That sounds like a good plan," Lance clapped him on the back as he walked toward his horse.

The rising sun found Keelan and Lance riding back toward Creekside. They rode in silence, but Lance could sometimes feel Keelan's gaze on him. He knew his friend had a lot of questions, and he didn't know how to answer them. Hopefully, he wouldn't ask questions until they returned to his ranch.

They were forced to camp one more night before returning to their homes. Lance busied himself taking care of the horses while Keelan set up camp.

When they finally settled down, Keelan said, "I don't know how to ask all the questions that are rattling in my brain."

Lance looked up at Keelan, "The only way to ask is just to do it," he said dryly.

"Right." Keelan nodded firmly. He was slightly distracted cleaning the cut on his cheek. Most of the pain had subsided but it still stung when touched.

Lance shrugged, "Bandits attacked us, and we took care of it."

Keelan stopped messing with his cut and looked at Lance, "That's not what I'm talking about, and you know it. Don't play games. I heard and saw things I can't explain."

Lance sighed, "I'm not a monster if that's what you're thinking."

"Why would I think that?"

"Because I'm different. That's all I can tell you."

Keelan gave him a look.

"Look, it's for your safety. But you just have to know I would never hurt anybody I care about. I need you to promise me that you won't tell anyone, including your parents, what you saw or heard."

Keelan stared at his friend with his mouth open, *My friend has a secret that he can't tell me, and he doesn't want me to share it for my safety,* he thought.

When Keelan didn't reply for a moment, Lance looked at him pleadingly, "Keelan, I'm serious, you have to promise me. Everybody in our village will be in danger if even one soul finds out, but as I said, I am not a monster, but what people don't understand. People fear."

Keelan looked at him. He seemed to tell the truth. "You're a good friend, Lance. I won't tell anybody what I heard or saw."

"Thank you." Lance smiled, thankful it was over.

"But," Keelan continued, "We need to get our story straight, then."

"As I said, four bandits attacked, and we took care of it."

"Nobody's going to believe that I could take care of any bandits. I am not a fighter. I've never been trained to fight; everyone will know that is a lie."

"Okay, then we'll just say that we got attacked by some bandits. We'll leave the exact number out; I've had sword training. That doesn't have to be a secret, and we can say that you got lucky and were able to evade your attacker until I was able to get rid of mine and came to your aid."

"That sounds weirdly plausible," Keelan frowned.

"Do you have a problem with that?"

"Not necessarily in the way we're going to state the story, only in my performance. It makes me sound like a coward and a weakling." He rolled his eyes.

"Well, we can change that."

"How?"

"My father taught me everything I know of the sword and fighting. I don't think he'd have a problem teaching you too. You have the strength. You just need to know the techniques."

"I don't know. I don't think my father will agree to that."

Lance waved his hand at him, "You just let my father worry about that. He'll convince him."

Keelan chuckled dryly, "Okay, sounds good to me. I didn't like the feeling of not knowing what I was doing and having to fight somebody who was so set on killing me." He looked away. "That was the worst feeling in the world." He reached into his pocket and pulled the pin he had found in Kingston a year earlier. After he had returned home, he cleaned and polished the bronze pin. The etching was still hard to make out, but it looked like a round shield with a sword and an arrow crossed in front of it and two battle axes with long spikes crisscrossed behind.

"What's that?" Lance asked.

Keelan flipped the pin to him. "I found this in Kingston last year."

Lance held it close to the firelight. "I've seen this before. This is the royal seal of the Kingdom of Oshana. The former rulers of this part of the continent."

Keelan held his hand back out, "I know very little about the history before Evansshire. I've never heard of them. How do you?"

Lance shrugged, flipping the pin back to him. "My father taught me. He loves history. You can't change the past, but you can learn from it, he always says."

Keelan nodded and pocketed his pin.

They fell into silence, listening to the crickets, owls, and the popping of their fire.

CHAPTER -9-

THE rest of the summer was uneventful, and everything went back to life as it usually was, at least mostly. Keelan's nights were troubled for weeks after the bandit attack. But slowly, his fears decreased, and the memory, as well as the scar on his cheek, faded.

While Keelan had been away on his name-day trip, his father had built a stall for Rogue.

He had told his parents about the bandit attack, but they said very little about it; they were just glad that he was okay. Nothing more was said about learning to fight, and Keelan had kept his promise to Lance and said nothing about the actual happenings of the incident. So Keelan's days were back to waking up early and helping his father in the farrier shop all day. On any days off that he got, he would grab Lance and go on short hunting trips close to town. While out on their hunting trips, Lance started showing Keelan how to weld a sword and a few attack moves. This, of course, was kept a secret from Keelan's parents as well.

Then, one day, as he was just about done cleaning up the shop for the evening, his father came back into the workshop. "Hey, son, stop for a moment. I need to talk to you about something."

Keelan put down the broom and sat on a hay bale next to his father.

"You've been doing really well around here lately, and I wanted to thank you for that. You're turning into a fine young man. And with becoming a man, you need to learn how to protect yourself."

Keelan said nothing but held his breath, waiting for his father to continue.

"I want you to start taking some lessons from Mr. Firestrum. You can work shorter days here, ride to his ranch, and learn to protect yourself."

"Are you sure? I know how you feel about fighting, Pa."

"No, I didn't say anything about learning how to fight. I said learning how to protect yourself, there is a difference. Going around picking fights is not what I want you to be able to do, but if the need arises, I want you to be able to protect yourself and those you love." He raked his hands through his hair. "My size has always deterred people from trying anything. Thankfully, you did inherit most of my size," he chuckled, "And working in the farrier shop has given you some muscles, but times are changing. Bandits are getting bolder, coming closer to town. I don't even feel safe letting your mother travel alone anymore into the capital."

Keelan had a flashback of the attack. All the blood, his heart pounding in his chest, the helplessness…

"Thank you, Father." Keelan didn't know what else to say. Elliot patted him on the knee and then left the shop.

Keelan woke up with a bounce in his step the following day. He hurried through his chores and helped his father in the shop. Soon, he found himself astride Rogue, galloping toward the Firestrum Ranch. Lance was out in the field rounding up some cows when he arrived; he waved and said something to the ranch hands before galloping toward him.

"So, I guess your father finally told you the good news, huh?"

"Yeah, last night. I can't thank your father enough for helping me."

"Oh, and believe me, convincing your father wasn't easy. Your mother was an easier sell," Lance laughed.

"My mother? How long have you known that I would be able to do this?"

"Almost two weeks now. I was sworn to secrecy and had to wait until your father came to terms with the decision. I guess it was your mother that finally convinced him."

Keelan grinned and shook his head; he never thought his mother would be the one to agree to let him learn how to fight.

Mr. Firestrum exited their newly finished ranch house. It was a large two-story house with a wraparound porch. Lance said they even had a pump in the kitchen. "Good to see you, my boy," Mr. Firestrum greeted Keelan. "We have a lot of work to do and not much daylight." He looked at Lance, "Don't you have some work to finish?"

Lance smiled, "Yes, sir." He spun his horse and galloped back over to the pasture.

"Soon, I will have you sparring with Lance, but first, there is work to do before we put a weapon in your hand."

Mr. Firestrum gestured for Keelan to follow him over to the arena. Inside the arena was an obstacle course: logs, bales of hay, and ropes.

"The first step is to teach you balance - at all times. I will run through this course once so you can see what you are to do, and then we'll see how you fare."

Keelan looked over all the obstacles and nodded, "Seems easy enough."

Mr. Firestrum bellowed out a loud laugh, "We'll see, my boy, we'll see."

Douglas Firestrum removed his coat and shirt and hung them on the fence. Keelan had always thought that Mr. Firestrum was older than his father, but seeing him about to run an obstacle course made him second-guess that judgment. Douglas Firestrum was extremely well-muscled in his arms and chest, even more so than Keelan's father.

When looking at him on an everyday basis, you would never guess the condition he was in. He stretched for a moment and then sprang into action. He crossed over balance beams, jumped over logs effortlessly climbed up ropes, and maneuvered through the tight places he had set up with hay bales.

When he returned to the start, he was barely breathing hard. "Okay, your turn." He smiled. "Let's see if you can make it through without falling. Don't worry about speed right now; just stay on your feet."

Keelan gulped down. He was a bit nervous but if Mr. Firestrum could do it without breaking a sweat, Keelan was confident he'd be able to make it through. It didn't look that difficult.

He walked up to the balance beam and made it about four steps across before he slipped and fell off. Laying flat on the ground, it took him a minute to register that he had indeed, fallen. He stood up and smiled sheepishly.

"That's alright, my boy!" Douglas said.

Keelan took a deep breath and got ready again. He took five steps and again, fell. He couldn't understand what was happening; why was he losing grip?

"Is there oil on this," he asked, looking at the balance beam.

Douglas laughed, "On your feet, boy."

Keelan bypassed the balance beam and started jumping over the logs. He made it about halfway up the rope before he slid all the way down. He tried to hold the rope for support but instead, his hands burned the whole way. He growled in frustration but refused to quit. The hay bales were the easiest to maneuver through, but he was winded beyond belief when he returned to the start.

Keelan tried to stabilize his breathing, "Wow, you made that look way too easy."

Douglas clapped him on the back, making him stumble forward, "Take a quick break, and then back to it. We'll get you through this cleanly by the end of the week."

"By the end of the week? After going through it once, I don't think I'll ever get through it cleanly." Keelan wiped the sweat off his shoulder.

Douglas tossed him a waterskin and gestured to the course, "When you're ready, proceed."

Keelan took a long swallow of the water, letting the cool liquid run down his burning throat, and then ripped off his sweaty shirt and threw it over the fence rail.

He tackled the balance beam again, moving extra slowly, but he only made it about four more steps. Instead of proceeding to the next obstacle, he returned to the beginning.

"Just continue through; we'll come back to that after."

"If it's all the same to you, I'd prefer to master one obstacle at a time. Once I have this down, I'll move on to the next. Is that okay?"

"Smart plan; most people don't do that. Proceed."

For the remainder of the day, Keelan worked on the balance beam; by the end of the evening, he was able to walk on it confidently at a quick pace but nowhere near as fast as Douglas had earlier.

"That's good work for today, Keelan. Let's call it a night. Now, your father mentioned that you'd be able to come here every afternoon. Is that correct?"

"Yes, sir, I'll be here."

Keelan fell into his new routine quickly. He worked all morning with his father, sometimes assisted his mother, and then spent the afternoon at the Firestrum Ranch. By the end of the week, true to his word, Douglas had Keelan walking through the Obstacle course cleanly but not at a brisk pace.

By the end of the third week, he could move through the course at almost the same speed as Lance.

At the beginning of the fourth week, Keelan found Lance and Douglas in an open field away from the obstacle course. Lance was holding two Bo staff.

When Keelan approached, Lance tossed one staff at him. Keelan threw a hand up to catch the staff and caught it clumsily in the air.

"We'll work on that too," Douglas said, "Lance will show you the basic moves we will be learning today. Everyone learning the sword starts with the staff; it can be welded like a sword but has its own style. Footwork and body positioning will be the biggest similarity.”

For the rest of the day, Lance showed Keelan how to stand and move his feet and the basics of how to hold and move the staff.

Keelan decided at that moment that he would enjoy the staff. Both of the boys laughed as Keelan fell, trying to balance it. But the decision to enjoy the staff soon changed by the end of the second day when they had their first spar.

The young men faced off and began their warm-up moves, swinging and slashing their staffs.

“Begin,” Douglas bellowed.

Quick as a viper, Lance lunged one foot forward, bringing his staff down on Keelan's knuckles.

Keelan cried out, dropping his staff to shake out his hand.

“I wasn't expecting that,” he moaned in pain.

“Always guard your hands; you have to be quick,” Douglas commented. “Again!”

Keelan did better the second time; he anticipated Lance’s quick movements and blocked his next attack.

The clack of wood on wood rang through the ranch for the rest of the afternoon. When both boys were dripping and tired, Douglas finally let them stop.

“Good work today, Keelan. We will work on these techniques for the rest of the week, and then we will see how you do fighting on the beams.”

“The balance beams?” He asked.

Douglas nodded, “Is that a problem?”

“Well, I don’t know. Is that even possible?”

Lance clapped Keelan on the back, “Not at first, but don’t worry, you’ll get it.”

Fighting with staff while on the balance beams turned out to be possible, but not without a twisted ankle, a jammed finger, and lots of bruises. But Keelan was finally able to master walking forward and backward, jumping over slashes of Lance's staff, and managed to remain on the beam.

Every day, Keelan's amazement at Lance's balancing ability and general agility was renewed. It was like he was not even human.

Finally, it was time to put a sword in his hand. He was a little surprised to find out that it was wooden, but at least it had the right shape.

"We will start with the wooden practice sword; then we'll move on to blunted steel before we put anything sharp in your hand. I don't want you or my son losing an arm," Douglas chuckled.

Keelan found himself falling into the rhythm of sword fighting quickly. He loved the idea of the sword dancing through the air at his command. Douglas correctly asserted that learning the staff first would give him the beginning skills needed. The footwork could be transferred over, and even some of the motions with the weapon.

Keelan just found everything about the sword comfortable and familiar. After the first week of training with the wooden ones and then the blunted, it was almost like he had been training with the sword his whole life. His feet and hand would move in rhythm – almost as if, Keelan had been practicing his entire life.

After one exhausting session, Douglas invited Keelan to stay for dinner.

"I am quite impressed, Keelan, with how you have truly mastered the techniques of the sword. From hearing the recounts of your run-in with the bandits and looking at you now, I would say you were playing back then. No one would guess that you have only been using the sword truly for a week."

"Thank you, sir." Keelan smiled. "That is high praise. When those bandits attacked, I fumbled with the sword, and I was just terrified. But now I can't quite explain it. When I grab a hold of the hilt, it just feels like an extension of my body. It feels… He struggled to find the right word.

"Right? It feels right?" Douglas completed his sentence and Keelan nodded.

"Well, that's definitely how it looks," Lance replied.

"I was originally going to run you through a couple of other weapons, but I think we found yours. There's no sense wasting time on anything else, in my opinion. From what Lance has said, you are an ace with a bow, and before winter, I think you will have mastered the sword as best as most men I know."

Keelan took a deep breath and looked at Douglas, "I don't know what else to say, but thank you, sir. The bow has always come naturally to me. My father was always impressed with my accuracy. And now, with a sword at my hip, I just feel complete." He smiled sheepishly. "I don't know if that makes sense."

"Oh, it most definitely does. We will begin with sharp weapons at our next session."

CHAPTER

-10-

WINTER hit with full force earlier than usual. Harvesting had been completed just three weeks ago, and already, it looked like a second blizzard was upon them.

Keelan, wrapped up tightly in his cloak while heading home from his latest weapons training at Firestrum's Ranch. Rogue traveled slowly and carefully with his head bowed against the biting headwind laced with ice, sleet, and snow. Snow was accumulating quickly on the already snowy roads.

"I hope we get home before this storm fully hits," he muttered to himself. He didn't know how, but he knew deep down that the eye of this storm was not on them yet; this was a massive storm system and would be sticking around for a couple of days. If he didn't know better, he would have said it didn't feel natural. But what else could it be? A storm was just a natural phenomenon.

"Help, help."

He reined up Rogue. "Did you hear something, Rogue?"

Of course, Rogue didn't reply.

"Help! Can anyone hear me?" The plaintive cry pierced the chilling air once more. "I'm freezing... I need help!" A woman's desperate plea echoed through the stillness.

"Is anyone there?" Keelan said.

"Please, I'm hurt and freezing. I can't move. Please, hurry!" The urgency in the woman's voice was unmistakable.

Keelan scanned his surroundings, attempting to pinpoint the source of the voice, but it seemed to surround him from every direction. "Speak again; I can't tell which way you are," he said to her.

Suddenly, a loud screech pierced the evening.

"What was that?" Keelan spun around, trying to find where the bird was coming from.

"Follow my call," the voice said.

Again, the bird called out; it was coming from his right. He led Rogue in the direction of the bird's call.

Soon, the snow was too deep for Rogue to continue; Keelan dismounted, secured Rogue's reins, and continued on foot. About one hundred yards off the road, the screeching stopped.

"Where are you?" he asked.

"Against the tree near your feet," the voice said.

Keelan froze; he was sure he heard the voice but somehow didn't hear it. It appeared to be coming from within his head like a second thought.

He shrugged off the feeling and looked around the tree near the base. Soon, he saw red feathers. He knelt, brushed the snow off the feathers, and found the strangest-looking bird he'd ever seen.

Oh, thank you so much for finding me

"What?" Keelan looked closely at the bird. "Did you…talk?" He jumped backward.

Please, don't leave me here.

Keelan's eyes widened. Her beak wasn't moving yet he could hear her speak, "How am I hearing your voice in my head? How is a bird talking to me?" He backed up a few steps, his hands shaking.

Oh, please don't leave me. I'm so cold, my wings are numb, and I think one is broken. You have to help me, please we can talk later. Please…

Hesitantly, Keelan walked closer to the bird and stooped to scoop her up. She was correct; her whole body was almost frozen stiff.

He gently cradled her in his arms, trying to wrap some of his cloak around her, and then returned to Rogue and the road.

As they traveled down the road, he kept glancing at the small bird in his arms and couldn't stop thinking about how he could hear the bird's voice in his head, not to mention the bird had a voice he could understand.

Soon, the little bird fell asleep.

Not knowing exactly what the bird was, he decided to keep it from his parents for now. His mother's reaction to his inquiries about elves and fairies made him wonder what she would do if she saw the strange bird. Would she deny the bird was in front of her, or would she try to hide her from him?

He got Rogue squared away in the stable and made a spot in the hay to place the bird so she would be warm until he could return for her.

"Keelan," his mother called from the kitchen when she saw him walking toward the house. "I'm so glad you made it back. Come in quickly and get warm."

His father was sitting beside the hearth smoking a pipe; his mother was busy cleaning up from dinner in the kitchen. He went to his room to get out of his wet clothing.

"When you're warm, come get some dinner," his mother called from the other room. When he returned to the main room, she was sitting next to his father, knitting something. They were speaking in hushed voices, but some of the words reached him. His mother was concerned about a new edict coming from the king, having something to do with births. Apparently, Consul Tybard had been at the house earlier trying to reassure his mother that nothing was truly changing in the law, this was just a further precaution.

He hurried into the kitchen, dished himself up some stew, and grabbed a large hunk of cheese and bread. He placed his dinner on the table and then called to his parents, "I forgot something in the barn. I'll be right back."

His father held up a hand that signified that he heard him. Keelan left the house to fetch the strange bird he had found earlier in the day. Thankfully, she was still sleeping.

He scooped her up gently and hurried back to the house. He grabbed his dinner and walked quickly to his room. "I'm gonna eat in here if you don't mind, and then I'm gonna hit the hay. It's been a long day."

"That's fine; just don't leave your dishes there tomorrow morning."

"Yes, Mother."

Once in his room with the door shut, he hurried over to his bed and placed the sleeping bird on his pillow.

Her eyes fluttered open but closed again just as quickly. He looked at her truly for the first time. She was about the size of a small hawk but with bright red and orange feathers, a definite bird of prey beak, and talons, but not a bird of prey he'd ever seen before.

"She mentioned that her wing was broken," he muttered. Gently, he stretched out one wing and then the other. It looked like she was right. He went over to his chest, pulled out an old shirt, and grabbed a small twig from his bedroom hearth. He made a splint with pieces of the shirt and bound it to her wing.

"I hope that works," he said to himself and then busied himself eating dinner. He couldn't help but keep glancing at the bird. Even though she was sleeping soundly, he was scared she'd wake up and make noise which would alert his mother.

She talked, He thought to himself, *I could hear her. How?* Before he could ponder over it more, he was fast asleep.

He woke the following day with a stiff back and a kink in his neck from falling asleep in the chair by the fire. He glanced over at his bed and saw two black eyes staring back at him.

The bird slowly turned her eyes to her wing as she moved it around slowly.

Thank you for fixing my wing, she said in his head.

[100]

He jumped. Hearing her voice in his head was still unsettling, "Stop doing that."

Doing what? She hopped forward.

"That! Stop talking in my head." He got on his feet.

The bird tilted her head a bit before her eyes fell on the bowl on the table. *Is there meat in that bowl?*

He looked down at his half-eaten stew and nodded. "Yes." The bird was looking at the bowl, "Would you like some?"

Oh, yes, please. It's been days since I've eaten.

He walked over to the bed and placed the bowl before her. She slowly picked out a few pieces of meat with her beak and swallowed them.

You are a wonderful cook.

"Oh well, my mother is. I wouldn't say I am," he chuckled.

The bird's head snapped back. *Are there other people in this house?*

"Just my mother and father."

Do they know I'm here?

He shook his head, "No, I figured it would be best to keep you a secret right now."

So, are they wizards, too, like you?

Keelan blinked at her word. "I'm not a wizard."

You are hearing my voice in your head, aren't you?

"Yeah, I was gonna ask you about that."

Only those with magic can hear me, she said.

He laughed suddenly, "I'm just a person. I don't have any magic."

If birds could frown, she was definitely giving him one. *Then you are the strangest human I have ever met, not that I've met very many, mind you.*

Keelan pressed his lips and nodded. "So, what are you exactly?"

Why, I'm a Phoenix; of course, have you never heard of one?

"I've heard stories of the phoenix, but I didn't know they really existed."

Where am I, anyway?

"You're in my house in the village of Creekside."

She looked at him intently.

"Um, we are on Oshana. Is that what you wanted to know?"

She shook her head, *Which Kingdom?*

"Evansshire."

She reared back and flapped her good wing, *Evansshire? Oh no, how did I get here?*

"I don't know. Why don't you tell me what happened?"

I was flying over the Sapphire Mountains when the storm suddenly hit. It came out of nowhere; I didn't even see it coming. It tossed me this way and that until I was flying completely blind. And then I crashed into a tree – it's quite embarrassing if you must know – Phoenixes are known for their impeccable sense of direction and our superior flying techniques and ability; that storm is just not natural.

Keelan couldn't help but smile. Not only was a bird talking to him, but a sassy one. "Well, I agree with you there. I don't know what that storm is, but it didn't feel natural to me either."

Didn't feel natural, huh? I know what you are. You're not a wizard; you're a Sorcerer.

"Like I told you before, I am just a person—a young man from Creekside in the Kingdom of Evansshire. My father is a farrier, and my mother is the town's healer."

Truly, a Healer? That's how you were able to fix my wing.

"Well, all I did was stabilize it. It's definitely not fixed yet." He pointed at her wing.

Phoenixes heal fast, you'll see, she said, puffing out her chest.

"What do I call you? Just Phoenix, or do you have a name?"

Of course, I have a name, just like you have one, don't you?

"Of course, my name is Keelan Keifman."

Nice to meet you, Keelan; my name is Aurora. She held out a clawed foot like she was asking him to shake it.

He hesitated a moment.

I'm not gonna claw you; isn't this how humans greet each other?

"It is. It's just a little funny when claws are attached to the hand," he chuckled as he tried to grip her taloned foot and shook it gently. "How do Phoenixes greet each other?"

We bow our heads like so, she said as she demonstrated.

"That appears to be much safer," he imitated her motion.

Would you be so kind as to move me closer to the fire? It's a bit cold over here.

He gently picked her up and took her to the chair he had been sitting in.

Closer, please.

He scooted the chair closer to the fire; *oh, that's much better*, she said as she ruffled her feathers slightly.

Slowly, she sat down until she was lying on her legs and looked like a wild feathered fire chicken. She closed her eyes, and soon, it appeared she had drifted off to sleep.

Keelan pulled another shirt from his chest and draped it across her to keep her warm.

Thank you, she muttered.

"No problem. But I have to go help my parents. It would be best if you stayed here today. I don't think I'm ready to explain you to them. Please don't make any sounds, if you need me…" He looked at her and sighed, "Just talk in my head, I guess."

That is the only way I speak to humans, don't worry, no one will hear me but you.

He made his way out of the room as quietly as possible. He saw his mother standing in the kitchen.

"Dinner was wonderful, Mother. I think I'm going to take an extra serving if you don't mind and then retire early," Keelan told his mother after dinner.

"Okay," She raised her brow. "You feeling okay?"

"Oh, I'm fine. Just didn't get much sleep last night. I don't think I ate enough yesterday with that snowstorm I got stuck in. And my fire burned down a little bit too much. I'll add more wood this evening."

"Well, tell me immediately if you're not feeling well - I can't have my only son coming down with a winter fever."

"I'm fine, Mother, just hungry," he chuckled. He grabbed an extra roll, a slice of pie, and two slabs of pork from the pork roast on the table.

Elliot laughed from his living room chair, "I think he's in for another growth spurt, Maya."

"Oh, good heavens. I'm going to have to be letting out his clothes sooner than I thought," she laughed with him.

Keelan shook his head at his parents and went to his room.

His fire had burned down to nothing but coals, so his room was dark. He walked carefully over to his nightstand and fumbled with his steel and flint to get his candle lit. Once he lit the first one, lighting the rest of the room was easy.

"Aurora, where are you?" He looked around his room but saw no signs of the Phoenix. His heart started racing; did she leave? Is she well enough to go? Did somebody find her? Questions rattled through his head.

He heard a small chirp coming from his fireplace. *I'm over here,* she projected.

"Where? I don't see you." *Hearing her voice in my head is so weird,* he thought, shaking his head.

Take a closer look, she replied.

He walked over to the hearth and saw the small bird lying in the middle of the coals. "What are you doing in there? You're going to catch on fire!" He exclaimed.

She laughed in his head as well as made small chirping sounds. ***I'm a phoenix, silly. We do not get burned by fire; we are actually born in fire. I thought you said you knew something about the Phoenix.*** She tilted her head to one side. ***A phoenix lays an egg in fire, and then and only then will the egg hatch. And if for some reason I am killed*** *prematurely, all you have to do is place my body in fire, and I will be reborn. You already knew this, didn't you? You're just teasing me.*

"Okay, I have heard that, but again, I thought they were just stories. I didn't know that was true. So, how will I know if you die prematurely other than, I guess, being murdered?"

Phoenixes live for hundreds of years. I will outlive you by years and years.

"How old are you now?"

Oh, I am still very young, about 20 years old.

"You don't know exactly how old you are?"

Of course, I do. But I've been told it's not proper for a lady to divulge her true age. Again, she started laughing in his mind.

"But you're a phoenix," he said, puzzled, "I think that only applies to human ladies."

I know I'm just teasing, she laughed.

"Your laugh is very pretty; it's almost like a song." Keelan smiled. "I brought you some dinner if you're hungry,"

Aurora immediately jumped onto her feet, shook her feathers out, removing coals and ash from her plumage, and then jumped onto the chair next to the fireplace. *I can eat,* she said.

"Do you need me to cut this into smaller pieces?" he asked, holding up the two pork slices.

She picked up a clawed foot and opened and closed her talons, *No, I think I can handle it.*

He placed the two pork slices on the chair beside her, and she immediately tore into it.

Keelan sat on the bed, finished his roll, and started in on the pie.

When she was finished eating, he asked her, "Are you feeling better today? How's that wing?"

Oh, it's doing much better; I think you could take off this brace.

"Are you sure? I don't want you to reinjure it by taking it off too soon."

If you insist, we'll leave it on one more day, but I'm pretty sure it's already healed.

"So, where will you go when you are all healed?"

I'm not going anywhere until spring, she said, ruffling up her feathers. *I don't like the cold.*

CHAPTER -11-

THE snow continued to fall for three straight days. Keelan kept busy ensuring the path from the house to the shop was cleared several times daily. Soon, finding places to pile all the snow became a challenge.

When he wasn't shoveling snow, he was helping his father perfect the snow skids he had been making. The skids would attach to the wagon wheels, allowing the townsfolk to continue their commerce and work.

Every evening, he would retire early to his room with his hidden stash of meat for Aurora. He ensured he worked extra hard during the day so his parents wouldn't suspect anything about him retiring early.

While she ate, Aurora would tell him stories of places she'd seen; different mountain ranges, an ocean, and a volcano - where her family had spent an entire month basking in the warmth.

She munched on the food he brought for her today. This evening, she was unusually quiet, "Are you okay?" He asked her.

She ruffled her feathers and then started to preen, *I've just run out of places to tell you about,* she replied.

Keelan nodded. He sat on his bed, looking at the ceiling. Doing all those chores actually had worn him out. He took a deep breath and suddenly, a question popped in his head, "I suppose you haven't come across any strange creatures."

Define strange creatures, Aurora didn't bother looking at him as she devoured the meat.

He laughed before replying, "Well, just a few weeks ago, I would have said a phoenix was a strange creature and something totally imaginary, a fable or a fairytale."

This time, she shot him a look, *I am not a fairytale.*

"I know that now, but two weeks ago, I didn't." Keelan dropped his shoulders casually.

Let me think, I don't know what you consider strange, she jumped off the side table and hopped onto the bed. *Let me see,* she paused for a moment, *you know about horses and cows. I'm sure you know about cats and dogs, boars, and rabbits. What about a Pegasus or a griffin? What about an elf, a fairy, or a dragon,* she said, making her voice a little sinister.

Keelan raised his brow, trying to look unimpressed, "You've met elves and fairies?"

Of course, I have. They are quite common when you get outside of Evansshire, but from what I've heard, there's even some here just in hiding.

"Hiding? How big is Evansshire?"

Not that big. The human Kingdom used to be much larger but it is much smaller now.

"If the kingdom used to be bigger but it's smaller now, what inhabits the rest of the land?"

People still live there, and elves and fairies and trolls and dwarves and all manner of beings.

Keelan was intrigued and couldn't hide behind his casual look anymore. "Do they have their own kingdom then?"

Not as a whole. My history knowledge is a little shaky. They used to be united, but they are fractured now, each ruling themselves.

"Tell me about elves and fairies?"

Why the interest?

Keelan glanced at his room's door before telling her all about it. "Last summer, I traveled to the Capital with my mother. On our return,

I met a girl who claimed she was an Elvenfae. My mother says she's never heard of one, so I didn't know if it was a joke she was playing on me or if this was something new: elves and fairies uniting. But keep in mind that before I met this girl, I thought elves and fairies were nothing but fairy tales."

Aurora nodded, *I can assure you they are quite real, and no, it is not common for them to unite. I've met a few who have lived together but never produced offspring. If your friend is truly a mix, she is one of a kind.*

"Interesting."

It sure is. She made herself comfortable in his bed. *Would you look at that? The sun is down. No wonder I'm tired.*

Keelan shot her a look. He labored all day and Aurora was tired? He shook his head and smiled.

"Of course, Aurora, get some sleep. See you in the morning."

As dawn broke, Keelan jolted awake, his senses immediately on edge. Beads of sweat formed on his forehead as he scanned his surroundings anxiously. His eyes fell on Aurora, who was sleeping soundly. He felt a sudden rush of relief finding her safely tucked in the blanket, but his heart was still pounding in his chest. "That was one heck of a dream," he murmured to himself, reclining once more in an attempt to grasp the fading dream.

He saw himself walking through an ancient castle; tapestries lined the walls between each floor-to-ceiling multi-colored stained-glass window. The tapestries showed landscapes and gallant knights riding into battle. Keelan walked down the long, dusty corridor, his boots clicking on the marble tiles.

At the end of the corridor, impossibly tall doors sat slightly ajar. Keelan stared up at the lavishly carved doors. Figures of dragons, knights on warhorses, and other fantastical creatures were cast in gold and silver.

He pushed one of the doors open and slipped into what appeared to be the throne room. The entire ceiling was crystal clear glass; the sun illuminated the area. A throne sat at the end of the long chamber before another large window. A glint of light caught his eye to the right of the throne. He moved quickly across the room, his entire focus on the object in the corner. A red tarp was half draped over a mirror. Keelan grabbed a corner of the tarp and pulled it off. With a loud swishing sound, the sheet slid off the mirror and pooled onto the floor.

Keelan stared at his reflection in the mirror. He was wearing fine clothing of green and bronze. His image in the mirror started to ripple and slowly change until he stared at Lance, his red hair and blue eyes unmistakable. He wore a high-collared white shirt with a blue vest and a purple doublet. Keelan and Lance gazed at each other, confused expressions on their faces. Suddenly, an image of a giant blue dragon surrounded Lance's image like a misty shroud. The sky above the castle turned dark, thunder shook the room, and lightning flashed. Keelan glanced around the throne room; the candles throughout the vast chamber had lit themselves. Looking back at the mirror, Keelan gasped in horror; the dragon opened its great maw. Keelan shouted at Lance to get out of the way. Lance smiled as a ball of fire left the dragon's gaping mouth and consumed Lance.

That's when Keelan woke, drenched in sweat and shaking. He found himself gasping for breath. He could still feel the chilling air of the temple biting his skin, sending shivers down his spine.

That dream felt so real, he thought. After shaking the feeling and scrubbing his face with his hands, he squinted at his ceiling with the light of predawn coming through his window.

"Good morning, Aurora," he said, as he had come accustomed to saying every morning when waking. He closed his eyes and waited for her chirpy greeting. But this morning was different; this morning, there was no reply. He bolted upright again and looked around his room. There was no sign of the Phoenix. The bundle of blankets next to his hearth was empty now and his window was open a little.

He jumped out of bed, threw on his trousers and boots, and grabbed a shirt as he rushed out the door. His parents were not up yet, thankfully. Looking for her, he glanced around the room and whispered softly, "Aurora, are you out here?"

Again, no reply. He rushed outside and ran to the side of the house that his window was on. A large snowbank came almost up to the windowsill, but no footprints from the Phoenix could be seen. Suddenly, there was a screech from above. He turned his gaze upward and saw the Phoenix streaking through the sky.

She screeched again, banked her wings, and slowly returned to the house.

You're up! she exclaimed.

"You gave me a mighty fright. I thought something happened to you."

Oh, something did. The sun has finally shown its face. I just couldn't stay inside any longer. I had to get out into the sky and soar. And let me tell you, it feels wonderful, she screeched again as she rose higher into the atmosphere.

"You might want to be a little quieter," he tried to whisper shout to her.

Stop shouting, you're going to wake your parents, she replied. *Just speak to me in your mind. I think you can do it.*

Really? he thought to himself, *Just speak to her in my mind, and she can hear me. This bird is out of her mind.*

Hey, you're out of your mind! she replied.

His mouth dropped open. *She hears my thoughts as I hear hers.*

Of course, silly, we've bonded. I'm familiar.

My what? Keelan looked at her.

Oh, never mind. She waved her feathers, *I'm going to go hunting. I'll be back later.*

Wait, don't go, he thought, *what if somebody sees you?*

No one will see me if I don't want them to. She winked. *Don't worry.*

With that, she disappeared into the woods.

Keelan stared after her vanishing form and chuckled, *This has been a crazy week.*

He hurried back inside to find his father in the kitchen.

"You're up and about early this morning," he replied without turning around.

"Yeah, I thought I heard something outside my window. I thought I should look, but I guess I was just hearing things, no tracks."

His father nodded his head. "I'll have breakfast ready in a few moments. Why don't you get warmed up? You really shouldn't go outside without your cloak."

"You're right, Father. How silly of me."

Later that day, while Keelan was still working in the shop, he heard a tiny chirp from the rafters. He looked up to see Aurora staring down at him. His eyes opened wide as he looked around to make sure no one was there. ***What are you doing here?*** He thought to her.

I'm watching you work, she said, tilting her head to one side and ruffling her feathers.

What if somebody sees you?

Like I said, I won't be seen if I don't want to be seen. You worry too much.

Keelan sighed and returned to work, trying to ignore the tiny eyes staring at him.

"Good day's work, son," Elliot said as he entered the shop. "With all this snow, I'm guessing you won't go to the Firestrums' ranch anytime soon."

Keelan gave him a tight smile. "No, probably not. It's a shame I was really enjoying the workout." He glanced at Aurora, but she wasn't there.

"There's no reason you can't work out here; come to the back with me."

They left the shop's main room and into the stable area. He looked behind them to see if she was following but he couldn't spot her.

A practice dummy was set up in the middle aisle between the stalls with hay bales all around it.

"Where did this come from?" Keelan asked.

"I made it today. I figured you might want to continue working out even when you can't make it out to see Lance and Douglas. From what I remember, practice dummies look like this. It should be about right."

"It looks spot on. Thank you, I can't wait to try it out. I can probably make myself a staff, but I don't think I will be skilled enough to make a sword." Keelan made a slow circle around the practice dummy, inspecting it.

"I can help with the staff part," Elliot reached behind the hay bale and pulled out a black staff with silver cuffs on both tips.

Keelan slowly reached for the staff, "Where did you get this?" he asked. It was beautiful.

"A merchant was traveling through town a month ago. I was going to hold it until your fifteenth name day," he chuckled. "But I think now is a good time to give it to you."

"I don't know what to say," Keelan smiled broadly, "Thank you, Father."

"No thanks needed. Now show me what you can do," he winked, gesturing to the practice dummy.

For the rest of the afternoon, Keelan went through all the moves he learned from Douglas.

His father watched the entire time with a proud smile on his face.

CHAPTER

-12-

A few days later, Keelan and his parents sat in the main room after dinner, playing cards near the fireplace. There was a pounding at the door. Elliot jumped up and rushed to the door to see who was there.

"Maya, I'm so glad to see you're home," the baker, Colton Greig, said with a troubled look on his face. He rushed into the house, completely ignoring Elliot.

Maya jumped up, "What's the matter? Is Emma okay?"

"I don't think so; there seems to be a problem. Alma, the midwife, requested that I get you immediately."

Elliot rushed off to grab her medicine bag and cloak.

"It must be something serious if Alma can't handle it," Keelan replied, "I'll come with you in case you need some help."

"No, you stay here with your father."

"I'm coming with you," he said sternly, throwing his cloak over his shoulders.

Maya looked at her son for a second. She took a deep breath. He was growing up into a fine man. She had to start treating him like one. She nodded and shrugged into her cloak.

"Good idea, son," Elliot said to him.

Maya, Keelan, and baker Greig rushed out of the house and hurried down the snowy street to get to his home. The evening sky was clear, with millions of stars twinkling down at them. They stayed in the middle of the street to avoid running into anything. With the new moon upon them, it was tremendously dark.

"Please tell me everything that's happened that you know," Maya said to Colton.

"I don't know, there's been a lot of screaming, and then Alma rushed out and said to get you. I didn't have time to ask questions."

Maya nodded her head but didn't say anything more.

The baker and his wife lived above the bakery. When they arrived, there were three horses hitched out front.

"Who in the world would be out at this time of night," the baker said.

Keelan looked at the saddle blankets and noticed the Royal seal on all three horses. He shared a quick look with his mother, but she shook her head and rushed up the stairs.

In the baker's home, three knights spoke with one of the midwives in hushed voices in the corner.

"What's going on here," the baker demanded.

"We are here to witness your child's birth as decreed by the King," the Officer replied with a scowl plastered on his face.

Maya gestured for the midwife to follow her, and they went into the back room.

Keelan and the baker sat down on the couch to wait.

Maya entered the back room to see Emma pale as a ghost and sweat-drenched. She rushed to her side and placed a hand on her head and her ear on her chest.

"Tell me everything that's going on, Alma," Maya said.

Emma groaned in pain.

Alma approached with a look she couldn't quite understand. "We think there's going to be two," she whispered.

Maya's face blanched; twins…And royal knights stood just outside the door—no way to hide one now.

Over the years, Alma requested Maya's assistance in hiding a couple of twins. Thankfully, there were never very many born, but the numbers did seem to be increasing.

"Get wet towels," Maya looked at Alma, "Lock the doors. Don't open them until I say so."

Sophia nodded and rushed to the door. Alma came with cold, wet towels and placed them on Emma's forehead, "She's burning, Maya."

"Emma, look at me," Maya said, "Stay strong, alright? Just a few more minutes." Emma moaned in pain as she shifted to her left and threw up.

"It's alright," Alma held her hair gently, "Let it out."

"What are knights doing way out here so far from the Capital?" Maya asked, nervously.

Sophia shrugged and looked over at the newest midwife, Heather. "You were out there speaking with them," Alma said to Heather. "Did they say what they're here for?"

"The King has decreed that all births are to be witnessed by an officer. You got the message just as I did," she replied coldly.

"But how did they get here so quickly? Her birth is early, and I have not been in contact with them yet. We just got the message from the King no more than a fortnight ago." Maya rubbed Emma's back.

Heather simply looked at both of them and shrugged.

Alma advanced on her and got right in her face. "I don't know you very well, and you don't know me, but if you know something, you better speak up." The Old midwife scowled at Heather with her hands on her hips.

Heather pressed her lips, "I'm from the castle. I have been sent by the King. Midwives have been sent all over the kingdom to ensure this decree is followed. Each town has a couple of knights stationed outside of it that come quickly when we call. No births will go unnoticed in the night," she said with her nose in the air and her face flushed.

Suddenly, Emma shrieked.

"We're here." Maya sank to her knees, ready to help Emma bring her child into the world. Within a few minutes, the voice of a child was heard crying; moments later, the second one came into the world.

"Oh, my babies!" Emma cried tears of joy and pain rolled down her cheeks.

Someone knocked on the door. "Open the door, by order of the king!"

Emma looked at Maya helplessly. "Please, don't let them take my babies for Ombrasia's sake! Please!"

Before Maya could respond, the door was thrown open, and the three knights marched in.

"Please, a little bit of privacy for the new mother. She needs time to recover." Alma tried to sound calm, but the guards weren't having it. "Hand over the children."

"Both?" Emma sobbed, "Please, don't take both; twins are nothing without their sibling," she begged. "Please for Ombrasia's sake. Please, let me keep one," Emma sobbed.

"The King has decreed that all twins - both children and their mother - shall be eliminated." The guard at the very front barked.

All the women in the room gasped at this announcement except Heather. Maya couldn't believe her ears.

"Eliminated? Killed?" Alma managed to ask, hoping she had heard wrong.

"Yes, killed."

"What do you mean killed? And the mother? How is she committing a crime? She only gave birth to the children. It takes two to make a child," Maya stood in front of them, hiding Emma behind her. "Are you going to kill the father too?"

"No, the King has discovered that twins run in the female line. All females who give birth to twins shall not be allowed to give birth again." The guard took a step forward. "Now, step aside."

Maya did not budge. She knew she couldn't win in this situation, but she wasn't going to give in. Before Maya could make another move, two of the soldiers grabbed Maya by the shoulders and threw her out of the room.

"Ma!" Keelan jumped to his feet, "Let her go! Now! Keelan ordered the guards. They dropped Maya on the floor and went inside the room. Alma and Sophia quickly followed.

"Ma, are you okay?" He sat on his knees, trying to help his mother.

"Emma!" The baker ran to the closed door, "No! Let me in!" He yelled, pounding on the door.

"What's going on?" Keelan asked in a panic. Tears rushed down Maya's face as she stood up. "I'm sorry," She shook her head, "I – I couldn't stop them."

"What are you talking about?" he asked a moment before they heard Emma's shrilling scream.

The knights and Heather marched out of the room. They pushed the Baker out of the way. The two knights each held a newborn baby in their arms. The officer was wiping his blade and then sheathed it.

"Where are you going with my child?" His eyes widened when he saw two bundles in their arms. His knees buckled, and he started to weep, realizing the birth was twins.

"Why are you taking the children?" Maya asked.

"They are to be brought to the capital, where they will be dealt with," the officer replied and marched down the stairs.

The baker ran behind the guards, but they had already left. He rushed inside to his room.

"Emma! Oh, Emma!" He screamed, crying out in disbelief, and dropped to his knees with his head on the bed next to his wife. He struggled to speak, choking out her name, "Emma, I was power – powerless."

Alma and Sophia clung to each other, sobbing hysterically. Keelan looked between them and his mother in complete shock. His mother backed away from the bedroom and dropped on the couch, her face ashen. Keelan rushed to her side, "What's happening, mother? Please, tell me.

Tears streamed down Maya's cheeks. "The King is wrong," she whispered.

"What?" Keelan asked, "What do you mean?"

Maya shook her head, "What?"

"What did you say about the King?"

Her eyes widened, "I – Never mind." She stammered. Her eyes fell on the room.

The baker sat on the floor beside the bed, holding Emma's hand; while she stared at the ceiling.

"What's happening here?" Keelan pressed.

"The King says all twins and their mother are…are outlawed."

Keelan whipped his eyes to the bedroom door; the baker was still inside, holding Emma's hand, "So, she's…" he trailed off.

Maya nodded her head but said nothing more.

Alma and Maya agreed to stay with the baker for the evening and help him with his wife's remains. Keelan stayed for a little longer before numbly returning to their house to tell his father what had happened.

When Maya returned to the house the following day, she was in no mood to speak about what happened. She entered her room and closed the door, asking to be left alone. Elliot tried asking her but left her to be with herself for a while.

A few hours later, after she was confident the two men in her life had left the house, she reached under the bed and pulled out a small trunk – a trunk she hadn't looked into in a very long time. On top was a pair of old shoes, Keelan's first. She put them aside and reached for a small book near the bottom; the cover was old and tattered. When she was young, she spent countless nights reading the passages within. The book was filled with stories of histories that had fallen into fairy tales and old prophecies that had come and gone. Even though she had not looked in the book since right before Keelan's birth, she thumbed through and quickly found the page she was looking for, searching for clues.

As soon as she read the first line, the remainder of the words came flooding back to her, and she recited the passage by heart.

"Forgotten Kingdoms lost to tyranny, the realm of beasts, and the realm of magic fade away. The birth of twins in the darkness of night, upon uniting, the fates of the Royal Lines shall intertwine. Infinity embraced; royal birthrights restored."

Something tapped at her window. She slowly opened her eyes and then jumped to her feet when she saw a Phoenix staring at her.

Hello Maya. My name is Aurora, the Phoenix said in her mind.

Where did you come from? Maya responded.

I've been sheltering with your family for a while now. I was injured; your son found me and healed my wing.

What brought you to my window?

I heard you speaking a passage from the Scrolls of Eldjren.

Maya nodded. *Do you know of the Twin's Prophecy?*

I know more than just that prophecy. My sire was Eldjren the Seer's familiar. He was with him when he prophesied the downfall of the great kingdoms and the coming of the twins to restore order. He even helped him unravel the riddles in his visions. The Twins' Prophecy has always been my favorite. Did you know there is a phoenix that assists the twins?

Maya shook her head, walking the short distance to the window and opening it. *I've heard pieces of the full prophecy over the years. But the full works of Eldjren were lost before I was born. I know Eldjren foretold the fall of the two kingdoms, but no one heeded his words.* She projected to the bird.

Indeed, he spent the last decade of his life trying to persuade people to believe him. He knew that the two great kingdoms would fall to tyranny and that the only hope for the future was the birth of Royal Twins. With the help of a lost phoenix, they would find the Infinite Medallion, unite, and save the world from The One.

"Who is The One? I always thought the twins would overthrow the oppressive powers that destroyed the great kingdoms. I never knew there was something else coming."

Oh, that's the most mysterious part. Eldjren didn't know who The One was, either. He was confident it wasn't quite human and definitely not a wyvern or dragon. Would you like to know what the prophecy fully says?

"Oh, yes, please?" She pleaded in a whisper.

Centuries long ago, peace and harmony ruled the land. Beast and man living hand in hand. Two mighty Kingdoms rose. Two Royal families came to power, one to rule the beasts, one to rule man. Their legacies were once aligned but still forever entwined. The two mighty Kingdoms will fall and lose their power. New blood would rise to rule and dictate. The kingdoms would divide, and tyranny would be unleashed on the realm. Beast and man are separated by hate and fear, and unity is lost.

But in secret, magic would survive. Freedom would dance, and unity would find its sacred room. Twins would be born from royal birthright in the darkness of night. The twins from the royal lines would be tested, their strength grown from strife. But the twins must unite; they must entwine their legacies to take a stand. With the help of a Phoenix, lost in the world, they will find the Infinite Medallion. Only with the medallion can they unite and save the land from tyranny while overcoming the shadow cast by The One.

I never knew all this. Why was it shortened so? Maya projected; her throat constricted with emotion.

To protect the twins, of course. Eldjren struggled with this prophecy more than any other. He knew he had to ensure their success when no one believed him. He wanted to give just enough information for twins to be treasured without The One being able to stop them. Before he died, he said he found the Infinite Medallion but hid it with his original writings. Only the royal line heirs can find it, and then they will know what to do. The Medallion will lead the way. But now I must ask you how you know about the Twin's Prophecy. It is not common knowledge anymore.

Maya glanced at her bedroom door and listened closely for any sounds, *I am of the Royal line.*

Truly! This is wonderful news. You must tell Keelan. He must know all that you know. Aurora opened her wings and ignited the tips of her feathers.

"NO!" she yelled and then clapped a hand over her mouth, *He is too young to be burdened with our history. Someday perhaps. He doesn't have magic; he can live a normal life. After he marries, I will tell him all he needs to know.*

He has magic, Maya. Why are you denying this?

"He has no magic. He is blessed," she whispered.

He can hear my voice. He has magic! Iton, the God of Wisdom has blessed him.

No, that can't be; it must not be. My son has no magic. She waved her arms at Aurora, trying to get her to fly off. *Go, go,* she projected.

Aurora fanned her tail out and spread her wings wide, the tips of her feather igniting in flame. *I will do no such thing. You know what I am; you know that we do not lie. You can live in denial all you want and keep secrets from your son. But I shall do no such thing.*

Oh, please don't tell him anything. It's unsafe for him to know any more than he already does, Maya pleaded with the bird silently.

He knows nothing! He thought that elves, fairies, and phoenixes were fairy tales. And when I told him he had magic, he rejected the notion. I have not pressed the issue, but that will only last for so long. You must tell him the truth!

I can't, not yet. The King's knights are in town killing women who are having twins. We are not living in safe times.

I will protect him. I am his familiar, now and always. Oshan, the Goddess of Life, guides my path.

Maya bowed her head and thanked the bird quietly. When she looked up, the phoenix was gone. Hastily, she closed the window, then placed the book in her hand back in the bottom of the chest and slid it back under the bed. She composed herself in her bedroom mirror and left her room to join her family. She knew she would have to tell them the truth someday, but not yet.

She could keep her secret a bit longer.

CHAPTER

-13-

THIS was Creekside's snowiest winter in recent memory. On the few days when it wasn't snowing, Keelan went to the Firestrum Ranch to continue his lessons, but most of the time, he stayed at home working with his parents and practicing with the staff in the barn.

On one of his trips out to the ranch, Douglas let him take one of the practice swords home so he could continue honing his skill.

Aurora was his ever-present invisible shadow. Wherever he went, she was close by. She would hunt if the weather was nice enough, and he would bring her food if she refused to go out. It turned into a comfortable partnership.

They also worked on their telepathy, stretching the distance she could travel and still reach his mind. Soon, they reached the distance from his house to the Firestrum Ranch before he couldn't pick up her thoughts anymore.

Spring is almost here. I can feel it, Aurora announced one day on their way out to the Firestrum Ranch. A slight breeze stirred the budding branches overhead and a few early spring flowers bloomed along the edge of the road.

Not too long now, Keelan agreed.

So what adventures are we going to go on?

Adventures? I really wasn't planning on leaving Creekside anytime soon. My parents need me. But you don't have to stay; you're a free bird.

Of course, I'm free. But our fates are intertwined. I am yours, and you are mine. That's just the way it's going to be.

Keelan chuckled as he watched her fly overhead.

When they came into view of Firestrum Ranch, Aurora disappeared into the branches of a tree. Having the ability to stay impossibly still, she almost appeared to disappear, the thousands of leaves breaking up her shape and concealing her. True to her word, no one ever saw her unless she wanted to be seen.

"Hi, Keelan," Lance greeted him from the field. "Are you ready for another grueling day of sparring?"

"Always," he replied, laughing.

"Great! Here, let me get out to the main road, and then I'll race you to the house." Rogue snorted a greeting to Lance's horse and tossed his head.

They raced down the road to the ranch house, skidding to a halt when they reached the barn. Both boys were breathing hard and laughing when they dismounted their equally exhausted horses.

"I think you two have way too much energy," Douglas said as a way of greeting. Watching the boys trying to stabilize their breathing, he said, "Grab your swords and a water skin. I want you to run to the glades and back,"

"The glades? But that's got to be at least two miles," Lance whined.

"Then you just better be glad I didn't say run to the Craigs."

"Oh, no, that's okay, sir. The glades will be just fine. We don't need to tack on another two miles on top of it," Keelan said, grabbing Lance's arm. A chasm called the Craigs was almost a mile deep and was at the edge of the Firestrum Ranch.

Both boys hurried to comply; they each grabbed a water skin and belted their swords to their hips. They took off at a brisk pace. They would jog there and back but would be required to sprint the last hundred yards. This was a run they had completed many times. It had gotten easier each time, but it was still challenging with a bouncing sword at your hip.

When they returned, they were no longer laughing and no longer full of energy. But now it was Douglas's turn to laugh. Both boys reached the barn and collapsed on their backs, breathing hard.

"On your feet, soldiers," Douglas boomed. "Time for the obstacle course." Both boys groaned but climbed shakily to their feet.

The obstacle course was similar to what Keelan had first done when Douglas had agreed to train him, but now there were a few twists. With the two of them running the course simultaneously, they were required to spar as they went. They hung up their metal weapons and grabbed their practice swords to begin their first run through the course. They might get lucky if they did it well enough, and Douglas would only have them run it once or twice.

After they completed their fourth run through the obstacle course, Douglas looked up into the sky. A red and orange phoenix was streaking toward them; she opened her beak and emitted a piercing cry and a stream of fire.

Keelan froze. Aurora was making an appearance, and she looked frightful. He never heard her make such a sound and had no idea she breathed fire. She swooped down and landed in front of him.

Keelan, you must return home quickly. Your mother's in danger.

Without thinking, he spoke aloud, "What do you mean my mother's in danger? How do you know?"

"Keelan, do you know this bird?" Douglas asked him.

"I've never been this close to a Phoenix before," Lance said in open awe.

"I really can't talk about that right now, sir. I need to get home." Keelan rushed over to Rogue and started to saddle him.

"Hold up there. Who is this phoenix to you?" When Keelan did not reply, Douglas turned to the phoenix. His gaze intensified, but he did not say anything verbally. Aurora returned his look and stared deeply into his eyes. She squawked and took flight, circling their heads.

What's wrong with you? Keelan projected to Aurora.

"Lance, I want you to go with them. Make haste, both of you. Oh, and take these with you." He threw them their real swords.

Lance nodded and saddled his horse.

Keelan was perplexed by what had just transpired, but he was in too much panic to ask any more questions. He mounted Rogue and rushed down the street to return to his house.

Aurora didn't say anything to him but kept pace, urging Rogue to go faster and faster.

When he saw his home in the distance, he noticed the King's knights were at his house. Two horses were riderless and being held by one soldier. Keelan and Lance slowed their horses to a discreet walk. Rushing in without knowing what was going on would not help anybody.

"Why don't I ride up alone? I'll go up to the house and ask your parents if they've seen you, and then I can kind of gauge the situation," Lance offered.

"Good idea," Keelan agreed. ***Aurora, can you keep an eye on him? I'll stay over in the woods.***

Of course, she replied. Within seconds, she was perched on top of the roof of his house.

Keelan veered off into the woods as Lance approached the house.

"Hello, wonderful spring day, isn't it?" Lance said to the soldier; he looked young, maybe only sixteen.

"Who are you, and what do you want?" the soldier asked him.

"My name is Lance. I've come to see if my friend Keelan's home."

"Go away!"

The front door opened, and the other two knights exited the house. "Why, hello, boy, what can we do for you?" the officer inquired. He looked like a seasoned officer, with gray hair lacing through his beard and temples.

"I was just telling your soldier here that I was looking for my friend Keelan. I wanted to see if he was available to go fishing."

"Keelan is not home, but if you see him, tell him he must get home immediately."

"Oh, I will, thank you, sir." Lance continued walking toward the house.

"You can go away now," the officer said curtly.

"I have business with Mr. Keifman too, sir. My father needs him to show me a couple of horses tomorrow. So, I need to see if he's available."

"All right, but make it quick," the officer told him.

The three knights mounted their horses and walked a little ways from the house.

Lance hurried to the house, tied his horse up, and went to the front door. The officer had left it open.

"Lance!" Elliot said, "Quickly get inside and close the door."

Lance complied, "What did those three goons want?"

"I'm not sure. They spoke with Maya, and now she's locked in her room. Where's Keelan?"

"He saw a boar and decided to go after it." Lance cleared his throat and spoke loudly, "I needed to ask you about shoeing a few horses for my father tomorrow."

"Yes, yes, I have time." Elliot played his part.

Maya peeked her head out of her bedroom, "Lance when you see Keelan, have him come to the back of the house. Tell him not to be seen by those knights. Quickly now, go find him before he shows himself," she slammed the door shut.

"What's going on, Maya?" Elliot tried the handle of the door, but it was locked again. He started pounding on the door. "Let me in," he said sternly.

Lance exited the house and mounted his horse, "Have a good day, officers," he waved to the soldiers and trotted back toward his house.

A streak of red caught his sight as the phoenix dove into the woods. *Keelan has a phoenix! I wonder how long she's been with him?* He thought. *I'm going to have to ask my father what this means.*

When he was far enough down the road that he could no longer see the soldiers, he veered into the forest. He whistled twice, and Keelan whistled once in reply.

"So, what do those knights want?" Keelan asked.

"I don't know. I guess they spoke to your mother; she locked herself in the bedroom and won't let your father in. She said to have you come to the back of the house and not let the soldiers see you. But she wants you to get to the house as quickly as possible."

"Okay, thank you, Lance. Maybe you should go home, and I'll sneak in through the barn."

"No, I think I'll stay with you. You might need backup. Those knights definitely didn't want me anywhere near the house and were very interested in your whereabouts."

"Okay, let's find a good place to hide the horses, and then we'll sneak in."

Aurora, can you be our lookout?

I'm on it.

They crept to the back of the barn, slowly opened the door, and peeked inside. When they didn't see anybody, they carefully made their way up toward the house.

The three soldier men are still out front, Aurora told him.

"I think the coast is clear. Let's hurry up to the back door," Keelan told Lance, who only nodded.

The house's back door was slightly ajar; Keelan slowly pushed it open and hurried inside. Lance followed closely at his heels. Once inside, they made their way to his mother's room.

Elliot nodded to the boys but remained seated by the hearth with the lamps turned down low.

Keelan knocked quietly on his mother's door.

She says to come in, Aurora projected.

She can speak to you? How does she know who you are?

Lance looked at Keelan; he stood still with his hand hovering above the doorknob, "Are you okay?"

"Um, yeah, come on," he opened the door and swiftly entered. The room was completely dark. The curtains were drawn tightly and the hearth and lamps were doused. A sliver of light peaked through a small tear in the bottom of the curtain.

"Quickly, shut the door," Maya said in barely a whisper.

Keelan and Lance carefully walked across the room in the direction Maya's voice had come from.

"Why are you in the dark," Keelan whispered.

"Shhhh, sit first."

Both boys sat on the floor next to Maya.

She held her hands out, and a soft glow surrounded them. Slowly, the light grew until the three of them were encased in a glowing bubble.

Keelan's eyes widened, but he remained silent, his heart beating quickly. He fought the urge to shy away from her. His mother was using magic, he started to shake, and he was having a hard time drawing a breath. He only started to relax when the soft glow slowly disappeared.

"My father mentioned a few things about you but didn't know if he was right. Nothing more than feelings, but I see now that he was right. He said you were the one we have been searching for," Lance said.

"Shhhh," Keelan whispered in surprise. Lance was not whispering.

"It's okay, son. We can speak naturally now."

"How, what…" He shook his head. "What's going on?"

"I will attempt to answer your questions." Maya reached out to pat Keelan's hand, but he flinched away from her. She frowned as she lowered her hand to her lap. "Douglas has been looking for me?" She asked Lance.

He nodded, but before he could say anything more, Keelan interrupted.

"How do you have magic?" Keelan asked quietly. Barely more than a whisper under his breath.

"I was born this way, but I will explain all that later."

"What did the knights want? Can we at least start there?"

His mother nodded, "That is why you are here. The king is getting increasingly paranoid."

"About what?" Keelan interrupted.

Maya raised her hand to quiet her son, "The current royal family has not been in power very long. Only a couple of generations. They seized power and have been trying to eliminate the former royal line. A prophecy foretold the fall of the old royal line and how they could regain their power. It appears that King Percival Theodoric is trying to ensure the prophecy is not fulfilled. I'm not sure what makes him think now is the time, but his actions against the baker's wife clarified his intentions."

"I know of this prophecy you speak of. Are you sure he is certain the bloodlines are close?" Lance asked.

Keelan looked between his mother and best friend, *What are they talking about?*

"I don't know about the Ragnis line, but I know the Vaelums are at least another generation away. What King Theodoric is doing now will not stop it from coming to pass."

"What are you two talking about?"

"We're talking about history that has been suppressed. There used to be two kingdoms that ruled this part of the world. Well over a hundred years ago, a prophecy foretold the downfall of those two kingdoms. Each kingdom was overtaken by tyranny independently. The prophecy spoke about the rebirth of the original birthrights."

"Okay, so let me get this straight: you two are talking about a 100-year-old prophecy, and this is history that has been suppressed and hidden from the public," Keelan scrubbed his face with his hands and then ran his hands through his hair. "So, how in the world do you two know about this?"

"Families from both kingdoms have vowed to keep the memories alive. Lance appears to be from one, and I am from another."

"This is a lot to take in. Does father know any of this?"

"Blessed Gods in Ombrasia, no!" Maya exclaimed. "There is much for you to learn about the kingdoms of old, and you must be very careful who you speak to about any of this information. Speaking of any of this where the King may hear comes with it a sentence of death. As I said, King Theodoric is paranoid that his reign will end. It will eventually, but I don't see that happening soon."

"How do you know? What is this prophecy? Can you tell me about it?" Keelan rambled.

Maya cleared her throat and started to smooth out her skirt, clearly stalling. As she opened her mouth, Lance interrupted.

"Forgotten Kingdoms lost to tyranny, the realm of beasts, and the realm of magic fade away. The birth of twins in the darkness of night, upon uniting, the fates of the Royal Lines shall intertwine. Infinity embraced; royal birthrights restored."

Maya stared at him with wide eyes. "You said you knew the prophecy. I didn't truly believe it. Please tell me how you know of this prophecy. Which family do you hail from?"

"I think that's a conversation you need to have with my father," Lance replied.

Maya nodded her head, "So I shall."

"Okay, mother. So, there's this prophecy about twins that will help bring the rebirth of the old kingdoms. I can see how that correlates with what King Theodoric is doing now. He is killing all twins and any mother that may give birth to them, but what if the twins come from the father? What if the father is the royal line, not the mother?"

Maya shrugged, "The knights said they had information that twins come from the mother's line. I don't know how they got that information or if it is even true. All I know is that women need to be careful."

"Okay, I have another question. What do the knights want with you? You didn't have twins. You just had me."

Maya smiled sadly, "They believe I knew Emma was carrying twins, and I was trying to hide it. They're coming after Alma as well," she sighed deeply, "I fear for her life."

"Then why do they want to know where I am?"

"That I really don't know," Maya looked down at her hands while she spoke.

Keelan just frowned, *She is still keeping something from me.*

"To be safe, I need you to go away for a while, just until things settle down."

"Where will you have me go?" He asked, concerned.

"I don't know, maybe just stay at the Firestrums for a while. Did you tell them your last name or where you were from, Lance?"

"No, ma'am, I just told them my first name and told them I was looking for Keelan."

Maya nodded, "I would appreciate it if you two would return to the Firestrum Ranch and then send Mr. Firestrum to see me. When he returns, we will have a better plan of what to do."

"Can you tell me more about your magic first?"

"There is no time right now. Let us get you safe and then I will tell you all you need to know. Now, you and Lance need to go."

"If you really think I have to mother, I will do as you say," Keelan said.

Maya nodded, tears glistening in her eyes, "Now, go and be safe."

Lance and Keelan snuck back out the way they came in, retrieved their horses, and made their way to the Firestrum Ranch, sticking to the forest as much as possible. Aurora joined them when they were far enough away from the village.

Douglas Firestrum rode out as soon as the boys told him what was happening; he told them to stay inside, stay hidden, and, if anybody came to the door, hide in the root cellar. Douglas returned shortly after nightfall.

"All right, boys, it has been decided that the two of you will go out to the line shack by the Craigs. I want you two to stay out there until we send for you. Right now, I think that will be the safest place for you both."

"Both of us? Why both of us?" Lance asked.

"You told the king's knights that you were friends with Keelan. They may try to use you to get to him."

"Why do they want me so badly? I haven't done anything wrong."

"That is what your mother and I intend to find out."

"What about my father?"

"I told him I was sending you and Lance to a special trainer for advanced swordplay. I told them it was time to increase their skills to the next level and that I was insufficient to do so."

"Okay, so we're going to go out to a shack out by the Craigs and wait for you to fetch us. But what happens when I return and don't know any more advanced techniques?"

"I've thought about that too. Don't worry; I will actually be sending a master swordsman out to you. He'll also be there to keep an eye on you to make sure you're safe."

"Are you sure this is the only thing we can do, Father? It's almost my Name-Day, Father." Lance stared at his father intently.

"That cannot be helped. It has come down to this, son. Now, pack up your stuff and grab some extra supplies for Keelan. I want you gone at first light."

CHAPTER -14-

AT first light, both boys were mounted and headed into the forest toward the chasm called the Craigs.

They rode silently for a while before Keelan spoke, "Your father is sending us to a shack to live and sending us a master swordsman to help us." He looked ahead, "This is all really strange. Do you know what's going on?"

Lance just shrugged, "Not much more than you do."

"What do you mean not much? You either know more than me, or you don't."

"All right, so I know a little bit more, but now is not the right time to talk about it."

"That's great. Everybody's keeping secrets from me. I feel great." Keelan almost snapped. "First, my ma, and now my best friend." He looked at the sky. Aurora was keeping pace with them. "You're keeping secrets from me too, aren't you?" Keelan mumbled.

I've never told you that I wasn't keeping secrets from you, Aurora said to him.

I know, and now I know you are, he projected to her.

Rest of the travel, Keelan kept his gaze forward. It was bothering him – people keeping secrets. He was not immature, nor was he a child.

They reached the Craigs by mid-morning. The mile-deep chasm was jagged and imposing. Short, twisted pine shrubs clung to the walls in various places, and a small herd of mountain goats grazed and walked along the impossibly thin trails they had created. The view was so impressive that Keelan forgot he was mad.

"I've been up here before but never seen the shack your dad spoke about."

Lance chuckled, "Oh, just wait and see. My father calls it a shack. It's anything but."

They traveled along the edge of the ravine for another mile. "I thought you said that your land ended at the Craigs."

"It marks our Western boundary, but we own a couple of miles this way," Lance replied, casually.

"Wow, the amount of land your father owns is impressive," Keelan said in all honestly.

"My father said nobody wanted it, so it was cheap."

Keelan couldn't believe nobody wanted that land. "It's absolutely breathtaking. Can't believe nobody wants to live here, and all the time we've spent up here, I've never seen anything remotely scary."

Lance laughed again but didn't comment.

A large rock formation appeared in the distance that looked almost out of place next to the rest of the topography. Soon, they were upon the outcropping and circling it. Once on the opposite side, Keelan could see that it was partially man-made and that the so-called shack was built inside.

"So, this is the shack," he realized.

Lance laughed again, "Just a little family joke, I guess. Come on inside. Let's get settled, and I'll show you around."

From the direction they came, all you could see were rocks, but once you ventured around the side closest to the chasm, the structure took shape. Numerous windows were carved in the rocks, giving the shack a great view of the Craigs. A giant porch platform cantilevered out over the chasm with the main entry at the back. When they reached the front door, it was opened by an old man wiping his hand on his apron and bowing deeply.

"Master Lance, what a pleasant surprise; I wasn't expecting you so soon and with company."

"Gregor, this is Keelan. Father sent us here to lay low for a while. The King's men are looking for Keelan, and we don't… know... why," he said the last three words slowly, one at a time.

Gregor nodded hurriedly, "Come right in, boys. I will have dinner prepared at dusk. Lance, you know your way around."

"Thank you, Gregor." He looked at Keelan, "Come on, my room's over here."

"Does he stay here full time?"

"Who? Gregor? Oh yeah, he's the caretaker here. The ranch hands come and go when rounding up cows that we have pastured up here. That's why it's called a line shack. It's along the line of the trail. I like to come up here occasionally, too, to get away."

"And he wasn't expecting you so soon?"

"Yeah, in a couple of days, Father and I were going to come up here for my name-day."

Keelan nodded, "I wish I had known your name-day was coming soon. I would have got you something. You're going to be fifteen like me, right?"

"Fifteen?" He looked at Keelan and then smiled, "Oh, yeah, fifteen. But it's okay. My family likes to keep our name-days more private than most people."

"That's okay. Every family has their traditions."

The entry into the rock house was at least two stories tall; a vaulted ceiling greeted them with numerous skylights. A large gathering room was in front of them, with hallways branching off on both sides. Gregor took off to the right; Lance led Keelan to the left. The hallway was wide and took several turns before it opened into another common room with a large fireplace and several couches.

"This is the sleeping wing, as we call it. My father's room is the first one. The ranch hands use this one, and then mine is furthest back here on the right-hand side of the fireplace." Lance led him to his private room.

The bedroom was massive, easily the same size as Keelan's house. Two large windows and a glass door overlooked the chasm. A large fireplace with a couple of chairs was on one side of the room, and a large bed with several dressers was on the other. But the double doorway that led outside caught Keelan's eyes the most. The doors were easily five times larger, in height and width than any door he'd ever seen. A mounted rider could ride their horse easily through the door and still not hit their head. Keelan walked over to the door and looked outside. Another large platform was just outside the door, cantilevered over the chasm. He looked over at Lance and gestured with his eyes, "So what's with these large platforms? You don't have a problem with heights, do you?"

"Those ledges were naturally formed. We just utilized them as a porch, I guess you could call it," Lance shrugged off the question.

Another thing that caught Keelan's eye was the huge rug in the center of the room. He walked over and placed his hands on it. It was almost as thick as a mattress and super soft. "This is some rug you have here," he remarked.

Lance chuckled, "Yeah, sometimes I just curl up on it and go to sleep; it's really comfortable. But I think the bed will do for us, it's pretty big. I think we can both sleep in it."

"Sounds good to me, but I don't think I'm going to be sleeping tonight. I have too many questions rolling through my head." Keelan chuckled dryly.

"That might change after you eat one of Gregor's meals. You'll be so full you'll just fall asleep. Come on, let me show you around."

For the remainder of the day, Lance took Keelan on a tour of the rest of the house and the surrounding area. They returned to the home a little before dusk to find appetizers spread out in the common room. Lance and Keelan grabbed a few things and sat down, waiting for dinner to start.

"Young Masters, dinner is ready," Gregor said from the dining area. The dining room was massive, as was every room in the 'shack', which made the large dining table, with twenty chairs around it, in the center of the room look grossly undersized. Two place settings were set on one side of the table. Keelan's eyes widened at the massive spread of food that was already in place.

"He does know it's just the two of us, doesn't he?" He asked Lance.

"I don't think Gregor knows how to cook for only two people," he laughed. "Don't worry, the ranch hands will be around soon. It will all get eaten."

The boys dove into a hearty meal of beef, lamb, numerous different types of roasted vegetables, sautéed vegetables, and bread. There was even a stew and some sort of a soufflé that Keelan couldn't quite identify the ingredients of, but nonetheless, it was delicious. When they stopped eating and couldn't possibly eat another bite, Gregor appeared with a platter full of desserts.

"I think I'm going to explode," Keelan said with a groan.

"How about dessert in a little bit? Gregor, I think we're going to go sit outside."

Gregor nodded and returned to the kitchen.

Lance grabbed another roll as they walked from the dining area to the platform off the house's entry. Keelan hadn't noticed before, but some chairs were off to one side.

Both boys sat heavily and groaned with pleasure, their stomachs full.

"I think that's the most food I've ever eaten in one sitting," Keelan laughed.

"Like I said, Gregor loves to cook, and there's never a shortage of food up here."

Keelan smiled. This shack was truly something he had never seen or dreamt of.

"Your father made it sound like we would be alone." Keelan said after a while.

"Yeah, sometimes I think he forgets Gregor is always up here."

"Does Gregor like being forgotten?"

Lance chuckled, "Yeah, I think he does. This place has been in the family for a long time, longer than we have owned the bottom land; that's what we call the main ranch. Gregor planted himself here long before I was born. If we linger too long, he kicks us out and tells us to get back to society."

Keelan nodded and they fell back into silence as night descended all around them.

When they finally entered the house, they grabbed a couple of dessert items before retiring to their room for the evening.

Keelan fell asleep on the surprisingly comfortable enormous rug in Lance's room but woke with a start. He bolted upright in a panic. *What was that sound?* he thought.

Do you mind not thinking so loudly? Aurora complained from where she was lying on the rug.

How did you get in here?

Lance sleeps with the window open, she said sluggishly.

What was that sound that woke me?

I didn't hear anything.

He stayed startled for a few minutes before he yawned, laid back down, and tried to fall asleep. He bolted upright again when he heard a roar. *I know I heard something that time. I wasn't sleeping.*

It was just an eagle.

That must be the biggest eagle in the world, then.

There are some mighty big eagles up here, she replied. *Please just go to sleep.* He could tell Aurora was sleepy and wasn't appreciating the 'disturbance.'

Fine, he grumbled, laying back down. He closed his eyes, and soon he fell back to sleep.

He woke the next morning to the sunlight peeking in. Keelan felt weirdly fresh and as if, he was reborn. *That was some sleep,* he thought to himself. He forced his eyes to open and saw Lance, already up and ready.

"Well, you slept awfully long." Lance smiled. "Good sleep?"

"Surprisingly yes. I feel fresh." Keelan replied shyly. Suddenly he remembered the noise he heard. "Although, I was wondering if you heard any strange sounds in the night?"

"No, I don't think I woke up once. What do you think you heard?"

Keelan shrugged, "I'm not sure."

"Well then it was probably nothing. Now, let's go get breakfast. I'm famished."

"How in the world can you be famished? I think I'm still full from last night," he chuckled.

"I'm a growing boy." Lance threw his hands in the air.

"We're the same age. I don't know how you can eat so much."

Lance shrugged and threw on his clothes and boots; Keelan quickly followed suit.

Just as with dinner, the table was laid out with more food than the two of them could eat. "Good morning, boys. I trust you slept well," Gregor greeted them.

"Like a log," Lance said.

"Yes! It was the best sleep I've had in a while. Although I did hear something last night, I think it was just my imagination, most likely just homesick."

"First time sleeping away from home?" Gregor asked him.

"No, sir, but knowing I can't return makes it difficult."

"Oh, stop with the sir business. Just call me Gregor, or 'hey you' will suffice," he laughed and left the room.

Lance dug into the smorgasbord of food on the table. Keelan grabbed a patty of sausage and a roll, "Want to sit outside again?"

Lance nodded and led the way.

They sat in silence, eating their breakfast.

Within a few moments, someone walked around the bend, coming into view. The man's build was almost the same as Lance's father.

Lance looked up and waved, "Hey, Uncle, didn't expect to see you so soon," he said.

The man nodded, "Your father requested my presence. When he calls, I come running. I hear a couple of young men need some advanced swordwork."

"That would be us. Uncle Cedric, I'd like you to meet Keelan. Keelan, this is my father's brother, Cedric."

No wonder he resembles Lance's father, Keelan thought before brushing his hands on his pants and offering his hand out, "Nice to meet you, Mr. Cedric."

Cedric grabbed his hand with a firm grip and shook it, "No, Mr. here, young sir, call me Cedric."

"Sir Knight Cedric, so good to see you," Gregor said, coming onto the platform. "Might I interest you in some breakfast?"

Cedric held his hands before him, "Gregor, it's a pleasure to see you again! And, no breakfast for me. I had my fill before I got going this morning."

"Knight Cedric?" Keelan asked.

"An honorary title. Nothing more, nothing to concern yourself about." He winked at Lance "Now, how about we put you two through some paces and let me see what I have to work with."

Keelan and Lance nodded, retreated into the house, and grabbed a couple of wooden practice swords near the door. "Do you always keep practice swords handy?"

"My father is always using any excuse to train. I think we have practice swords stashed all over the ranch." Lance ran outside, "Come on, let's not keep my uncle waiting."

The rest of the morning was spent sparring and showing Cedric the techniques, they knew.

By midday, both boys were exhausted. "I think you young men deserve a break. You have an hour to yourself, and then we will get to work."

"What we did wasn't work?" Keelan leaned close to Lance and whispered in between trying to stabilize his breathing.

"Not by his standards. Come on, we better take advantage of this hour." Lance replied, panting.

They went into the main common area, each took a couch and instantly fell asleep.

Cedric woke them both by tossing them off the couch in what seemed like no more than five minutes. "Up and at'em, lazy bones, we've got work to do."

Keelan groaned, followed by Lance. "Already?"

"What was this? Five minutes?" Lance rubbed his eyes.

Cedric sat on his knees and looked at them, "Get up and get moving before I get water." The boys fumbled to get on their feet while Cedric made his way out, "And for the record, it was an hour," he called out.

The rest of the day, Cedric showed them new stances and moves, and by the time dinner rolled around, they were too tired to eat.

The next couple of days had the same routine: practice until they couldn't move, eat, practice again, and fall asleep.

CHAPTER -15-

"**LANCE,** why don't you and Keelan go down into the chasm today and release some energy?" Cedric stood at the corner of their usual training spot.

"That sounds like a great idea, Uncle. Thank you," Lance grabbed Keelan by the sleeve and dragged him out of the house.

"Why are you in such a hurry?"

"I don't want to give him a chance to change his mind. Follow me. I know the path down to the bottom. It'll take us a good hour, but once down there, it'll be worth it."

They made their way down the steep switchback trail. It was like being in an entirely new world. The humidity rose as they descended, and the vegetation changed from scrub and pine to ferns and vines. Their horses' hooves slid on occasion on the loose shale.

The rocky game trail opened into a small clearing. A creek traversed along the bottom of the ravine and pooled into a decent-sized pond. The bottom of the gap looked to be about a hundred yards across. The opposite wall was a sheer cliff face; there didn't appear to be any paths leading to the top of the other side. Lance dismounted next to the pond.

"How about a swim?" Lance ripped off his shirt and tugged off his boots before diving in.

"That didn't sound like a question!" Keelan laughed, "You forgot your pants!" Keelan removed his clothing down to his small clothes and jumped in. His head promptly burst up from the water. The chilled water hit Keelan like an avalanche. He almost forgot to breathe.

"How is this water so cold?" he gasped for air.

Lance laughed, splashing him in the face, "This creek comes from a glacier not too far from here. It's always cold. Now, you know why I left my pants on."

Keelan swam around the pond, looking at the strange plants surrounding it, then flipped onto his back and floated with his eyes closed. Lance dove under the water.

After a few minutes, Keelan started to look around for him when he didn't resurface. Concern grew to panic as the minutes ticked by. Finally, Lance surfaced with an enormous wiggly fish on the end of his dagger.

"Hungry?" Lance smirked.

"Starving!" He added, "How did you hold your breath so long? That's impressive!"

"Large lungs, I guess," he said dismissively.

"Large lungs?" Keelan shot him a look and nodded slowly, "Yeah, I guess," he chuckled, eyeing his friend.

Keelan got out of the chilly water and shook his head, sending water droplets flying all around him. Still dripping wet, he started to search for wood to build a fire. He gathered as much as he could and started walking back toward Lance. Something caught his eye, sparkling at his feet. He placed the wood down and picked up the object. It was about half the size of his palm, thin like a pottery shard, smooth to the touch on one side and rough on the other. The object was bronze and slightly warm. He stared at it momentarily before stuffing it into his pocket and gathering the wood again. Once the fire was ready, Lance placed the fish between a couple of sticks and leaned it over it.

Keelan sighed contently, stretched out on the lush grass, and patted his full stomach, "Where to next?"

"Hmm, there are some caves downstream. I've found some gems in them before. We can try our luck if you want."

Keelan sat up quickly, "Free gems just lying around?" His brows shot up as his face broke into a smirk, "You bet, let's go."

Lance chuckled at his reaction, "We can leave the horses here; come on."

Both boys took off at a jog. Lance picked a game trail to the left that followed the creek's bank. He slowed and crossed the stream at a shallow spot twenty minutes later. The creek was narrow but surprisingly deep in most places.

"We have to climb a little."

Keelan nodded and followed Lance up the cliff. Well-worn hands and footholds were in just the right places. "Come here often?"

Lance turned and smiled at him, "I told you; we spend a lot of time at the shack, not much to do on top."

They scaled the rocks, and just when Keelan thought he couldn't keep going, they scrambled onto a small ledge in front of a cave. The cave entrance was only three feet tall, "Do we have to crawl the whole time?" Keelan asked, losing his patience and strength.

"No, only the first ten feet or so," Lance went to the right of the cave and pulled two torches from behind a small bush. He handed them to Keelan as he fished his striker from a small bag at his hip.

With both torches lit, Lance led the way into the small opening.

Crawling while holding a torch was slow going, but thankfully, sure enough, after about ten feet, the ceiling soared above their heads. Standing and turning in a complete circle, Keelan whistled, "Wow, this place is huge!" His voice echoed off the walls.

"Shhhh, whisper." Lance said hurriedly, "We don't want to cause a cave-in."

Keelan brought a hand up to cover his mouth and ducked his head. He stared wide-eyed at the ceiling and walls. No rocks moved; slowly, he let his breath out and sighed, "Sorry," he whispered.

Lance smiled and gestured for him to follow. They walked deeper and deeper into the cliffside. They made so many turns and took several different forks that soon Keelan was beyond lost, "How do you know which way to go?"

"I've spent a lot of time in here. Come on, I know the spot I want to search."

They took a couple more turns and paused at an opening with another low entrance. "I've only been in here once; keep quiet and keep a lookout."

Keelan wasn't sure if he was scared or excited. The ceiling was low but not quite as low as the cave's main entrance. They stooped over deeply and slowly walked through the passage. After fifty feet, the ceiling allowed them to stand erect again.

Lance motioned with his head and then walked toward another branch. After another ten minutes of walking, they found themselves in a large cavern with sparkling walls. Lance walked over to one twinkling star and, with his dagger, pried it loose and then tossed it to Keelan.

Keelan held it closer to his torch; the small stone was rough to the touch but sparkled brightly with a brilliant blue color.

"Sapphire," Lance's voice broke his thought.

Keelan nodded, "Are all these Sapphires?"

He shook his head, "Well, kind of, but there are a couple of different colors here. Mostly blues and greens, but a few yellows can be found. I found a small thread of red in a different area. I've been told they are all the same type of gem, but the color varies by the actual location you find them in. Let's see how many we can collect. Only dig out the shallow ones, though. We don't want to weaken the walls."

Keelan nodded and excitedly went to work. He filled his pockets with rough-cut gems of varying shades. After half an hour, he stuffed both his pockets and was now out of breath. He headed toward Lance. "My pockets are full, and I need some fresh air."

Lance nodded, "Just a couple more, and then I'll get you out of here."

The canyon was cast in shadows with the late afternoon sun hidden by the high walls. Torches still in hand, they walked back toward the horses. Keelan rubbed his fingers against the object he found. It warmed his pocket. The stone definitely looked different than other stones he had picked.

Maybe Lance knows what it is.

Rogue nickered in greeting as they neared. But what made the boys freeze mid-step was their fire from lunch was fully ablaze, and two men sat around it. Both men looked up when Rogue nickered. The curious warm object instantly forgotten.

"Welcome back, lads; thanks for collecting all this wood."

Lance and Keelan gave each other a look before they started walking again, slowly. Neither of them had their sword on them, only their daggers. They needed to get to their horses to arm themselves.

"What were you two doing so far from your horses and weapons?" the same man mocked. He was dressed in little more than rags and was missing several teeth.

"Out on a lover's stroll, just look at 'em. So finely dressed. Rich boys, for sure," the other snickered.

Keelan looked down at his clothes.

Finely dressed? He thought. While his clothes were clean and relatively new, they were just ordinary.

Do you need assistance? Aurora projected.

Keelan smiled to himself. **Not yet, but stay close.**

"What do you want?" Lance asked boldly.

"Everything you own, and if you cooperate, you can keep your lives," the first man winked.

"Don't promise something you don't have any control over," a familiar voice said from the trees.

Lance and Keelan spun around to see four more men walking up the trail. Lance kept his eyes on the four newcomers while Keelan turned his gaze back to the other two, but now five men were standing by the fire.

"As you can see, you are surrounded and vastly outnumbered. So, just empty out your bulging pockets and back away." A new man entered the clearing; he was the best dressed and had two swords strapped to his hips and one across his back. It was the same leader from their last bandit run in.

"Do you think they found gems in that cave, General?"

"I would say a whole lot of 'em," General Lucas answered. "We watched you go into Gem Cave, and you went deeper than anyone I've ever met who still returned." He gave them a tight smile. "Find any diamonds back there?"

Lance emptied his pockets on the ground, "Just sapphires, here take them all."

"Thanks for offering." He countered back immediately. "We shall and more. Oh, I remember you two. Let's see how lucky you are this time." General Lucas' sword made a swoosh sound as he unpinned his and pointed towards the boys, "Show them no mercy."

The three men advanced slowly. Keelan moved his eyes to the advancing men, to the horses and their swords, to the ones that were watching and waiting, and back to the men advancing. All the mercenaries grinned and laughed manically. Keelan felt anger rising in his chest; his hands grew warm, and his face flushed.

Keelan glanced at Lance, and he shook his head. *Was Lance getting bigger?* The closest warrior raised his sword and swung it toward Keelan's head; time slowed; Keelan easily ducked, stepping out of the way, but was almost run through by another bandit's sword. He jumped backward, holding his hands out in front of him. His hands felt numb, but his fingertips were tingling. The first bandit recovered from his missed swing and readied his sword for another try. Keelan thrust a hand in his direction, and a bolt of blue light launched from his palm. It struck the attacker in the chest and threw him back into a tree. The man crumbled and didn't rise again. Keelan shook out his hand, staring in disbelief. *What just happened?* He thought.

Wake up! Behind you! Aurora shouted in his head as she uttered an ear-piercing screech.

Keelan snapped out of it and saw another attacking bandit closing in on him. The mercenary was just as shocked as he was at what had just happened.

Aurora dove down, shooting a stream of fire at the attacker, causing him to stumble backward. Suddenly, Aurora's whole body ignited in flame. She screeched again, flying circles around the bandit. The man screamed as he held his arms over his head. Aurora circled the bandit while slowly shrinking her dizzying path. A bright light flared as Aurora screeched and then shot straight into the sky. The bandit screamed and then fell in a heap as the flames consumed him.

Keelan stared at the charred body and then up at Aurora as she circled and swooped back down. *How did you do that?*

No time. Watch out!

He nodded, set his feet, and braced for another attack as another brute rushed toward him. The new attacker slashed his sword back and forth; Keelan jumped and retreated backward, knowing exactly where he would strike before he did. The tingling in his fingertips intensified. With only one thought in his head - get back - he thrust his hands at the bandit; the same blue energy light erupted from both hands and struck the bandit in the chest; he was hurled backward. Not knowing what was going on but willing to go with it, he spun around, trying to find Lance and the other bandits. He was suddenly struck from behind with a misplaced slash. Thankfully, the flat of the sword hit him and not the edge. He stumbled forward, getting his feet underneath him before he fell to the ground. He executed a crouching spin and threw his hands in the direction of the attack; another bandit took flight.

On the ground, now! Aurora yelled at him.

He dropped to the ground and grabbed his head with both hands as her thoughts ripped through his skull.

An earth-shaking roar ripped through the air, and an intense heat seared his back.

Screams were the next thing he heard: the screams of the bandits and the terrified screams from their horses. Another scream raged through Keelan's body; it took him a few seconds to realize that the scream was coming from him.

The heat stopped as quickly as it started. Keelan cautiously raised his head and looked around. Charred bodies and blackened trees surrounded him. A snort sounded from behind. He rolled over quickly to a sitting position, looking for the cause of the sound. His eyes widened; his jaw dropped open. Standing about ten feet from him was a blue dragon with a phoenix beside it. The blue dragon loomed before him, its massive form casting a shadow that seemed to swallow the very air around it. Scales the colour of a stormy sea glinted in the dim light, each one reflecting the flickering flames of the nearby torches. The dragon's wings, folded against its back, seemed capable of unfurling to blot out the sky itself.

Its head, crowned with sharp horns and adorned with piercing sapphire eyes were looking directly at him. Smoke curled lazily from its nostrils. With each breath, the air trembled, carrying the faint scent of brimstone and power.

Keelan shuffled backward on his behind, his heart hammering in his chest, his breath coming out in ragged, panicked gasps.

"Lance, Lance!!" He yelled. "Lance, where are you?"

Calm yourself, Keelan. This is Lance, Aurora projected.

"Where?" He looked around, and his eyes fell on the creature. "No…" He couldn't believe his eyes or ears. "What the hell is this? That's not possible. Dragons don't exist. What kind of magician's trick is this?"

Aurora hopped over to him, ***Keelan, stay down!*** He was trying to regain his feet. She opened her wings, igniting the tips of her feathers.

Keelan shielded his face with his arms against her flames, "How can that be Lance?"

It just is.

"No."

Yes!

"No, Lance is a boy like me, a fifteen-year-old boy, not a dragon."

Hi, Keelan, Lance's voice said in his head.

Keelan shot to his feet, looking at the dragon. "Where are you?" he shouted, "Show yourself!"

The dragon stepped toward him and lowered his head. *I'm right here,* he projected.

Keelan looked at the dragon in front of him in bewilderment. He was over twice the size of Rogue, cobalt blue with shimmering scales from snout to tail, with twisted horns on top of his head and small silver spikes down the ridgeline of his neck that stopped at his shoulders. Lance stood on four strong legs with talons the size of Keelan's arm. Lance stretched his leathery wings out, easily twice the length of his body, blue on top and black underneath. Lances' tail was long and slender with spikes along the top and three long spikes on the tip. It was the dragon from his dream.

"How – how are you a dragon? Who did this to you?" Keelan couldn't find the right words.

No one did this to me. I am a dragon; this is how I was born.

Anger filled Keelan's body. He felt betrayed by his best friend. "When were you going to tell me about this!"

Keelan, I –

"How do you change into a human? Can you do it again?" Keelan added breathlessly.

Slow down and breathe, Keelan. The transformation is magical. I've never bothered learning the why, only the how.

A cloud of blue and black swirls appeared between Lance and Keelan. Keelan fell over and scooted away, "Aurora, what is happening?"

He's transforming.

Within less than a minute, Lance, in human form, stood where a dragon once did.

"Is this better?" Lance asked.

He was glad to see his friend standing before him again, but his heart was still racing. Dumbfounded by what he had witnessed, Keelan nodded.

Lance walked to the pile of sapphires he had dumped out of his pockets and scooped them all up. "Let's go check on the horses, and then we can talk."

Keelan nodded numbly again before following his strange friend. *Should I tell him about the dream?* He thought. *Maybe later.*

Rogue and Lance's horse, Ripper, were just fine. They had moved a short distance from where they had been tied up but seemed content to graze and not wander off.

Lance stoked the fire and sat down. Keelan hesitated for a moment before sighing and joining his friend.

"So…" Keelan started and paused, not really sure what to say. "How long have you known? Does Douglas know? Oh, man, this is going to be a weird conversation with him. Does he know his son is a dragon?"

Lance stared at Keelan for a moment and then started to laugh. It was a few minutes before he composed himself to speak again. "Sorry, I thought you were joking. When I figured you were serious, I couldn't stop laughing. Of course, my father knows. Keelan, he's a dragon, too. Actually, everyone that works for us but one is a dragon."

Keelan's mouth fell open, "I had no idea."

"That was the idea. No one was supposed to know."

"So, the primal roar I heard from you before was just your true side coming through?"

"Both forms are my true side. Dragons are hatched from an egg in dragon form, but we can change to human form within a few years."

Keelan frowned, "All pictures of dragons I have seen have two back legs and two wings with claws, but you have four legs and two wings. Is that common?"

"Those creatures you have seen are not true dragons; they are wyverns. They cannot change into human form. They have usurped the dragon throne and disrupted the world's order. Nothing but vermin," he spat.

Keelan nodded and took a deep breath. "Wow, I've never seen you so passionate about anything like that."

"Sorry, the subject hits close to home."

"In dragon form, you can only talk telepathically?"

"Dragon lips don't form very many words properly. I can speak, but it sounds funny."

"Aurora?"

Yes, Aurora landed next to him.

"Did you know Lance and his father were dragons?"

Of course, I would be a poor excuse for a magical creature if I didn't recognize another magical creature.

He shot her a look, "Why didn't you tell me?"

It wasn't my place to tell.

Keelan sighed, "That's fair, I guess." He turned to Lance again, "So, what now, Lance? Do you have to eat me or something? So, I don't tell anyone."

Lance's face twisted in disgust, "Humans taste bad; no, I won't be eating you."

"How do you know humans taste bad?" Keelan panicked.

Lance started to laugh again, "I don't, just assuming. Don't worry; my family has always been allied to humans; we don't eat people. I'll tell my father, but honestly, he is prepared for you to find out about it on this trip."

"How so?"

"I can stay in dragon form for as long as I like. However, I can only stay in human form for up to a year. Every year on my name-day, I will turn back into my dragon form whether I want to or not, which is in two days."

Keelan chuckled, "Were you just going to turn into a dragon in two days and say surprise?"

"No, my uncle was going to send you on a solo hike, and hopefully, by the time you returned, I would be able to transform again."

"Some friend," Keelan frowned.

"No offense, but it's a family secret. We are living in dangerous times. Trusting normal people is hard to do lately." He took a minute before adding, "I'm sorry, Keelan, I wanted to tell you right off…"

Keelan held up his hand, "I'm joking. Don't worry, I'm not mad. Maybe at the start but not anymore. The opposite actually, I'm honored to meet my first dragon and call him my friend."

Lance smiled, "Thanks that takes a lot of pressure off." He shot him a look, "Now, how about telling me about yourself?"

Keelan gulped, "Wh – what do you mean?"

"I saw what you did earlier. I saw the magic. You have a phoenix that you speak to, so I know you hear her. Who are you?"

Keelan looked at his hands and then over at Aurora, "I don't know. Truthfully, I was just getting so mad at being attacked again. My sword was not with me; we were in danger and outnumbered. My hands went numb, and then my fingers started to tingle. The bolts just came out. I couldn't control it."

Lance nodded, "I understand. What were you thinking just before the energy bolts came?"

"Get away. I just wanted the bandits to back off and get away from me."

"They certainly did that," he said with a chuckle.

But Keelan had a serious face. "What am I?" He asked.

"I'm no expert, but I would say a sorcerer."

"Sorcerer?" Keelan repeated, "How would that be possible?"

"From what I know, and mind you, it isn't much; anyone can learn the tricks of a magician; some can learn to cast spells and be a witch or wizard, but only those with magic in their blood can do magic as a sorcerer. Only sorcerers can use magic without casting a spell or using a potion. I have only met one before, and that was at least twenty-five years ago."

"Wait, what? Twenty-five years ago? I thought you were fifteen like me?" Keelan said, surprised.

Oh, boy, Aurora projected before flying up into a tree.

Lance gave him a guilty smile, "By human standards, that's true; I am about fifteen. Dragons live a long time, so we age slowly."

"So, how old are you? How long ago were you born?"

"Forty-five years ago, but believe me, that is the same as a fifteen-year-old boy. I won't be considered an adult until I am almost sixty."

"But when I'm fifty, you will only appear to be in your late twenties. Wow, that's not fair," he started to laugh.

If you two are quite done, I think you should get back up top before dark, Aurora projected to them both.

Aurora sounded like she was speaking in a cave; her voice was echoing. "Are you okay? Your voice echoes."

I am projecting to both of you now, not just you, Keelan.

"Oh, okay. That's good to know. I forgot you said you can speak only to magical beings. Did you speak to Douglas before we rushed back to my parents?"

Yes, I told him what I knew; that's why he sent Lance with you.

Keelan nodded, "I'm glad he did. I still don't know why those knights are looking for me, though."

"Maybe the King knows about your powers," Lance said.

"How would he know when I didn't know until today? I could understand it if I had had accidents in the past. This is the first time anything strange has manifested itself." He paused, thinking back to his trip to Kingston and the strange things that had happened there.

Lance shrugged, "Maybe he only suspects then. Your mother is a healer who was not Healing Council trained, and they said the King discovered that magic runs in the female line."

Keelan shook his head, "No, they said twins run in the female line, not magic."

Lance looked up at Aurora and sighed, "You're right. I don't know what they were looking for. Come on, let's get these rough-cut gems and see what Sephra can do with them."

"Who's Sephra?"

"She's our Gemist," he said, "Oh, and also a witch; she cuts and polishes the gems we find."

Keelan nodded, "I was wondering how we were going to get these sellable."

"We might raise cattle, but that is not where we get most of our money. This mine and others have been in our family for generations."

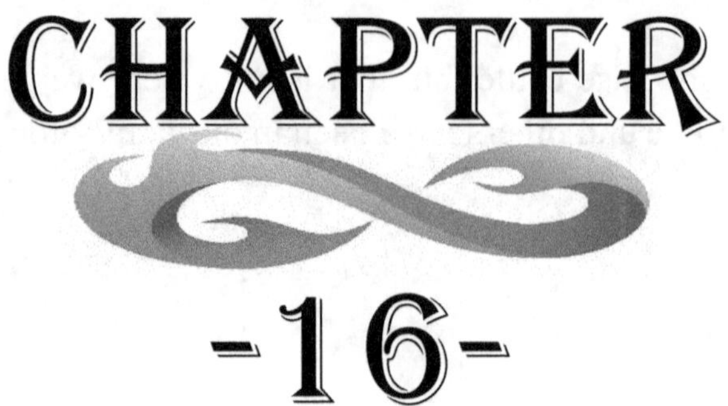

CHAPTER -16-

WHEN they returned from stabling their horses, Cedric was waiting on the main platform. It was almost dusk, and the moon was high overhead, and the first star twinkled dimly in the distance.

"You two were gone longer than I thought you might be. I was about to go looking for you." He eyes fell on Keelan and needless to say, his mouth dropped open, "Keelan, why do your clothes look singed? It looks as if you were rolling in a fire."

"Long story, uncle. Can we tell you over dinner?"

Cedric nodded and swept his hand toward the front door, "Gregor has dinner ready; clean up first, though. This looks like an interesting story."

They hurried to the dining room after changing their clothing and wiping off the worst of the day's adventure. Cedric sat at the table with his hands steepled before him.

Gregor appeared immediately and began placing food on the table.

Cedric waited and watched as the boys piled food into their mouths like they hadn't eaten in a month. He laughed, watching them eat and drink, almost in sync.

"What's so funny?" Lance asked with his mouthful.

"You two. What did you do to get so hungry?"

Lance slowly placed his fork down and cleared his throat. "We had a run-in with some bandits."

Cedric's face flashed with worry and anger, "Were either of you hurt? Are they still a threat? Tell me what happened from the beginning."

Lance nodded and began their story at the beginning with heading down the switchback trail, the quick swim, and fish lunch. He showed him the gems they collected and then paused.

"What about the bandits?"

Lance looked over at Keelan.

Keelan nodded, "Tell him everything. I have nothing to hide from your family."

"When we returned to the horses, a couple of bandits awaited us. Soon, others joined them, and we were surrounded and outnumbered. Our swords were with the horses."

Cedric frowned but motioned for Lance to continue.

"The bandits attacked, and we attempted to evade while edging closer to the horses. Neither of us was making headway. Suddenly, I saw a brilliant, blue flash come from Keelan's direction out of the corner of my eye. I thought one of the bandits was a mage, but instead of Keelan being blasted, I saw a bandit get thrown into a tree. I kept my cool, but then Keelan was struck from behind, and I couldn't control myself." Lance hung his head, "I transformed and burned all the bandits after Keelan took out two more."

Cedric's expression was like cold steel, "How did you avoid Keelan?"

"Keelan has a phoenix; she told him to get down."

"Mage or sorcerer?" Cedric asked.

Keelan and Lance stopped eating and looked at each other, "Sorcerer," Lance said. "I don't know," Keelan said.

"You don't know?" Cedric asked Keelan, "How do you not know?" Keelan shrugged, "Did you cast a spell or just react."

"Definitely just a reaction, sir."

"Sorcerer then." He looked at Lance, "Mother, father, or both?"

"Mother, definitely," Lance said, stuffing his face with food.

Keelan looked at him, "How are you so certain?"

Lance paused and looked at Cedric, "She knows the prophecy."

Cedric stopped eating and looked at Lance. "Are you sure?"

Lance nodded.

Cedric nodded slowly. "Do you or did you have a twin, Keelan?"

"A twin? No, I'm an only child," Keelan replied.

"Perhaps," Cedric leaned back in his chair and folded his arms. "Since you know our family secret, Keelan, there is no need to send you on a solo trek. Get some rest; I'll see you boys in the morning."

Both boys nodded and left Cedric sitting at the table, deep in thought.

Cedric nodded and mumbled to himself while he contemplated what to do next. Finally, with a subtle sigh, he stood, scooped up all the sapphire rough gems the boys had collected, and hurried through the kitchen and out back. Sephra's cabin was far from the main house and the stable. They offered her a place in the house, but she declined, saying she liked her space and tranquility.

He knocked gently on the door, "Come," a soft voice answered after his second knock.

"Good evening, Sephra. I come bearing gifts." He held up the two sacks full of gems.

Sitting at a table in the middle of the room was a slender woman with coal-black hair and olive skin. She looked up at him, her brown eyes shining in the candle light.

"Evening Cedric, I didn't know anyone was harvesting this week," she gestured for him to place the sacks down.

"Lance and a village boy named Keelan found them."

"I've heard a little about Keelan."

"Well, I just learned a lot more about him." He sat down and told her all he knew.

Keelan and Lance were up early the following day and already running through their drills before Cedric arrived with Sephra.

"I have something for you both," Sephra said, brushing her long coal-black hair behind her shoulder.

Breathing hard, Keelan and Lance approached.

"This is Sephra." Cedric gestured toward her as she showed Lance a couple of polished sapphires and then handed him his bag. "These are all ready for you, nice find." She then turned to Keelan. "Keelan, you found some rare and exquisite star sapphires." She showed him five stones. All five were brilliant blue with white streaks that looked like a starburst.

"I have placed a protection spell on each of them. Give these to people you want to protect. Hold the stone in your closed fist and whisper their name while holding their image in your mind. The stone will then only protect them. I made two of them into necklaces, one as a bracelet and two as bracers." She held one bracer tightly in her hand; he felt the air around Sephra get heavy and thick. She whispered his name and then clipped it on his wrist.

A jolt of uneasiness hit him from the sound of her voice whispering his name. Immediately, he felt a peculiar sensation of warmth flow up his arm and pass through his whole body, causing him to wince. "That was strange. Was it supposed to feel like that?" He asked. "It was a little unsettling."

"That is the best way to describe the feeling. These stones won't protect you from everything, but surprise attacks will be more difficult."

Aurora? he projected.

Instead of responding immediately, she screeched as she dove from high in the sky. Like a flaming arrow, she streaked through the air, banking at the last moment to land gracefully before him. *Yes,* her echoed projection reached everyone.

He knelt and showed her the bracelet with the star sapphire.

That is very pretty, she said, ***oh, is that a guardian stone?*** She hopped a step closer and peered at the stone intently.

"Yes, Sephra made it. I would like to give this one to you."

Aurora's eyes widened as she took a step back. ***Me? Oh, I would be honored. But how will I wear it?***

Keelan looked up at Sephra. She smiled, her green eyes dancing, and held her hand out. "If you come with me, I will make you something that should work perfectly." Aurora nodded. "Keelan, try to perform the protection spell."

"Me?" He looked at Sephra, "I – I don't know how to do it."

"Just do as I instructed. Try to remember what you felt when I cast my spell."

Keelan nodded. He wrapped his hands around the stone in the bracelet, pictured Aurora in his head, and whispered her name. The stone flared bright blue for a few seconds. Slowly, he opened his hands; the stone was still glowing.

Sephra approached and took the bracelet from him, frowning. "I have never seen a protection stone so strong before. I wish you could have done your own, but it isn't possible." She mumbled with a frown, "I will have this on Aurora before nightfall." Sephra and Aurora departed.

Keelan looked at the other three stones in his hands. "Lance, I want you to have the other bracer."

"Are you sure? These should be given to people close to you, people that you care for deeply," Cedric said.

Keelan shrugged, "I grew up an only child. I have friends in the village, but Lance, you feel more like a brother to me than just simply a friend. Even best friend doesn't seem sufficient. If anything happened to you, it would feel like I lost a family member. Please, let me do this for you."

Lance looked at his best friend speechless. He smiled and nodded as Keelan wrapped his hand around the other bracer, pictured Lance as a human and as a dragon in his mind and whispered his name. Nothing happened. Keelan opened his hand and frowned, "Why didn't that work?"

Cedric and Lance shared a look, "You didn't say his real name," Cedric replied.

"Lance Firestrum isn't your name?"

Lance shook his head in guilt, "About that. Uh, not entirely. My name is Lancet Lapis Firestorm."

Keelan shot him a look, "So much for being best friends." He mumbled, loud enough for Lance to hear. Lance mouthed 'sorry' as Keelan continued, "Firestorm, though? Sounds about right. That's not a very human last name. Lancet is different, but why not use that?"

He shrugged, "My father always called me Lance; my mother used Lancet. That name sounds strange coming from anyone else."

Keelan nodded and tried again using Lance's full real name. He never asked Lance about his mother and didn't think now was the right time.

The stone in his hand flared brightly and then dimmed but still glowed. He smiled at his success and clipped the bracer on Lance's wrist.

Lance grinned and shuddered as the warmth spread through his body.

"All right, boys, playtime is over. Draw your weapons; let's see which of you can get through my defenses. Now, coordinate your attack. Begin!"

For the rest of the morning, Keelan and Lance tried to get a hit on Cedric while attacking simultaneously. Cedric's defenses proved to be too much for their skill level. Lance came the closest, having had decades more training than Keelan.

Later that evening, Aurora came to show off her protection stone. Sephra had fashioned the bracelet into a chest plate that circled her neck, down her breast, and then under her wings to clasp on her back. The leather was coal black with the star sapphire placed in the center of her chest.

"Are you able to fly all right wearing that?" Keelan asked her out loud.

I didn't think I could at first, but Sephra made this so perfectly. I hardly notice it at all. How does it look? She projected to everyone present.

"It looks great," Keelan said.

"Makes you look like a member of the Warbirds," Cedric smiled at her.

Truly, a Warbird?

"What's a Warbird?" Keelan asked.

"Long ago, during the War of the Lost, there was an order of phoenix. They worked alongside the dragons and The Circle of Illumination, a group of sorcerers, but it wasn't enough to stop the Wyverns; there were just too many of them."

"I really want to learn more about the history and happenings," Keelan said eagerly. "Maybe then people," He glanced at Lance, "Would stop keeping the truth from me." Keelan rolled his eyes and Lance gave him a look.

"Stop being dramatic." It was Lance's turn to roll his eyes.

Cedric shook his head, "The history, someday perhaps. But let's concern ourselves with survival techniques for now. Let's go!" He roared.

CHAPTER
-17-

ONE month passed before Douglas sent word for them to return and with haste.

Keelan and Lance dropped what they were doing, grabbed the few items they came with, saddled their horses, and raced back to the main ranch house.

Keelan had received two letters from his parents over the past month. His father missed him but was managing the shop in his absence. His mother was keeping busy and two more women in town had given birth under the watchful eyes of the knights. Other than that, she had seen little of them. Keelan had returned one letter to them but hadn't found the time to reply to the second. Keelan's mind raced in time with Rogue's footfalls as the landscape rushed past them.

Douglas was waiting on the front porch, sitting in a rocking chair, when they arrived – their horses were lathered and breathing hard.

"I said to make haste, not kill your horses," he shouted at the two boys. "Come inside while they recoup."

A ranch hand led the two winded horses away after they dismounted.

Douglas showed them into the house. On the floor in the main room, they saw saddlebags and gear laid out.

"Are you going somewhere?" Lance asked.

Douglas shook his head, "No, you two are. As soon as your horses are fit for travel, you need to head back to Keelan's." He looked at Keelan. "Your mother is sick. My healer has done all she can for her. Your mother has one last idea, it's a longshot, but we see no alternative."

"What's wrong with her?" He asked, concerned. Douglas did not reply. Is she dying?" Keelan blurted out.

Douglas hung his head.

Keelan gasped in shock but quickly recovered, grabbed half of the gear, and marched out of the house without saying anything.

"Keelan, you can't leave now. Your horses are not fit for travel. Killing your horses before your journey starts will only negate your mother's chances of survival."

Ignoring Douglas's warning, Keelan continued to the stable. Their horses were breathing better, but their coats were still slick with sweat. The fire of emotions within Keelan cooled a little. He couldn't risk Rogues' life. Douglas was right; if he was to save his mother and journey somewhere to find something or someone to help her, Rogue needed to be strong. He approached his horse and pressed his forehead to Rogues'. He took a deep, steadying breath in and out while running his hands up and down his neck. Keelan felt his hands start to warm and tingle. Slowly, a bright light penetrated his eyelids. He opened his eyes and saw a bright light engulfing him and Rogue. Rogue sucked in a surprised breath and then shuddered. Rogues' hide was now dry and only slightly warm to his touch. His eyes were bright and full of energy. Rogue nickered and shook his head. "What happened? What did I do?"

Douglas chuckled, "Good work. I see your powers have manifested after all."

"Powers? You knew?"

"About you being a sorcerer? No, not fully. Just suspected. But do not tell your mother any of this. She is too weak, and the revelation might be too much to take, and most certainly do not tell your father. He is a nonbeliever; I don't know what his reaction would be."

Keelan nodded. "I better see if I can help Lance's horse."

Douglas shook his head, "No, save your strength." He turned to his son, "Lance, saddle a different horse."

A few moments later, Keelan and Lance were trotting down the road.

Not knowing if the Keifman's were still being watched, they decided to play it safe and sneak in through the back door again.

Elliot was in the kitchen when they entered. He spun around with a kitchen knife in his hand, his eyes wide with fright. "Keelan! I'm so happy to see you." He rushed over and enveloped Keelan in a crushing hug. "Did Douglas tell you about your mother?"

"I'm happy to see you too, father." He managed a smile and continued, "Only that she's ill and wanted to see me."

Elliot nodded and gestured to his bedroom, "She's in there; go quickly."

The room was dimly lit, with only the tiny fire in the hearth giving off light. Maya lay in bed tightly bundled up and appeared to be sleeping. Keelan walked to the side of the bed and sat on a chair next to her.

"I'm so glad you're here," Maya whispered without opening her eyes.

"I got here as fast as I could, Maa. How can I help? Do you know what's wrong?"

She nodded weakly, "I have what was once called The Wasting; Douglas didn't believe me at first until his healer confirmed it."

"Is there a cure?"

She nodded once, "It is a rare affliction but one that used to be treatable. Since the banishing of magic, no one has heard of it, so the remedy is not readily available."

"Why did the banishing of magic get rid of The Wasting?"

"The Wasting only affects those with natural magic. When magic was banished, those with natural magic were slaughtered or forced into hiding and fled."

Keelan nodded. "Is there unnatural magic?"

"There are those that are born with the full flame of magic; they are called natural magic users, also called sorcerers and sorceresses." Maya coughed. "Then there are those that are born with a spark. This is much more common. Those born with the spark can learn to use magic but must use an artifact to control it and spells or potions to enact it. Natural magic is controlled with thoughts, emotions, and pure will."

"So, those with learned magic were not targeted when magic was banished?"

Maya shook her head slowly, "Oh, they were, but they can also hide and suppress it easier. When you are born with magic, it would be like not using your eyes or ears. It can be done, but it is most definitely not easy to do and keep hidden."

"How have you done it?"

Maya smiled weakly, "My father was a strict man and a desperate one as well. We lived in seclusion until I was about ten. Then we moved to Kingston. What better place to hide than right under their nose, he always used to say. He was discovered when I was twelve. Jonal took me in, changed my name, and taught me to be a healer."

Keelan's eyes widened. "What was your name?"

"Mayriana Vaelum."

"Vaelum?" He connected the dots, "As in the old kingdom?"

"Yes, Princess Mayriana. Until you were born, I was the last living descendant of the old royal line."

Keelan didn't know what to say. He took a deep breath as he tried to ask the right questions. "Who are the Ragnis?" he asked quietly.

"Do you remember the prophecy, realm of beast, realm of magic?"

Keelan nodded.

"The Vaelum's are the realm of magic, the Kingdom of Oshana. The Ragnis line is the realm of beast, Kingdom of Iton."

"What kind of beast?"

"Dragons," she whispered.

He stared at her momentarily. An image of Lance converting into the dragon flashed before his eyes, but he kept his mouth shut. "How do I find this cure?"

Maya barely smiled, "That's a good boy. You will go to Jonal. He knows how to find it."

"Is Jonal a natural or learned?"

"He is a learned but the most powerful I have ever met."

"And Sally and Esther?"

Maya chuckled softly before a dry, raspy cough ripped through her lungs. Keelan quickly gave her a glass of water. Maya shook her head.

When she recovered, she sighed wearily, "Sally is a sorceress; Esther is a witch."

Keelan blurted, "Witch?"

"I am so sorry to have raised you in such isolation of who I am, but it was necessary. A witch or mage is a magic learner. If they are powerful like Jonal, they are referred to as a wizard."

Keelan fell into silence.

"What am I?"

"You are blessed to be a normal like your father," she fixed her gaze on him and nodded.

"How is that a blessing?" He frowned. *Should I tell her?* He thought.

She might be too weak to handle that at the moment, Aurora said to him.

He nodded and then caught himself, his mother didn't know he was hearing a voice in his head. "Is it safe for me to go to Kingston? Do you think they will know who I am?"

Maya was silent and then sighed, "I don't know truthfully."

"Can't we send a letter to him?" Sweat started to bead on Keelan's head.

His mother shook her head, "I think any letters I send are read before they are sent. I don't think I got sick out of chance."

Keelan leaned forward, "What do you mean?"

"The King has been trying to rid Evansshire of magic. I wouldn't put it passed him to release an illness that affects magic users."

Keelan sat back, thinking about what she was telling him. Finally, he nodded, "I will go to Kingston and bring Jonal here." He started to stand.

Maya reached out and grabbed his hand. "I have something to tell you and your father. Go get him, please."

Keelan nodded and returned a moment later with his father.

Elliot sat on the edge of the bed and grabbed Maya's hand.

"First thing I must tell you, my love, is that Keelan will be going to Kingston to fetch a healer, my good friend Jonal. He may have the cure I need."

Elliot nodded slowly, "If you think he might, then Keelan will leave immediately."

Maya held a hand up, "But before he leaves, I have something to tell you. The night Keelan was born," She looked away from Elliot's face, "There was another baby born."

Elliot's face paled, and his thumb stroking her hand froze.

The room fell into silence. Maya continued, "Keelan, you had a twin sibling."

Keelan's voice was barely audible, "Had?"

"Alma and the other midwives," a sob ripped through Maya, "helped me hide the fact that I gave birth to twins. You were born first, Keelan, your twin died at birth. You were both so small that we never suspected I was carrying twins..." Tears fell down Maya's face. "I couldn't bear the thought of losing both of my children; I had waited so long to conceive that I had to save you, Keelan. I have always known I was the last of the line, and when I failed to get pregnant, I felt I had failed the prophecy." She took his hand in hers, "When you were born, hope was rekindled."

Aurora broke into Keelan's thoughts, *Now, you know why I won't leave you. I am needed. Your descendants will need the help of a Phoenix to fulfill the prophecy.*

Elliot sat in stunned silence for a few moments. Keelan could only guess he was trying to comprehend everything he was being told, "What prophecy are you speaking of?" he finally choked out.

"My love, my dear Elliot. My last name is not Flim. Keelan and I are the last of the Royal line Vaelum's."

"No, that can't be right. The Vaelums were evil magic users; they were all defeated."

"None of them were evil. Magic in itself is not evil; only man can be evil. Most Vaelums' were hunted down and killed like animals or captured and tortured, but my great-grandfather was the youngest son of the last King; he was just an infant and was smuggled out of the kingdom right after his birth. His birth had not been announced yet. My grandfather was his son, he had one child, my father."

"But you aren't cursed with magic." He tried to make sense of the situation.

"Magic is not a curse, but it is a difficulty nowadays," Maya held up her hand, and a small ball of light bloomed in her palm.

Elliot jumped backward and fell off the bed, shielding his face with his arms. "Who are you?" he screeched. "Keelan, get away from her!"

Keelan stood up but stayed near his mother.

Maya's face contoured with pain and grief. "You know who I am. I'm still the same person you fell in love with. This is who I have always been."

Elliot shuffled away on his backside, "But it's all been a lie! You are a liar. Is Keelan cursed, too?" Elliot shifted his gaze to his son, his eyes wide and fearful.

Maya shook her head, "No, thankfully, Keelan has been saved from your bigotry. Twins are two parts of the same energy. If his twin had survived, their bond would have ignited his magic, and it would have manifested by now."

Elliot recovered enough to get back on his feet. He stared at Maya for a moment and then fled the room.

Keelan stared after his father's fleeing form, shocked that his father was so closed-minded.

"Don't hate him. He has been lied to his entire life; it's not his fault."

"How can you forgive him? He looked at you like you were a demon."

"I'm used to it. I've seen that look before." Maya gave him a tight smile.

Keelan pondered his next words. He needed answers, but how much information could she handle hearing? He sighed loudly, "Why did you lie about me?"

"What do you mean?"

"When we went to Kingston. I knew things, and things happened to me. Jonal saw it, Sally saw it and so did Esther. I have magic, Mother!"

"No, your twin died!" she exclaimed with a panic squeak. "Your magic is locked inside of you. It will never fully manifest. You only have a shadow of magic, but you will be able to pass it on to your children. My grandfather was born a twin; his brother died when they were five before they manifested their magic." She coughed. "Keelan, please go get Jonal and bring him back quickly. Can you do that?"

"Of course, but what about you? You can't take care of yourself, and I don't think father will do it now." He shouldn't have pressed the issue. He knew he had magic, he would just have to learn on his own.

"Douglas and his healer are coming today. I will see if they will take me to their house to wait for you."

"I'll have Lance go and fetch them."

She patted Keelan on the arm, "You are a good boy—my miracle. Our family line ends with you. You need to survive and marry. When I was a young woman, I hoped I would have twins to bring the end to Evansshire, but after marrying and moving here, I knew I would never be able to hide their births." A tear dropped from her eyes, "I thought about trying to get your father to move to Threndy, but I was never able to convince him Elves and Fairies existed. I gave up all hope. Have lots of kids; maybe you will be the lucky one to have the prophesied twins. Raise them and guard them well. Then, search out the Ragnis line and bring order back to the world." She patted his hand weakly, "Now go and return quickly."

"I will, mother, rest easy." Keelan leaned over and kissed her on the forehead. He glanced at the table beside her bed and noticed a few strange looking feathers, large bright blue ones and a few smaller yellow ones. He frowned at them but shrugged, he had a trip to take.

"How's your mother?" Lance asked.

Keelan shook his head, "Not well. I have to go to the Capital and bring a healer back here with the cure. It is rare, and she hopes he can find it."

"So, she knows what she has?"

"Something called, The Wasting."

Lance sucked in a sharp breath, "This healer from the capital knows the cure?"

Keelan nodded, "He's a wizard. I met him a few years ago. My mother told my father and me about her true past and that she has magic. My father didn't handle it well. Your father and healer are coming here today to check on her; she wants to move to your house. Can you go back there and have them hurry?"

Lance shook his head, "I'm going with you."

"I can't ask you to do that."

"My father packed enough for both of us to go to the Capital. You need backup. I'm going. The knights are most likely still looking for you," Lance said sternly.

"Thank you," Keelan grabbed Rogues' reins and mounted. They stuck to the forest trails for the rest of the day until they reached a fork in the main road. Keelan was silent, deep in thought the whole day. There were so many questions in his head, yet he didn't understand which one to ask first. In the past couple of weeks, he had seen so much – learned so much. His mind wandered to his twin. What would it have been like to grow up with a brother or sister? Would his magic have manifest earlier? He shook his head, wondering about what might have been was not going to help him.

After the horses and camp were ready for the night, Lance broke the silence, "So, how did the conversation with your mother go?"

Keelan remained silent for a few minutes before he retold the whole conversation.

Lance listened to Keelan, letting his questions build and grow.

When Keelan finished the story, he stared into the fire, sitting stiffly.

Lance sighed, "That's a lot to take in. Wow, you had a twin. Did you tell your mother that your magic manifested even without it?"

Keelan shrugged, "I started to, but she is so weak, and she is certain that I am better off without magic."

"Do you trust this healer? If he is truly a wizard, he can start your magic training. And since he raised your mother for a while, he obviously knows how to train a natural born."

"My mother trusts him, so I have no reason not to. I just hope we can get into Kingston. They have tight security. If they know what I look like, I might be seized. What I don't understand is how does the King know about me?"

"Your mother said they were questioning her because they suspected she knew that woman was going to have twins and that she would try to hide one. They weren't interested in your father, so I don't know why they wanted you."

"Maybe Jonal will have more answers. We will be at the Kingston's gates tomorrow."

"Didn't you say you had to stay at two inns before reaching the gates?"

Keelan nodded, "We traveled in a wagon with an aging horse. We'll be moving much quicker and already have been. The first inn is behind us a ways."

CHAPTER

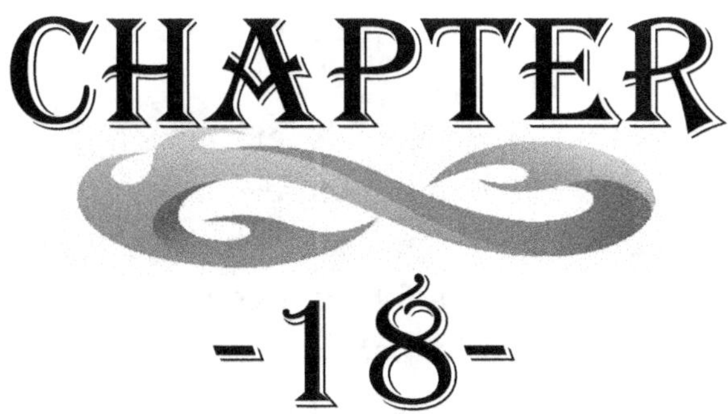

-18-

"PURPOSE for your visit?" the inspection officer snapped impatiently.

"Visiting a friend," Keelan answered.

"Friends name?"

"Jonal Bertlesen, the Healer."

The officer looked at Keelan for the first time then his gaze fell on Lance. Slowly his eyes narrowed, "Healer Jonal, you say?"

Keelan nodded, trying to keep his face neutral but friendly.

The officer sifted through the scrolls in his satchel and scribbled on it quickly before thrusting it into Keelan's outstretched hand. "You have one day. Next!" he yelled, looking at the wagon behind them.

Keelan and Lance passed through the gates into the darkening canyon. With the sun close to setting, the only light to see was the torches lining the path.

Keelan wasted no time and headed directly to Jonal's small house from memory. He led Lance to the rear of the house, where they tied their horses to the fence. Keelan walked up the steps, taking two at a time, and rapped on the door firmly.

"Who's there? Who's at my back door at this time of day?"

Jonal swung the door open, holding a frying pan like a weapon. His eyes went wide, "Keelan, my boy. What are you doing here?"

"Can we come in?"

"Of course, of course. Come in, please. Is everything all right?"

Within moments, the three men were sitting at Jonal's kitchen table, a cup of tea in front of them.

Keelan wasted no time jumping into his story. He started back with the birth of the twins' months before.

Jonal sat quietly listening to the retelling, his tea untouched, his frown deepening as the story unfolded. Keelan skipped over their time at the line shack and rushed forward to his mother's illness. When he mentioned The Wasting, Jonal leaped to his feet and rushed into the other room, the rest of the story untold.

Lance and Keelan looked at each other before jumping up to follow him.

Jonal was at his bookshelf, grabbing books and tossing them aside.

"Can you help my mother?"

Without pausing his frantic search, he said, "I hope so." Jonal thrust four books into Keelan's hands before he rushed into his bedroom. He returned a moment later with a bag and bedroll.

"Go saddle my horse while I empty my pantry. Hurry, now!" Jonal shooed them out of the house.

"I'm glad he's taking this seriously, but he's scaring the tar out of me," Keelan said.

"Glad it's not just me," Lance agreed.

Jonal handed each of them a saddle bag stuffed with food and then mounted his small horse, his tall, lanky frame making it look even smaller. Suddenly, he froze and then turned in his saddle to look at Keelan, "Do you think the knights are still looking for you?"

Keelan nodded, "Even the gate officer narrowed his eyes at me. I don't think he recognized me, but he looked suspicious."

Jonal turned his horse to face the two boys, "Hold absolutely still." Jonal pulled a long, thin stick out of his cloak; he cast a quick look around them before closing his eyes. He muttered something under his breath while pointing his stick at Keelan and Rogue. A green mist poured out of the tip of the stick and quickly closed the distance between them. The green mist engulfed Rogue and then surrounded Keelan. The temperature inside the cloud was frigid. Keelan gasped at the sudden change in temperature. When the mist slowly dissipated, Rogue was no longer a blood bay; he was a flea-bitten gray.

"You look good, Keelan; the gray hair is a nice touch," Lance laughed.

Keelan looked at his hands, he now looked to be older than Jonal. He patted his face and found wrinkled and worn skin, a large nose, and a massive beard. "How did you do that?"

"I'm full of tricks, my boy. Hold still, Lance." He repeated the steps, but this time, a rose-colored mist came out of his stick.

When the mist cleared Lance's black horse had changed to a silver dapple.

Keelan busted out a roaring laugh when the mist revealed Lances' new features.

"What's so funny, old man?"

Jonal chuckled, "I apologize, Lance, I only have two forms I can change people into, and I can't have you looking like elderly twins."

"What do I look like?" he asked panicked. He dismounted and rushed over to the horse trough to gaze at his reflection. A startled cry ripped from his throat.

"Don't speak, though; I can't change voices."

Lance glared at Jonal, "You couldn't have made Keelan look like a young girl? Why me?" Lance locked eyes with the teenage girl in his reflection. High cheekbones and jet black hair tied in a long braid. Even his clothing changed color, but at least he wasn't wearing a dress.

"It's only temporary. Mount up. We need to be out of Lower City before this enchantment wears off, and we have one stop to make first," he shrugged.

"After you, miss," Keelan said politely. Lance scowled, stalking back to his horse.

Lance mounted and followed Jonal and Keelan to the main road.

"What's our back story?" Keelan asked.

"You and I are brothers. Your name's Colin, and your granddaughter," He pointed at Lance, "Alice."

Jonal led them through the city until they reached Sally, the Herbalist. "Come inside, but don't speak."

Jonal entered the shop, which was still open at this time of night. A tiny bell chimed, announcing their arrival. Sally and a large, burly man came from the back room.

"Jonal, what are you doing here at this hour?"

"We need to talk. Wait here," he said to his companions.

Jonal and Sally retreated to the back room only to return a few minutes later. Jonal rolled up a scroll in his hands and stuffed it into a pocket of his cloak.

"Take this, last resort only, mind you." Sally glanced at the other two people in the shop, a smile bloomed on her lips. "Nice to see you again, Keelan; age looks good on you. And a pleasure to meet you, Sir Flyer." Lances' eyes widened in shock. Sally approached Lance and grabbed his wrist. She brought the bracer up, staring at the star sapphire. "I knew you were a special young man," she said, looking at Keelan, "No training, and you still managed to do this."

"What are you talking about?" Jonal asked.

Sally looked at Jonal, "Keelan made a protection stone for his friend." She grabbed Keelan's bracer next, "Too bad you can't make one for yourself. This one is good, but not as powerful as the one you made. I am looking forward to meeting you again after you grow into your powers." She smiled at him. "Now go, save your mother." She came closer to him and whispered, "Stay hidden, but don't hide when it matters."

Jonal took a bag from the counter and then motioned for the two boys cloaked in illusion to follow him.

"I think you need to finish that story."

"I will, Jonal, I will. Let's get out of town first."

"Good evening, Healer Jonal, a little late for a stroll," the officer at the gate said.

"A healer's work is never done."

"When will you return?"

"I never know," he chuckled, "I never know. These two are with me." Jonal held his stick in his hand as he gestured. Keelan didn't see any mist coming from it this time, but he felt and saw a shimmer in the air.

"Colin, I'm glad you found your brother so quickly. Do you have your entry pass?"

Jonal nodded to Keelan.

Slightly stunned, he pulled his entry scroll from his cloak and handed it over.

"Safe travels," the officer said without looking at the scroll. The officer turned his attention to the next traveler but stumbled and accidentally dropped the scroll into the torch next to him. The officer cursed and scrambled, but the scroll was nothing but ash.

Jonal snickered quietly and spurred his horse into a brisk trot.

They made their way through Lower City and out into the surrounding woods. Keelan recognized this as the way to Esther's small cottage. Once they were far enough away from the city, Jonal cast a spell, and a small glowing orb floated in front of his horse, lighting their way slightly. Keelan saw a flash of red off to his left. A sense of relief passed through him, seeing Aurora again.

They continued until they saw Esther's cottage glowing in the distance. Jonal reined up his horse, and with a squeak of the saddle, he dismounted, throwing his mount off balance. Keelan and Lance started to dismount, but Jonal held up his hand to halt them. Retrieving his stick from his cloak again, Jonal held it up in the air and said a few foreign words. Blue and purple sparks flew from the stick and sparkled in the air.

"That looks just like the illusions the magician made," Keelan remarked.

"This is not an illusion," Jonal harrumphed. "That magician was just a charlatan; these sparks are true magic. That performer had nothing but illusion; you could put your hand in his sparks, and nothing would happen, but I assure you if you try that here, you would get burned."

In the distance they could see the door to Esther's cottage swing open; green and pink sparks shot into the air.

"Come on it's safe to approach now."

"What would have happened if we had approached without signaling?" Lance asked.

"All three of us would be having a very bad day, Esther doesn't trust unexpected company at night," Jonal replied.

"I didn't expect to see you here this time of night," Esther's raspy voice echoed through the night. "And who's that with you?"

Jonal held his stick in the direction of Keelan and Lance. A white mist surrounded them, the first thing that Keelan noticed was Rogue looked like himself again.

"Is that you Keelan? My, oh my, you have grown."

"Quickly stable the horses and come inside." Jonal told the boys.

Keelan and Lance took care of the horses while Jonal went inside. When the boys entered the house, they found two large bowls of stew and a fresh loaf of bread on the table. Jonal was already digging into his bowl.

"So, Jonal here tells me you have a story and that he hasn't heard the whole of. So, eat and then spin your tale," Esther cackled.

Keelan smiled and complied. Neither of them had eaten since midday and they were beyond famished.

When the rabbit stew was done, and the dishes put away Esther herded them into her main room and stoked the fire.

"Now I want you to start at the beginning for when you met Lance here."

"That far back?"

"Every turn of events is important. I thought about having you start from when I last saw you, but it's getting late."

Keelan nodded and began his tale of meeting Mr. Douglas and Lance, to their first run in with bandits, to being trained in the art of the sword. After he told of the baker's wife and being sent to stay at the Firestrums line shack with Lance, Jonal finally perked up as this was getting to the new stuff. Keelan left out any mention that Lance was a dragon though.

"After Mr. Douglas told us to get back to my mother's house and that she was sick, my mother told me about her past. That she is the last of the Royal line."

"Not the last anymore my boy," Esther interrupted.

Keelan nodded and then continued. "She then had me get my father and she told us both about her past, that she is a sorceress, I guess. She said that she was a natural born magic user."

"And how did your father take this news?" Jonal asked.

"Not well at all. He actually fell off the bed and scooted away from her. I've never seen my mother so sad. But that's not all, she also told me that I had a twin, but it died at birth. I couldn't tell her that my powers had manifested."

"You didn't tell her?" Esther inquired.

"I started to but she's already so weak and she is certain that I am better off without magic. I couldn't bring myself to press the issue and couldn't tell my father, seeing his reaction. From what little I know about twins, mine must still be alive if my powers have manifested, correct?"

"Twins are not very common, so I don't know much about them," Jonal said. "It is written that if twins are separated at birth their powers will not manifest until they meet each other again. But how true that statement is, I do not know. I would venture to say that it is not true. Your mother told me that your twin died, never taking a breath."

"So, what of the prophecy then?" Lance asked.

Esther looked at Lance, truly looked for the first time. "What are you boy?"

"I am a dragon," Lance paused and looked at Keelan, "I am the last of the Ragnis line."

"Oh wow. The last? Why didn't you tell me this?" Keelan said surprised.

"I didn't know if it was important until I found out that you were a twin, and your mother is a Vaelum. But out on the road, in the middle of nowhere, I didn't think it was an appropriate time to tell you. I'm sorry I kept it from you."

"Don't be." He waved off Lance's concern. "So, how does this affect the prophecy? If my mother is of the Vaelum line and she had twins as the prophecy suggested, but one did not survive, is the prophecy broken?"

"No, only delayed. Your grandfather was a twin, the other boy perished when he was five. Everybody thought that it was too soon for the prophecy to be fulfilled, only a generation out. It will now be up to you to produce the twin."

"But doesn't the prophecy talk about the Royal lines intertwining how does that happen?"

"That's the problem with prophecies they're always full of riddles; they're never clear," Esther grumbled.

"Maybe the fact that you two have met and have become friends is the start of that entwinement," Jonal remarked. "Only time will tell. We just have to keep both of you safe. But first things first, we need to heal your mother."

"So, what do we need to do?" Keelan asked.

"I consulted with Sally, and she is certain that a grove of firebush still exists, but it's deep in the sacred mountains guarded by the griffins."

"Griffin's? Those actually exist too?"

A knock on the glass startled all of them. Keelan jumped up and went to the window. When he threw it open, Aurora fluttered in.

Of course, griffins are real, just like phoenixes, she projected as she puffed out her chest.

"So, you have found a familiar already," Esther said.

"Sorcerers don't need familiars," Jonal scoffed.

"Of course, they don't need one, but that doesn't mean they can't have one," Esther smacked Jonal on the shoulder. "Did she join you before or after your powers showed themselves?"

"Before, I guess, but I've been doing strange things since coming to Kingston that first time. Remember the festival and knowing those things about that woman?"

Jonal nodded.

"That would explain the full manifestation of your powers. Phoenixes are very powerful familiars. They are also very picky about who they choose, and a bond with them is the strongest there is outside of a firedrake or a vaskakat. I knew you were special the first time I laid eyes on you," she cackled.

"I've never heard of a firedrake," Keelan said.

"It's a moderate-sized lizard about the size of a cat that can fly and shoot flames like a dragon," Lance told him. "I had one when I was very young. I don't remember what happened to him."

Jonal started to laugh.

"What's so funny?" Lance asked. A flash of hurt crossed his face and his cheeks flushed.

"The image of a dragon in dragon form with a firedrake perched on his shoulder as his familiar."

Lance's face twisted into a scowl before he broke out laughing, "I guess that is kind of a funny picture, but it could happen, couldn't it?"

"Of course, it could. I've never met a magic-wielding dragon, but I have heard of it."

"You've never met a dragon," Jonal said to Esther.

She started to laugh, "That's true but, I still say I've heard of it."

"So how do we find this grove of firebush and the griffins that are guarding it?" Keelan inquired.

"We leave at first light."

PART TWO

Shaylee

CHAPTER -19-

SHAYLEE ran out of the barn and around the backside of the inn.

Keelan was an interesting boy, she thought. *Strange that he had similar eyes without my heritage.*

She sprinted into the forest, taking deer and rabbit trails she knew so well. She lingered in Verndale longer than she should have. Her parents would be furious if they knew she went there again. She couldn't understand why she was drawn to the humans, but she found them fascinating.

Lyra leaped from Shaylee's shoulder to fly just behind her.

The game trail widened slightly before giving way to a small meadow filled with wildflowers. Shaylee exploded into the field without slowing, scattering butterflies into the sky. Lyra swatted at any that got too close to her flight path.

On the far side of the meadow, a small stream meandered lazily.

Shaylee bounded through the meadow and leaped over a narrow section of the Blackbane River. Once deep in the forest again, she slowed to a jog. She concentrated on her breathing and keeping her heart rate in check.

Continuing on well-worn game trails, she traveled through the forest, across an old lava flow, and around the remnants of the extinct volcano core. On the far side of the ancient core, the terrain changed from a mostly pine, oak, and maple tree population to redwoods, ponderosa pine, cottonwood, and madrone trees.

Dusk was approaching quickly; soon, the ground grew too dark to see. Shaylee knew right where she would stop for the evening. Ahead stood a majestic pine tree, its branches stretching low to the ground like protective arms. Shaylee approached the sheltering pine, gently parting the branches to reveal a hidden hollow. Retrieving her bag from the snug nook at the tree's base, she uncovered a blanket and some cold rations she had stashed there earlier on her journey to Verndale. Settling down beneath the comforting branches, Shaylee pondered her travels, accompanied by the soft presence of Lyra curled up beside her. Before she knew it, she was fast asleep.

She woke up the next morning to the sounds of birds chirping. She quickly packed her blanket and got on her feet to leave. Lyra followed her as she made her way out. She walked slowly through the forest, listening to the birds and squirrels. She knew she would be back home soon. The varying flora of the area helped hide the small village of Threndy.

Just after midday, she passed underneath the first sentry. High in redwood tree branches. The elf looked down at her with his bow nocked and drawn. She raised her right hand and made the 'all clear' signal, followed by a sharp whistle. The sentry whistled in return, lowering his weapon.

She continued, knowing that at least three other sentries followed her progress.

Threndy was an old establishment; no one knew quite how old, but the guard post trees - enormous redwoods surrounding the village - were several hundred years old and planted in just the right places. As she proceeded on her path, she gained more sight. The towering trees, with their full canopy, shaded the ground, not allowing the underbrush to grow. Houses along the outer ring were hidden entirely within the towering trees, either carved inside the mighty trunks or high up in the canopy.

Most elves preferred to live on the ground, but the fae liked the treetops. The village was a mixture of elves and fairies living together but separated simultaneously. Shaylee's family was the most unique because she was the only Elvenfae. She was the only one in the world, as far as she knew. Her mother was Rosepetal Faeven, a fairy, and her father was Talon Sprucebough, an elf.

Shaylee Faeven had her mother's surname, as was the fairy way. She had her father's rich tan skin, but other than that, she looked nothing like them.

Shaylee ambled her way through the sleepy village without thought like she'd done countless times before. The image of the boy she met earlier in the day and her conversation with him replaying in her head obsessively. Abruptly she came to a stop as she ran straight into a clothesline strung across the path.

"Oh!" she exclaimed, thinking she had wandered off her route. She frantically tried to keep the freshly washed linens from falling into the dirt. "Why would someone put this here?"

An elf rushed out of the house and helped Shaylee untangle herself from the wash.

"Fawn, what is this line doing here?" Shaylee asked.

"The line came untied," Fawn pointed to a tree about ten feet from her home. "I couldn't reach the branches to tie it back, so I tied it to this shrub." She pointed to the shrub across the path. The weight of the line had broken the branch she had tied it to. Fawn was only a year younger than Shaylee but she was very short for an elf. Shaylee was always self-conscious of her height, but compared to Fawn, she was tall.

"Why didn't you get help?" Shaylee said, looking down at Fawn.

The young elf sniffled and wiped her turquoise eyes with the back of her hand, "Pa's not here, and Ma's sick."

Shaylee gasped, "Oh my." Fawn's father was a ranger, and they patrolled out far sometimes. "Has my mother been here?" Shaylee asked.

Fawn nodded, "Yesterday. She gave her something to make her sleep. I didn't want to wake her." Fawn absentmindedly pulled her golden blonde braid across her shoulder and was twirling the end between her fingers.

"Let me help you with this." Shaylee spent the rest of the evening helping Fawn relocate her clothesline and rewash the items that had fallen on the ground.

By the time Shaylee made it home, she was exhausted.

"Shaylee? Where have you been?"

Tsk. Shaylee knew what was coming.

"You were supposed to come home at first light this morning. Your friend Amelia said you told her you were coming straight home." Her father said sternly, the tips of his pointed ears turning red. Her father was a stickler for rules. Her mother's parenting style was much more carefree. But then everything a fairy did was carefree.

"I was just out exploring, and on my way home, I stopped to help Fawn with her laundry. Did you know her mother is sick?" She expertly changed the subject.

"Yes, poor little thing." The anger on Talon's face was replaced by sympathy, "Your mother was over there with her for almost the entire day yesterday. I'm glad you were able to help." He tapped on her head. Talon towered above Shaylee. She strained her neck looking up into his blue eyes. "I guess, go in and help your mother with supper since it's too late for our training." He gestured toward the house, his long blonde, almost white hair tied in a ponytail flipping over his shoulder.

"Oh no. I missed training." Shaylee tried to fake her disappointment as she turned around to leave.

"Double training tomorrow to make up for today." Her father called from behind her. The mischievous smile on Shaylee's face dropped as she turned to face her father – who was smiling now.

Shaylee groaned but did as she was told. Her days consisted of learning the art of the staff and archery with her father, learning to be a ranger and track, helping her mother with her healing arts or the garden, and preparing dinner. There were a few rare moments here and there when she was allowed to venture off on her own.

But helping with dinner was always a must. Like all fairies, her mother was a vegetarian, but she and her father couldn't stand meal after meal of only vegetables. So, Shaylee's job was to prepare the meat for herself and her father.

"How is Fawns' ma doing?" Shaylee asked while helping her mother with the dishes after dinner.

"Not good, I'm afraid. I don't think she will make it to spring, the poor dear." She shook her head. Her curly red hair bouncing as she shook her head. Rosepetals alabaster skin was almost glowing in the candlelight, her long-pointed ears curling at the tips whenever she was sad.

"When do you think Joran will return?"

Her mother shrugged, her golden eyes glistening with tears, "No one knows for sure. The Rangers left before sunrise. It could be days or weeks. Talon sent a bluebird. He hoped they were staying on the surface, but since the bird hasn't returned, it hasn't found them yet."

"What will happen to Fawn if Flora passes before Joran returns?" Shaylee looked down at her mother. A fleeting thought entered her mind, the only adults she was taller than were the fairies.

Her mother sighed, her four golden wings drooping, "She will live with us, of course. I just hope I can figure out what's wrong with her."

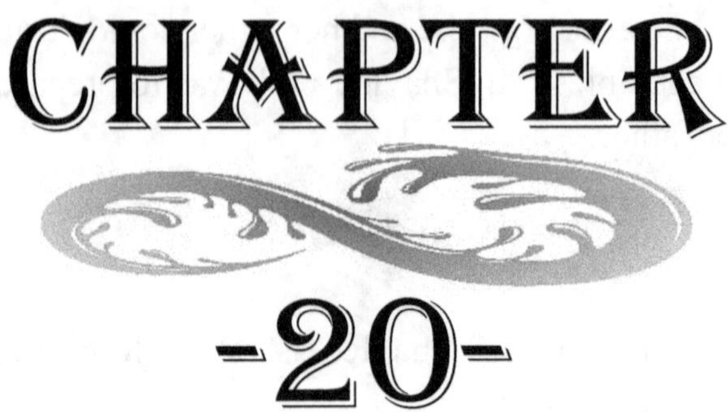

CHAPTER -20-

LYRA'S growling woke Shaylee up before daybreak. "What is it, girl?" she whispered into the darkness of her room.

Lyra jumped from the windowsill and glided to the bed. She hopped twice, landing on Shaylee's stomach, "Oof, you're getting heavy." Shaylee complained to her growing kitten. Ignoring her comment, Lyra walked up her chest and pressed her forehead to Shaylee's. Images instantly transferred. A shadow lurked through the garden, followed closely by another. She knew who it was.

Shaylee groaned, "We better go look into this."

Lyra hissed and flew to her pillow on top of Shaylee's dresser. Shaylee crawled out of bed slowly and walked over to her. She scratched Lyra's chin causing a deep purr, "Thanks for waking me," she whispered. Lyra closed her eyes a soft chirp-like meow followed.

Shaylee threw on a pair of pants, a shirt, and her boots and quietly exited the house. *If father catches those two raiding our garden again, he'll lose it.*

She crept along the side of the house, staying in the deep shadows. The full moon bathed the garden in a silvery glow. Jurren and his brother Elas were bent over, filling their sacks with squash and melons.

Shaylee inched closer and closer to the marauders. With a garden rake in one hand and a large rock in the other, she got as close as she dared before releasing her stone into the back of Jurren's head, the stronger and elder of the two.

Jurren uttered a startled grunt, dropping to his knees, holding the back of his head. He swayed slightly before falling face-first on top of a pumpkin.

Elas spun around, hands held out before him, "Who's there? Show yourself!" He whispered.

Shaylee advanced, twirling her rake like a staff. Elas's eyes snapped open in surprise, taking several steps backward. He shielded his face with one arm and cast out with the other. Green and black sparks erupted from his fingertips but fell short of reaching her.

She swung her rake in an arc and brought the handle down on his left shoulder with a crack. Elas yelled out in surprise and pain grabbing his shoulder with his other hand. Shaylee spun in a tight circle repositioning her weapon and hooked his right foot with the rake head and yanked him off his feet. She spun her weapon a couple of times before placing the butt of the rake in the center of his chest. "Take your brother and leave. I don't want to see you two stealing from us anymore," she said sternly.

Jurren growled and pushed himself up to his knees. "I'd like to see you try those fancy moves on me, Nubla," he spat.

The word hit Shaylee like a punch in the stomach, *Nubla*. She gulped and blinked away the tears the dirty slang he threw at her caused. Even though old elven was not spoken anymore as a common language, a few words hung around. It wasn't her fault her magic hadn't surfaced.

Jurren rubbed the back of his head and slowly stretched his neck, with a couple audible pops, while shaking his hands. Shaylee swallowed a lump in her throat slowly sliding back a couple of steps.

He sneered as he rolled his hands together; a golden glow surrounded them which grew into a one-foot sphere.

Shaylee started to panic, her heart hammering in her chest and her breathing becoming ragged. With no magic of her own, she only had a flimsy rake with which to protect herself.

Jurren continued to grow his magical sphere until it was about three feet across. He threw both hands at her with a mighty grunt and hurtled the ball of light. She turned her back and dropped to her knees covering her head with her arms. "STOP!" she screamed moments before the magical incendiary exploded like a crack of thunder. Shaylee fully expected to be engulfed in the magical blast, but she didn't feel burned or singed. Slowly she peeked through her arms and saw a shimmering shield surrounding her. Wondering where the shield came from, she frantically looked around.

Elas was kneeling next to his brother with his hands held in her direction, sweat beaded his forehead, and he was as pale as a ghost. A few moments later, he collapsed, and the shield failed. Shaylee let out a shuddering breath of relief. Trembling she tried to regain her feet. All the vegetables around her were signed and smoking. The pungent air was thick with ash causing her to choke and cough.

Jurren locked eyes with Shaylee, "How are you untouched?" He then looked at his brother's crumbled unconscious form next to him, the remnants of Elas's last cast still glowing on his fingertips.

"Ish," he cursed in elvish and kicked his brother in the ribcage.

"What's the meaning of this?" Talon's voice roared from behind them. He walked calmly from the house, but his facial features told the true story of his emotions.

Jurren turned, ready to flee and abandon his brother, but he was unable to move. Shaylee looked at her father's hand, it was glowing bright silver; a thin thread of magic snaked from his wrist and was swirled up Jurren's legs, like a vine, holding him in place.

Talon strode forward, placed two fingers on Elas's neck, and then looked at the bag full of pilfered vegetables.

"I can explain…" Jurren started.

"Quiet." Talon said with a flick of his other hand. Jurren's scarf untied itself from his neck and wrapped around his mouth like a gag. Jurren continued to explain his actions though everything he said was muffled.

Shaylee knew her father had once been a head ranger, and of course, he had magic, he was an elf. But he never used it.

Talon knelt beside Elas and placed his hands on either side of his head. Elas's eyes popped open, and his head flew back in surprise.

"Oh, my head. What happened?" He whined, shaking his head and slowly rubbing his temples. When he looked up his mouth dropped open, "Oh, hello, Ranger Talon. I… I can explain."

"Start with when Shaylee confronted you. No explanations of why you're here… yet." His voice was cold and hard.

Elas looked at his frozen brother and nodded. "Shaylee snuck up behind us. She threw a rock and hit Jurren on the head, causing him to fall. Then she attacked me with a rake. She wielded it like a staff!" He glanced at her with surprise etched across his face, "She dodged my cast, cracked the rake across my shoulder, and then hooked my heel, bringing me down," He paused for a moment to look up at Jurren's sneering face. "Jurren recovered then, called her, oh, .um, never mind, and then told her to try her fancy moves on him…"

Shaylee's father held a hand up, "What did he call her?"

"Um… I really don't want to repeat it, sir." Elas glanced at Talons' face and gulped, closing his eyes tightly he whispered, "Nubla."

"Continue," was Talon's only reply. Shaylee kept her eyes downcast; she couldn't bear seeing any disappointment from her lack of magic on her father's face.

"Jurren spun a spell, and I didn't want to see Shaylee get hurt. I cast a shield over her, a shield! I actually did it…" Elas stopped talking and looked at his hands. Shaylee knew his magic was weak and never did what he wanted it to.

"Thank you for telling the truth. What spell did Jurren cast?"

"Circle of Torchictum," he said with a wince.

Shaylee's father turned his attention to Jurren, still frozen in place. "You know the rules." His eyes narrowed, and his jaw tensed. "That spell is only to be used when your life or the life of a fellow ranger is on the line. It is not to be used against a girl protecting her family's garden with a rake." He clapped his hands, releasing his spells around Jurren. Jurren stumbled forward, landing heavily on his knees.

"Why isn't he a Ranger anymore? I've never seen a spell so powerful. He needs to return and teach." Elas whispered to Shaylee, who in return whispered.

"How would I know?"

Talon heard the whisper and shook his head. "I had my reasons, Elas." He looked at Jurren again. "But you," he pointed at the frozen-in-place young man. "You won't have to worry about who's teaching the Rangers anymore. You will not be returning to their ranks."

"What? You must be joking. I'm at the top of my class. You aren't a Ranger, and you don't get to decide. All because of a simple prank; come on, we need this food," Jurren rambled.

"You may be at the top of your class, but you are not mature enough for the level of spell you just cast. That spell would have killed my daughter."

"She's not worthy of being your daughter." Jurren turned his hate-filled eyes onto Shaylee.

Talon backhanded Jurren, spinning him off his feet. "Being born who she is, is not a crime. As for this," he gestured at the garden, "was this a prank or theft? Explain?"

Jurren's eyes burned with anger. Elas spoke instead, "Our father is still on patrol, and mother just came down with a sickness. Jurren and I aren't farmers; our garden is dying, and Mother needs food."

"Why didn't you come for my mother, she can help yours." Shaylee finally spoke.

Elas hung his head, "Mother doesn't trust fairies; she forbids it."

Talon sighed heavily. He was tired of hearing that sentence. "I know that your father's patrol is overdue. We sent another one to find them. I suspect they will all be home soon." Talon turned towards Elas, "Take this food back with you." He pointed at what they had collecte. "Jurren, you will be coming with me. Shaylee, go with Elas and see if she is afflicted with the same illness Fawns' mother has."

"Others are sick?" Jurren asked, surprised.

"Fawns' ma became ill yesterday. Now, go!" Shaylee's father flicked his hand; the sacks of vegetables tied themselves up and flew to Elas.

Elas caught them just before they barreled into him. "You, come with me," he said to Jurren.

Shaylee and Elas walked silently back to his home. Elas led her to the back door, which in turn led into the kitchen. He placed the vegetables near the sink, grabbed three cups from the cupboard, and placed them on the table. He grabbed a cold teapot and held the bottom with both hands; soon, the pot whistled.

Elas filled the three cups with boiling water and added a tea strainer. "I'm going to go see if Ma's awake." Shaylee nodded, breathing in the steam from her cup. Her eyes still stung from Jurrens words earlier and then seeing Elas, a weak magic user, being able to boil water so quickly, she felt like she was just punched in the stomach.

A moment later, Elas returned, "She says you can come in."

Shaylee quickly wiped her eyes and followed him. She'd never been in their home, but it looked like her elven friend Amelia's: simple wood furniture and a few pictures on the walls. The only thing that looked similar to her own home was the multitude of flowering plants everywhere.

Elas's mother was propped up in her bed, wearing a deep scowl, "What do you want, Fae child?"

Shaylee frowned, "I am half elf too, you know?"

She waved her hand dismissively.

"When did you first notice you were ill?" Shaylee asked her.

"Four days after Lans left." She coughed and stared at the ceiling, "I was out in the garden. I remember the moment quite vividly. I was taking a break, stretching my back, when I saw a bright blue bird with strange yellow feathers throughout that made it look like it had small yellow spots everywhere, flying overhead." She shook her head slowly,

"I had never seen a bird that looked like that before. It circled and then landed not more than five feet from me. It squawked loudly and then flew off in a hurry, leaving a bunch of feathers and pollen behind." Her eyes widened and narrowed as she continued, "It was quite a mess. I don't know how the bird wasn't bald by how many feathers it left behind. After I cleaned up all the feathers, I almost immediately felt weak and lightheaded. The next day, I couldn't get out of bed." She closed her eyes and a tear fell down. "I am just so weak."

"Ma…" Elas couldn't stand seeing his mother in this state.

She opened her eyes quickly and gathered herself. She looked at Shaylee and nodded firmly, "Nothing else seems to be wrong. Weakness. That's all there is to it."

"Thank you, ma'am," Shaylee dipped her head and departed. She needed to tell her mother about this, but she wanted to make a stop first.

The sun was brightening the eastern sky when she skidded to a halt in front of Fawns' home. She hesitated; her hand hovering close to the door; it was pretty early. She sighed and gently knocked.

"Who's there?" a weak voice asked.

"Shaylee, ma'am. Can I ask you a question?"

"Come in, dear."

Shaylee walked into the house. It was decorated like the last one she was in. *It must be an elven thing,* she thought.

"I'm back here."

Shaylee walked to the rear of the house, "How are you feeling?"

"Same, just so weak."

"Do you remember when you first started feeling sick? Did you happen to see a bright blue bird with yellow spots?"

Flora's eyes widened, "I did; it was the strangest-looking bird. It landed next to me…"

"Let me guess, it squawked and flew away, leaving nothing but feathers and pollen everywhere."

Flora nodded slowly, "How do you know that?" she asked, fear lacing her words.

"Elanor is sick too. I just came from her. That was her story, but that was almost four weeks ago."

"Four weeks? And she's no better?"

Shaylee shook her head.

"But no worse?"

"She says it has been the same weakness every day."

Flora slumped into her bed, "At least it's no worse. Can you please have your mother come see me when she can?"

"Of course, get some rest."

What kind of sickness is that bird giving and how many villagers are sick? She thought, *hopefully, Ma knows what it could be.*

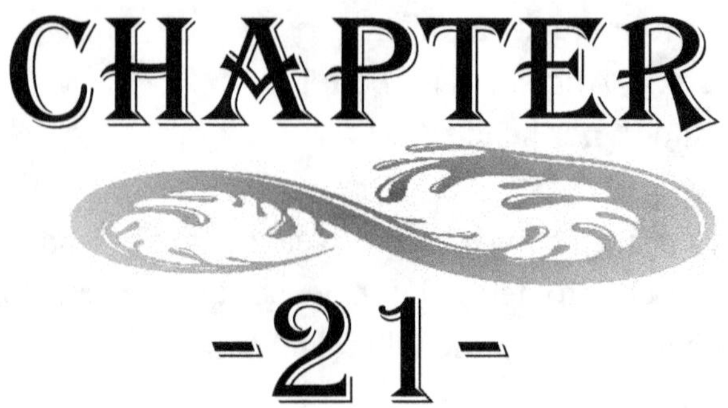

CHAPTER -21-

WHEN Shaylee arrived home her father was already back. "Is it the same?" He asked.

Shaylee nodded, "She told me she felt sick immediately after a strange bright blue bird with yellow spots shed a bunch of feathers and pollen next to her. I went to Flora, who said she saw the same bird and then felt sick. It must be connected - this sickness, this weakness, and the bird. Do you know if anyone else is sick?"

Shaylee's mother flew into the kitchen, her blue slippers a few inches off the floor. "Eight that I know of. Many like Elanor don't trust fairies, so they won't let me see them."

"I have always thought it was strange for a group of elves and fairies to live in the same village but not like each other," Shaylee stated.

Talon sighed, "Safety in numbers will lead some to live where they might not otherwise. Speaking of safety," He turned towards Shaylee with a stern look, "Ranger Wolic saw you coming from the direction of Verndale yesterday. We told you never to go there. Didn't we? You said you were staying with Amelia."

Shaylee's mother elevated a few feet, leaning forward with her fits on her hips and gave her a look.

Shaylee looked between her mother and father. "Yes, but nobody saw me – well, at least no adults saw me," she said, her eyes downcast and shoulders slumped.

Her mother's face reddened, and she started to elevate her voice to yell but caught herself and turned into a very stern whisper, "Who saw you?"

Shaylee looked at her feet. "Just a boy who was traveling through town with his mother. We only spoke for a few moments, and then I left. I'm sure he won't tell anybody." She barely whispered.

"What did you tell him?" Her father asked his voice flat.

Shaylee thought about her conversation with Keelan and decided it was probably best not to tell her parents everything just yet, "I told him my name was Shaylee and that I was not from Verndale."

Rosepetal sighed. "It could have been worse, Shaylee. Do you understand?" Shaylee nodded. "But no going back there or staying overnight with Amelia," Rosepetal said shaking her finger at her. "It is not safe for our kind around non-magical humans. Now tell me everything that Elanor and Flora said to you."

Shaylee told her parents about the strange bright blue and yellow spotted bird that both ladies said they'd never seen before. "So, do you know what this could be?" She asked her mother; glad she wasn't the topic anymore. "Could the bird have brought whatever is afflicting them? It seems like such a coincidence that the bird landed next to them weeks apart with the same flurry of feathers and pollen, and then both instantly become sick."

"It does seem like a bit much to be a coincidence," Her father agreed. "Why don't you go get that sleepy pet of yours up and fed? You have a long day ahead of you today."

Shaylee shuffled out of the kitchen and returned to her bedroom to get Lyra and put on some decent clothing for the day.

Shaylee and her father spent the morning sparring with staffs. The early morning quiet was shattered with the cracks of the wooden staffs connecting as they traded blows back and forth. Shaylee spun, jumped, and dodged her father's attacks. Like always she was on the defensive.

Her father dipped his left shoulder–a tell she had learned that meant he was going to spin to his left while lashing out. She braced herself and readied her staff. When he spun, she reacted, bringing her staff up to stop his downward movement and save her shoulder from the blow. The staffs clacked together with a sharp sound and then her staff broke in half. Shaylee cried out in shock and pain, dropping both halves shaking out her stinging hands. Talon wasted no time and swung his staff around connecting with her calves sweeping her feet from under her. Shaylee landed with a huff.

Talon chuckled, "Always watch yourself especially when you have been disarmed."

Shaylee nodded accepting his outstretched hand to get to her feet and then he handed her a waterskin.

After a long pull from the waterskin, she looked at Talon and finally asked the question that had been wandering on her mind, "So, what's going to happen to Jurren and Elas?"

"Jurren is being punished; the council has decided not to remove him from Ranger training, much to my protest. But I do have to agree we need every elf we can get in the ranks. He, however, will be much lower in seniority now, and his magic is being restricted until he can prove that he is more mature."

"How do you restrict magic?"

"With magic, of course," he winked. "Now, shall we get back to our lessons?"

"In a moment, I wanted to ask you something first." She paused for a moment picking some leaves off her pants, "Do you ever think my magic will surface?" She pressed her lips, "It's just not fair. You have magic, and so does mother. Why was I cursed to be a Nubla?"

"Don't ever use that degrading word in my presence," he snapped. Shaylee looked at her father's stern face. Talon sighed as his features softened, then he grabbed her hands, "You are no such thing, Shaylee. You are unique; your birthright will reveal itself when it is ready. I don't want you to ever think of yourself as being less of an elf or fairy than anyone else in this village.

"You have every right to be here as any of them. The Kingdom of Evansshire, where our little town resides, hates, and fears each and every one of us. That is why we are on high alert all the time. That is why we send out patrols constantly. That is why you and I train and spar every day. The current King is nothing but a human, a non-magic-wielding human. And he, unfortunately, hates all magic. Everything that is magic and anything that uses it. We must keep our wits about us and protect each other. Do you understand?"

Shaylee was silent for a moment, "Yes, I think so. Thank you."

"For what?"

"For talking to me like an adult. For trusting me with knowledge I have never known before. It has changed my whole way of thinking and given me much to think about."

He clapped her on the back, "Let's get back to work, shall we?"

Lyra soared overhead pawing the air like she was swimming, Shaylee smiled at her. Still feeling the sting from the last knockdown, she winced and nodded.

The following day, Fawn came to live with them. Flora's condition hadn't changed, but a few elders had designated a house for all those who had come down with this new illness to be grouped so they could be properly cared for. Fawn would stay with them until her father returned or Flora recovered.

Their house was small and only had two bedrooms. Shaylee gladly took Fawns' belongings and set up a cot in her room.

"I've always wanted a little sister," she beamed at Fawn once all her belongings were stored away.

Fawn looked up at her with tears in her eyes, "I always thought it would be nice to have an older sister. Thank you for letting me live here."

Shaylee wrapped her in a big hug, "There's nothing to thank. You are part of our family now for as long as you need it." Fawn smiled back at Shaylee. "So, what do you usually do throughout the day?"

Fawn sighed, "Ma has me help in the garden and with preparing meals. Pa was teaching me how to read."

Shaylee thought for a second. "That's great; I can have you help my mother with the garden, and all three of us will help with the meals. I can also help you with your reading."

Fawn's face broke into a huge smile. "That sounds good. What do you do all day long?"

"Gardening, reading and my father is teaching me how to be a Ranger."

Fawns' eyes opened wide, "But girls can't be Rangers," she said in a hushed voice.

"Can you keep a secret?"

Fawn nodded.

"My magic hasn't manifested yet, so Father received special permission to train me so I wouldn't be vulnerable."

"No magic? But you're so old."

"I'm not that old," she frowned. "I'm only thirteen. My mother says my powers will take longer to manifest since I am a cross. How long have you had yours?"

"I've had them for almost six years now." Fawn levitated a book on Shaylee's desk; it spun around and then softly landed back in place. "I'm still learning control though. Ma didn't want me to learn too quickly. I am already teased because I'm so short."

"Wow, I've never heard of anyone so young coming into their powers. I bet you'll be very powerful when you get older."

"That's what my ma tells me," Fawn smiled shyly.

The following few weeks turned out to be more challenging than Shaylee thought they would be. Having Fawn to talk to and play games with was great, but she started seeing a shift in her parents. Fawn was a full elf and was already coming into her powers. She needed instruction to grow them and develop control, and both her father and mother jumped at the opportunity to help.

Shaylee's magic was still locked away. Her mother could feel it just below the surface, and over time, Shaylee had been able to detect it just sitting there. But still, she couldn't touch it. It was like an itch just out of reach but never going away.

Fawns' magic developed rapidly under the tutelage of Shaylee's parents. By the end of the second day, she had no issues levitating buckets, firewood, and the fruits and vegetables from the garden. Her control and strength were developing so rapidly that by the end of the week, she could even levitate herself for a short period of time.

By the end of the second week, Fawn continuously used magic for every task she completed, even eating. She never seemed to lift a finger anymore. She would think about what she wanted done, and it would be done.

The only times Shaylee found herself remotely happy were the few short hours every day when Fawn visited her mother. Shaylee knew she was not being fair, and it wasn't Fawns' fault that she had no magic, but it was hard not to resent how easily magic came to her. For everyone in the household's sake she tried to pretend that she was happy when they were all together.

She thought she had everybody fooled for a while until she started being punished for her attitude. She found herself being asked to do tasks alone. Her parents never talked to her outright about it, but she knew they were disappointed in her attitude.

Shaylee didn't know what she would do all winter when there were fewer things to do. Their harvest was almost complete, and parts of the garden were already set up for winter slumber. With fewer obligations in the garden, her sparring with her father usually picked up, but now that he was teaching Fawn how to control her magic, he had less time for her. Sure, they still did their daily lessons, and he gave her extra tasks to complete independently, but she missed the one-on-one time she had with him.

Today, after their daily lessons, he gave her a message to take to one of the furthest outposts of the village's perimeter. It would take her all day to get there and back.

Shaylee took the message, placed it in her satchel, grabbed a waterskin, and left quickly. She didn't want her father to see the tears shining in her eyes. She had woken up extra early that morning to complete all her chores, so when Fawn took off in the middle of the day to see her mother, she could try to get some extra time with her father. But now she was being sent off to deliver a message. She grumbled to herself as she jogged through the forest, "Stupid message, I'm not a messenger. Maybe I can spar with him before dinner if I hurry back."

She sprinted through the forest with Lyra flying through the treetops. At least she still had her vaskakat, and their bond seemed to be strengthening. Her mother said it was a good sign that her powers were starting to strengthen and come more to the surface, even though a bond with a familiar was not something elves or fairies were supposed to be able to do. In the past, she and Lyra had to touch their foreheads together to receive images from each other; now, as long as they looked into each other's eyes, she could see the pictures clearly. She even started hearing whispers, too faint to make out, but Lyra was definitely trying to speak to her.

It was almost midday before she saw the Outpost ahead. To the untrained eye, it looked like nothing more than a common redwood, but Shaylee saw the small hand, and footholds notched into the tree that allowed the scouts to get up and down quickly. As well as the small platforms that were hidden throughout the tree's boughs, giving the sentries places to sit.

Today, she saw something that she'd never seen before. She saw the tree shimmering. Her father told her that magical spells were placed on the trees and that anyone with magic could see the slight shimmering surrounding it. She had never seen it before. Her heartbeat quickened.

Could it be possible that my magic was finally about to awaken? She tried to calm her thoughts. *There's no sense getting all worked up only to be disappointed if it wasn't true.*

A sharp whistle rang out from the top of the tree, she returned the whistle with two short chirps. Within moments, an elf descended the branches and stood before her.

"What are you doing here?" He asked her gruffly.

"My father instructed me to bring you this message," she told him with a scowl. She didn't understand why he was so cross with her.

He held his hand out and flicked his fingers impatiently, "Well, then hand it over and get back to the village. This is no place for the likes of you."

"What do you mean the likes of me?" she said, holding the paper close.

"Nublas should stay in the village proper where they can be cared for. It's too dangerous out here. You have no magic to protect yourself, no ability to fight, and you aren't even carrying a weapon."

Shaylee drew a small dagger from her hip and showed it to him, "I am not completely useless just because I don't have magic yet."

He laughed abruptly, "Come on, hand over the message. Some of us have important things to do."

She glared at him as she thrust the piece of paper into his hand. "Now, off with you. Get back to the village," he said with a dismissive flick of his hand.

She clamped her mouth shut tightly to keep from uttering the words she wanted to. She was still a child and could not speak so to adults. She turned and stomped away, "I'll go home when I feel like it," she mumbled. Lyra landed in front of her and gazed up at her; an image of a crystal-clear pond popped into her head, and a faint voice that could just barely be heard, **Let's go here.**

She smiled broadly, "I heard you! I really did! Lead the way."

Lyra led her through the brushes and brambles to a small clearing with a little pond. No stream fed into or trickled out of it. Shaylee walked up to the pond and leaned close to it, smelling deeply of the water, "No sulfur," she said to herself. She dipped her fingers into the pond and tasted a couple of water drops, "Must be artesian."

Placing her lips to the water, she drank deeply and then flopped onto her back, staring at the sky through the canopy.

Go back now? A small voice asked in her head a few moments later.

"You were drinking from the pond. We weren't even looking at each other that time," she said, astonished.

Lyra looked up. *Yes, of course,* she projected.

With newfound energy, she jumped to her feet and started back through the forest to get to the main trail.

When she returned to the trail leading back to the village, she heard loud grunting, roaring and screams from the outpost. "What's going on?" She asked aloud looking around for signs of danger. Lyra took flight and headed back toward the outpost.

Images fluttered into Shaylee's mind; two trolls and an ogre were attacking the outpost. The Rangers were firing arrows and magical attacks down at the invaders from the tree, but they couldn't penetrate their thick armor and hides. *Oh, no this is a junior patrol group. Their magical attacks are too weak against ogres and trolls,* Shaylee thought.

The trolls attacked the tree with large, long, double-sided axes. Their blows shaking the mighty tree causing one elf to lose his grip and tumble out of it. He regained his feet only to take the ogre's club across his skull. A couple of the other Rangers leaped from the tree and started attacking the invaders on the ground. They drew their swords both attacking the one ogre. It was no match for their skill with a blade, but they were no match for its brute strength. Their blades landed on the thick arms, chest and legs of the ogre but it just laughed, his hide absorbing the attack.

A loud crack echoed through the forest, which Shaylee could clearly hear with her own ears. The tree was breaking. A roar pierced the air, and a large black shape streaked through the canopy. Lyra couldn't get a clear visual of the item that crashed into the tree until the tree splintered the rest of the way and crashed to the ground.

A large, winged creature stood up, stretched its wings wide, and roared again. Shaylee had learned about wyverns, but she'd never seen one before. This creature that Lyra was seeing was most definitely a two-legged dragon. Its black scales looked greasy, and its thin bat-like wings had tiny claws at the ends. It had a long, slender neck with spikes that ran up the length and encompassed its head in a sort of spiked collar. It had a large almost crocodile-like face with long teeth that stuck out from its snout. Its tail whipped back and forth, slashing the tree and anything else that got in its way. Razor-sharp spikes lined the tail all the way down to its spear-like tip.

The wyvern didn't attack the elves, it just watched with curiosity as the trolls and the ogre defeated the four elves they battled. The last elf was grabbed by the throat and thrown into the bushes. When it did not rise, the trolls and the ogre roared triumphantly. After a moment, the wyvern joined in.

The trolls gathered up any weapons they found and lumbered in her direction.

Hide! Lyra shouted into her mind.

Shaylee dove into the bushes; her breath was ragged, and her heart raced.

Calm yourself and look to your right.

Shaylee tried to do as instructed, she closed her eyes and concentrated on her breathing, after a few seconds she opened them up again. To her right, on the ground, was something long and spiraled. It was pure white and smooth to the touch. She picked it up and turned it, looking at all sides; it was almost the length of her palm and about the thickness of two of her fingers at the base. *What is it?* She thought.

It is a young unicorn horn. Now, hold it tightly and think about being invisible.

How are you hearing my thoughts? Shaylee thought, her heartbeat increasing again.

The same way you hear mine, now quickly, do as I say. Hold the horn and think about being invisible.

With nothing else to do and the sounds of the trolls getting closer, she held the horn tightly with both hands and thought about being invisible. Completely hidden from sight and smell. Totally hidden.

The trolls and the ogre stomped by her hiding spot without stopping. The sound of enormous wings beating flew overhead. A few minutes later she was alone again with nothing but her heart beating frantically.

How did I do that?

Unicorn horns are very magical, even young ones; you can channel your inner magic through them. Very good.

How did you know this would work?

Lyra swooped down and landed on her shoulder. *I didn't, it was worth a try.*

Shaylee pushed her off her shoulder playfully. "How did you know this was here?" She said aloud.

I could feel its magic, not important. We need to move on.

"Do you think I can make it back to the village before those vile things? We need to warn everyone."

Try the horn again—picture where you want to be and go there.

"How can I picture a place and go there? That's impossible even for magic."

Lyra growled and hissed. *Stop doubting and just believe. Hurry, we have no time to lose. Stop thinking, just do.* Lyra jumped back onto her shoulder, wrapping her tail around Shaylee's neck. *I can read your thoughts and see deep inside of you. I know who you are. Believe in yourself.*

Shaylee sighed. *Here goes nothing.* She held the slender horn tightly with both hands again and pictured her kitchen.

Make sure each detail is crystal-clear, Lyra whispered.

Shaylee nodded and focused on the little details. The kitchen table and chairs with every crack and knot, the tiny flowers painted on her mother's favorite mugs, and the flowers and herbs on the windowsill.

The image was so vivid she thought she smelled a pie cooking in the wood oven. ***I want to go here. I need to be here now***, she thought. Her hands started to get hot; her fingers began to tingle. A bright light erupted around her, so bright that she felt blinded with her eyes closed. Her head started to spin; it felt like the world was spinning; she threw her arms out to steady herself, making sure to keep one hand on the horn.

CHAPTER

-22-

"**SHAYLEE?** How did you get here?" Rosepetal's startled squeak made her eyes pop open.

"I did it! Ma, I did it."

"What did you do?" Rosepetal asked.

"No time to explain. Where's Father?"

"Answer my question first, young one."

"Mother. Lives are in danger; where's father?" Shaylee said sternly.

Rosepetal looked at her in surprise, having never been spoken to by her daughter like that; Shaylee was on the verge of tears, her eyes glistening and filled with fear. "Where's father?" She asked again Her voice elevating to almost a shout.

"Outside with Fawn, what's wrong?" Her mother asked softly.

Shaylee tore out of the house into the backyard with Rosepetal close behind.

"Shaylee, how'd you get back so fast? What's wrong?" Talon asked when he saw her pale face.

Without speaking, she walked up to him, holding her new horn in one hand and placing her other hand on his temple. She closed her eyes and willed the images Lyra shared with her to flow into his head.

He gasped but didn't break contact.

"How did you do that?" he asked in barely a whisper when the images stopped.

She shook her head, "Not now. Lyra shared those images with me; the outpost is gone. I had already delivered your message. The attackers are on their way here."

His face went grim. "Stay inside; share that with your mother if you can. Don't leave the house until I return." He motioned for Fawn to follow Shaylee before he sprinted out of the yard.

Shaylee grabbed Fawn's hand and led her into the house.

"What's going on, Shaylee?" Rosepetal almost shouted after she closed the door.

"Please sit, ma."

Rosepetal slowly complied sinking into a chair. Shaylee approached and repeated what she had done to her father. Rosepetal stared at her in disbelief.

"How did you do that?" She finally asked. Shaylee held up the unicorn horn. "Where did you get that?"

"Lyra found it for me. I could make myself invisible to the trolls and the ogre, and I was able to will myself into the kitchen instantly."

A crash behind Shaylee made her jump and turn around, hands held out before her like she saw Elas doing. Fawn was scrambling backward and knocked over a chair. "That's not possible. Elves and fairies do not have that type of magic!" Fawn exclaimed, "We can't use artifacts to enhance our magic. What are you?" She screamed.

Rosepetal jumped from her chair and grabbed Fawn by the shoulders," She's my daughter. You have never met an Elvenfae; you don't know what they can do." Rosepetals' eyes were filled with fright.

"Ok, I'm sorry." Fawn whimpered.

Shaylee wrapped her arms around Fawn's shoulders, "Ma, you're scaring her."

Rosepetal wrung her hands floating backward, "I'm sorry, those images caught me off guard. I didn't mean to scare you, Fawn."

"It's okay. I didn't mean to yell," Fawn said quietly, eyes downcast.

Rosepetal tried to smile, but it came out sad and strained.

"Father said to stay here until he returned, but I think I can help." Shaylee started to walk to the front door.

"NO!" Rosepetal shouted flying around her to get between her daughter and the door, "If he said to stay, then you stay. You and I must protect Fawn."

"I can handle myself!" Fawn pouted with her arms crossed.

The front door flew open with a crash into the wall, making all of them jump and spin around. Talon walked in and slammed the door shut. "Pack quickly. We are leaving."

"Wh – what, why?" Rosepetal stammered.

"These fools think I am lying. Since the sentries have not sounded the alarm, they say we are safe."

"You told them what I showed you, right?"

Talon's eyes darted to his feet.

"You didn't tell them?"

"Shaylee, dear. You saw Fawn's reaction. Do you think the elders and Rangers would be more receptive? What did you tell them?"

"That Lyra could link with me and show me what she saw."

Rosepetal sighed, "Of course, they didn't believe that. What are we going to do?"

"We are going to flee and hope others can do the same. We will help any survivors."

"Can't we tell everyone and convince them to leave with us?" Fawn asked.

"There's not enough time, I'm afraid. Quickly pack, and we will see if we can save Fawn's ma. Now, hurry!"

Everyone packed essentials as fast as they could and then hurried out of the house.

The Sick house, as it was starting to be called, was a little way from the village proper. Set off by itself next to a small artesian pond.

Talon rushed into the house to warn the residents, with Fawn at his heels.

"Fawn! What are you doing back today?" Flora said weakly.

"We are about to be attacked; we have to get you out of here," Talon told her.

She shook her head, "No, leave me. I'm too weak to travel. If I die, it was meant to be." She took Fawn's hand, "Talon is your guardian now. Treat him like a father and do all that he says."

"No, mama, no. You have to come with us!" Fawn started to sob.

"I cannot. You must survive and be strong. I know you can do it. Now, go before it is too late." Tears streamed down her cheeks.

Talon thought about arguing with her, but the look of determination on Flora's face stopped him; he nodded grimly, gently grabbed Fawn's shoulders, and started to lead her from the house. Fawn numbly allowed her body to be turned, but her eyes continued to look into her mother's eyes. As they neared the door, she broke free from Talon and threw herself onto her mother. Flora gasped with pain and shock at the little girl's weight on her chest.

"I can't leave you." Fawn sobbed.

Slowly, Flora wrapped her arms around her daughter and held her as tightly as she could. "It will be okay, Fawn, my precious. We will see each other again, if not in this life, then in the next for sure. Ombrasia exists; the afterlife is our second chance at happiness. You will be rewarded if you lead a decent life and help those in need whenever possible. We will see each other again, I know it. Now, go. Please." A sob ripped through Flora as she tried to push Fawn away. Talon picked up Fawn and carried her out of the house, as she cried and struggled to get down.

Rosepetal and Shaylee followed Talon into the woods, tears streaming down their cheeks.

CHAPTER -23-

THEY sprinted for as long as possible and then broke down to a light jog for almost an hour. Shaylee was beyond tired, and Talon looked spent, carrying Fawn the whole way. Rosepetal fared the best as she flew the entire time. At some point during their mad dash, Fawn had fallen asleep draped over Talon's shoulder. When they stopped, he gently laid her down, waking her up.

"Have they attacked yet?" she asked quietly.

"I don't know," Talon replied. He found them a cave in a hillside to spend the night in. He gathered pine tree boughs and a few boulders to hide the entrance.

"Do you think they will come this way?" Shaylee asked.

Talon shook his head, "I don't think so. There are no settlements in this direction, and we snuck between the outposts this far out."

"Shouldn't we have alerted them, Father?"

"I don't think it would have done any good. Lyra, can you venture out and alert us if they get near?" Lyra nodded her head and then took flight.

Shaylee frowned, "What if that wyvern sees her? I don't like her being out there all alone." Suddenly, everything Lyra was seeing entered Shaylee's mind.

I will share my sight with you, Lyra projected to her.

"What is it?" Rosepetal said when Shaylee smiled.

"Lyra is sharing her sight with me. It – it's like I'm flying along with her."

Lyra flew through the trees, staying below the canopy. She flew past the last outpost before faint sounds of fighting could be heard. She slowed down and started leaping from branch to branch to stay hidden better.

The fighting sounds grew louder and louder; then, suddenly, they were gone. Lyra continued to venture closer. Up ahead, she saw the bulking hide of an ogre. He was looming over a small group of elves with his club raised high.

The wyvern crashed through the canopy with a snarling roar. The captives screamed and huddled closer together, hoping for protection. The wyvern slowly stalked closer to his terrified prisoners.

He snaked his lethal neck from side to side, hissing. "Where is she? Where's the human?" The wyvern was challenging to understand as he hissed the s's and slurred his speech. His snake-like tongue flicked back and forth.

"What human? No humans live in this village?" One of the elders said.

"Don't lie to me. I can smell her," he hissed.

"Honest, we don't know any humans. Their closest settlement is Verndale. It's that way," the elder pointed.

The wyvern growled, swinging his tail around, and stabbed the elder in the chest with his long tail spike. Everyone screamed as the elder slumped to the ground without a sound.

The trolls arrived, pushing a few more survivors into the huddled group.

The wyvern growled and barked at them.

"This everyone alive," one troll garbled out, "all fairies and elves, no humans."

The wyvern raised his head and roared; sparks and a bolt of lightning followed. The lightning hit a tree with a deafening crack.

"Kill them all, no witnesses."

The trolls and the ogre grinned menacingly, readying their weapons.

Thunk, thunk, thunk, the rapid firing of three arrows felled the ogre where he stood. The trolls whirled around, looking for the attacker.

Two men strode into the village, one with a bow with an arrow nocked pointed at the closest troll, the other held his hands in front of him, both hands glowed bright blue.

"I don't think we will let you kill anyone else today," the one with the bow said.

"This doesn't concern you. Leave now, and you may live." The wyvern barked, a puff of smoke escaping his mouth.
"The Order of the Chosen begs to differ. We are making this our business, and you may not leave," the magic welder said. He thrust both hands at one of the trolls, uttering a primal scream; blue lightning streaked from his hands, striking squarely into the troll's chest. The troll grunted at the impact and was thrust backward; it hit a tree with a sickening crunch. The man with the bow fired three arrows in quick cession into the other troll. Two in the chest, the third struck it in the eye. The troll crumbled to the ground with a startled grunt.

Both men turned to face the wyvern, bow and glowing hands ready. The wyvern looked at its three companions and then at the two warriors walking purposely toward it. It hissed and growled one last time before springing into the air. Both men let their weapons fly. One arrow bounced ineffectively off the black scaly hide, and the wyvern dodged the lightning bolt that careened for its head.

"Damn it. It got away. I knew we should have attacked it first."

"That would have been too dangerous. Come on, we have work to do."

The two men helped the remaining villagers to their feet and then led them back to the village.

Lyra left her hiding place and started to head back to Shaylee. The link between them stopped. Shaylee rubbed her temples and eyes; sharing someone else's sight was a strange sensation.

"What did you see?" Talon asked.

Shaylee took a couple of deep breaths and relayed everything she saw.

"So, not everyone was killed?" Fawn asked, "Did you see my ma?" She sounded hopeful.

"Lyra didn't concentrate on the villagers' faces; I couldn't make out anyone but the elder." Her father's eyes burned with interest, "It was Tolec."

"So, what now?" Rosepetal chimed in.

"We head back and see how we can help. Maybe our two saviors will still be there." Talon replied.

They left the protection of their cave and jogged back to the village. When it got too dark to see, Talon and Fawn conjured a couple of glowing sun-orbs to light the way.

They made it back well after midnight. Fires were a glow all around the village square and in most of the homes. Sentries were placed every few feet surrounding the village.

"Halt, who goes there?"

Talon strode forward without a reply.

"Ranger Talon, thank all the Gods you're back; we thought you were dead. Come with me quickly."

Talon turned to his family, "Go check on Fawn's mother; I will find you soon."

The girls all nodded. The Ranger that greeted them led Talon to the council building. The small hut near the center of the square was where the elders and Rangers met to discuss anything concerning the village.

Talon ducked in through the doorway of the council hut. The soft glow from torches and candles illuminated the small space. Three Rangers and two strangers sat in a circle around the center fire pit.

They all looked up when he entered; the eldest leaped to his feet grabbing Talons shoulders in greeting, "Ranger Talon, thank the Gods in Ombrasia you're alive."

"Where are the elders and Ranger Lorsan?"

"All dead, sir. You are now the senior elder and senior Ranger."

He nodded his head solemnly. The two strangers stood and approached.

They both bowed deeply, *an elf and a human; interesting*, Talon thought.

The elf spoke first, "It is an honor to meet you, Ranger Talon. I have heard of your times as a Ranger, but I thought you retired, Sir."

"I did, but it looks like that was just ended for me. What brings you to our village in this time of great turmoil?" Talon didn't want to reveal that he knew what transpired, not just yet. He needed to judge the intentions of these strangers.

The black-haired elf spoke again, "May I introduce ourselves first? I am Tarrid Norell, son of Ranger Taegan, and this is my companion, Leo'venath Spencer. We are warriors of The Order of the Chosen." He pointed at his companion. Leo smiled and bowed his head in greeting causing his shaggy dirty blonde hair to fall over his eyes.

"I did not know The Order had officially reformed. When I was young there were only fragmented groups calling themselves members of the Order, but nothing organized."

"These are trying times we find ourselves in. It has called for the awakening of the old ways. A High Shepherd was chosen and has taken up residence at the Sanctum."

Talon nodded. "Please sit and tell me your tale."

"How far back should I go?"

"What brought on the need to reawaken The Order?"

Tarrid nodded, "After the wars, life was strained for magical folk, as you well know. We weren't welcome in the land of dragons or the land of men. Our kind stayed out of both fights and found ourselves homeless.

"A few found hiding places in both kingdoms, like here in Threndy and my home of Thanbel, deep in the heart of the Wyvern Empire. But unlike here, we had to be on the constant move. We were always hunted, scared, and hungry. I think it was this upbringing that led to the organized rise of The Order. My father's generation was tired of running. We left the Wyverns territory and ventured across the waste, but life there was no better. When I was six, my father said we had to fight for the life that was stolen from us or die trying. Staying out of the last wars was a mistake. When the kingdom of men fell, the dragons should have assisted them, as should have we.

"Being neutral led to our downfall. When the wyverns attacked, the dragons sought our help and the help of humans, but again, we said no, and the fight was extinguished from the humans that were left. Now humans suffer under tyrannical governess. Magic folk in Evansshire must stay hidden and live in fear of discovery. Dragons live in slavery, locked in their human forms under the wyvern's dictatorship - magical folk live in even more fear - the fear of being eaten if found. Most have left; let me tell you, the Waste is no place to live. The land yields little crops and the wildlife is dangerous."

"Why do you travel with a human?" One of the Rangers asked.

Leo'venath cleared his throat, "Many humans are tired of the ruler we have. Most do not know we are fed lies from the cradle. We grow up learning that elves, fairies, dragons, and magic are fairy tales, all fake." A collective gasp sounded in the small hut. "Some families teach the old ways, in secret, of course. But there are those of us who do not want to hide anymore. I am one of those who wishes to hide no more. I journeyed off on my own in search of the truth. I found Tar."

"Who found whom, Leo?" Tarrid interrupted.

Leo'venath coughed, a small smile tugged at his lips, "Tar found me about to be eaten by a young wyvern. I was taught they were real, but until you meet your first one, you don't know what to expect. I have been traveling with Tar ever since; we are trying to find like-minded elves, fairies, humans, and dragons, if we can find any, to join our cause."

"And what cause is this?" Talon asked cautiously.

"To take back what is ours. To help fulfill the prophecy if we can," Tarrid explained.

The hut fell into silence. Everyone pondered the newcomers' words.

"I can't speak for everyone, but I have a family to look after…" Talon began.

Shaylee rushed into the hut, "I will help," she blurted.

"You will do no such thing, Shaylee. Go back to your mother." Talon thrust a finger to the door.

Shaylee placed her hands on her hips and stuck her chin in the air, "Times are changing, Father. I will be changing with it," she said defiantly.

Talon stared at her for a long moment and then sighed, "It has been a trying day. Let us resume these talks in the morning. Watches rotate every two hours, even during daylight, six hours off between shifts," he told a junior Ranger.

The Ranger snapped to attention and departed.

"I will see you both at my house for breakfast, please," he said to Tarrid and Leo'venath, both bowed their heads. "Come, Shaylee, we need sleep before we talk about our next steps."

Shaylee looked at her father. He seemed to have aged ten years in a single day. She nodded and followed him back to their house.

Even though she had been there just after midday, it felt like a lifetime ago as she walked through the front door. So much had changed.

Thoroughly exhausted, they all retired to their rooms for the evening.

CHAPTER -24-

TARRID and Leo'venath requested to help with the watch and took the two hours right after daybreak. When their watch was complete, they went to Talon's home.

It looked like every other elf house in the village, single-story, clay bricks with a sod roof and lots of windows. Most homes had a small garden beside it, but Talon's garden was the one thing that set his house apart. The garden was easily five times larger than anyone else's. Vegetables, fruits, and herbs of all sorts graced the large plot.

As they neared the house, they saw no activity inside at this early hour, so they sat down to wait.

Closing his eyes to rest, Tarrid thought back to the meeting the night before. This poor village was just thrust into a war they didn't know existed, a war he didn't know how to tell them about truly. Talon seemed to be a cautious but intelligent man, but it was his daughter that he found his thoughts centering on. She looked to be thirteen or fourteen, short for an elf and headstrong, but there was something else about her that he couldn't quite place. With long brown hair and dark eyes, she was stunning. She had a slender athletic frame, but something about her features just didn't look right.

"Morning." A woman's voice brought him back to the present, and he opened his eyes. A fairy hovered in front of him. Her flame-red hair, a mess of curls on top of her head, made her pale skin look even whiter.

"You must be Tarrid and Leo'venath. My husband told me a little about you last night. I'm Rosepetal. Come on inside; breakfast will be ready shortly." She fluttered past him with a large basket of freshly picked strawberries on her golden wings.

"Husband? She doesn't mean Talon?" Leo'venath whispered.

"Surely not; fairies and elves don't marry, and fairies don't live on the ground." He pointed to the tree houses scattered through the village.

Leo'venath shrugged and followed the fairy into the house.

Talon was in the kitchen when they entered. Rosepetal fluttered up to him and kissed him on the cheek. "Good morning, dear," he greeted. "Welcome, men; please sit; breakfast will be ready soon," he said to the two.

"You said two men were coming for breakfast? These two look barely past boyhood. How old are you?"

"Rose, that is rude. I apologize for my wife's fairy carefreeness." Talon bowed. Rosepetal's face turned beet red.

"No apology needed, and no offense taken." Tarrid bowed in return. "I am sixteen, Leo is eighteen, ma'am."

"Sixteen? How does one so young know so much? My husband says your magic skills would rival him."

"That is high praise for sure, thank you. I grew up in a difficult atmosphere. The wyverns, with their trolls and ogres, hunted us constantly. All the other children and I learned to harness our powers at a young age. And before that, we learned hand-to-hand combat and sabotage techniques. You can say we were bred for war."

"I'm so sorry your childhood was robbed from you." She fluttered closer to him and then wrapped him up in a big hug. A cloud of magic engulfed them. Tarrid felt warmth and love pour out from the fairy.

"Get a hold of your emotions and magic fairy," Talon chided. "I apologize again for my wife. Fairies are highly emotional."

Rosepetal released him, backing away, clearly embarrassed.

"Again, no apologies necessary. We have numerous fairies working for our cause. They are marvelous scouts and keep our spirits up. I know I am young, ma'am, and much younger than most of The Chosen's leaders, but difficult times have led us to make difficult choices."

"Shaylee, Fawn! Time to get up. Help me set the table," Talon hollered.

Tarrid turned to see two girls walk in. Shaylee, he met briefly. The other girl, Fawn, was younger but clearly an elf. She was a little shorter than Shaylee, with long blonde hair and striking turquoise eyes. Her hair was pulled back in a simple braid pushed behind her pointed ears, whereas Shaylee's braid hid her ears.

"Girls, this is Tarrid Norell and Leo'venath Spencer." Shaylee and Fawn both smiled at the two strangers in their kitchen. "Shaylee is my daughter; you met her briefly last night. Fawn is a neighbor who has been living with us for a while; her mother is sick."

"What kind of sickness?" Leo'venath asked.

"I'm not sure exactly. We have eight women, all elves, who saw a strange bird land beside them, and now they have no energy. They are simply wasting away," Rosepetal said sadly.

Tarrid and Leo'venath shared a look, "The bird wouldn't happen to a bright blue with strange yellow feathers that almost look like spots?"

Shaylee and Rosepetal nodded. "That's what they all said they saw," Shaylee said. "Do you know what it is?"

Tarrid nodded, "We are currently looking for the cure. That is our primary mission; our secondary is looking for those willing to fight."

"We believe you should abandon this village and come with us. All of you." Leo'venath spoke carefully and slowly, knowing this was a sensitive subject.

"Now look here, Tarrid and Leo'venath…" Talon began.

"Please, just Leo and Tar," Leo interrupted.

Talon nodded, "We are grateful for your assistance, but we are not looking at moving. You defeated the intruders. We have nothing more to fear."

Tar shook his head, "I'm afraid all we killed was the trolls and the ogre; the wyvern escaped. It will be back."

"What is it looking for?" Shaylee asked.

"Food," Leo stated.

"No, it was looking for a human. It was questioning everyone."

Tar turned his eyes onto Shaylee. "How do you know this?"

"A friend of mine told me last night," she said, her eyes glazing over. Suddenly, Shaylee found it very hard to think straight. The truth itching at her throat, trying to get free.

"Shaylee, hello, Shaylee," Fawn waved a hand before her face.

"Oh, sorry. I guess I'm still tired from last night."

"Understandable. As I was saying. Your friend is right. The Wyvern is looking for a human, but we don't know why," Leo told her. "I apologize for lying just now." He bowed slightly. "I didn't wish to worry anyone."

"It will be back, though," Tar stated.

"How will we convince everyone to leave?" Fawn asked.

"Everyone probably won't, but we will move all those that will."

"What about the sick? My ma?"

Leo touched her shoulder, "We can move her if she wants to come. It will be her choice, however. The only thing we know about this sickness is that fairies are not afflicted, and it doesn't spread from elf to elf. Direct contact with the bird's feathers is needed."

"Avian Weakness."

Tar looked at Shaylee, "What was that?"

"Avian Weakness, that's what I started to call it."

He nodded, "Fitting name. Now we have plans to make. Are there any others we need to include in this conversation?"

"Yes, they should be here shortly. Let's eat."

As they ate, Shaylee's heart hammered in her chest. The looks Tarrid gave her made her feel comfortable with him and made her want to tell him the truth, but she couldn't. Elves weren't supposed to have a familiar connection; neither were fairies. That was a strictly human ability.

Fawn is right. What am I? I am not a human, but the wyvern did say he was looking for a human. It felt like a part of her was screaming, trying to tell her something. She shook her head, *No,* she told herself, *I am the daughter of Talon Sprucebough and Rosepetal Faeven; I am an Elvenfae, Shaylee Faeven, one of a kind,* she thought.

CHAPTER -25-

"I'M not leaving my home. I was born here, and my father was born here. This is where I belong," Ranger Wolic shouted from among the villagers.

Talon raised his hand in a calming nature, "No one is saying you – or anybody – has to leave; we are only saying that it would be best… for now. The wyvern could return at any moment with reinforcements."

"Wouldn't our rangers protect us?" A woman cried out.

"Our rangers are trained to fight clumsy humans." Talon glanced at Leo and bowed his head slightly, "no offense, Leo. I am referring to those without magic."

Leo waved off his comment with a grin.

"We are not prepared to fight dragons. We didn't stand a chance yesterday unless you've forgotten," Talon said, looking at all the faces of those gathered. He raised his hand to shade his eyes from the sun blazing overhead, even though the air was crisp and cool with the coming of fall.

Leo stood, "We have been fighting these adversaries for decades. Our trainers will be able to teach you - every one of you, man, woman, and child, how to evade and fight if needed," he said sternly.

Talon nodded, "We leave at dawn tomorrow. Anyone who wishes to come is welcome. We will have litters available for those who cannot walk. For those that wish to stay, we wish you all the safety and blessings that Iton and Oshan can bestow on you," he bowed deeply.

Murmurs and soft conversation broke out as everyone dispersed.

"That went about as well as I thought it would," Talon said, pinching the bridge of his nose with his forefinger and thumb.

"How many will join us?" Leo asked.

Talon looked at the many people eyeing him like a crazy man. Some stood with tears in their eyes, some looked furious. He slowly shook his head. "I don't know, Leo." He sighed "I truly don't."

Shaylee sat by herself with closed eyes, listening to the adults argue, Lyra on her lap purring contently.

"Fine vaskakat."

Tarrid's voice startled Shaylee, who jumped, causing Lyra to spring from her lap, hissing and digging her back claws into Shaylee's legs.

"Ow, Lyra, watch the claws." She grabbed hold of her legs, rubbing them.

"I'm sorry to startle both of you. My deepest apologies." He bowed deeply.

"It's okay," she said sweetly, as she glared daggers at him. "So, has my father agreed to leave here?" She asked.

Tar smiled, "Yes, I'm pleased your father agreed. I only hope most will follow him. Your father…" he paused, looking over his shoulder and then raised an eyebrow leaning forward. "Talon is a smart man."

He seemed unsure of his words. Shaylee narrowed her eyes, looking up at him. "My father is a smart man," she said without a doubt in her voice.

"May I?" He gestured at the ground beside her.

She nodded.

"Were you born in Threndy?"

She shook her head, "No, my parent's marriage was frowned upon. They lived alone and traveled a lot."

"Your father's a ranger, but what does your mother do? How long have you all lived here?"

"Mother would offer her healing abilities whenever they came near a village but never let anyone know they were a couple. It wasn't until after I was born that my father convinced the elders here to allow us to stay. They did so for 'the sake of the innocent baby.' It took me a long time to make friends."

He nodded, "But you do, right? Have friends? They survived?"

She sighed deeply, "Thankfully, yes. Amelia, she's an elf, was out gathering with her mother when they attacked; her father is out on patrol, and they don't know when he will return. Sparrow is a fairy; they stayed hidden in the trees."

"Do you think they will leave tomorrow?"

She shrugged, "I don't know about Amelia; with her father gone, I don't think they want to leave until he returns. Sparrow told me all the fairies were leaving. She doesn't know if they are joining your group or not, though."

He nodded, scratching his chin. "I didn't see many fairies in the group this morning."

"They live here with the elves but mostly keep to themselves. Safety in numbers, not by desire, I guess." She shrugged.

He nodded. A comfortable silence settled upon them until he asked again, "How are you feeling about all this?"

Shaylee shrugged her shoulder, "Confused, scared…" she trailed off and stared at Lyra flying toward her. Her tail was puffed up three times its normal size

"Is there something wrong?" He prodded.

She jerked, "Something's coming." She jumped to her feet. Lyra circled above her head, hissing.

"What do you mean something?" He stood and looked around, "How do you know?"

"Lyra smells something." Lyra screeched and dove, landing on Shaylee's shoulder. Shaylee's eyes grew wide as she got into panic mode, "The wyvern is coming back; it's almost here."

"How do you know that?"

"This is not the time or place. We have to warn everyone." Shaylee took off at a sprint, "FATHER!!" she yelled at the top of her lungs.

Talon rushed out of the council hut, "What's wrong?"

"The wyvern's coming back. Lyra smells it."

Talon's face grew pale, but it only took him a second to bounce back, "Is it alone?"

Shaylee paused briefly. "She doesn't smell anything else."

Talon nodded and started shouting orders. Everyone scattered into the forest. Houses and belongings could be replaced, but family members could not.

A loud roar shattered the calm morning.

Elves and fairies scattered in every direction, running for the safety and cover of the trees. It was happening.

The wyvern landed on top of the council hut. His back talons sank deeply into the sod roof with a loud crunch as the rafters were snapped in half.

Shaylee watched the scene unfold from her hiding place. Talon and Tarrid beside her.

The wyvern stretched his bat-like wings out wide and lifted his beak-like snout to the sky. When he opened his mouth to roar, lightning bolts shot into the heavens.

"I thought they were fire breathers," Shaylee looked at Tarrid with fearful eyes.

"Most wyverns and dragons are, but some have more than one attack."

When the wyvern inhaled finally, he lowered his head and looked around at the deserted village.

"RUNNING AND HIDING LIKE THE MICE YOU ARE," he yelled in slurring speech. "WHERE ARE YOUR SAVIORS NOW." His words echoed through the empty streets, met only by the silence of abandonment. A contemptuous sneer twisted his scaly visage as he widened his jaws, stretching them impossibly wide, reminiscent of a gigantic python unhinging its jaw. With a mighty exhale, an inferno erupted forth, a thick green foam that engulfed every structure below, igniting them in emerald flames that burned hotter than any blaze Shaylee had ever known. Even from her hiding place, she could feel the searing heat licking at her skin as the fire devoured the elven homes and consumed the surrounding trees.

When the wyvern finally closed its maw, most of the houses were nothing but smoldering ashes. He looked around the village again and emitted a strange sound that sounded somewhere between a laugh and a struggling cough. Nothing moved in the village except the wind and a few loose leaves. With a sharp bark-like chirp, he jumped off the council hut, smashing his spiked tail into it three times until it collapsed in a heap. He slowly circled the village before leaping into the air and flying north. When the sound of his wings was no longer audible, Lyra told Shaylee that it was all clear to come out.

Shaylee was the first to emerge from their hiding place, Lyra perched on her shoulder. Talon tried to grab her arm, but she moved too quickly. With his bow drawn, Tarrid jumped up and was beside her in a flash.

He made a quick survey of the village and the surrounding sky. When he was sure it was safe, he slung his bow over his back and quivered his arrow. Slowly, others from the village walked out from the forest, hand in hand. They solemnly looked at their burned town. Everything they owned was gone. There was nothing left to stay for.

Leo and Tar motioned for everybody to gather. Leo held his hand up until everybody was silent. "We are genuinely sorry that this has happened to your village. Everyone is welcome to come with us. Where we are going, we have plenty of resources, at the moment, to help you all."

Someone from the crowd's rear hollered, "Well, of course, we're coming with you. There's nothing left for us here, obviously. I can't speak for everybody, but my family will not be staying there long. This all just seems too convenient. We were attacked, and you encouraged us to leave our village. Most of us decide to stay, and then the village is leveled. If I didn't know any better, I'd say you perpetrated this."

"Samson, is that you?" Talon strained to see who had spoken. No one fessed up as to who the speaker was. "No one has to come with us, but those that do will not speak such. While I do not know these two gentlemen who have come to our aid. I do know about The Order of the Chosen, as I was one when I was young."

A collective gasp echoed through the crowd; Leo and Tar looked at him in surprise.

"The Order of the Chosen is a secretive society. They have the full blessing of Iton. They are not liars and only look out for those in need and strive for righteousness. Gather anything that you can; we leave in one hour."

In less than an hour, no one was left in the village. Most of the fairies had flown off independently, and several elven families went their own way. The rest of the villagers were quietly following their last elder into the unknown. Tarrid and Talon took point while Leo and a few younger Rangers brought up the rear.

Rosepetal and Fawn kept close to the middle of the group, but Shaylee insisted on staying with Talon.

"How long until we reach your village?" Shaylee asked Tarrid.

"The village is a couple of hard days' ride from here. At our current pace, it's over a week." He wiped the sweat from his forehead. "Our camp isn't far; that is where we are heading first. I could make it by midday tomorrow, but traveling at this pace will take us a couple of days."

They pushed on as fast and far as possible for three days before Tarrid announced they would be at his camp that evening.

The camp was little more than a ring of a dozen tents, a string of twenty horses, and a large fire pit.

"Welcome to my home." Tarrid smiled for a second then his smile faded, "Well, home for now anyway," Tarrid gestured broadly with his arms.

Several men and a couple of women–all elves that Shaylee could tell–came out to greet them. They quickly took action and got everyone set up next to a tent, if not in it, and brought food and drink for everyone.

The rest of the evening was spent recovering from their journey and reflecting on what they had just been through. That night, the sounds of people having nightmares from all around the camp kept Shaylee awake.

Lyra slept curled in a ball next to Shaylee, utterly oblivious to the sounds around her.

Shaylee was still awake as the sky started to brighten. At the edge of the camp, she saw several sentries walking the perimeter and tending to the smaller fires. Tarrid exited his tent and relieved one of them. He made one complete loop around the camp, stoking up a few of the fires before sitting on a large rock.

Leaving Lyra sleeping, she slowly made her way over to Tarrid. She was almost upon him when he spoke.

"Can't sleep?"

She stutter-stepped, caught off guard. A small smile crept onto her lips. *He didn't even turn around.* Without answering, she climbed up the rock and sat next to him. "How did you know it was me?"

He shrugged, "You wouldn't believe me."

"Try me."

He turned to look at her, "I could sense you. It was like I could see your shadow in the back of my mind."

Shaylee smiled shyly, "Why do you have so many fires set up? They don't seem to serve a purpose, no one is sitting around them," Shaylee asked.

"It's an old Ranger trick. We need to be either completely unseen or give the illusion of a larger force. Wyverns will attack smaller groups. Perimeter fires serve two purposes, make us look like a large gathering and combat fire blindness."

She gave him a puzzled look, "Fire blindness?"

"When you sit close to a fire, you can't see what is coming at you, but they can see you. Perimeter fires illuminate the entire area, so you are not blinded by a single fire."

"Huh. I never learned that."

They sat in silence until the sun fully crested the eastern horizon. Shaylee was leaning backward, her hands resting on the boulder behind her, and was just about to nod off when Tar spoke.

"How did your family find themselves far from the village before the attack? And some of the other families said they had advance warning as well. Who gave that warning?"

Shaylee jerked awake and sat up straight, "Umm…," she trailed off, rubbing her eyes.

"Shaylee!" Talon called from across the camp.

Her eyes opened wide, "That's my father. I have to go. Talk to you later," she vaulted from the boulder and sprinted across the compound.

"Strange elf," he muttered to himself.

"I don't think she's an elf and definitely not a fairy," Leo said, walking up behind him.

Tar shook his head, "The only non-elf that can sneak up on an elf," he chuckled.

"Taught by the best." He bowed. "Find out anything?"

"No, I waited too long to ask any questions. I will, though." Leo looked at him with his head half-cocked. "What? I will. Don't you have someplace to be?"

Leo barked out a laugh, "She's just a kid, you know."

Tar looked at his friend with his jaw dropped, "I wasn't thinking anything like that."

"Sure, you weren't," Leo kept laughing as he walked around the encampment.

Tar frowned at his friend's back. *Well, what if I was thinking that?* He thought to himself. *We're about the same age.*

Movement caught his eye as Shaylee's vaskakat took to the air. She was snow white with black points, a very striking coloring. The vaska soared close to the trees, changed directions suddenly, and dove into the underbrush, only to emerge a moment later with a fat vole in her mouth. She took flight once again and disappeared into the camp.

He surveyed the waking camp and watched the newcomers mingle with his fellow followers. Everyone's faces were a mixture of fear and relief.

In the distance, he saw Shaylee speaking with Talon. The fairy and the young elf were with them. Shaylee took the young elf's hand and turned to walk in his direction. Talon and the fairy started to argue, throwing their hands toward the two girls. The fairy's hands shot upward, and a small show of magic shot from them; Talon backed away briefly before closing the gap between them and wrapping the fairy in his arms. She crumbled into him, hugging him back.

Shaylee and the young elf were heading in his direction, right to him, as a matter of fact.

"Tarrid, I have a favor to ask you," Shaylee said when they approached.

"Please, just call me Tar; what can I do for you?"

"Teach us to fight with magic."

"Both of you?" He said, surprised.

She nodded, "My father taught me the bow and the staff, and he started Fawn's magic training. But we need more, now more than ever."

"Is your father okay with this?"

She nodded again.

"And your mother?"

She shrugged. "She will be; it just takes her longer to come around to new ideas."

"OK, well, my shift ends in about an hour. I will meet you here then."

Both girls nodded with serious, grim looks on their faces, trying to hide their excitement.

CHAPTER -26-

"OKAY, let's see what you know, and then I'll know what to teach you. I have four targets set up," Tarrid gestured to a row of trees with painted circles on the trunks. "These are set at twenty, forty, and sixty yards. And then two hundred yards, way out there."

"Two hundred yards, that's an impossible shot!" Shaylee exclaimed.

"We'll see. You first, Shaylee," he smirked.

Shaylee grabbed her bow and quiver and approached where he gestured to stand. She steadied her breathing, looked at the first target, nocked her arrow, took aim, and let loose—Bullseye. She smiled at Tar; he did not comment, and his posture was stiff. She steadied her heartbeat and aimed at the next one. Bullseye, again, no comment from Tar; Fawn clapped loudly, though. *Fine, I'll show him,* she thought.

Calm your thoughts; this is not a time to show off and brag. Just do it, Lyra's voice drifted into her thoughts.

Shaylee rolled her eyes and took a deep breath. She held the breath while she aimed. She let out half, held it, and let loose. She missed the bullseye but was still within the circle.

"Good," Tar finally spoke, "now the two-hundred yards."

She huffed, "Come on. That's impossible. You're just setting me up to miss," she repeated herself.

Tar just stared at her.

"Fine," she mumbled as she gazed into the distance. The circle on the tree was probably the same size as the last three, but from this distance, it looked tiny. Knowing she would have to aim higher, much higher than where she wanted the arrow to land, she chose a small branch in the tree. She repeated her memorized routine and then let her arrow fly. Her arrow fell short of the tree. She turned to Tar. "See," she said.

Tar looked puzzled but said nothing to her. He grabbed his arrow, took aim, and fired before he even stopped moving. She watched as his arrow sailed through the air and landed with a satisfying *thwack* into the red circle on the far tree.

"How did you do that?"

"Oh wow!" Fawn exclaimed.

He looked at her, his puzzled expression deepening. "It's just like any other shot. I used my magic to help the flight; you just have to concentrate a little harder to get it to travel that far. If you had used magic, you would have hit the two-hundred-yard tree."

Shaylee looked at the ground.

"What?" He asked.

Shaylee continued to look down at the ground, not speaking. Finally, Fawn walked up. "Her magic just manifested the day of the attack," she said quietly, "because she's a mixed breed."

Tar's eyes grew wide, "So, you never use magic to assist your flights?"

"No, sir," she replied quietly.

Tar smiled and used a finger to lift her chin to force her to look him in the eye, "That's nothing to be ashamed about. Actually, it's quite impressive." His expression showed his surprise, he nodded with an eyebrow raised. "We will work on other techniques until you master control of your magic."

She looked down to the ground when he removed his hand, "I should already have control at my age."

"Magic doesn't appear at the same age for everyone," he said in a kind voice.

"But I'm thirteen. I'm so much older than I should be. My parents told me my magic will be unpredictable since I'm a cross."

"That makes sense." He shrugged. "How long have you been working with yours, Fawn?"

"Going on six years."

"Six years? I've never heard of one so young. Manifesting powers at six?"

Fawn shrugged, "Magic runs early in my family."

"How are you with the bow?"

"Talon has only just now started teaching me. I might be able to hit the first target."

"Has he been teaching you how to augment?"

Fawn shook her head, "No, he said I needed to learn strength, skill, and accuracy first."

"That was very smart of him. I've met many an elf who couldn't hit the broadside of a hut without using their magic."

He handed her the bow and an arrow and gestured for her to try it. Fawn steadied her breathing as Talon had instructed. She raised the bow, aimed, and released. She hit the tree but just outside the circle.

"We will continue working on your strength and accuracy before I teach you to augment." He turned to Shaylee, "As for you, we will start gauging your magic." Tar looked up and saw Leo heading their way; he raised his hand and motioned for him to hurry.

Leo jogged over, "What's the matter?"

"Just target practice. Fawn here is learning archery. I'm going to work with Shaylee with her magic. Can you help Fawn with her accuracy?" Tar pointed to the tree.

"This is what… twenty yards?" Leo asked. "That's not a bad spot. At least you hit the tree. How long have you been working with archery?"

"Only a couple of weeks."

He grabbed an extra bow and started working with Fawn. Tar beckoned Shaylee to follow him. He took her back to the boulder they had been sitting on earlier in the morning. But instead of sitting on the boulder, he sat behind it, hidden from the camp's view. Sitting cross-legged, he straightened his back, rolled his shoulders, and neck a couple of times to loosen them. He then placed the backs of his hands on his knees and nodded to Shaylee. She sat down, mimicking his posture.

"Whenever you're doing anything that requires accuracy, whether a weapon, a craft, or magic, centering yourself and focus is primary. When you started your weapons training, I imagine Talon taught you to clear your mind and focus on the task." Shaylee nodded. "Good, magic is the same way. Elves, fairies, and human sorcerers have it easier than witches and mages. We are born with magic. We do not have to learn how to do magic; we only have to learn how to control it. Much the same way that we learn to speak and walk. We are born knowing we will eventually do these things, but perfecting it takes time and practice. You would not expect a newborn to sprint a hundred yards, nor do we expect somebody whose magic has just manifested to be able to do everything someone ten or even twenty years older can do." Shaylee smiled and shook her head. "Good." Tar said. "And remember that using magic takes energy just like any other task. If you overexert yourself, you can cause harm."

"That makes sense," Shaylee agreed.

"Now close your eyes, focusing on your breathing."

Shaylee closed her eyes and slowed her heart rate and breathing as her father had taught her.

She felt a soft breeze flow across her skin; she heard birds chirping and squirrels chattering in the trees, and all her senses came alive. Every touch, every smell, every sound was amplified.

She marveled at how fragrant the flora around them was. The rich smell of bark coming from the redwoods and madrone trees. A faeberry bush was close, she could smell its sweetness. The sounds from the camp reached her ears next. She could hear the soft voices of conversations and the laughter of the children playing games.

A tiny insect landed on her hand. She ignored the urge to wipe it away and concentrated on the touch of every one of its legs. She could hear its tiny wings carrying it across the sky when it flew away. A small smile tugged at the corner of her lips.

Tarrid watched her relax and slip into Schen. "When magic first awakens, there is a period of adjustment to the new life inside you. You must bring your whole being into a state of calm and oneness, the Schen. Then and only then will the magic flow and follow directions. Schen takes time to nurture at first until it becomes second nature like breathing," he whispered softly.

She nodded slightly before starting to rock gently from side to side.

"Picture your right hand in your mind's eye." Her fingers twitched. "Now, picture your fingertips glowing. Just light, no heat, no flame. Just a gentle glow."

Shaylee concentrated on her fingers. "Just a gentle glow," she mumbled. Her brow furrowed and sweat beaded her forehead. She focused until she was breathing hard.

"Open your eyes and take a deep breath," Tarrid said gently.

She opened her eyes and saw him smiling at her.

"I failed. Why are you smiling?"

"You did well for your first time; I could see when you reached Schen, when you relaxed and opened yourself. Could you feel the roll of your magic just under the surface?" She nodded. "I couldn't feel your magic, but I think you almost had it. The level you were just at takes some elves months to achieve."

Shaylee frowned. Lyra appeared out of nowhere; she swooped down and landed on Shaylee's lap.

Try it again, she projected, ***and this time, grab your horn.***

Shaylee nodded and closed her eyes; she stroked Lyra's soft, fluffy fur and reached up to the horn under her shirt. She grabbed the horn but left it hidden.

"Take a break. You don't need to try again today. We will try again in the morning. You need rest."

Suddenly, Shaylee's hand ignited in blinding white light. Tarrid grabbed his cloak beside him and threw it over her hand to snuff out the light. "How did you do that?"

She looked at him wide-eyed, "I don't know, I just did as you told me." She released her hold on her shirt and scratched her vaskakat's chin.

He looked at the vaskakat and then at Shaylee, *It was almost like… no*, he shook his head. *Elves and fairies don't have familiars; certainly, a hybrid couldn't. That is strictly a human thing.*

"Did I do well, though?"

He snapped out of his thoughts, "Yes, extremely. Better than anyone I know for their second attempt. Are you sure you've never done this before?"

She shook her head.

"Explain what happened when your magic first manifested."

Shaylee blanched, "I don't really know what happened."

"Just try; it will help me. I've never met an Elvenfae, but I believe that is what your mother said you prefer to be called." She nodded. "Your magic is all new; I want to understand so I can help you."

Tell him it'll be ok.

She nodded, "I was delivering a message from my father to one of the outposts. After delivering it, I was returning when I heard a frightful roar. Lyra flew back to see what was going on. She relayed what she saw…"

"How?" he interrupted, his eyebrows raising.

"At the time, she could send me pictures of what she saw. We used to have to touch foreheads to transfer the images, but we started being able to send them when we couldn't even see each other. Suddenly, I could hear her voice in my head. It was weak at first, but it quickly grew stronger." Shaylee had closed her eyes while reliving what had transpired. "Lyra told me to hide and then told me to pick up a unicorn horn," without thinking, she pulled it out of her shirt. "Lyra told me to picture myself as being invisible. She told me the horn would do the rest. The trolls and the ogre walked passed me, and they couldn't even see me. At this point, I was desperate to get back to the village to warn everyone. Lyra told me to picture the village in my head and will myself there.

"Suddenly, I was standing in my kitchen. I told my parents of the attack. My father tried to warn the village, but nobody believed him. So, my father did the only thing he could do. He took us, and we fled." She finally opened her eyes and looked at Tar. She narrowed her eyes and groaned, rolling her shoulders, "I knew I shouldn't have told you. You don't believe me."

He tried to smooth his features and placed his hand over the top of hers, "It's not that I don't believe you." He hesitated momentarily, "This is just something I've never heard of an elf or fairy being able to do. I have heard of sorcerers being able to do what you described, but you are not a human."

She pulled her hand away, her face flushing with anger. "You don't have to make fun of me. I know I'm different—some strange freak to be made fun of—but I have feelings."

Hurt flashed across his face, "I am in no way making fun of you. Your magic is something new and unique. I would love to be able to help you on your journey of developing your magic if you will let me." He scratched his head, "It will take some time knowing that you can do things I didn't think possible."

Shaylee frowned and looked down at Lyra. When she looked up, her face was more at peace, "I'm willing to try if you are," she said.

"For the time being, I think we should keep the fact that your magic has manifested a secret; your village has been through so much, and times are changing so rapidly. I don't know how anybody will handle something so new," he said cautiously.

She nodded enthusiastically, "I'm so glad you said that. My whole life has been a secret. I want to keep it that way for as long as possible."

"That's good; then it's settled. Since you seem to have the abilities that sorcerers do, I think Leo should also help, though. "

"He's a sorcerer?"

Tar nodded.

"If you think it might help, I prefer fewer people knowing."

"Okay, I will see what I can do for now." He grabbed her hand again. "I won't tell anyone else without speaking to you first."

Shaylee smiled, "Okay, then, should we meet here at the same time tomorrow?"

He nodded, looking into her brown eyes. The green flecks in her eyes caught the sunlight and seemed to dance in time with his heartbeat.

"Are you ok?" She asked him, tilting her head slightly to one side.

"Um, yeah, just not much sleep lately; see you tomorrow."

Shaylee smiled and patted him on the shoulder before skipping over to where Fawn awaited her.

Leo walked over and sat on top of the boulder. His face was neutral as his eyes scanned the forest.

"What? Out with it," Tar snapped, jumping up.

Leo held his hands out, "I didn't say anything."

Tar squinted his eyes; he could tell Leo was having difficulty keeping his composure. "Say what's on your mind."

"It's nothing; it's just that you looked like you were having a pretty intense moment there."

"What?" He looked at him in disbelief. "It was just a magic lesson, that's all. Her magic hasn't fully surfaced yet, and I was just giving her some pointers."

Leo frowned.

He rolled his eyes, "What now?"

"Fawn told me she teleported into her kitchen and can speak to her vaskakat. That sounds like some intense magic and quite unusual for an elf fairy."

Tar briefly looked at Leo and scanned the camp to see if Shaylee was nearby. He saw her across the camp, walking into the medical tent with Fawn.

"You must keep this between us. She doesn't want anyone to know about her powers. She has some unique abilities, and as you said, not ones common amongst elves or fairies, more like a…" he trailed off.

"A sorceress," Leo finished for him.

Tar nodded, "I don't know what to think. She says her mother said her powers will be unique like she is."

"Do you think they are her birth parents?"

He shrugged, "I have no evidence to the contrary right now. I will see how I can train her, but it will be in secret. I told her you may need to assist, but she can't know I told you any of this before she's ready."

Leo nodded and placed a hand on his shoulder. "You have my word, brother."

CHAPTER -27-

INSIDE the medical tent, Fawn hurried to her mother's side. "How are you today, Ma?"

Flora looked at her daughter with tears in her eyes. "Same as always," she replied.

"Then why are you so sad?"

"You are growing into such a beautiful woman, and I'm missing it."

Fawn gently hugged her mother. A handkerchief floated out of Fawn's pocket into her hand. She wiped her mother's eyes and then her own.

"I see you are developing fine control."

Fawn nodded, "Talon's been teaching me. Today, I started learning how to properly shoot a bow," she said proudly.

"Truly? The elders are allowing it?"

Shaylee stepped forward, "My father is the eldest now, ma'am. We have left the village and joined a group of… I guess you can call them rebels."

Flora nodded, "I was told we moved; I am glad they made me sleep for the journey."

Shaylee nodded and sighed, "They thought it would be best given your and the other's conditions." Shaylee and others had questioned that decision, thinking it was not kind, treating them like infants and toddlers. She was happy to know no hard feelings were being expressed.

"I need some rest, but I expect you to visit me daily," Flora said.

"Of course, ma. Of course. Get some rest."

The two girls quietly exited the medical tent together. Fawn stopped and turned to look at the tent flap. A beautiful silver fox with an enormous bushy tail tipped in blue was portrayed standing proudly over the doorway. Rei, the Blessing of Wellness, stood guard to protect the sick. Her striking blue eyes looking for illnesses to defeat.

"Ahara will look after your ma, Fawn," Shaylee said when she noticed Fawn's hesitation.

"I know. The Goddess of Healing and her spirit helper will heal them in their time." Fawn nodded and gave Shaylee a tight smile.

At daybreak the next day, Shaylee sat on the boulder, waiting for Tar to finish his watch. He saw her from a distance, "Okay," he mumbled to himself. "I can do this. I can keep this professional. She's only thirteen, Tarrid. Keep your thoughts on the task at hand. She's not the first pretty elf you've seen." He sighed, "Only the most beautiful Elvenfae I've ever seen." He squared his shoulders and forced himself to walk over to her.

Shaylee's whole face lit up when she saw him coming in her direction.

"What do you have planned for today?" she asked. Lyra meowed at him while she soared overhead. Shaylee reached into her shirt and pulled out the small unicorn horn she had tethered around her neck.

"I was thinking about keeping it simple. Every elf learns how to make light first. We tried that yesterday, but I want it to be controlled and with intent this time."

Shaylee nodded as she hopped off the boulder and sat on the ground, hidden from the camp.

She readied her breath and thoughts while waiting for instruction.

"Now, I want you to create a sun-orb, just a small one."

She nodded, moved one hand to grasp the horn, and wiggled the fingers of her free hand. Slowly, a small light bloomed on her fingertips; the glow grew and swirled until it formed a small ball of bright purple light.

"Good, now hold it and open your eyes."

"Oh, it's purple!" She exclaimed.

"Were you thinking about a color?"

"No, I don't think so," she frowned.

"Well, now I want you to think about a color."

The orb slowly turned purple to blue then pink and yellow, and finally white.

"Very good."

They spent the next hour moving the glowing ball out of her hand to hover in front of her and then move it to various places nearby.

He called for a break when sweat started to bead on her forehead.

Over the next few days, they worked on similar items, and each day, he was more and more impressed with the level of control she could exhibit and how quickly she caught on to his lessons.

By the end of the week, one of their long-range sentries returned, saying there had been another attack and that they were currently tracking the wyvern. Several members of The Order prepared to leave at once.

Shaylee had thought that Tar would stay behind and continue to mentor her, but she found him outside his tent fully packed. "You're going with them? What about my lessons?"

"You're doing just fine. A small break won't do you any harm. Just keep working on the lessons I've already taught you, and I'll be back before you know it."

"But will you?" she said with a slight pout.

He stopped and reached for her hand. "I'll be back; this is just routine. There's nothing to worry about."

Shaylee nodded once and sniffled, "OK."

Tar didn't know what to do, pat her on the head like a little kid, or hug her tight and never let go. He decided on a gentle bump on her shoulder and lifted her chin so she would look at him, "I'll see you soon."

She nodded, turned, and ran away.

Tarrid watched her fleeing form and sighed; he was not a romantic by any stretch of the imagination. *Did I handle that right?* He thought. *Will she hate me? Will she wait for me? What am I saying? She's only thirteen. Get a hold of yourself.* He groaned audibly, "Keep your head in the game," he mumbled.

Shaylee watched as Leo, Tar, and a dozen others left the camp in the early morning light; no one knew when they would return.

Hours later, she was still sitting in the same spot when Fawn found her.

"Are you just going to sit here all day, or will we train?"

Startled out of her daydream, Shaylee turned to look at her, "What do you mean train?"

"I saw Tarrid working with you and your magic. I don't see any reason why we can't continue what he started. And I'm sure your father will help. You haven't spoken much about what happened before the attack, but I think now is the time."

Shaylee chuckled, "When did you start sounding like an adult?"

Fawn shrugged, grabbed Shaylee's hand, and yanked her off the boulder. Together, they walked back to the camp to find Talon.

During the next several days, they fell into an easy routine. Shaylee would help Fawn with her archery without using magic, and Fawn and Talon would help Shaylee learn control over her magic. It was frustrating, as her magic didn't work like theirs. They both shrugged it off, saying it was the fairy magic mixing with the elven. But even when Rosepetal tried to help and guide her using fairy magic, it just didn't seem quite right. She couldn't feel them using their magic, and they couldn't feel hers either.

"Don't let this discourage you," Rosepetal told Shaylee one morning. "It'll get easier. I'm sure of it. You'll get the hang of it."

Shaylee sighed and nodded, "I know, Mother. I have to try harder."

Weeks and months passed before Tarrid, Leo, and the others returned. The leaves were changing into the brilliant autumn colors of oranges and reds.

The weary group arrived early in the morning; all were bruised, some were limping and bandaged, and a few were missing. The camp was immediately awake, fires lit, and breakfast prepared.

The Order of the Chosen members huddled closely together to hear the news. Talon and a few from Threndy were also invited to the meeting.

Tar stood to direct all eyes to him. When the crowd hushed, he hung his head in silent prayer; all The Order's members mirrored him. After a few moments, he looked up and addressed the crowd.

"We lost three of our brothers-in-arms. They fought bravely; we would not have been victorious without their sacrifice. We stopped three ogres, eight trolls, and two wyverns." Everyone was quiet. They didn't know whether to celebrate the stopping of their enemies or feel sorrow for the lost brothers.

"Unfortunately, we did not stop all that we faced. Aggression is increasing, and more villages are being attacked. Our methods worked in the past, but they are insufficient for the new level of threats. Time for action is upon us. We need allies. We need to take the fight to them. Living in fear and only acting when the fight has already begun will lead to our demise."

Several people spoke up at once, shouting and crying in angry voices. Tar held up his hand, asking for quiet. An older member of The Order stood and waited patiently to be called on. Tar locked eyes with him and then motioned for him to speak.

"I have been a member of The Order of the Chosen longer than most of you have been alive. And while I know that we have always chosen those with the strongest magic to lead us and you, Tarrid, are well on your way to becoming a full Shepherd of Iton, a little wisdom shared occasionally is needed. We have always been the champions of the downtrodden and the ones who were always available to clean up the mess. We have been chosen for this high honor. We do not start wars."

Leo bolted to his feet, "That is true, brother; we do not start wars, but is there anything in the doctrine that says we cannot finish one?" He paused briefly, "If we keep doing what we are doing, we will lose. And when The Order falls, who will be left to clean up the mess? As you stated, who will be left to provide refuge for the downtrodden? Chapter one is over; the war has already begun. Now is the time to start a new chapter, and we must be the main characters."

"And how do you propose we start this next chapter?" A woman from The Order stood and asked, "We are just a small fraction of The Order; we do not dictate for all."

"You are correct; I will go to the Sanctum of Iton and speak to the High Shepherd himself. Along the way, I will gather as many supporters as I can. We will make them see that the time for action is upon us," Tar stated.

"And if they say no?" Somebody in the crowd shouted.

"They will not say no!"

As the sun set, Tar found Shaylee out by his makeshift archery range, working with Fawn at twenty and sixty yards. Fawn was hitting every target within the faded bullseye ring. Shaylee was hitting everything in the very center of the ring.

He clapped his hands as he approached; they both stopped and smiled. "Can either of you hit the two-hundred-yard?"

Shaylee shook her head, but Fawn beamed. Fawn grabbed her next arrow, took a steadying breath, knocked, and released. Tar could see the shimmering around her arrow as she guided it toward the distant target. With a satisfying thud, her arrow found the very center of the bullseye.

"Excellent, Fawn." He turned to Shaylee, "Have you tried?"

She sighed, "I just can't feel the magic that Fawn is using; I can't duplicate it. My father has also tried to teach me, but I can't sense what they're doing for some reason. It's very frustrating. If I am given verbal instructions and told what to do with some tasks, I can do it, but when asked to copy the feeling, I don't feel anything."

"I think it might be time to speak with Leo. Maybe he has some insight being a sorcerer."

Shaylee gave him an exasperated look. "How can a sorcerer help an elvenfae?"

"I don't know, but it's worth trying, right?"

Lyra hissed at her from her perch in a tree branch above them. Shaylee looked up and narrowed her eyes. Lyra hissed again and then opened her mouth. A stream of something bluish-white came out and streaked toward her, hitting her on the shoulder. Shaylee jumped backward, rubbing her shoulder, "Lyra that was cold, ouch. When did you get ice breath?" Lyra growled down at her. "Fine!" Shaylee threw her hands in the air, "What could it hurt? Call Leo, let's see if he can help me."

Tar raised his fingers to his lips and let out a shrill whistled; it was an ear-splitting sharp whistle that made Shaylee and Fawn abruptly cover their ears.

"What in the world was that?" Fawn screeched.

"That's my 'get over here immediately' whistle for Leo. It can be heard over a great distance," he smiled.

"How about a little warning next time?" Both girls said simultaneously.

An answering whistle pierced the air as Leo sprinted toward Tar. "What's wrong?" he asked in a panic.

"Nothing, I just needed you to help me with something."

Leo frowned, "You know that whistle's only for emergencies." He crossed his arms over his chest.

"This is an emergency," Tar explained, "We have a magic emergency."

Leo tilted his head slightly, "Magic emergency?" He asked with a half-smile.

"As you know, Shaylee is a unique blend of elf and fairy."

"Okay," he said, drawing out the syllables.

"She is just now starting to gain control over her magic, but she's having problems feeling elf and fairy magic. They each must be blocking each other."

"That makes sense. I guess. I'm not sure how I'm supposed to help with that."

"Well, I just have a theory, so hear me out. If Shaylee is given instructions on what to do, she can complete the task, but when asked to watch how something is done, she cannot see it or feel it. When I do something with my magic, can you see or feel it?"

"No, I just see it being done if it has a visual effect," Leo answered.

"Okay, well, let's try something." Tar took his bow, knocked an arrow, and aimed at the two-hundred-yard target. "Did you see my magic around the arrow?"

Leo shook his head, "No, didn't see a thing. Just an arrow flying impossibly straight through the air. What about you, Fawn?" Leo asked.

"Oh yes, when Tar or any other elf uses their magic, I see a shimmer around it. Can you use magic to make your arrow go further?"

Leo nodded and then demonstrated; Shaylee sucked in a sharp breath. She could feel and see his magic. Leo looked over at Fawn, "Did you see anything?"

"No, only like you said, an arrow flying impossibly straight but no shimmer. What about you, Shaylee? Did you see anything?"

She hesitated, afraid to answer, not sure what it meant that she could actually see a human's magic.

"What's the matter?" Tar asked, "It's okay. You're among friends. Did you see anything?"

She nodded, "I could see and feel something."

Leo's face fell, and Tar's lit up. "What did you feel?"

"It's hard to explain, but I could see the magic leave Leo's hands and travel with the arrow. And it was almost like I could feel a heaviness in the air. Does that make any sense?"

Leo and Tar shared a look, "It sounds exactly like what a sorcerer feels when another human magic user is doing magic, and we can tell who is casting it."

Now it was Shaylee's turn to frown, "Why did you use that word? Human magic user? And not just sorcerers. That is what you are, isn't it?"

"Yes, I am a sorcerer. But I'm also referred to as a natural magic user. With humans, you are born with the full flame of magic and referred to as a sorcerer or sorceress, or you're born with a spark of magic. Those people are called witches or mages, and they can learn how to harness magic through spell-words and by using a magical artifact like a wand." He continued, "As a sorcerer, I can feel magic being cast by any other human, know who cast the spell if they're in the vicinity, and I can tell what magic was cast. I instantly know what they did and how to do it.

"A witch, on the other hand, will be able to feel the magic being cast, and if they're strong enough, they can tell who cast it, but they will not be able to duplicate it without being taught the spell word that controls it. And not everything that a sorcerer can do can be tied to a spell word, so they are very limited in their abilities."

"Well, why was I able to feel what you did? I am not a human and certainly not a sorceress."

"I don't know," Leo admitted, "Maybe your unique blend of magic more closely mirrors the natural magic a human has; nobody knows exactly where or how humans first got their magic. Some say with the help of dragons, but maybe we have elf and fairy blood from thousands of years ago. Do you think you could mimic what I did?"

Shaylee thought back to what she witnessed. "Maybe if I saw it again?" Leo nodded and shot another arrow. Shaylee could feel the magic, and almost like a tiny bolt of lightning hitting her deep in her core, she knew she could do it. She grabbed her bow and an arrow. Her hands were shaking; she tried to steady her breath and heartbeat, finding it more challenging than usual. She remembered the feeling of the magic she just witnessed, concentrated on her arrow, and told it to fly straight. She barely felt her fingers leave the string as she watched her arrow fly straight and true and smack into the distant tree.

Fawn hollered and jumped for joy, "You did it, Shaylee! You did it. This is wonderful." Fawn looked at her and furrowed her brows, "Why don't you look happy?"

She shook her head, "I don't know. This is all just so new. Leo, would you be willing to assist me more?"

"I would be happy to."

Her parents weren't happy during the first two days of Shaylee's new lesson plan. The idea that a human could help their daughter better than them did not sit well with them. Talon argued at first, saying it wasn't possible. Rosepetal accepted it more readily but seemed deeply saddened that she couldn't help.

Over the next couple of days, Shaylee's ability improved dramatically with the help of Tar and Leo.

Just when she was getting used to the daily lessons and looking forward to spending time with Leo, Tar, and Fawn without her parents' constant scrutiny, it ended with Tar announcing it was time for him to travel to the Sanctuary of Iton.

"How long will you be gone this time?" Shaylee asked.

"I'm not sure; traveling straight to the Sanctum will take me about a week…"

"So, about three weeks?" Fawn interrupted.

He shook his head, "No, I really need to find others that feel the same way we do. We must convince the High Shepherd that this is the right direction for our continued survival."

"If the war is escalated, won't that kill more?" Shaylee pried.

"Maybe, maybe not. So many of us are dying every year anyway; we need to take the fight to them if we have any chance of ending this."

Shaylee hung her head, "Okay, I see your point."

Fawn looked at Shaylee with her mouth open, "That's all you're going to say? You're going to let him go?"

Shaylee looked at Fawn, "I can't stop him."

"You can try!" her voice elevated. Her eyes filled with tears that started to stream down her cheeks.

"It will be ok, Fawn. Leo and I will return."

"You don't know that. You can't say that," she yelled and ran off.

Tar started to follow, but Shaylee stopped him.

"She just needs time; I think she sees you as a big brother or father figure. Her father never returned from his last patrol." She pressed her lips, "Just be safe and return to us."

Tar stared into Shaylee's glistening eyes, "I will, I promise."

She gave him a lingering hug before she sprinted off after Fawn.

CHAPTER -28-

WINTER in Threndy had always been a challenge—keeping walkways clear, water sources free of ice, and ensuring food stores lasted the entire winter. The camp proved to be much more difficult. It lacked any permanent structures, and tents had to be constantly brushed off to keep snow accumulation from seeping through.

The Order's warriors were not farmers and had to forage and hunt for everything. So, foraging and hunting continued throughout the long winter.

The newest experience for both Shaylee and Fawn was the scarcity of food. Sure, they had been hungry if they missed a meal, but missing two or three days at a time was new and foreign.

Talon tried to keep their spirits up by making sure they practiced their magic every day. Shaylee and Fawn both grew in their control and abilities, but Fawn seemed to grow faster, which frustrated Shaylee.

When spring arrived, one of Tars's group returned, a fairy named Lark. Everyone rushed out of the tents to meet her, sadness in their eyes that she was the only one to return. She held a hand up to quiet the murmurs.

"Don't worry, everyone is fine. We've sustained some injuries but no losses. We have been traveling all winter and successfully found numerous groups that will join us."

"Why have you returned, Lark?" Someone shouted.

"There have been numerous attacks, and the wyverns have been increasing their aggression. I am here to lead all of you to a more permanent location where others will join us. Everyone pack as fast as you can. Let's try to leave tomorrow."

The camp came alive; their belongings and the little food they had left were packed. The following morning, the tents were broken down, as the sun climbed in the sky. The morning air was light and crisp with a breeze stirring through the still bare tree branches.

Soon everyone was ready to go. The gathered group of close to fifty stood waiting for Lark to lead them. The sick elves were being strapped to stretchers and getting ready to travel as well.

Shaylee saw her father speaking with Lark in the distance. He had a grim expression as he approached Shaylee, standing next to her mother. Shaylee looked around for Fawn and waved her over.

"What's going on, father?" Shaylee asked when he arrived.

"I told them that we will not be joining them."

"What?" Shaylee and Fawn both yelled at the same time.

"We must go and make our own lives. Your mother and I traveled through these forests for years before you were born, Shaylee. We will find a new home."

"What about me?" Fawn asked, panicked. "What about my mother?"

"Your mother has requested that she go with The Chosen. I assume you will want to go with her, but of course, you are welcome to stay with us."

"Of course, I want to stay with her, but I don't want to leave you either." Her face flushed.

"I'm staying with Fawn," Shaylee announced.

Rosepetal shot into the air, her wings moving like a hummingbird's. "You will do no such thing!" She exclaimed crossing her arms across her chest.

"I'm sorry, mother and father, but I want to help. I need to help. I can't explain it, but I am supposed to do this."

"You are only thirteen. How do you know what you are supposed to do?" Rosepetal shouted.

Talon touched Rosepetal's arm and gently pulled her to the ground.

"We stick together," he began. Shaylee opened her mouth to argue, but he continued before she could, "We will stay with The Chosen."

Rosepetal's eyes and hands started to glow, and her hair rose all around her. Shaylee stared at her mother like she'd never seen her before. The apparition before her was angry and ugly. Rosepetal's features twisted in a snarl of hatred aimed at Shaylee.

"Rosepetal!" Talon said sternly. Her gaze shifted to him; Talon's hands were held before him, ready to cast if needed.

Her features softened immediately, and she crumbled to the ground sobbing.

Shaylee rushed to her side after a brief moment of indecision.

"I'm so sorry, Shaylee, I'm so sorry," Rosepetal sobbed.

Shaylee had always heard that you should never anger a fairy, but until now, she didn't know why. All the fairies she knew were kind-hearted and carefree. She had never seen an angry one before; it was pretty terrifying.

"It's… ok." She struggled to bring herself to say 'ma.' She looked at the fairy, sitting on the ground with tears running from her eyes.

"How can you say that? You want to stay here and learn how to fight."

She pressed her lips. "I don't want to; I-I have to."

Rosepetal sniffled, looking up at her, and nodded, "I know."

Shaylee looked at her, puzzled.

"I've always known you were bound for great things. You are special, my wonderful, found miracle."

Talon carefully cradled her in his arms and lifted her off the ground. "Grab your bags, girls; we don't want to be last."

Talon slung his and Rosepetal's bags over his shoulder while still carrying Rosepetal. She sobbed quietly into his shoulder.

It took almost a week of hard days before they spotted sentries sitting in trees. Happy faces whistled and waved as the group slowly walked underneath them.

"How much further?" Fawn asked.

Talon glanced into the trees and nodded at the two sentries. "Lark said two days past the first sentries."

"Two days? That's a big perimeter," Shaylee remarked.

The forest was heavily wooded, which made following the trail difficult. The game trails they used were only wide enough for them to walk in a single file. Lark had made it abundantly clear that they could not widen the paths by even one leaf.

One of the sentries jumped out of his tree and took up the rear. Fawn watched him intently as he cast a spell to remove their footprints on the path.

The settlement came into view only moments before they entered it.

"I haven't seen a concealment spell this big in decades," Talon whistled.

An elder elf approached them wearing the ceremonial robe of The Order, "Welcome all. I welcome you to our village for however long you wish to stay. I only wish you were here in better times. I am Shepherd Halfar. Please, come, come."

"Stay here; I'll see where they want us to stay," Talon said, then departed.

Shaylee looked around at the village. It seemed so similar to her own village that she found tears springing to her eyes. Every house was made of mud bricks with sod roofs. Flowers adorned every window. She even saw some fairy huts high in the treetops with woven grass walls with leaf roofs.

"This way," Talon called from where he stood with Shepherd Halfar. The Shepherd led them to the far side of the village. Here, they had dozens of tents set up.

"Take your pick. You are the first to arrive, but we expect many more."

Talon picked the first one they came to. "This one will be fine. Thank you, Shepherd."

"I will assist you with handing out the rest."

Rosepetal grabbed Shaylee's and Fawn's hands and led them into their new home. "First things first, girls, we have flowers to pick and a garden to grow. Shaylee, go and see if anyone is selling seeds. Fawn, go into the surrounding woods just a short way and pick some flowers and all the roots, mind you. I will see if healing is needed."

Fawn and Shaylee smiled at the 180-degree change in Rosepetal's attitude and then got to work.

By the time Talon returned, flowers in three pots were placed in front of the tent flap. Shaylee looked out of the tent at him with a grin on her face. He smiled. "Things were going to be all right."

Shaylee and Fawn walked together around their new village; whether temporary or permanent, they did not know. The morning was calm and cool, with barely a breeze to blow the bare branches of the slumbering trees.

Lyra glided overhead, purring loudly. She swooped low over their heads and shot a couple of frozen streams of ice breath at them playfully.

Fawn danced out of the way after Shaylee was struck on the shoulder, Shaylee looked up at the playful cat and, with a wave of her hand, caused a gust of wind to push the vaska into a bush.

Lyra hissed and growled as she disentangled herself from the branches. Fawn and Shaylee laughed at her antics.

"Come on Lyra," Shaylee called to her.

I'm going to watch out for that next time, Lyra laughed in Shaylee's mind.

At the edge of the village, she saw a small group forming and staffs being handed out. "Come on," she said to Fawn.

They quickened their pace. An elf about the age of Shaylee's father was speaking to the group of elves and a lone fairy. "Welcome to day three of your third week of training. Today, we will begin with the staff." His eyes left his students and settled on Shaylee and Fawn. "Can I help you?" He sounded a bit impatient.

"Can we join you?" Shaylee asked.

He shook his head, "I don't have time to start at the beginning; you will have to wait for the next session."

"When does that start?" Fawn asked.

"In the fall." He immediately tore away his gaze back to the students, "Now where was I?"

"But we already know how to use staffs. My father was a Ranger; he already started our training." Shaylee interrupted.

"The Order is more advanced than the Rangers…"

"Tar and Leo already started our training with magic and bows," Shaylee interrupted him again.

He harrumphed, "Fine, I will test you so you will stop interrupting me." He looked back at his students, "Pay attention, class; this is how you deal with those who think they are your equals." The class snickered. A couple of the boys whispered to each other, and a girl glared at them.

"One at a time, or both at once?" Shaylee asked.

The teacher scoffed, "One at a time, I am evaluating your abilities." He threw a staff at Fawn, which she snatched out of the air easily, swinging it in precise, practiced moves. A student came forward, an elven girl about their age, the one that glared at them.

She bowed to Fawn, "Ashryn Roslyn," she said. Ashryn was easily six inches taller than Fawn, with honey-blonde hair and copper eyes.

"Fawn Carric," Fawn said with a quick bow.

The teacher nodded, "Begin."

Fawn attacked first; their staffs clacked together, breaking the silence. The students quickly formed a circle around the duo. Blows were traded back and forth; Fawn swooped for her legs, which she easily jumped over. Shaylee saw Ashryn's hand start to glow, but Fawn must have seen the shimmer when she first started her cast; she dodged to the side and cast her own spell at the same time as Ashryn cast hers. Ashryn's spell hit one of the students squarely in the chest simultaneously as Fawn's collided with Ashryn, sending her sprawling backward.

"Very good," the teacher chuckled dryly. "Your turn," he said to Shaylee without looking at her.

Shaylee nodded, her confidence waning. Her control over her magic was reasonable, but she wouldn't have the same reaction time as Fawn since she couldn't feel elven magic. She took the staff from Fawn and twirled it around.

The teacher smiled, "Simon," he shouted.

A student from the group's rear approached; he was a muscular boy a few years older than Shaylee. He had red hair and the start of a red mustache. He was taller than her but shorter than most elves.

"Human?" she asked. *Elves and fairies don't have facial hair,* she thought.

"Simon Onate," he bowed with a flourish of his arms. "Do you have issues fighting a human?"

"No, I was just curious," she said with a grin. She planted her feet and got ready for the fight.

Simon smiled broadly and attacked first.

She nimbly stepped aside from his clumsy, slashing attack. She spun and hit him solidly on the back. He stumbled forward but was able to catch himself. Shaylee felt the air thicken around him; he was getting ready to cast. She dove to the ground, flattening herself as a bolt of black magic shot through the air where she had just stood, creating a dark sphere above her. *A capture spell,* the thought sprang into her head; the black globe hung just inches above her head. Without thinking, she cast the same spell at him but made sure to aim lower and adjust the bubble to fit his bulk. Her black sphere caught him before he could cast his next attack. He let out a startled yell as her spell lifted him several feet in the air.

"Bravo," the teacher clapped his hands. "Who taught you that spell?"

"Um, no one," she said meekly.

"No one? Then how did you do it?" Simon grunted as he crumbled to the ground when she released her spell.

"I'm just unique, that's all. I can see, feel, and copy human magic."

Whispered mumbling broke out amongst the students. The teacher frowned, "How so?" He looked her up and down, taking in her obvious elven attire.

"I'm an Elvenfae," she replied.

"No such thing," Someone yelled.

"My father is Ranger Talon of Threndy and a former member of The Order of the Chosen, and my mother is Rosepetal, a fairy."

"I think that does it for today's class. Same time, same place tomorrow," he boomed.

No one moved; everyone continued to stare at Shaylee.

The teacher clapped his hands together, creating the loudest clap Shaylee had ever heard and causing her heart to jump into her throat.

"Dismissed," the teacher said forcefully. "Except you two, please," he said to Shaylee and Fawn. The class slowly retreated, looking back at Shaylee and Fawn.

"Nice work, you two." He smiled at them. "I would be honored to have you both in my class. I will assign a tutor to you for the next couple of weeks to help you get caught up. Welcome to The Order," he bowed slightly and departed.

"We are members of The Order now?" Fawn glanced at Shaylee, raising her brows.

"I guess so." She dropped her shoulders. "That was easy."

It turned out not to be as easy as she thought. Being three weeks behind everyone else meant they had a lot to learn in very little time. The lone fairy in the group was assigned as their tutor; she was the teacher's assistant and had very little patience for them.

Shaylee and Fawn were expected to join the rest of the students and then study with Solara in the evening.

Most of the students met their teacher, Devnar Paran, every day at sunrise to work on magic control; it turned out that there were five humans in the class: one sorcerer, Simon, one witch, Kate, and three non-magic users, Peter, Kevin, and Trevor. The three non-magic users would join them after their midday break for weapons training. They worked on hand-to-hand combat the first three weeks, and now they were learning the staff. It was at least something Fawn and Shaylee already knew. After the rest of the class was dismissed for the evening, they met with Solara.

The first two nights with Solara were beyond frustrating. She had no patience and expected them to remember what she told them immediately and without fail.

Fawn was ready to give up, but Shaylee convinced her to stick it out. Shaylee had something she wanted to try.

After their third tutoring session, Shaylee led Fawn to the back of their tent. She lit a small fire and gestured for her to sit down.

"So, what is it that you wanted to try?" Fawn asked.

"This," Shaylee said; she rubbed her hands together and placed them on a large rock in front of her. Fawn jumped as Solara's voice drifted out of the rock, saying the exact same things she did earlier that evening.

"How did you do this?" Fawn looked at Shaylee in surprise.

"I'm not sure," she replied, touching the rock to stop Solara's voice. "After our first lesson, I tried to remember everything Solara told us and couldn't remember much of anything. She gives us so much information. After yesterday, I knew I had to find some way to 'replay' what she had said. I couldn't sleep at all last night."

"That explains weapons training today," Fawn giggled.

"I'm exhausted," Shaylee smiled, hunching her shoulders. "I came up with this. I don't know what to call it, but I can capture her voice and replay it later."

"How long does it last?"

Shaylee shrugged, "I don't know, but we better listen in case it's not long."

They spent the next couple of hours listening to Solara's lesson over and over until they felt pretty confident that they would remember most of it. The first watch was being relieved before they crawled into bed and fell asleep before their heads hit their pillows.

Talon had been watching them all night; after he was sure they were asleep, he went to bed, immensely proud of them and their dedication.

The rest of the week went better, and Solara seemed impressed at their retention. By the end of the week, she declared them caught up with the class.

Shaylee and Fawn soon became the two to beat when it came to staffs and archery, although neither of them had the upper body strength for swordplay. With magic, Fawn was the evident leader amongst the entire class. Shaylee could only compete with the two humans, which irritated her, so she focused on improving her archery.

Additional refugees from the ongoing conflict with the wyverns appeared just after magic practice one day. The group consisted primarily of humans, with a few elves mixed in. A tall, thin, elven woman seemed to be the leader. She had silver hair and violet eyes. She spoke with the Shepherd and started assigning tents to her people. She then approached teacher Paran. "Good day," her voice was almost like a melody. "Do you have any room for additional students?"

Teacher Paran frowned, "It depends on their skill level. I don't have any room for beginners," he said roughly.

Teacher never speaks with pleasantries, Shaylee chuckled to herself.

"Well, do you have any advanced students willing to teach beginners? We are going to need all the help we can get. Every man, woman, and child needs to be taught how to defend themselves."

He lowered his staff and looked at her. His face turned sober. "Is it getting that bad?"

She nodded.

He nodded firmly. "Very well then. I will find you after my classes are complete this evening. We will restructure the lessons. I want to ensure my students still advance, but it sounds like we need to get everybody else up to an acceptable skill level."

The silver-haired elf nodded and departed.

"All right, you all heard it. Back to work. Tomorrow, I will have a new schedule for you."

She spotted Jurren and his brother Elas watching their class a short distance away.

She leaned down to Fawn, "We'll have to see if anybody from Threndy wants to learn," she said, nodding to the two elves in the corner.

Fawn looked in their direction, scowled, but nodded. "I suppose we need everyone that is willing."

CHAPTER
-29-

THEY met in the town center the following day like they always did. The morning was crisp with the threat of rain in the air.

The students always arrived before the teacher, but he was later than usual. When he finally arrived, the silver-haired elf was with him.

"Everybody, I would like you to meet Aspen. We have devised a new schedule to utilize your blossoming talents to help train all the new people. We will still meet here every morning. We will have advanced magic from sunrise to mid-morning; anybody new will join us after, and you will each be given a student or two to mentor. Your job will be to get them up to your level as quickly as possible." He looked around at his gathered students and then continued, "After our midday break, we will have weapons training. We will start with stations with several of you leading. We expect numerous refugee groups over the next several weeks, with every group having different skill levels. Aspen and I will evaluate each of them and team them up with those we think will be able to help them the most." He paused and looked at the students for any questions. He clapped his hands together loudly, "Let's get to it then."

At the mid-morning break, a large group had gathered at the town center. Old and young, men and women, from the new refugees and from Threndy, all huddled together. Some looked around confidently, but most, especially the women, looked nervous and unsure.

"Welcome, welcome," teacher Paran said. "Today will be a little bit slower than in the coming months. We need to evaluate where each of you is sitting. The group standing behind me is my current class. They will be assisting in your training. Each and every one of them shall be treated with the same level of respect that you show me and Aspen. Aspen, if you will take all the women, I will take all the men, and we'll see if we can get through this as quickly as possible."

For the rest of the day, the current students sat and watched. Most of the men had some level of weapons training or magic training. Most of the women had neither, especially the humans. Shaylee watched as Jurren was placed into an upper class, most likely because of his Ranger training, and it appeared he convinced them to allow his brother to join him. She hadn't seen much of him since they left Threndy, which suited her perfectly.

She was surprised to see her friends Amelia and Sparrow in the women's group. She hadn't seen much of them either lately. Few fairies had traveled with them, and most family groups stuck close and only ventured out a little. Once they were in a beginner's group, Shaylee decided to go over and say hi.

"I'm glad you two are out and about," she said cheerfully. Her friends saw her, squealed with delight, and threw their arms around her neck.

"You know how overprotective my mother is," Amelia said, her black eyes dancing in the defused sunlight. "She wouldn't let me out of her sight."

Sparrow was so happy she started fluttering a few feet off the ground, her silver wings flapping rapidly, "And my father kept us in the air constantly while we were traveling. He said the ground was no place for a fairy," she giggled, her blue hair whipping around her face as she twirled in the air. "What have you been up to?"

"My father allowed Fawn and I to start training soon after we arrived. We're in the advanced group. I might even be your teacher," Shaylee said with a smile.

"That would be the best thing in the world," Amelia said.

Sparrow composed herself, floated back to the ground, and leaned close to Shaylee, "Has your magic manifested?"

Shaylee nodded.

"Oh, that's wonderful!" She exclaimed loudly. "Show me, show me," she said excitedly.

Shaylee looked over at a small rock and caused it to levitate and then float over to her friend's hand. Amelia and Sparrow both frowned at the rock as it floated. "What's the matter?" Shaylee asked.

"Your magic is different," they both said simultaneously.

Shaylee's shoulders slumped, "I know. Being an elvenfae makes my magic not like an elf or fairy. For some reason, it's more like a human's."

Both girls gasped, their hands flying to their mouths.

"How is that possible?" Sparrow asked in a hushed voice, her silver eyes growing wide.

"Do you remember the two men who helped us after the wyvern attack?" They both nodded. "Leo'venath said that he thinks that sorcerers–that's a human with natural magic," she explained to their confused expressions, "Might have elf and fairy blood in them from generations past. He thinks that's how they got their magic."

"Well, that makes sense, I guess," Amelia said with a frown, "And since you're a mix of both magic, you would have magic that more closely aligns with them, or maybe they have magic that closely aligns with you."

"I guess, but it's strange. I wish I were just one or the other."

"Don't say that," Sparrow said, fluttering her wings. "You are who you are because of your mix. If it weren't for you, I wouldn't have Amelia as a friend, and if you were a full elf, I wouldn't know you either." Amelia nodded in agreement.

"Thank you so much." The three friends embraced.

Teacher Paran clapped his hands together, augmented by his magic, startling everyone to attention. "Everyone is dismissed. Come back here at midday tomorrow for your assigned groups."

Shaylee looked around at all the gathered current and new students as they were slowly separated. Jurren and his brother were together with one of the advanced students. Aspen had a group of ten around her, and Devnar Paran had what looked to be twelve hovering next to him.

"They must be more advanced skill leveled," Fawn remarked.

Amelia was teamed up with Fawn, which made Shaylee immensely happy. Sparrow was teamed up with Solara, the teacher's assistant, and the two other fairies.

So far, Shaylee had no one. She frowned and looked around. Then she saw two humans walking toward her. Neither looked happy.

"Are you Shaylee?" One of them asked.

"That's me. What's the matter?" She asked. Both were scowling.

"I don't see why we were paired with an elf and not with the sorcerer or even the witch. Doesn't make any sense to me," the woman said.

"I'm not an elf."

"Well, you're not a fairy either," the man replied.

"Yes and no, I'm an elvenfae, my father is an elf, and my mother is a fairy. Are you a natural or learned?" She asked them

"I'm a natural," the female said. "Name's Amanda."

"I'm neither, so again, I'm not sure why I'm being paired with you. I see two human males over there. I should be paired with that group."

Shaylee thought for a moment, "Any good with a sword?"

He shook his head, "Never used one."

"How about a staff or bow?"

"I'm a farmer, so I guess a staff would be the closest thing I could wield."

"That must be it then. I will teach you the staff and the bow. Those two," she pointed to the men referenced before, "Are good with the sword but terrible with staffs and bows."

"What are you going to teach me then?" Amanda asked, rolling her eyes.

"How much magic do you know?"

"Very little, I was orphaned as a toddler; a non-magic family took me in. I only recently found out I had magic."

Shaylee floated a rock up in the air, and Amanda's eyes snapped open, "I can feel what you are doing," astonishment in her voice.

Shaylee smiled, "See if you can duplicate it."

"Can you explain how you did it?"

"I don't have to. Concentrate on what I'm doing, really feel it, and then don't think, just do."

Amanda nodded, "Ok, here goes nothing."

Shaylee floated another rock up and spun it in the air.

Amanda took a deep breath and held her hand out over a rock; the rock shot up into her hand.

"Good," Shaylee beamed. "Now try it without using your hand. Sometimes, we need our hands to direct the magic, but something like this should be pure willpower."

Amanda lowered her hand and concentrated on another rock, which levitated slowly into the air. She smiled broadly.

"Good, now make it spin."

The rock spun like a top floating three feet in the air.

"Ok, good first lesson. Now, let's go to the archery range." She turned toward the man, "Um, sorry, I don't think I caught your name,"

"Benjamin, but just call me Ben."

A few days later, a new group of refugees arrived, and more followed over the next week. There needed to be more room for everyone in the town proper. A meeting was called, and leaders of every group were required to attend.

Shepherd Halfar stood before the assembled, "Thank you all for coming. I wish it were under better circumstances. I am truly sorry for the losses you have all suffered." He hung his head for a brief moment of silence, and the assembly did the same.

"I have asked you all here tonight to discuss our next steps. I know that since you are here, you have all met Tarrid and Leo'venath." Murmurs of agreement rang through the group. "Then you all know what we are facing and what we are trying to do. The fact that you are here leads me to believe you are willing to follow us."

"But how can we build an army to stop the wyverns?" Someone yelled.

"By teaching everyone and anyone willing to fight how to fight. As soon as Tar and Leo return, we will know more. For now, our primary concern is shelter and food for all. Our gardens are still growing, but the forest is plentiful. We need volunteers for hunters. We must venture a little way from the village with so many here. We will have hunters and lookouts. Have volunteers report to me at daybreak. Any that want to learn to fight, man or woman over fourteen, have them meet Devnar Paran," he pointed to the teacher, "daybreak as well."

"Fourteen? That's too young," a woman shouted from the crowd. Several others joined her.

Halfar held up his hand, asking for quiet, "While I would have agreed with you a year ago, today, we live in desperate times. Consent of the parent will be required for all those under sixteen." That seemed to appease most present. "Thank you all."

The group at mid-morning increased threefold. *We definitely don't have enough teachers now,* Shaylee thought.

Don't worry, I'm sure they have a plan, Lyra projected. She was perched on her shoulder, watching the growing crowd.

Devnar Paran addressed all the current students, "Please continue your lessons. I will speak with you all tonight."

Shaylee and Fawn took their students to their usual spot. Archery targets were set up at twenty, forty, and sixty yards. All three students could hit the twenty-yard target with ease. Ben was the only one to hit the forty-yard within the target circle. He could hit the tree at sixty yards but not within the painted circle every time.

"Amanda and Amelia, today we will be teaching you how to control the flight of your arrows," Shaylee said.

"Isn't that what you have been teaching us?" Ben asked.

"No, I have been teaching you how to aim, release, and build strength. Amanda and Amelia can use their magic to increase their distance."

"Impossible," Ben said, crossing his arms.

Shaylee smiled, "See that tree over there beyond the sixty."

Ben squinted and saw a small painted circle on a tree in the distance, "You mean that one out there?" He pointed.

Shaylee nodded.

"That's got to be two hundred yards."

"Two hundred and twenty-two, to be exact," Fawn said, reaching for her bow.

Shaylee reached for hers, "Now, you two pay close attention." Shaylee and Fawn nocked their arrows and released them while still looking at the students.

"You didn't even aim!" Amelia exclaimed.

Shaylee and Fawn turned their attention to their arrows and concentrated on the flight path. Amanda and Amelia had the same look of surprise and then determination on their faces. Within a few moments, the resounding thud of the arrows to a tree reached their ears.

"But you didn't even aim," Ben repeated.

"It's ok, Ben; I know it's not fair to use magic, but we each have to use our strengths to their potential," Shaylee approached him, reaching up to place a hand on his shoulder. "Before I learned to use my magic, I learned to hit the sixty-yard tree with ease. I will get you there. You are far stronger than me; hitting one hundred with a proper bow shouldn't be out of your reach."

"Thanks, Shaylee, I needed that," Ben said sourly, but soon his face cracked, and he started to laugh.

Paran gathered his original students as the sun set in the west. Grumbles could be heard; everyone was ready to retire for the evening.

"First, I would like to say how proud I am of every one of you. You stepped up, learned to teach, and continued growing your abilities. It has been decided that we have to start doing things differently with so many new students. We have also received word from Tarrid; he wants us to move the village."

"Where, too?" Lark squeaked.

"The Monastery of Iton."

"The Monastery? Why not the Sanctum?" Someone asked.

"He didn't say. We leave in two days; lessons continue as normal tomorrow, and there will be no work the following day as we prepare to leave."

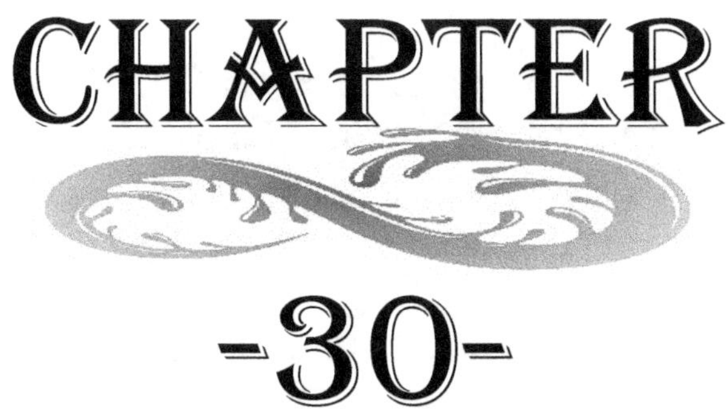

CHAPTER -30-

IT took them several weeks to reach the Monastery. It was set in a small valley rung by a thick forest to the east and a small mountain range to the west. An active volcano loomed over the other mountains, with a thin trail of smoke lifting into the sky. Paran told them there was also a deep ravine along the north side of the forest. The Monastery sat on a small mesa above the surrounding forest.

"This doesn't look like a very good place to live," Rosepetal remarked.

"I hear that volcanic soil is quite fertile," Talon said in passing.

Rosepetal perked up a little at that.

The Monastery grounds were enormous. They were told that the monastery building was nothing but gathering rooms, a kitchen, and a few living quarters; it was the surrounding grounds that were truly impressive. Hundreds of two-room cottages surrounded the main building on one side, while the entire rear area was dedicated to farmland. A large stable and training area graced the remaining side. The Monastery was enclosed by a tall wooden wall, with the main gates open and awaiting their arrival. A spacious courtyard lay between the gates and the steps leading up to the monastery."

"So, where do you want to request our house to be, dear?"

"As close to the garden as possible," Shaylee answered for her.

Rosepetal laughed and fluttered her wings. "Of course, exactly," she beamed.

On top of the steps of the Monastery, Tarrid and Leo'venath waited with their hands clasped behind their backs.

A hush loamed over everyone as they gathered as close to the steps as possible. Once the last of their group walked through the gate Tarrid addressed them.

"Thank you all for journeying here. I hope it is not for naught," he said somberly but loud enough for all to hear.

"What's happened?" Talon asked loudly.

"The Chosen have decided now is not the time to act."

Shouts of outrage and confusion rippled through the crowd.

"So, what are we to do?" Someone shouted above the others, using their magic to augment their volume.

"I will not stand by and let the wyverns destroy any more lives than they already have. I made this clear to the High Shepherd. He is digging his grave and the grave of all those who blindly follow him. I am going to fight," Tarrid's voice rang out with conviction.

"We are going to fight," Leo'venath echoed.

"But how, without The Chosen, we are nothing," a voice drifted to them.

"Together, we are everything. This," he gestured broadly, "is our stronghold. We are no longer The Order of the Chosen. The order has forsaken us. We are our own people; we are freedom fighters in our own right. All those that stand with us shall be known as The Blade of Freedom."

"What if we don't choose you?" A voice carried through the air.

"You are a free people. You can choose your own path. The Chosen have offered sanctuary at the Sanctuary of Iton to those who wish to remain with them, promising protection. However, I caution you that the wyverns are becoming more aggressive, and unless we stand up, freedom will be lost."

"What of the prophecy?" Another person shouted.

"The royal lines went into hiding years ago. Until the heirs show themselves, we must continue the fight and look for them," Leo said.

"Everyone is welcome to stay here and recover from their recent trip. Shepherd Halfar, can you gather decision-makers and have them follow me?" Tar asked.

The Shepherd bowed his head.

Talon, Aspen, Halfar, and three others from the newest refugees joined Tarrid and Leo'venath inside the Monastery a few moments later.

"First off, I would like to thank you all for coming this far. I hope it has not been for naught. Shepherd." He bowed his head, "I am sorry I left The Order, and I am sorry that I am fracturing it further."

"Be at ease, Tarrid. I do not know why the High Shepherd has forsaken your cause, and rest assured I will get answers. I will lead all those who wish to go to the Sanctuary. I will return if the answers I seek are not favorable."

"Thank you, Shepherd. You are more than welcome here, and if you return, you will have a spot of honor in my new order. And if by some miracle The Order of the Chosen changes their mind, I will atone and rejoin." He bowed deeply. Shepherd Halfar placed a hand on Tarrid's head and said a quick prayer to Iton before departing. Tar turned to address the others, "It's wonderful seeing you again, Talon. It has been a while."

"That it has. You seemed to have keep busy in your absence."

"That I have. I want each of you to speak with your people. Anyone who wants to leave can join Shepherd Halfar. Anyone who wants to stay is welcome with open arms."

"I do not need to speak to my people; we are with you," Aspen said with a bow. "Now that you are no longer a warrior of The Chosen and in line to be a Shepherd, what will you be called?"

Tarrid smiled, "I am still a warrior. Our followers are not sheep to be herded. Our followers are the blades to be guarded. Our warriors will be ranked by weapon size and type. Our leaders are their shields."

Aspen smiled broadly and bowed deeply, "Shield Tarrid the first," she said.

"Talon, do you need to speak with your group?"

"Yes, I'm afraid so. My people are simple folk, not warriors."

"What of your Rangers?" Leo asked.

"Most never returned from their last patrol. We lost two patrols before the wyvern attacked. And the wyvern along with his ogre and trolls killed most in the outposts surrounding Threndy." He shook his head, his words laced with pain.

"What of you?" Tar asked.

"My wife and I would like to set off on our own. We lived in solitude for many years before Shaylee came to us."

"You will be missed…"

"But…" Talon interrupted, "Shaylee and Fawn have been training to fight. I will not be able to persuade them. We will stay."

"Glad to hear it," Leo chimed in.

"And you all?" Tarrid addressed the other three leaders amongst them.

"I will speak with my people, but I think most will stay."

"Agreed."

"Agreed."

"Wonderful. You can't imagine the stress load that just left my shoulders. Tomorrow, we will start organizing our people and resources."

Tarrid walked along the upper ramparts of the Monastery. He gazed down at all the people getting settled for the evening. So many had come, but how many would stay? A gust of wind blew across the rooftop rustling his hair and threatened to extinguish the torches that lined to roof.

"Am I interrupting?"

Tarrid turned to see an elven woman in long flowing robes walking toward him. He immediately knelt and bowed his head, "Thank you, Prioress, for allowing my people to stay here."

"Rise, child, you do not need to kneel before me. It is my pleasure and duty to open the doors to all seeking refuge." Her emerald eyes brightened as she smiled.

"Even when the High Shepherd has declared us criminals and outlaws?"

She chuckled softly, tossing her platinum blonde braid over her shoulder, "The High Shepherd and I do not always see eye to eye."

"But you are second to him; didn't he choose you?"

"There is much for you to learn about Iton. Hundreds of years ago, when we first started to worship the God Iton, the Prioress was the leader of the followers. When turmoil arose, and The Order was called upon to protect our flock, the Shepherd emerged to fulfill their calling. Much of our history has been lost, and much has been corrupted. The High Shepherd may lead the flock, but he does not speak for our God. You are following the righteous path. The Blades of Freedom are his new champions."

Tarrid's knees buckled, and he again knelt before her. "I am truly blessed."

"You are what we truly need. I heard Shepherd Halfar will leave for The Sanctum in the morning. I am sending along two scrolls with him: a plea for the High Shepherd to join your cause under your leadership, and when he refuses that one, he shall be given the second scroll, dissolving his order and removing his blessing from Iton."

"Is that truly necessary? We need to be united, not at war with each other."

"So, you do not think folding him into your group is wise."

Tar paused briefly, "Only if he truly wishes it. Bringing him in against his will only causes a rift. The Blade must be firmly united if we are to succeed."

"But if there are two champions for Iton, The Chosen and The Blade, you may be unable to recruit all those you need. Some may see you as usurpers and try to bolden The Chosen."

Tar thought for another moment, "Our successes will show people our true intentions. I hold no hard feelings for any member of The Chosen. Everyone must choose their path in life. This…" he gestured to the Monastery and the people below, "this is my path. This is the path I have chosen and the path that those following me have chosen. I only hope The Chosen will see the wrongness of their ways and join us in the fight. I do not wish to dissolve The Order of The Chosen; I only wish to stand beside them and bring order back to the kingdoms. I will find the prophesized twins; I will find the lost bloodlines. And together, we will defeat the wyverns and right the wrongs."

"Spoken like a true leader," the Prioress praised. "No scrolls shall be sent." She bowed her head slightly and left him alone with his thoughts.

CHAPTER -31-

SHAYLEE aggressively dug a small hole in the ground with her spade and slammed a tuber root into it, pushing it down firmly before covering it with loose dirt.

"Now, Shaylee, that is no way to plant vegetables," her mother scolded.

Shaylee sighed as she dug up the small root and placed it into a different hole.

"I'm sure they're going to start training again soon," her mother said.

"But when? I'm so bored."

"There is nothing wrong with a little bit of manual labor to pass the time," Rosepetal hummed to herself.

The root Shaylee had just planted was the last for the row; grateful, she stood and stretched out her aching back. Rosepetal took flight, flew over the row of freshly planted tubers, and showered the fresh plantings with her magic. Satisfied that the little plants would start well, she nodded and went to the next row.

"Shaylee, look!" Fawn said from her side of the field. Shaylee looked in her direction and saw her pointing toward the Monastery. She saw her father speaking with Tarrid. They'd been at the Monastery for over a week, and she'd seen very little of him or Leo. She had hoped to be able to get him alone so she could show him how far she had come in such a short time with her magic. But the little that she did see him, he was never alone. Their former teacher, Devnar, Aspen, or one of the other newly appointed leaders, was always around him. The one that bothered her the most was Aspen. Shaylee didn't know why the woman infuriated her. She seemed like a nice enough person and highly skilled, and when she first met her, she didn't have any issues with her, but now, every time she saw her standing next to Tarrid and always a little too close, she just felt anger rise inside of her.

"I wonder what your father is saying to him," Fawn said.

"Hopefully, something about getting training going again. We've been sitting here too long. I thought the whole point of us being here was to train for the fight to come."

"Your father's coming this way. Let's ask."

"Wait…" Shaylee said, but she was too late; Fawn was already sprinting toward Talon.

"Has he set a date?" Fawn asked as she skidded to a halt.

"A date for what?" Talon grinned.

"A date for training to start, of course."

"Not yet, but we are close. Don't you two have some vegetables to plant?"

"We are tired of planting vegetables, father. We should be preparing. What if the wyverns attack here?"

"Back to work, you two. We will discuss this later. Right now, we have the Spring Equinox to prepare for."

"Spring Equinox? What is that?" Shaylee asked.

Talon grinned, "The Spring Equinox and Winter Solstice are special days for those who follow Iton. It's in one week. Ask your mother if she can hurry up any vegetables. If we can secure enough food, there will be a feast."

"A feast! Oh, I can't wait," Fawn squealed.

The evening of the Spring Equinox was surprisingly very warm. Hunting parties were gone from sunrise to sunset, and Rosepetal worked herself ragged every day to ensure the feast would succeed.

Several fires burned brightly, cooking everything from tubers and peppers to rabbit, boar, and elk.

The smells coming from the front of the Monastery made Shaylee's stomach growl loudly. Since coming to the Monastery, they had been eating little to ensure that everyone was fed and, it seemed, to prepare for this feast.

Shaylee and Fawn put on their best clothing after washing. Shaylee looked down at her pants and shirt. She sighed as she glanced at her boots. Even though she cleaned everything and stitched a couple of holes in her pants, she still felt way underdressed. She used to have a couple of dresses, but those were long gone.

Fawn came out of their shared room wearing a light purple ankle-length dress. She spun around quickly, flaring her skirt out. When she stopped, the dress wrapped around her legs, showing her bare feet. "How do I look?"

Shaylee smiled, "You look beautiful, but why are you barefoot?"

"My boots looked silly, and I left my slippers behind. I didn't even know I had this dress with me."

Shaylee frowned and looked at her clothing again.

"I wish I had something for you to wear," Fawn said.

"What? Oh, don't be silly. My clothes are clean. That's the important thing. I'm glad you have something so pretty to wear. The light purple dress looks great on you."

"I can change," Fawn offered.

"Don't be silly, Fawn. You're beautiful. Come on, shall we?" Shaylee reached for her hand.

Hand-in-hand, they walked to the festival.

Standing at the Monastery steps was the Prioress wearing a bright blue robe. Standing beside her were Tarrid and Leo'venath; Shaylee's heart skipped a beat as she caught Tar's gaze. He smiled and waved; his eyes left her as he looked at Fawn. His smile faltered and then grew. Shaylee looked over to Fawn, and her face beamed with the largest grin she'd ever seen on the young elf's face.

Tar's gaze was again interrupted by Aspen's appearance. She strode in front of Fawn and walked directly up to Tarrid.

"Look at what she's wearing; that is highly inappropriate!" Fawn said with a scowl.

Fawn was right; Aspen wore a wispy, sheer white outer robe that didn't hide the fact that she only wore skin-tight britches that came up to just below her belly button and a top that only covered her breast while leaving her stomach and shoulders wholly uncovered.

"She's not leaving much to the imagination," Fawn grumbled.

"Jealous?" Shaylee asked.

"Who me? Of course not. If she wants to walk around half-naked, that's her business," Fawn said, though clearly upset.

"Let's go get something to eat before it's all gone." Shaylee had to drag Fawn away. Her eyes were glued on Aspen as she approached Tarrid and hugged him.

Halfway through the evening, everyone relaxed and had a good time as bota bag wineskins were passed around and bellies were filled.

Shaylee and Fawn sat with Amelia and Sparrow on the top step of the Monastery, watching Jurren, his brother, and a couple of other elves their age roughhousing below.

The sun was setting behind the western mountain range, and the first stars were just starting to twinkle in the night sky. A warm breeze rustled through the monastery grounds, bringing with it the sweet smells of the first spring flowers in bloom.

"They're all drunk," Sparrow giggled.

Jurren struggled to stay on his feet while trying to catch Elas. Elas darted just out of his brother's reach, shaking the wineskin at him and taunting him to take it. Elas stumbled over a rock and almost fell but caught himself. All the boys roared with laughter.

"I think those two have had a little too much," a woman said behind them. The four girls looked behind them and then scrambled to their feet.

"Good evening, Prioress," they all said, bowing their heads.

The Prioress waved her hand at them, "Be seated."

Shaylee remained standing. "I'm sorry. We should have asked permission to sit here," she said, her head still bowed.

The Prioress smiled kindly at her, "You must be Shaylee."

"Yes, ma'am."

"It is a pleasure to meet you, child. You all are fine sitting here." The Prioress swept her hands out, pointing to the steps. "The Monastery doesn't belong to me. It belongs to the people of Iton. I am only its caretaker." She paused for a moment, looking out over the people dancing and laughing. "I hear that training will be resumed. Are you ready?"

"It is? I mean, yes, ma'am, I am more than ready. I've been asking my father daily when it would start up again." Shaylee's eyes lit up with anticipation.

"What is that around your neck?" The Prioress asked suddenly, her eyes seeming to bore a hole through Shaylee's shirt.

Shaylee's hand flew to the unicorn horn she always wore under her shirt. *Is it visible?* She thought, her heart starting to race. "Nothing, ma'am," she swallowed, trying to calm her heartbeat. "Just a necklace. You can see it?" She looked at her shirt and didn't even see a bulge to give it away.

"No," she replied flatly, lifting an eyebrow. "I can feel it. May I see the horn?"

Shaylee let out the breath she held while pulling the horn out from under her shirt. She slid the leather necklace over her head and held the horn out tentatively.

"I will give it right back, child. Do not fear."

Shaylee looked at the Prioress; she was still smiling. Reluctantly, she handed the horn to her. Shaylee immediately felt her connection with the horn break. Her shoulders slumped a little.

"Interesting. You've made a connection with it," she whispered. The Prioress studied the horn for a brief moment more before handing it back. Her smile grew when Lyra glided down and landed on Shaylee's shoulder. "You and I must speak more when the time is right. Come and find me; I will have the answers you seek."

The Prioress turned and walked gracefully away.

"What was that about?" Fawn asked, coming up the steps to stand beside Shaylee.

"That was weird. How does she know 'she will have the answers you seek when the time is right'?" Sparrow asked, trying to mimic the tone of the Prioress.

"What answers do you seek, Shaylee?" Amelia inquired.

Shaylee held her hands out hopelessly, "I have no idea what she is talking about. But I have a whole bunch of questions right now."

CHAPTER

-32-

SHAYLEE raced through Newhaven as fast as she could. Shortly after the Spring Equinox festival, the village surrounding the Monastery of Iton was given a new name. Newhaven was a fitting one.

She saw Fawn and her mother in the fields up ahead. She spurred herself to go faster. They had to hear the news from her. She smiled at the feeling of her legs and lungs burning. All spring, they had done nothing but grow food, an important endeavor but boring, nonetheless. Summer was upon them, along with Shaylee's fourteenth name-day. Training resuming was the best name-day gift Shaylee could think of.

"Shaylee, what's wrong?" Rosepetal said in a panicked squeak.

Shaylee stopped and bent over, trying to catch her breath. She held up her hand, asking for patience. "Training… starts... tomorrow," she managed between gasps.

"Shaylee! You had me worried beyond belief. Did you really have to race here to tell us that?" Rosepetal scolded her.

"Yes, she did!" Fawn exclaimed, jumping for joy. "Where do we meet? What time? Sunrise like before? Can we work a little on our own this afternoon?" Fawn rambled.

"We meet in front of the Monastery after the first call."

"So late in the morning. I don't think I'll sleep a wink tonight."

"First call isn't that late. You will be fine," Rosepetal told her. "Now, back to work, both of you. If your training resumes tomorrow, I will be losing my helpers." Rosepetal clapped her hands and fluttered her wings with a spray of magical sparks.

Both girls giggled and got back to work.

The sun slowly peaked above the forest to the east of the Monastery. A few songbirds took flight to welcome the new day. The day promised to be clear and calm. Shaylee and Fawn were already sitting on the steps of the Monastery waiting for Newhaven to slowly awaken. Neither slept much that night and had all their chores done before dawn.

The day's first call was a bell that rang, waking everyone in the Monastery. The second call was about an hour later, calling the Priors and Shepherds to prayer.

Shaylee and Fawn's faces lit up when the bell rang high on the Monastery steeple. The bell chimed three times, and an echo continued for a moment after the third gong.

Shaylee started counting the minutes as they ticked by, wishing the Monastery had a clock like the village of Verndale.

Slowly, people started to join them. Some people stood alone; others grouped in small clusters. Amelia and Sparrow joined them on the steps. Shaylee saw Amanda and Ben off to one side together.

"I'll be right back," Shaylee told her friends.

She jogged over to her former students and said, "Hi, I haven't seen much of you two lately."

"Hi, Shaylee." Amanda said, "I've been helping with the school uniforms." She smiled, her eyes twinkling.

Shaylee smiled, "We're getting uniforms?"

"Well, kind of, you'll see," Amanda said with a wink.

"What did they have you doing, Ben? I didn't see you in the fields. Didn't you say you were a farmer?"

Ben shrugged, "I farm, I smith—a little of everything. I guess. They had me in the forge all spring."

"What were you making?"

"You'll see," he said with a grin.

"Why all the secrets?" Shaylee frowned at her two former students.

"Tarrid's orders," they both said together.

"Hmm, do you want to wait over there with me?" She pointed to her friends.

"Sure," Amanda replied.

Ben shrugged but followed them.

Finally, Tarrid, Leo'venath and the Prioress exited the Monastery. Shaylee and her small group quickly darted down the steps to stand with the others.

The Prioress circled her hands before her and then nodded to Tar.

"Thank you, Prioress," he said, his voice amplified so all could hear him, "and thank you all for coming. As you have heard, we will resume training for all those interested." The crowd broke out in excited murmurs, "BUT," he thundered, waiting for everyone to quiet, "we will be doing things differently. Times are changing, and just like the rebirth of The Order of the Chosen, we must reawaken the practices of old. We will open a training academy—the Norell-Spencer Academy of the Blade.

"That's a mouthful!" Someone yelled.

Tar held his hands out. "I know. Unfortunately, I didn't have the last word on the name," he said with a smile, stealing a glance at Leo and the Prioress. "The Blade Academy is fine with me. Anyway, with the gracious offer from Prioress Leilatha Moryra, we will be using the Monastery of Iton until we can find a more suitable location. Everyone in Newhaven is welcome to request admission."

"How young will you accept?" A man yelled.

"As young as ten will be admitted with parental approval."

"Ten?" A woman screamed, "Ten is too young to learn to fight."

"At age ten, they will not learn to fight. Rest assured, I believe we have considered everything. At age ten, they will learn magic control and discipline. The bow will be taught at age twelve. Staff and hand-to-hand will be taught as maturity grows. Sword and magical warfare last. We will have full magical theory classes, history classes, and everything else you would expect in a school."

A collective groan resonated through the crowd. "Now, now." Tar smiled broadly. "The scholars here at the Monastery and my trainers have devised a series of placement tests. Your scores will determine your schedule. We will begin with the theory and scholarly tests after midday today. Those who do not wish to gain entry are free to return to the jobs they have been requested to do, seek a new position, or leave. You are a free people; we wish you the best but hope you will join us."

Tar, Leo, and Leilatha walked down the steps to mingle and answer questions.

"So, what are you going to do, Shaylee?" Amanda asked. Her small group turned all eyes to her.

"Take every test they have. Maybe I'll test out of most of them." She shrugged.

Everyone else nodded in agreement.

Shaylee immediately regretted taking any of the tests. Other than being able to read the words on the pages, she knew next to nothing and didn't think she answered a single question correctly.

Everyone who had gathered that morning spread out across the village with four test scrolls in hand. Every chair was taken, and every rock or log that could be used as a chair was occupied; Shaylee and Fawn sat on the ground with their backs to a tree while using a plate as a table on their laps.

Shaylee glanced over to the table at the top of the Monastery stairs. No one else had walked up the steps to hand in their scrolls, and if anyone else was finished, they didn't want to be first, either.

Finally, a couple of people handed their scrolls in. *Might as well get this over,* she thought. When she stood, Fawn stood as well.

"All done?"

Fawn blushed, "As much as I could."

"Me too, don't worry, we'll be in all the same classes."

Fawn grinned, "That bad?"

"Not a single right one, I think."

They walked up the steps together and placed their scrolls in the appropriate stack.

"Are you going to tell us how many we got wrong?" Fawn asked shyly.

The Shepherd looked up at them and smiled. "Don't worry, only the grader will know the score. You will be given a pass out of the class, or you'll have to take the class."

"Ok, good," Fawn said with a relieved gush of breath.

"When will the weapons test start?" Shaylee asked.

"Be here at the first bell."

"Thank you, sir." Shaylee bowed her head.

Once down the steps, they returned to their tree to wait for the others.

"So, who didn't you want to know your score?" Shaylee asked Fawn once they sat down.

Fawn blushed fiercely, from her neck to the tops of her pointed ears. "No one in particular," she said, trying to sound uncaring.

"Ahh, why don't I believe you?"

"Really, I don't care who knows. I know I will have to take all the classes."

"Oh, so you wouldn't care if Leo knew your scores."

"Nope," she said.

Shaylee watched her for a reaction, but nothing.

"What about Tar?"

Fawn's cheeks flared, "Nope," she repeated, but her voice squeaked slightly.

"Tar? You don't have anything to worry about. You're like a little sister to him and could never truly disappoint him."

"Little sister! I'm not that much younger than him; I'm already thirteen. He's what, sixteen?"

"Seventeen now, I think. Wait, did you say you were already thirteen? When was your name-day?"

"About a month ago." Fawn looked at the ground.

"Why didn't you say something? I know my parents would have loved to celebrate that with you. Did you do anything?"

"That was the day I spent the whole day with my ma."

Shaylee nodded. "I'm glad you did that, but why didn't you tell us?"

"I didn't want your parents or you to make a fuss. I'm already staying with you; your parents have done so much for me. It… just felt awkward."

Shaylee draped an arm around Fawn's shoulder, "You have nothing to feel awkward about. You know how we feel about you. You are part of our family. Will you help me celebrate mine?"

"Of course; when do you turn fourteen?"

"In a couple of days."

The following morning, the prospective students were taken out into the valley surrounding the Monastery. A series of stations had already been set up.

"Good morning, everyone. I hope you slept well and are ready for today's tests," Leo thundered. "Each of you will be required to try each station. Do not worry if you don't know how to do something; give it your best. Remember, every one of you has already been accepted into the Academy; we do not have the luxury of picking and choosing. Every

[298]

single one of you is important to our shared cause. Pick a station to start with and remember to visit each. Begin!"

Shaylee and her growing group of friends decided on the obstacle course first.

Leo was the course evaluator. "Good idea, get the most exhausting station out of the way first. I will be timing each of you." He held up a sand dial. "If you fail to complete a task, a tally will be marked with your name. Now, who's first?"

No one moved. Finally, Ben squared his shoulders and stepped up.

"All right, I like the initiative. Whenever you're ready," Leo said.

Ben walked up to the starting spot. The first obstacle was thirty yards away. Ben shook out his legs and arms and then took off at a sprint. Leo turned the sand dial over as soon as he crossed the second line painted on the ground.

Ben sprinted to the first obstacle: three logs placed several paces apart. He easily jumped over all three. The next obstacle was a rope hanging from a tree. Ben tackled the rope and started to climb. Once at the top, he reached over his head and rang a bell. Ben shimmied down the rope and sprinted to the next obstacle, a balance beam. He took three steps and fell off. He landed with a grunt but got up and ran to the next. Another rope dangled in the middle of a decent-sized mud puddle. Ben looked at the rope for a moment before walking back several steps. He hopped up and down and then ran forward, leaping for the rope and swinging across the puddle. The finale of the course was another sprint back. When he returned, he was breathing hard but smiling.

"How did I do?"

"Not bad. Who's next?" Leo asked.

Shaylee went next, Fawn followed, then Amelia, Amanda, and finally Sparrow.

Shaylee overcame all the obstacles; Fawn and Amelia struggled with the rope, and neither reached the top to ring the bell. Amanda also failed at the rope and the swinging rope. She could jump and grab the rope but didn't get enough swing going. She got stranded on the rope, dangling limply in the middle of the mud. After a few costly seconds, she let go of the rope, falling into the sticky mud before finishing the course. Sparrow had the best time, but with her wings helping her the entire time, she was as fresh at the end as she had been at the start.

"I don't see how using your wings was fair," Ben complained.

"You use what you were born with. That is not cheating," Sparrow said, sticking up for herself.

"She's right. We utilize everyone's strengths, whatever they are. Fairies make great long-range scouts because of their endurance," Leo told him. "Don't worry, fairies are judged differently than everyone else. All right, on to your next station."

"Where to next?" Fawn asked.

"I say archery before staffs and swords," Ben replied.

"I agree, come on," Shaylee said.

The archery range was the busiest, which suited them just fine. They all needed to catch their breath. The range consisted of four targets at distances very familiar to all: twenty, forty, sixty, and two hundred yards. Anyone with any experience could hit the twenty-yard and most the forty-yard. Only a few men could hit the sixty-yard. But only the elves that had started training before coming to the Monastery could hit the two hundred yards. Those that didn't have that training failed to use their magic. After Shaylee's group succeeded, a couple of magical humans and the elves were able to mimic their success.

The staff was at another station that came relatively easily to their group. They were instructed to pair up and spar with each other as Aspen evaluated their techniques.

The final station was the sword. Again, they were paired up and sparred with each other. Tarrid evaluated this station. Fawn and Shaylee shared a quick look, knowing they were going to spar with each other. Neither of them wanted to look like a fool in front of Tar.

When it was their turn, they nodded to each other and then stepped into the painted circle.

"OK, as you've heard before. The swords are blunt; three touches, and you lose; a foot leaves the circle, and you lose. Begin."

Both girls attacked immediately; their swords cracked against each other. Back and forth, they traded blows; Shaylee was pushed backward a couple of steps before she forced Fawn to retreat. Shaylee got the first touch on Fawn, but Fawn countered immediately with one of her own. After a few intense minutes, Shaylee won out with superior size and forced Fawn to retreat to the circle's edge. One foot slipped out of the circle.

"Shaylee, winner!" Tar announced. "Good job, both of you. Have you done the other three stations?"

"We've done all of them," Sparrow said bubbly.

"Great, only one to go then."

They all looked around, "Where is it?" Amanda asked.

"Meet back here at dusk."

"Right, so where is the last test?" Ben looked at Tar and then the field again.

"The last test takes place tonight. See you all then. Ok, next group," he turned his back on them.

"What kind of test could they have in the dark?" Fawn asked.

"I'm not sure. Also, other than arrow flight, our magic wasn't tested either," Shaylee told them.

"Oh, no. You don't think they're going to test magic in the dark." Amanda shook her head, "I don't like attacking something I can't see."

"I think that might be the point," Shaylee replied grimly.

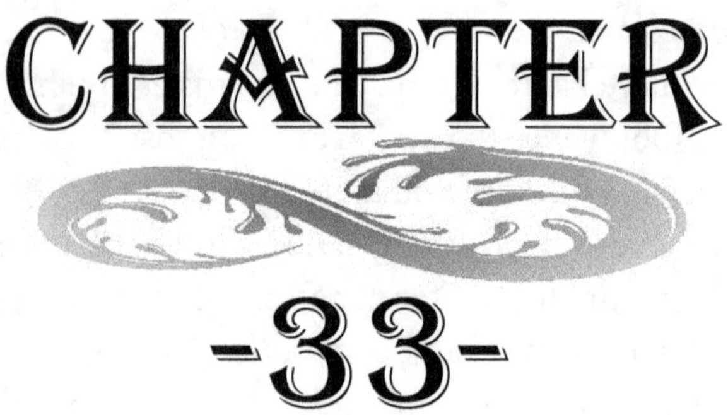

CHAPTER -33-

THE sun set behind the mountains surrounding the west side of the Monasteries valley, casting the valley and gathering hopefuls into shadow. Tar, Leo, Aspen, and Solara stood in the middle of the testing ground, each with a torch. The four torches gave off little light in the coming darkness.

"We will be breaking into four groups. This will be an exercise of cooperation. Somewhere in this valley, there is a wyvern captive; you must find and rescue him before he is eaten."

"Eaten!! Is there really a wyvern here?" Someone yelled.

"No, this is only a test," Solara said, rolling her eyes.

"Fairies will go with Solara, humans with Leo, female elves with Aspen, and the men with me. Your chaperone is there for protection and evaluation only. They will not help you. I can tell you that the captive is under a cottonwood, and he will call out when someone is close."

Shaylee raised her hand.

"Yes, Shaylee, you have a question?"

“Yes. Um… Which group do I go with?” She asked shyly.

“I sorry, I forget your uniqueness sometimes. You pick elves or fairies?”

“Elves,” she said. “I’m sure the fairies will want to fly.” She frowned when he nodded. *Was his forgetfulness endearing or insulting?*

“Ok, then let’s get ready. The test ends after the first group finds the captive or daybreak. Whichever comes first.”

Everyone broke into their groups. The fairies took to the sky right off, leaving the other three groups to search on foot. Lights bloomed all around the valley.

“So, where do we search?” Fawn asked.

Ashryn and a few others huddled together and spoke in hushed voices.

“We need to work together on this,” Fawn said to them.

“You are welcome to join us, Fawn, but not Shaylee,” one of the girls said as she played with her purple hair that was pulled into a tight braid.

Shaylee tried and failed to remember her name, “You heard Tar, I was given the choice of which group to join.”

“Well, we think you should have your own group; you don’t belong with us,” Purple-hair said.

“Hey, that’s not fair. Shaylee is no different than us,” Amelia said.

“Oh yes, she is. I think you should join your friend as well,” Ashryn said.

"Fine, come on, Fawn, we will be Shaylee's group," Amelia replied.

Aspen stood off from everyone watching the interaction but said nothing.

"I don't think that's smart. We are being tested on cooperation, remember?" Shaylee said to all of them.

Ashryn stood tall in front of her cluster of friends, "Aspen, split our group in two, please."

"I don't have that authority," she replied coldly.

"You are the evaluator; just evaluate our groups independently."

"You're wasting time," Aspen said.

"Let's just work together on this; I'll stay away from you all after tonight. What do you say?" Shaylee pleaded.

"You don't have to be around people that obviously don't like you," Fawn said, "let them go their way, and we'll go ours."

Shaylee shook her head, "The instructions were for us to work together, all together as a group." She circled her hands around.

"Do what you want, just don't follow us. Aspen, are you coming?"

"No, this isn't right, I agree with Shaylee. We are supposed to do this together, and we are wasting a lot of time," an elf Shaylee had never met before spoke out.

"It's ok, Sarya. Go with that group and report to me after daybreak. I will travel with this group," Aspen said.

"Are you sure, sister?"

"Yes, use our usual signals. Be safe."

Shaylee looked between the two elves; now that she looked closer at them, she could see the similarities.

Ashryn lifted her chin, "Fine, see you after daybreak, after *we* find the captive."

Shaylee watched as most of the girls followed Ashryn into the woods. She then turned her gaze to those left behind—Fawn, Amelia, and two others, as well as Aspen, of course.

"I'm Shaylee," she said to the other two girls.

"I'm Mira, and this is Dilya. I hope you don't mind us coming with you?"

"Of course not. I'm glad you're here."

"Where should we start looking?" Amelia asked.

All eyes turned to Shaylee.

"Well, the only clue given was that the captive was under a cottonwood. I don't see any around here."

"Where do cottonwoods grow?" Fawn asked.

"Our village had a grove next to a lake. That was the only place they grew," Dilya answered.

"OK, where is the water? The monastery's water supply is from a well. I don't see any rivers or lakes around," Fawn commented.

"There has to be," Shaylee said mainly to herself. She closed her eyes. ***Lyra, is there any water around here?*** She projected.

To the west, Lyra answered.

Any cottonwood trees?

A couple, do you want me to scout ahead?

Not yet. But if you see or hear any of the other groups, let me know.

Ok, I'm on it, Lyra projected.

"I think we should go west," Shaylee said out loud.

"As good a direction as any other," Mira said.

Slowly, they made their way through the woods, with Shaylee taking point and Aspen trailing behind them. Each girl had a sun-orb floating in front of them.

The woods thickened, with the underbrush becoming too thick to travel through. Shaylee stopped to wait for everyone.

"What's the matter?" Fawn asked.

"The underbrush is getting too thick. Does anyone have a solution?"

"I can burn a path for us," Mira volunteered.

"That might draw attention to us; we have to pretend the wyvern is on the lookout for a rescue party," Amelia offered.

"Is there really a wyvern here?" Dilya asked in a hushed voice.

"Of course not. Dilya, I swear sometimes," Mira chided her.

"It's okay; we should be thinking there is one. We have to pretend this is real and that there is a threat to our safety and the captives," Shaylee said calmly.

"Good thinking," Fawn praised.

"Any other suggestions?" Shaylee asked.

"How about you make us an air bridge so we can walk just under the canopy of these trees? It would give us a vantage spot, and we would be ultra-quiet," Fawn offered.

"Impossible, there is no such thing as an air bridge," Mira said, crossing her arms.

"Maybe there is," Shaylee said; she walked a couple of steps away from the others and reached for her unicorn horn. She closed her eyes and pictured an invisible bridge several feet above the ground. She imagined it leading to water and cottonwood trees. When she opened her eyes, she saw the faintest shimmering of something solid in front of her; she reached out and felt what felt like a stone bridge. Her breath quickened; it was working. She closed her eyes and added steps to her bridge, and then a dull silver glow that could only be seen from standing on top of the bridge.

"How did you do that?" Mira asked.

"That's impossible. Elves can't do something like this!" Dilya exclaimed.

"My big sister is an elvenfae; she can do things no elf or fairy can do. Come on, we're wasting time."

Fawn rushed up the steps, followed by Amelia. Slowly, Mira and Dilya followed, obviously nervous.

Aspen approached and studied the air bridge, "Well done, shall we?" She gestured for Shaylee to go before her. Shaylee hurried up the bridge and retook point.

They walked and walked, but still, the bridge continued. Midnight was almost on them when the end of the bridge could be seen.

Do you see anyone? Shaylee projected to Lyra.

The humans have an easy path, but they are further away. The male elves are almost here.

What about the fairies? Shaylee asked.

I haven't seen them yet.

Shaylee stopped and listened, "Do you hear that?" She asked.

Everyone stopped moving. Fawn hopped up and down, "The river!"

"I think we are close. Keep your eyes peeled."

They descended the bridge and slowly crept forward until they reached the river.

"Spread out. If you see the captive, do not approach; he might be booby-trapped; send off a purple flare if you see him," Shaylee told them.

"Why purple?" Amelia asked.

"We should see it without it being too bright; now go."

The five girls spread out, walking up and down the river, looking for the cottonwood and the captive.

Shaylee kept her eyes roaming, looking for any signs or a flare. Suddenly, a purple flare appeared downriver. She turned and hurried in that direction.

Mira was the furthest downstream. She crouched near a cottonwood at the edge of a cottonwood grove. When the others arrived, she pointed toward the river. A man was tied to one of the trees with his back to the river.

"How do we rescue him?" Shaylee asked.

"Just being here, isn't that the end?" Mira inquired.

"I don't think so," Fawn said, "I think Shaylee's right; we need to rescue him. See there?" She pointed to the other side of the grove. A small trail of smoke floated up through the trees. "He's being watched."

Everyone nodded.

"We need a distraction," Shaylee said. "I will send Lyra into the woods behind the guard. One of us needs to sneak up behind the captive and untie him. Any volunteers?"

"Who's Lyra?" Dilya asked.

"My vaskakat. Any volunteers?" She repeated.

No one spoke up.

"OK, I'll go. You all stay here. Can you detain the guard if he doesn't fall for the diversion?" Shaylee asked.

"I have that covered. I've been practicing that capture spell of yours," Fawn said.

"Good. Be safe." Shaylee backtracked a little way before circling back, heading toward the river to get behind the tree and the tied-up victim.

How many are guarding the prisoner? Shaylee asked Lyra.

Only one.

Good, when I am behind the prisoner, can you make a distraction to lure him away?

I know just the thing, wait for me. I will let you know when I am ready.

Ok, hurry, though; I don't want another group messing this up.

Don't worry. The humans and other elves won't make it in time, Lyra purred in her mind.

Shaylee positioned herself two trees away from the captive; he appeared to be sleeping. From her vantage point, she could see the outline of the guard on the other side of the small grove.

Get ready, Lyra projected.

A loud crash sounded behind the guard; he swiveled his head toward it.

Another crash and a horse screamed, or was it a horse? Shaylee frowned, *That sounded like a horse with a beast in its throat.* **What was that?**

Our distraction, go! The guard is investigating.

Sure enough, the guard jumped up and rushed toward the screaming animal.

Shaylee quietly approached the captive, "Be quiet and don't move. I'm here to rescue you."

"So glad to see you, Shaylee. Congratulations on being first," Devnar said. He moved his hands from behind him and stood. He walked under a break in the canopy and shot bright yellow and white sparks high into the air. A few heartbeats later, four more streamers of magic appeared in the sky.

"Well done," Devnar praised again. "Come out, all of you."

Aspen and the four girls from Shaylee's group emerged from the trees.

"Where's the rest?" He asked Aspen.

"A story for another time. Don't worry, my sister is with the others," Aspen lifted her hands into the air and shot a stream of red and blue into the sky; it was returned with a stream of green and blue. "Sarya will wait for us, let's go."

Back in the valley in front of the Monastery, the prospective students gathered together, waiting to be addressed by the evaluators, who huddled together, speaking in hushed voices. Sun-orbs danced around the students, showing tired and mostly disappointed faces.

"So, how did you do it?" Ashryn sneered, walking up to Shaylee with her hands on her hips.

"Superior tracking abilities," Mira said haughtily.

"Whatever," Ashryn walked away.

Tar clapped loudly to get everyone's attention. "Congratulations to half of the elven women. Fawn, Amelia, Mira, Dilya, and Shaylee found our captive, Devnar, first using proper cooperation. Off to bed, all of you. We will have your class schedules before the last call tomorrow evening.

Last call couldn't come soon enough for Shaylee and Fawn. They busied themselves as much as possible, but the sun moved far too slowly across the sky.

[311]

Rosepetal and Talon prepared a special dinner that evening. As it was Shaylee's fourteenth-name day, it was the only day of the year she didn't have to help.

They prepared her favorite meal - roasted silver grouse and peppers with rosemary mushroom gravy and goldhorn fruitcake for dessert.

Shaylee had a hard time forcing herself to eat; she was nervous and excited, but she did. Her parents worked hard to make something just for her.

After dinner, Shaylee was ready to dart out the door; she wanted to be the first to arrive.

"Before you go, we have something else for you—both of you, actually. This is for you, Shaylee, and this is for you, Fawn. We missed your name-day, but we had to get you something," Talon said, holding out two bundles. Both girls took their packages and tore into them.

"Oh, my, it's beautiful!" Shaylee exclaimed. She pulled out a purple dress. "Can I wear it tonight?"

"Of course, go change," Rosepetal shooed her away.

Fawn pulled out an identical styled dress; only hers was green. Both rushed to their room to change.

When they emerged, Talon whistled, "You two are beautiful."

Shaylee spun, her mid-calf-length dress flaring around her. She smiled broadly and rushed over to the mirror. Their dresses were form-fitting in the bodice, tied at the waist with a black sash, and had three-quarter-length sleeves and a V-neck collar.

"And you'll each need these," Rosepetal said, handing them black slippers that tied high up on the ankle. "Perfect," she beamed after they slipped them on their feet.

"Thank you so much. This is the best name-day ever," Shaylee beamed.

"Now go before you're late," Talon told them.

Shaylee looked outside. The sun was just starting to set, "We'd better hurry!"

It turned out they weren't the only ones excited to receive their class schedules; a fairly large group was already waiting.

Amanda and Amelia were standing together near the back. Shaylee sighed; she wanted to be at the front. *Oh well,* she thought, *I'm still getting into the academy. It doesn't matter if I receive my schedule first or last.*

Sparrow landed a moment before Shaylee and Fawn joined the others.

"You two look so pretty," Sparrow fluttered her wings so hard she lifted off the ground again.

"Is that your name-day gift?" Amelia asked.

"Oh, that's right. Happy name-day, Shaylee!" Sparrow shouted.

Amanda smiled, "How old?"

"Fourteen," Shaylee replied.

"Almost a woman. Happy name-day," Ben said from behind her.

"Thanks. Have we missed anything yet?"

"No. Oh, look, Tar and Leo just came out," Amanda said, pointing to the steps.

Shaylee looked up at the Monastery. Tar, Leo, and the other evaluators, and by the looks of it, every Shepherd and Prior were just exiting the Monastery.

Tar held his hands up, waiting for everyone to be quiet. "Thank you for coming here tonight and for all your hard work these past couple of days. I hope it will be worth it for all of you. When I call your name, please approach. You will be given your uniform, schedule, and ranking pin. Most of you will receive the Dagger, the symbol of all first-years.

"Some of you will be given the Staff or even the Bow. These pins show everyone your level in the Academy. First-year - Dagger; second - Staff or Bow, your strongest weapon; and third – you might get a sword if the sword is not your preferred weapon, a shield with either a Staff or Bow on it. No one will be starting higher than the second year tonight, though. Those who want to specialize in magic only will have their own ranking system." He nodded at the small cluster of fairies. "Further rankings will be learned later."

"Everyone will take at least one classroom class, and the rest of your day will be filled with hand-to-hand combat and weapons training. Let's begin."

With a loud but melodious voice, a Prior started calling out names, beginning with the humans. She only paused for a moment before reading the next. One by one, they approached and accepted a small bundle from one of the shepherds. The fairies went next.

Sparrow zoomed back to them after receiving hers. She looked at the pin and frowned, "Why did I get a dagger? I won't be using weapons."

"He said everyone gets a dagger as a first year, and second years will get a different one," Shaylee replied.

"Fawn Carric," the Prior called.

"That's me!" Fawn rushed to the steps, accepting her bundle. When she returned, she was wearing a large smile. "Look, I got a bow!"

"Of course you did." Shaylee smiled, shaking her head.

"Shaylee Faeven."

Shaylee's heart stopped briefly and then started hammering in her chest; she walked quickly to the steps. She wanted to sprint, but, in a dress and wearing slippers, she thought better of it. Her palms were sweaty, and her breath was coming fast when she finally reached the steps. Tar and Leo smiled down at her; she felt her cheeks flush bright red, suddenly very glad that only torches and floating sun-orbs illuminated the square.

She curtsied as she accepted her bundle and then hurried back to her friends.

"A bow, I knew you'd get one too," Fawn said happily.

When the last name was called, Tar clapped his hands loudly, augmented with his magic to regain control of the crowd.

"Congratulations, everyone. I look forward to you all receiving your second and third-year pins quickly. As the first class at The Blade Academy, we will accelerate you as quickly as possible. Future class years will progress much slower.

"Before you retire for the evening, I want to thank you all again for joining us in this fight for our freedom. I would also like to introduce you to some new allies who will also be assisting us. The world we are trying to save doesn't belong solely to elves, fairies, and humans. Many other species have been affected by the tyrannical rule of Evansshire and the Wyverns. These courageous few will be joined by many more to come over the next few months."

He raised his hands, magic spewing from his fingertips. The night sky illuminated to reveal a dozen large, winged beasts circling overhead. One by one, they landed. "Please welcome the griffins and pegasus to our Academy as well as their land-bound fellows," he pointed behind the group of students, "the unicorns and the great stags." The gathered mass split into two. Three unicorns walked through the monastery's gates. Their pure white hides almost glowed, and their horns of silver and gold sparkled in the torchlight. Their golden hooves clacked on the cobblestone walkway as they trotted in. Behind them, four enormous stags walked more slowly but no less regal. On top of their heads was a mess of gnarled, twisted antlers. The males had two sets of antlers that spanned off each side of the massive animals at least three to four feet. Even the females had antlers, just slightly smaller. Their hides were about the same shade as an elk, but they had glowing silver dapples on their rumps. The crowd seemed to hold their collective breath as the newcomers approached the monastery.

Shaylee's eyes moved back to the steps. She locked eyes with one of the pegasus. It stared back at her and nodded its head. The pegasus' silver forelock flipped messily around her ears and covered one blue eye. Her silvery white hide sparkled in the light of the sun-orbs. Her white wings were tucked in close to her sides, but the multi-colored tips were still visible. The blues, purples, and golds of the wingtips caught the light.

Hello, Shaylee Faeven.

Shaylee's mouth dropped open. The pegasus was projecting to her and knew her name.

PART THREE

Ashrozo

CHAPTER

-34-

PRINCESS Ashrozo glared down her nose at the male slave prostrated in front of her.

"Please forgive me, Drakaina Ashrozo. I did not know you were here."

"How dare you use my name with that vile tongue of yours? I should have it removed."

"Forgive! Forgive!" The slave cried, pressing his head onto the floor. "Princess Drakaina, please forgive me!"

"Get away from me," she said with a dismissive flick of her wrist. The slave rushed to his feet and hurried out of the chamber. *The nerve of that slave sneaking up on me like that,* she thought angrily.

Ashrozo stomped over to her dresser, picked up a brush, and then threw it into the mirror, cracking it and causing her reflection to split and splinter.

She smiled, *I look better like this,* she thought. She picked up the brush and raked it through her long auburn hair. Her father insisted that she always maintain a clean and tidy appearance. "A clean and tidy human appearance," she growled out loud.

She looked at her now combed hair and the disgusting human dress she was forced to cover her body with.

Ashrozo scowled as she took in her white complexion and silvery blue eyes. The silver accents on her black dress sparkled in the torchlight. Everything about her appearance irritated her. All she wanted was to look like her father and not like her mother.

She shuddered and shook her head. Thinking about her mother would just put her in a bad mood. She was still young; she had time to show her father that she was worthy of his name… and love.

A knock on the door brought her thoughts back to reality.

"Enter," she said coldly.

"Your presence has been requested, Your Highness," a meek voice said.

Ashrozo spun away from the mirror; her attendant peeked her head into the chamber, *Afraid to enter fully, as she should be*, she thought.

Without a word, she followed Lura to the throne room. Lura scurried in front of her with her head bowed and shoulders slumped. Ashrozo scowled at the humans' back. *They are such disgusting creatures, so weak and soft*, she thought. And she was cursed to look just like them. Her true form was locked away inside her; she could feel it, just under the surface.

The main hallway through the fortress was plain and unadorned with pale gray walls and ceiling and white marble tiles, but it was massive. The ceiling soared above Ashrozo's head, making her feel inferior and puny. She drew her shoulders back and lifted her chin. Soon, she would walk down these halls in her true form and make all the humans scurrying about feel real fear in her presence; a smile bloomed on her face.

The thick black iron throne room doors towered above her. She craned her neck to see the tops of the doors, and a small smile tugged at the corners of her lips. These doors even towered above her father. Thanks to her mixed heritage, she might even tower above her father when her true form emerged. Her smile instantly disappeared; her mixed heritage was also locking her in this cursed form.

Four humans stood on one side of the massive doors. Together, they turned a giant wheel, causing the doors to open slowly. Warm air blasted into her, pushing her backward slightly, blowing her hair from her face, and whipping her dress around her legs. Lura disappeared as soon as the doors started to open. Ashrozo made a mental note to punish her later for not being there to help her smooth her dress and hair.

Regaining her composure as quickly as possible, she entered the throne room. Her father sat on his throne, surrounded by his most trusted advisors. As she entered the enormous chamber, the council swiveled their heads to stare at her. Several hissed at her, their forked tongues flicking out of their snouts, tasting, and smelling the air. She suppressed an involuntary shudder that threatened to ripple through her body.

Her father's cold gray eyes watched her every movement.

The room was uncomfortably warm, just like her father liked it. Four fireplaces roared, two on each side of the room.

Every time she entered this room, its ambiance took her breath away. The clear glass ceiling showed the night sky, millions of tiny stars twinkling against a black velvet canvas, and the perfectly centered full moon shining brightly.

"Welcome, daughter. Please be seated," he said in the typical slurred speech shared by all wyverns. The hissing and garbled speech made it difficult to understand. "As I was saying. We will increase and expand our search. The human must be found."

A wyvern scout stood off to one side of the counsel table with its head bowed. "With the help of the pixie, we tracked the human to Threndy. I could smell it, but it was not there anymore. I will continue the search," the scout said.

"Be gone then; do not return without the human," the King snapped.

Ashrozo watched the wyvern crawl backward out of the chamber. A large sparkling blue firefly buzzed around the wyvern's head. Ash looked closer. *No, it was not a firefly. That's the pixie,* she thought. The wyvern snapped his jaws at the pixie and then shot a small bolt of lightning in its direction. Twinkling laughter echoed through the chamber as the pixie easily evaded the attack.

"What about our other issue?" An adviser asked.

The King nodded his great, spiky head. "The Order is fractured. The new threat must be dealt with." His inky black wings snapped open, his gray eyes smoldered, and a thin trail of smoke escaped his flaring nostrils.

A young wyvern sitting to the King's right lifted his head high. His scales and wings were the typical inky blackness like most wyverns, but each of his scales was rimmed in silver, making him shine and almost sparkle. "I will infiltrate their ranks. I will disrupt them from the inside," he slurred.

"And how do you plan to do that?" One of the advisors sneered.

The young wyvern turned his intense blue eyes to the advisor and closed them.

Ashrozo's breath caught in her chest. *He wasn't, he wouldn't*, her thoughts raced.

A mist of black and silver swirled around the young wyvern.

The king's advisors all hissed and spread their wings out in surprise.

When the mist cleared, a young, black-haired, dark-skinned, blue-eyed boy sat where the wyvern once was.

"I will infiltrate their ranks and disrupt them from the inside," he repeated. His speech now clean and clear.

"How is this possible? No wyvern can take a human's form. Imposter!" Avaaz screamed from his place of honor to the King's left.

"My son shall not be spoken to so. I was there for his conception, and I was there for his hatching," he snapped his long, pointed jaws inches from the advisor's face.

Avaaz snaked his head back with a soft hiss, "My apologies, my King. I mean no disrespect; I was only surprised at this development." Avaaz looked at the human sitting where a wyvern had been just a few moments ago and flicked his tongue in his direction.

Wyverns were smaller than their dragon cousins but still larger than humans. Ashrozo watched Avaaz narrow his eyes; one bite would end the wyvern in human form. She glared at Avaaz and her father.

They were speaking to each other like she didn't exist. Like she wasn't a wyvern stuck in human form.

The King glared at Avaaz for a moment, then moved his gaze back to his son. He glared for a few more breaths before his lips peeled away from his razor-sharp teeth. "Excellent, son. Make it so."

Ashrozo jumped to her feet without thinking, "I want to help!" She blurted; all eyes turned to her, and she resisted the urge to shrink away from their beady gray eyes. "I will go with my brother. We will destroy the threat together."

The chamber erupted in wyvern laughter.

"You will stay here, daughter. The world is not ready for you yet," her father said in his emotionless manner.

She sat back down and folded her hands in her lap. She nodded to her father and smoothed her features. For the remainder of the meeting, she did as she was expected. Be seen and not heard, keeping her features neutral. Her heart hammered in her chest; why had she spoken up? Why did she bring their attention to her at all? Her being in this chamber was pointless. She sat without speaking and without being spoken to. As a firstborn, she should be seated to the king's left instead of her brother, but his advisors would never tolerate a human-looking wyvern sitting in a place of honor.

When all the advisors departed, and no one remained but the King, Ashrozo, and her brother, she finally let her shoulders relax.

"Approach," the king said to his children.

Zarret didn't have to move and stayed in human form, but Ashrozo was near the back of the great chamber.

She walked quickly and sat to the left of her father. The chair was enormous, but she had years of practice climbing into it while retaining the refinement her father demanded.

"What are your thoughts, Rozo?"

The question took her by surprise. He never asked for her opinion. She cleared the look of surprise off her face as soon as it appeared, "Thank you, Father, for the honor of speaking," she began, "First off, I think sending someone trusted to infiltrate these traitors is a sound plan…"

"You have misgivings?" The King asked.

"I do not think Zarret is the one to send," she said plainly.

"What?" Zarret elevated his voice.

"I love you dearly, brother, but you just found your human form not more than a month ago. It is not second nature to you. I don't think you can pull it off. They will know you are not human."

"And you are the better choice?" Zarret asked, his voice edged with aggression.

"I have lived my whole life in this cursed form. I know no other." Ashrozo held her hands out wide.

"Ah, but you hold a deep hatred for humans in your heart," King Ichakik slurred.

"No more than Zarret does," she defended herself.

"Not true, dear sister; I hold no hatred for humans. They are below me; they do not deserve my hatred, my pity, or my consideration."

King Ichakik sat as still as a statue while he pondered his children's words. Ashrozo and Zarret sat quietly, waiting for him to speak.

"It shall be as Zarret recommended. You, my daughter, shall teach him to be human."

Her mouth flapped open, "How can I teach him? I am stuck in their form, but I do not interact with humans or know how to be one. I am a wyvern, not a human."

"Then how were you the better choice?" He spat, then shook his spiked head, "You are a wyvern-dragon hybrid; you have the ability to change into their form because your form includes theirs. You will do as you are told. Learn from our numerous slaves. You have until spring."

Ashrozo clamped her mouth shut and nodded her head. King Ichakik stood and left his children staring at his empty throne.

"I don't like this, Zar," she finally said.

"You don't have to; it is Father's decree."

"Well, you need to change your name then." She looked over at her brother. He was looking at his dark, nearly black hands and arms. She frowned; why was she cursed to look like their mother. Zarret's human skin color more closely matched that of a wyvern's coloring versus her white skin. "What's the longest you've been able to maintain?" She said with a sigh.

"Two days. Hey, why do I have to change my name?"

"Zarret, the Prince of the Wyverns, is a name known to many, and besides, Zarret doesn't sound human or even elven."

Zar pursed his lips in thought, "How about Zarren? My last attendant's name was Darren; that's close."

"That should work." She nodded her head slightly.

"You know who we should speak to, don't you?"

"I don't want to see her."

Zarret put his hands down and looked at her. "She's your mother; why do you hate her?"

"Because she's not a wyvern," she pouted. "It's because of her I have this, this… body. It's not fair that your wyvern body came first. I'm older; I should have the right chair to father."

"You'll get your wyvern form; just give it time. We are the first and only hybrids. What we can do is not fully known yet. Come on. I told Mother I would see her today anyway."

"How can you stand being near her."

Zar shrugged, pushed his tight, curly but shaggy black hair out of his eyes, and jumped to the ground, "Her dragon form's not bad, just too many legs, that's all. Father likes her, doesn't he?"

"No, dear brother, he does not." Ashrozo jumped gracefully down and walked with her brother out of the throne room. "He only took her for his mate because she is the heir to the Ragnis bloodline. He needs her to give him the prophesied twins so he can destroy them and save his reign."

Zar frowned, "That doesn't make sense."

"What doesn't," she said, exasperated, looking at him out of the corner of her eye.

"If she is the last of the bloodline, then why keep her? Why didn't he just kill her and end the prophecy?"

She stopped and turned to look at him. "Oh, little brother, you are not much younger than me, but you are still so naive. She is not the last of the bloodline. We have a half-brother."

Zarret's deep blue eyes widened and then clouded with anger, "Then… I will help Father set his reign in stone."

"And how do you plan to do this, pray tell?" She rolled her eyes.

"I will destroy The Order, and this fractured group, and then I will find our older brother and deliver him to Father. The prophecy will be broken, I will take father's place someday, and wyverns will rule forever."

TO BE CONTINUED...

PROPHECY FORETOLD

Forgotten Kingdoms lost to tyranny, the realm of beasts and the realm of magic fade away. The birth of twins in the darkness of night, upon uniting, the fates of the Royal Lines shall intertwine. Infinity embraced; royal birthrights restored.

Centuries long ago, peace and harmony ruled the land. Beast and man living hand in hand. Two mighty Kingdoms rose. Two Royal families came to power: one to rule the beasts and one to rule man. Their legacies were once aligned but still forever entwined. The two mighty Kingdoms will fall and lose their power. New blood would rise to rule and dictate. The kingdoms would divide, and tyranny would be unleashed on the realm. Beast and man are separated by hate and fear, and unity is lost.

But in secret, magic would survive. Freedom would dance, and unity would find its sacred room. Twins would be born from royal birthright in the darkness of night. The twins from the royal lines would be tested, their strength grown from strife. But the twins must unite; they must entwine their legacies to take a stand. With the help of a Phoenix, lost in the world, they will find the Infinite Medallion. Only with the medallion can they unite and save the land from tyranny while overcoming the shadow cast by The One.

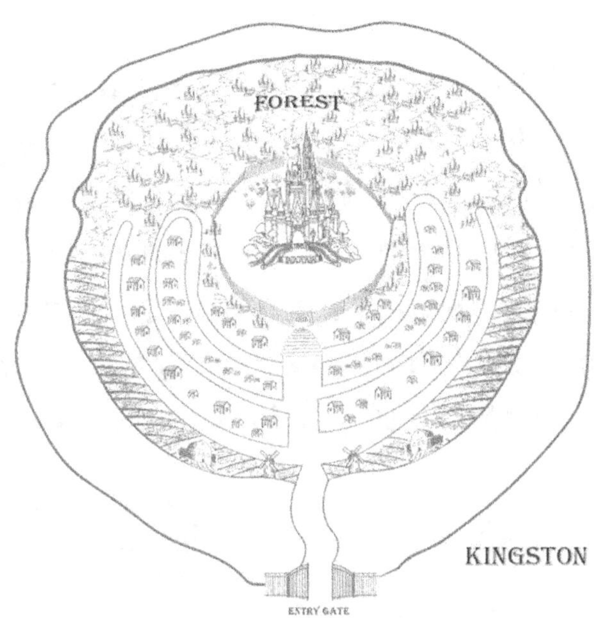

FOREST
KINGSTON
ENTRY GATE

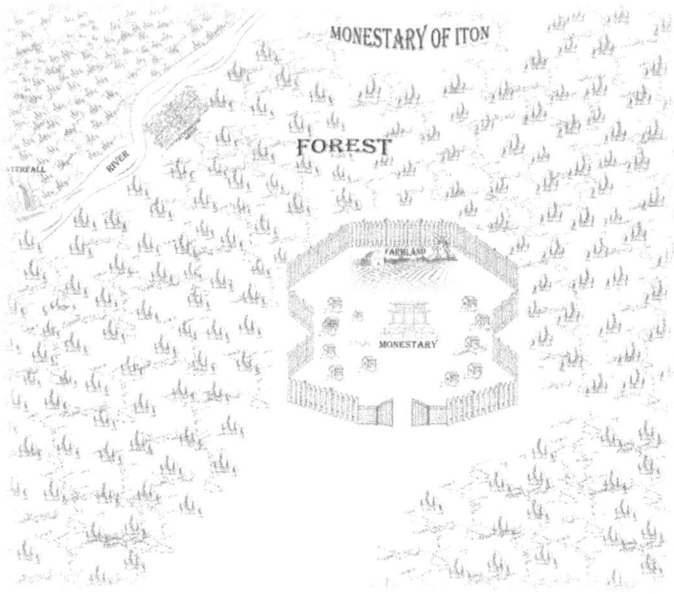

MONESTARY OF ITON
FOREST
WATERFALL
RIVER
FARMLAND
MONESTARY

Sarah M. Wasson

Within the shimmering embrace of Las Vegas, Nevada, I dwell with my beloved husband and son. My heart is imbued with the spirit of enterprise, juggling my pursuits as a pet groomer, amateur golfer, horse whisperer, falconer, and devotee of the fantastical realms of sci-fi.

www.FantasicalRealmPublishing.com

FantasticalRealmPublishing@gmail.com